Any Way You Want Me

Lucy Diamond lives in Bath with her husband and their three children. When she isn't slaving away on a new book (ahem) you can find her on Twitter @LDiamondAuthor or on Facebook at www.facebook.com/LucyDiamondAuthor.

BY THE SAME AUTHOR

Novels

Over You

Hens Reunited

Sweet Temptation

The Beach Café

Summer with my Sister

Me and Mr Jones

One Night in Italy

The Year of Taking Chances

Summer at Shell Cottage

The Secrets of Happiness

Novellas

A Baby at the Beach Café

Ebook novellas

Christmas at the Beach Café

Christmas Gifts at the Beach Café

PAN BOOKS

First published 2007 by Pan Books

This edition published 2016 by Pan Books
an imprint of Pan Macmillan
20 New Wharf Road, London N1 9RR
Associated companies throughout the world
www.panmacmillan.com

ISBN 978-1-5098-1114-4

1 3 5 7 9 8 6 4 2

A CIP catalogue record for this book is available from the British Library.

Typeset by Intype Libra Ltd
Printed and bound by CPI Group (UK) Ltd, Croydon, CR0 4YY

For Martin

Acknowledgements

I am very grateful to all the people who've helped me along the way with this book. Thanks are due to Sue Roe and Umi Sinha at the University of Sussex CCE for their brilliant tuition and inspiration on the novel-writing course. To Jo Thulborn, Bernadette Alves, Jo White and Deborah Smith who all read the first draft, and were so positive and encouraging. To my fab agent Simon Trewin, and to Imogen Taylor and Trisha Jackson at Macmillan, for saying yes, and making this happen. To my brother, Phil Mongredien, for hours of proofreading. And, of course, to my family, especially Hannah, Tom and Holly Powell, who always put everything in perspective.

I couldn't have written this book without Martin Powell. He gave me the time and space to start writing, and the love and support to see it through. Thank you.

Chapter One

'So, what do you do?' he said.

'I'm a . . . scriptwriter,' I said. That was my first lie.

He raised his eyebrows. 'What sort of stuff do you write?'

I tried to sound modest. 'TV dramas mostly. The odd film.' I gave a tiny shrug and dipped my head, trying to imply that this was not a big deal.

He leaned in a fraction closer, close enough for me to smell him. 'Really? Nice one.' He smelled expensive. He looked impressed. He seemed to think it *was* a big deal.

Rather a shame that it was all lies. I didn't quite know where they were coming from. It was as if someone else was speaking to him, not me. Five minutes later, and I'd been nominated for a BAFTA, had an office in Soho and was thinking of setting up my own production company. Well, I figured I might as well enjoy myself – and I was hardly going to tell him the truth. That would have sent him packing within seconds.

I wasn't lying for any sinister reason. I'd been minding my

own business, wondering if my trousers looked as tight as they felt, while I waited for Becca to come back from the bar with our drinks. Then he'd appeared beside me, sliding along the couch, one arm slung over the back of it. Jack. A pretty boy in a loud shirt. Young and cocky and definitely, oh, *transparently,* on the pull, but he'd been so charming and funny and . . . OK, then, he'd been so damn good-looking, I couldn't resist playing along with it, trying on a new persona to see how it fitted. And for ten minutes, it fitted wonderfully. I even convinced myself.

Then my phone bleeped. A message.

I glanced at it covertly. **NATHAN HUNGRY**, it said. The two words were enough to make me break off right in the middle of my Hollywood story. Nathan hungry? *Already?* Oh God.

Don't . . . don't go and LEAK now, I told myself fiercely. I could feel that familiar tingle starting at the very thought. *Please* don't start leaking here in public, not when I'm wearing my best dry-clean-only Kenzo top . . .

'Sorry,' I said to Jack. I pulled a rueful, shit-happens face. 'Gotta make a call. I'm meeting someone else for a drink and they seem to be early.' It was the most truthful thing I'd said all night.

'Oh,' he replied. He looked up at me through lashes so sooty and thick they should rightfully have been on a woman. 'Can I take your number, then?'

'Tell you what,' I said, 'I'll take yours.'

We shook hands. 'Nice talking to you, Sadie,' he smiled. His hand felt cool and firm. Long fingers. No rings.

'Nice talking to *you*, Jack,' I said. I meant it. I hadn't felt so creative for weeks.

I dialled home as soon as he'd made the return swagger to his mates, who promptly started slapping him on the back and making simian whooping noises. 'Alex, it's me,' I said. I kept my voice low; Jack had obviously made some comment or other about me as his whole posse were straining their designer shirt collars, leaning over for a good look. 'Is everything all right? He's not due a feed in ages. Are you sure he's hungry?'

'He's been bawling his head off, Sade. I've checked his nappy and that's OK, and he's not too hot or too cold or anything . . .'

'He's probably tired. Or windy. He can't be that hungry, I fed him just before I came out.' I could hear a wail down the receiver behind Alex's words. My boy. How could I have abandoned him? I felt like running out of the bar there and then in my best strappy heels, sod the stupid night out.

Before I could move, though, Becca walked into my line of vision and plonked two tall glasses on the table in front of me. The ice clinked, and my mouth felt dry.

'He's just tired,' I repeated into the phone, more forcefully this time. I couldn't take my eyes off the gin swirling languidly through the tonic. It looked so wonderfully viscous, so wonderfully . . . *alcoholic*. 'He didn't sleep much today. Why don't you try putting him in the sling and walking him about? Please, Alex.' We'd only just got here and I was about to be magicked back to Motherhood Central before I'd even had a chance to lift my drink. Maybe it was a punishment for all those lies.

'All right,' he said. He didn't sound convinced.

'And if that doesn't work, there's some breastmilk in the fridge,' I said. I looked around to see Becca looking grossed-out, and a couple on the next table with *do-you-have-to?* faces. I turned away hurriedly. 'You'll need to sterilize a bottle, remember, and . . .'

'All right, all right,' Alex said.

The wailing started up again and I squeezed my eyes shut. This was a mistake. I shouldn't have come.

Becca grabbed the phone. 'She'll call you back in ten minutes, OK? Bye now.'

I took a thankful swig of my drink. The ice cubes rattled down to butt my lips, and tonic bubbles popped on my tongue. The alcohol sank into me deliciously. I imagined it swirling through my bloodstream in the same languid way.

'Thanks, Bec,' I said.

She was staring at me, brown eyes scrunching up into a frown. 'Sade . . . I think you're . . . I think something's happening,' she said. She gestured to my top. 'What's that?'

I glanced down to see a telltale wet patch on my chest as the milk seeped sweetly out of me. 'Oh, Christ,' I moaned, trying and failing to cover it up with my arm. 'Oh, *bollocks!*'

The cab sped through the dark city, and I leaned my hot cheek against the window.

'Don't worry,' Becca said, giving my arm a squeeze. 'We can try again next Saturday.'

'We're going to dinner with Alex's sodding boss next Saturday,' I reminded her. I grimaced. Mine and Alex's first night out together since Nathan had been born five months ago – and it wasn't going to be quite the romantic get-away I'd been hoping for. We could hardly start holding hands and snogging drunkenly over the table at his new boss's dinner party. Not unless I was planning to *completely* ruin Alex's career anyway.

'Sometime in the week, then,' she said. 'Look, it's not a big deal. Honestly. If you've gotta go, you've gotta go.'

I returned the squeeze. 'Cheers, Bec.' I sighed. 'I'm sorry – I'm sure there's nothing wrong, but—'

'I know. I know! It's all right, you don't have to say it.'

People were spilling out of bars and restaurants, loitering in clusters on the pavement, heads tipped back in laughter under the flashing neon signs. They had all the time in the world to hang around. Maybe they'd go on to a club now or over to someone's house for a smoke. They could stay out until the first pink blush of dawn, if they fancied it, then lounge in bed all the next day, read the Sunday papers with their feet on the sofa, doze in front of the *EastEnders* omnibus. Bacon, eggs, fags, coffee, hangover. Such enviable freedom. Such a different world.

'There's Pete!' Becca said suddenly, banging on the car window and waving like a maniac. 'And Zoe!' She leaned forward. 'Could you stop here a second, please, mate?'

As the cab pulled in to the roadside, she turned to me. 'Mind if I jump out? I haven't seen them for ages,' she asked. Then she paused. 'Or – do you fancy joining us?'

I shook my head. 'Duty calls,' I said after just a tiny hesitation. 'Have a good one.'

I watched out of the window as she went. She turned and waved, her long dark hair tumbling over her pale suede jacket, and then she was gone, linking arms with Zoe, swallowed up by the crowd.

As the cab roared away towards Battersea Bridge and home, I lurched on the slippery vinyl back seat and had the sensation that I was being pulled in half. Part of me wanted to yell to the driver, Stop! I've changed my mind! Pete and the others would be going clubbing probably or to someone's house party and there would be loads of speed and E around. It had been so long, God, just SO long since I'd done anything like that, what with pregnancy and motherhood and all the zombifying tiredness . . .

NATHAN HUNGRY, I remembered. And the very thought of his frantic wailing face was enough to kill stone dead in an instant any ideas about going out clubbing. So that was that.

'Sorry,' I gabbled to Alex when I got back, and Nathan was still scarlet-faced with sobs. Alex was jiggling him around as best he could, but every jiggle just seemed to shake another cry from our son's unhappy red mouth. I reached over and took him, and his breath gasped out into my shoulder at once, in hot, tearful relief.

'Here I am, sweetheart,' I whispered, hurriedly undoing my top and letting his mouth fasten upon me. 'Mummy's home.'

My night out had vanished into the ether. Already, the feeling of being in the bar, the squishy couch beneath my legs, the smell of smoke and perfume and beer – already, it seemed like fragments of a dream I was struggling to remember. It was slipping further and further away by the second.

Nathan sucked hard and frantically for a few moments, then his body relaxed against mine in limp exhaustion, and his breathing slowed. His eyes shut dreamily and his face softened in the ecstasy of warm milk. My boy. My ever-ravenous boy. I stroked his cheek, held him tight to me.

'He just wanted you,' Alex was saying again, shrugging his shoulders in a *What was I supposed to do?* gesture. 'He went mad when I tried the bottle. It was like I'd offended him. He just—'

'It's OK,' I said, not looking up. 'Don't worry about it.'

Like a well-oiled machine, Alex's hands moved for the remote, his beer and today's paper at my words. *Permission to relax again, sir!* He sat down and opened the newspaper with a flourish.

As I leaned back carefully on the sofa, Nathan still attached, I felt the rustle of paper in my pocket. Then I remembered. Jack's phone number. Jack! He had been nice-looking, hadn't he, with his dark lashes and laughing mouth? He'd liked me, too. Well, he'd liked the BAFTA-nominated scriptwriter, anyway. Probably would have run a mile in those expensive leather shoes of his if he'd known the truth.

I tried not to smirk too obviously at the novelty of having been chatted up. It had been a long time since anybody had given me so much as a *first* look, let alone a second one. Not that I was *wanting* second looks, you understand, I was a million miles from those out-on-the-pull days but . . . Well, you know. Nice to be noticed, wasn't it? Looked at as somebody to desire again, rather than looked straight through as one more child-bearing mothering machine behind a buggy. And it was dead flattering that somebody as good-looking as Jack had seen something else there, some last vestige of sex-kittenness inside me. Well, hopefully, anyway. Of course, maybe he had just been on the lash, and desperate.

Nathan opened his eyes and blinked, his curled pink fists resting contentedly on me. My deliciously chubby boy with his dimples and solemn blue gaze. I ran a finger down the side of his face and felt a twist of guilt at the sight of a tear still clinging to his eyelashes.

The washing machine chuntered in the background. The telly's drone was interspersed with periodic bursts of moronic-sounding canned laughter. Alex poured me a glass of red wine and flicked through the newspaper. Everything – and everyone – was in their place.

I reached out a hand to him across the chasm of sofa between us and he took my fingers, stroked them absent-mindedly as he frowned at the sports pages.

Then he looked up. 'Sorry,' he said.

'What for?'

'For wrecking your night out. For dragging you home.'

I heaved our son up to my shoulder and patted his pyjama'd back gently. He had fallen asleep and his breath sighed out, sweet and milky against my face. 'It's all right,' I said, trying to ignore the flash of resentment I'd felt. I could do it again another night, after all, couldn't I? 'Honestly. Becca was cool about it. She saw Pete and Zoe on the way back, so she went off with them instead.'

Alex looked faraway for a moment, and I knew that, like me, he was wondering which club they were all at, imagining thudding bass-lines, amphetamine-fuelled dancing, sweat and shouting and bare flesh.

He rolled his eyes. 'It's great having kids, isn't it?'

'Oh yeah,' I agreed. 'Who needs a social life, anyway?'

'Exactly,' he said, reaching over to grab the remote and flip channels. 'Especially when *Match of the Day* is about to start.'

I put our full-bellied, slumbering son back in his cot and watched him for a couple of minutes as he lay there breathing in the half-darkness. Then I tiptoed into Molly's bedroom and tucked her duvet around her. She was cuddling her Fizz doll in her sleep, and smiling, her hair a mass of blonde fluff on the pillow.

My beautiful children. I was grateful, really, of course I was. I wouldn't have swapped them for the wildest social life in the world. It just seemed a shame that one life had to end so abruptly when another began.

I didn't mind the sacrifice of endless nights in front of the telly so much but I worried that Alex did. He'd been the uber-party animal in the pre-kids days, always getting invites for the hottest nights out, scoring the best drugs, suffering the worst Sunday come-downs. When we first started seeing each other, I had felt swept along by his energy and stamina, his passion for life, love, everything.

Those days seemed long gone. In my most miserable, sleep-tortured moments, I couldn't help wondering if he was secretly longing to escape the domestic confines of parenthood, and abandon us for some dark-eyed, lithe-limbed lovely in a sweaty nightclub, where life was easy and everyone was dancing.

I went downstairs again, suddenly anxious to know if this was indeed what he was feeling, but he was snoring on the sofa. Gary Lineker burbled away about Arsenal's defensive tactics in the background as I shook awake south London's one-time party king. Then we went to bed.

The thought of Jack and my aborted night out stayed buried beneath an avalanche of more pressing things until the following Monday morning. Twenty minutes or so after I'd put the first load of washing on, I remembered.

A scribbled phone number on a page torn from his diary, stuffed in my trouser pocket. I knelt in front of the washing machine and watched helplessly as the assortment of babygros and cot sheets and Angelina Ballerina vests swirled and churned with Alex's boxers and my vile nursing bras and . . . and, yes, there they were, my best black trousers.

I sighed. It wasn't as if I was going to *call* him or anything. It wasn't like I was going to . . .

'What Mummy doing?'

I put an arm around Molly's shoulders as she crouched next to me. She had pink felt-tip pen all over her cheeks. I kissed her blonde hair and she leaned into my side.

'Just thinking about life, Molls. Wondering where it's going.'

Her blue eyes were thoughtful. 'Where it going,' she repeated solemnly. 'Where it going?'

'That, my love, is the killer question,' I said. Then I stood up and grabbed her, lifting her top to blow raspberries on her creamy-white belly. 'And who's been drawing all over your face?' I asked. Her body was shaking with giggles. 'Was it Nathan?'

'Molly,' she spluttered.

'Was it . . . Doug next door?'

'Molly!'

'Was it . . . Grandma?'

'MOLLY draw on me!' she shouted. '*I* draw on me!' She was beaming with pride.

I gave her a kiss. 'Still haven't mastered the art of lying, have you, Molls?' I said. Unlike your bullshitting mother, I thought. 'Come on, let's go and clean you up. We're going to Tumble Tots in a minute.'

'Mummy, I done beautiful picture for you,' Molly announced, snuggling in to me as we went through to the front room.

'Have you? Aren't you . . .' I stopped. Aren't you lovely, I had been about to say. As I saw the felt-tip explosion in the front room, I had to bite my tongue not to launch into a round of expletives instead.

'Oh, *Molly*,' I said, putting her down abruptly. My mouth tightened. 'How many times have I told you – we draw on *paper*, don't we? Not on the sofa. And not on Nathan!'

My eyes bulged in horror at the sight of my precious boy with green streaks all over his cheeks and forehead, although he was beaming gummily under the baby gym, more concerned with pulling the rattly giraffe off its ring. I surveyed the damage wearily. One brown scribble on the sofa (thank Christ for washable covers) and some experimental pink lines on one of the cream walls. Marvellous. Truly avant-garde.

The budding artist, sensing all was not well, rushed to my side and did her best to cuddle me. 'I love you *very much*, Mummy,' she told me earnestly. Then, knowing it usually turned me to sentimental mush, she threw herself on her baby brother. 'I love you *very much*, Nathan,' she said, sneaking a look at me to see if it was working.

Nathan burst into howls as her bony elbows dug into him.

'Molly, you're squashing him. Get up!' I found myself yelling. 'Look at this mess! I can't leave you for two minutes!' My fists were clenched. 'Get off him! He doesn't like it!'

Now they were both crying. I stared helplessly at their wide red mouths and the tears that were springing out of their eyes. I snatched up a packet of baby wipes and started scrubbing the pen-marks off their faces. Oh God, now we were going to miss the start of Tumble Tots and the smug mum collective would purse up their lipsticked mouths as, once again, we crashed the double buggy in there late, guilty apologies pouring out of me. Sod it. Sod them. Why wouldn't this green come off Nathan? He was staring at me as if he hated me for wiping his cheeks so frenziedly.

'Molly, go and find your shoes.'

'I want my wellies.'

'I said shoes, not wellies.'

'I want my *wellies!*'

'OK, fine, get your wellies, then.' Get your sodding bollocking wellies, see if I care.

There, one small boy de-greened. 'Right, let's get the buggy out,' I said. 'Here's your coat, Molly. Oh, you put your wellies on all by yourself, well done. Do you want me to put your coat on?'

'I do it.'

'OK,' I said, fingers twitching as I watched her stuffing one arm down the wrong sleeve, upside down. 'Shall I just start you off . . .?'

'*I* do it, Mummy! Let *I* do it!'

'Right, fine, you do it. Let's go.'

We were ten minutes late for Tumble Tots in the end. Not exactly a crime against humanity, although you might be forgiven for thinking so if you'd seen some of the arched eyebrows, and heard the tutting.

A couple of the other mums waved knowingly across the

hall and I smiled gratefully back. Not everyone was in the motherhood mafia, at least.

'You'd better join this group,' Debbie, the Marlboro-voiced, scarily tattooed Tumble Tots leader told me, pointing to one corner where ten or so toddlers were dementedly rampaging up and down climbing frames. 'Hello, Molly – been drawing, have we?'

I tried to smile but couldn't remember how to do it. Instead, I grabbed Nathan and followed my daughter, who was pelting towards another group of kids altogether, having seen her friend Ella whizzing down a slide.

'I go with Ella,' she was shouting.

Ella's mum, Anna, elbowed me as I went over. 'Remember, we're *pleased* we've got feisty daughters, really, Sadie,' she told me. 'We're glad we've got independent, free-spirited . . .' She caught sight of the look on my face. 'All right, we're wishing they were obedient, passive little flowers, then, I admit it.'

We watched as our obedient, passive little flowers started bouncing alarmingly high on a mini-trampoline, holding hands and singing. 'WIND the bobbin up! WIND the bobbin up! Pull, pull, clap, clap, clap.'

'Wind the mummy up, wind the mummy up,' Anna sang softly.

'Pull, pull, smack, smack, smack,' I added, with feeling.

*

I stopped off for a coffee at Anna's on the way home. I'd met Anna when we'd both been hugely pregnant with our second babies, while breathlessly chasing our first ones around at a music class in Clapham. Ella was every bit as strong-willed as my own daughter, and Anna became an ally immediately. Nathan and Theo had been born within weeks of each other, and our friendship had deepened as we'd weathered the hellish early months together through coffees and large sugary doughnuts and plenty of crying.

'Anna, do you ever wonder if there's more to life than this?' I asked. We'd left the girls to trash Anna's sitting room while we sat in the relative peace of the kitchen. Nathan squirmed on my knee, brandishing a teaspoon with an air of triumph, and I wrestled to keep hold of him with one hand, clutching my coffee cup with the other.

Anna was frowning and sniffing Theo. 'Have you just . . .?' she started asking him. Then she pulled a face. 'Do you mean, is there more to life than stinking nappies and wind the bloody bobbin up and arguing about why your daughter can't wear her new coat in the bath?'

'Yes. That's exactly what I mean.'

She looked at me as if I was mad for even asking. 'God, yes, of course I wonder. Last night, I found myself trying to work out how much money I'd be earning now if I hadn't given up my job and had kids.' She gazed down at the table, and traced a pattern in the spilled sugar with her finger. 'It was so depressing and I felt so *guilty* for finding it so depressing that I went to bed instead.'

'Quite.' I took another slug of hot coffee. 'And it's not just the job and money stuff, it's the what's-happened-to-*me*? thing that I can't bear. The where's-my-life-gone? feeling.' I sighed and kissed Nathan's head, feeling bad for even saying the words out loud.

She was nodding. 'I know. It's like, what happened to the Anna who used to have a packed diary, gym membership, exciting sex-life, amazing career prospects? Where the hell *is* that woman? I really used to enjoy being her.' She swilled her coffee around. 'It was like she just melted away. She disappeared.'

I stared at Nathan as he patted my hand, his fingers closing around my thumb. 'Do you think our mums ever had this sort of conversation?' I asked.

She shook her head. 'No way. Not mine, anyway. My mum always says it was the happiest time of her life when me and my brother were tiny. The happiest time! Some days it feels like this is the worst thing that ever happened to me.' She bit her lip. 'Only some days. I mean, most of the time, it's great and lovely, but . . .'

There was a moment's silence. She didn't have to say the 'but'. We both knew what the 'but' was.

'You know, the stupid thing is, if I didn't have kids now, in my mid-thirties, I would be desperate for them,' I said, to spare her having to finish the sentence we all avoided saying. 'And here I am, with them, and all I can think about is how I want to feel like . . . like a sex kitten again.'

Anna spluttered, but then stopped as she realized I wasn't joking. 'Seriously?' she asked. 'Blimey, I wish I had the energy to even consider sex these days. What's got into you? Are you mad?'

She was smiling at me but I couldn't smile back. 'Anna, the other night, I went out and I ended up pretending to be someone else, just because the thought of my own life was too boring to think about.' I grimaced. 'And also because I really enjoyed talking to this guy. You know what, it was great to be talking to a man where the conversation didn't revolve around why no one had paid the gas bill and how the mortgage was going to be a struggle this month. It was just . . . fun. And flattering.' I looked across the table at her. 'Does that make me an awful person?'

A scream of rage interrupted us then and we rushed into the sitting room to find Ella and Molly both clutching the same fairy wand and shrieking at the other one to let go, even though there was another wand, exactly the same, on the carpet next to them.

'Molly, give it back to her!'

'Ella, let her have it!' Anna and I shouted in unison.

CRACK! The wand promptly broke in half and both girls fell over and started sobbing.

'Come here, Ella, love, you're all right,' Anna said, trying to cuddle her two children at once and nearly toppling over as she lost balance. Then she looked at me, her hazel eyes serious for once. 'It doesn't make you an awful person at all. You're a mum. We all feel like that.'

You're a mum. We all feel like that. Her words kept coming back to me as I heaved the double buggy back home. Did being a parent automatically mean you couldn't be the complete package of the person you wanted to be? Why *couldn't* you be sexy as well? Why couldn't you be a high-flying career woman without the guilt? Why did you always have to give something up?

I looked down at my children and felt like weeping as I saw Molly trying to hold Nathan's hand. 'Hello, little babe,' she was saying. 'Hello, little fella.'

They were so lovely but they were so bloody exhausting. Surely there had to be some kind of middle ground, one where you didn't necessarily concede your whole life to these small tyrants who deafened you with their cries and smothered you with their love – or was that just wishful thinking?

Chapter Two

On Saturday night, my mum came over to babysit, and suddenly I wasn't so sure if I wanted to escape the kids any more. Nathan was full of mashed potato and milk, and snoring contentedly in his cot, but Molly was tired and clingy. 'I be little baby,' she kept begging, crawling up onto my knee. 'I go back in Mummy's tummy.'

'Let's find your pyjamas, Molls,' my mum suggested. 'Do you want the Tweenies ones or the pussy-cat ones?'

'Pussy-cat,' she decided, leaping off my knee again. 'I put them on all by *myself!*'

I watched them go. My mum was one of those super-capable women whom children automatically seemed to obey. She had a way with them, as my dad was always saying proudly. She'd brought up me and my two sisters with a tidy two years between each of us and, like Anna's mum, professed to have loved every minute of it. She was either lying, deluded or suffered acute memory loss; I wasn't sure which.

'Let's go,' Alex said, checking his watch. His eyes flicked to the door. 'Your mum can manage now.'

'I'll just say goodnight.' I raced upstairs, half-anxious, half-ecstatic at the prospect of us both leaving the kids. I stroked Nathan's hair softly and watched as his eyelashes fluttered mid-dream. Then I went into Molly's room and kissed her goodnight.

'You got your beautiful top on, Mummy,' she said approvingly.

I hugged my mum. 'Thanks for this. Ring us about anything, won't you? Anything. We'll come back straight away if you need us. And . . .'

My mum put her hands on my shoulders. 'Relax!' she told me. 'These two will be a doddle compared to my year tens.'

I smiled faintly. 'Giving you grief, are they?' I asked.

She cocked an eyebrow. 'They try their best,' she said. 'They think all of us dinner ladies are fair game, but I tell them—'

'SADIE! Taxi's here!' Alex bellowed from downstairs.

'OK, coming. Bye, darling. Bye, Mum. See you later.'

'Have a great time,' my mum said, holding Molly up to wave.

A great time? I wasn't too sure about that. Dinner with Alex's new boss and some other people he worked with . . . It wasn't exactly what I'd have chosen, but still. We were going out, just the two of us, for an evening of good food – that I hadn't had to cook – and sparkling, intellectual, adult conversation. That was the main thing.

'Come in,' the man said, waving us inside. He was tall and square-shouldered, with neat, dark hair, and eyes so blue I wondered if they were colour contacts. 'You must be Alex and Sadie.'

'Hello,' said Alex, putting out a hand to shake. 'You must be Mark.'

'Hi, Mark,' I said. He looked as if he'd stepped out of a Paul Smith shop window with his white linen shirt and dark jeans. 'Nice to meet you.' He kissed me on the cheek and I breathed in his spicy scent. His skin was warm, soft as a child's.

'Come on in,' he repeated. 'Let me take your coats.'

Alex and I stepped inside onto the cream hall carpet. Thank God we weren't there with the kids, was my automatic first thought. Pure wool, I reckoned, trying to work out how much it must have cost. I shuddered, imagining the same carpet in our house. It would have lasted ten minutes before a trashing from Molly's muddy boots, or an explosion of carrot-coloured sick courtesy of Nathan. My children, arch-destroyers of anything remotely tasteful. I raised my eyebrows a fraction to Alex, and his grin told me he was thinking the same thing.

The immaculate carpet ran all the way along the hall and

up the stairs. There was not a miniature-sized welly or snowsuit or woolly hat to be seen on the coat pegs – just several well-cut winter coats, in black, charcoal and camel colours, a couple with glistening raindrops still on the shoulders, plus – oh God! – what looked like a Lulu Guinness handbag. There were four or five lighted church candles on the windowsill at the bottom of the stairs, flames wobbling as Mark closed the front door. And the house smelled fantastic – of vanilla, beeswax polish and the drenching perfume from a vase of white lilies on a side table. Their elegant, wide trumpets splayed out rakishly, showing the golden filaments within.

'What can I get you to drink?' Mark asked. He hung up my coat – my shabby, two-seasons-old Gap coat – and it looked like the scruffy kid in class next to the fawn cashmere number swanking on the neighbouring peg. 'We've got gin or vodka, red or white wine . . .'

'A gin and tonic would be great,' I interrupted eagerly. A bit too eagerly maybe, because Alex gave me a look, and Mark grinned at me.

'One of those days?' Mark asked.

'It's been one of those years,' I replied, trying not to blush.

'Gin, for me, too, cheers,' Alex said, squeezing my hand.

Even though I'd lobbied hard all week for dinner *à deux* somewhere expensive and luxurious, I was starting to think Alex had been right to talk me into coming here. It was going to be like stepping into someone else's life for an evening.

'You know we'll only bang on about the kids all night if it's just the two of us,' Alex had reasoned. 'We do enough of that at home. At least when there are other people around, we'll have to talk about other things.'

Other things? I'd thought at the time. *What other things?* Alex had a whole raft of 'other things' aside from family life, yeah – he had football and stag dos and a social life for starters. His 'other things' hadn't stopped, whereas my whole life was meshed together with Molly's and Nathan's. We had become a three-headed beast, a triptych. As a separate entity again, what did I have to talk about?

Three years ago, I used to say things like this:

No, I agreed with the judges. He definitely deserved to win the Booker. He has such an original voice.

And six years ago, I might have said:

I've been to every single shoe shop in the King's Road today and I still can't find the right shoes for Saturday night. My life is in ruins!

These days I say things like:

I tried Nathan with sweet potato today – he loved it!

Or:

Molly had a full-on, lie-on-the-floor-screaming tantrum in Sainsbury's this morning. It was so embarrassing!

Still, I was sure I could get back in the swing of adult conversation – especially after I'd downed a couple more of Mark's kick-arse G&Ts. Hmmm . . . Quick, Sadie, think.

Topics of conversation that had gripped me over dinner in the past . . .

> *Who was shagging who (friends).*
> *Who was shagging who (celebrities).*
> *What happened on* EastEnders *last night.*
> *Office gossip.*
> *Other people's office gossip.*
> *Shoes.*

'Hello, Alex, so glad you could make it,' a woman said, appearing in the hallway. Alex's new boss, Julia, presumably.

I eyed her over my glass, and mentally rejected the whole list. She looked far too scary to swap gossip with and not exactly the kind of person who would willingly discuss *EastEnders'* plotlines unless forced to do so at gunpoint.

As she walked closer, I found myself wishing I had bothered doing more post-natal sit-ups. All right then, *any* sit-ups at all in the last five years. She was tall and slim-hipped, with long, thick, chestnut hair that lay obediently waved on her shoulders. She had cheekbones you could cut your finger on, and clear green eyes. I wondered uneasily why Alex hadn't mentioned how good-looking she was.

'And Sadie, hello!' she smiled, looking me up and down. I could see her teeth, neat as a string of pearls, apart from a couple of wolfish-looking incisors. 'Nice to meet you. I've heard so much about you.'

'You too,' I lied, returning the smile in all its fakeness. I'd heard she was a bitch in the boardroom, yeah, but I hadn't heard that she had long hair and great boobs and dressed in what looked like Dolce & Gabbana. 'Pleased to hear that someone's kicking Alex and the team into shape.'

'I do my best,' she said. Her tone was light-hearted but I noticed her squaring her shoulders as if preparing for another business meeting. She practically radiated power. My heart sank.

I was *definitely* going to need a few drinks to see me through this one.

We followed the trail of Julia's musky perfume down the hall. Entering the living room was like stepping into a photograph straight out of *Elle Decoration* magazine – everything in tasteful neutrals. A sleek brown-leather sofa stretched along one wall with cream-coloured mohair cushions artfully arranged at the ends. My fingers itched to stroke them; my mind fought against mentally pricing them up. Heavy linen curtains hung in swags at the window and there was a fluffy pale carpet underfoot.

'What a gorgeous room,' I said to Julia, trying to keep the envy out of my voice. I was already feeling a creeping dread at the thought of having to throw a return dinner party and invite her round to our own bearpit. Julia, would you prefer a

Bob the Builder yoghurt, or a Petit Filou? I could imagine myself saying. Oh, and our starter tonight is lukewarm Tweenies spaghetti, served on toast – don't worry, the crusts *have* been cut off. Now, would you like a pink fork, or would you prefer to shovel it in with your fingers?

Julia put a hand lightly on my arm, and I looked at her *rouge noir* nails, long and polished. No chips. 'Alex, you know Matthew, of course. This is Alex's wife Sadie and Matthew's wife Chloe.'

'Partner,' I said, correcting her. 'We're not married. Hello,' I added to Matthew and Chloe.

There was just a tiny flicker in Julia's eyes at my words, but the rest of us had launched into the round of hellos and how-are-yous, and she didn't comment. Was it that she didn't like being put right or that it made Alex even more interesting? I wondered.

I vaguely recalled meeting Matthew at one of the newspaper's infamous office parties. He was the sports editor, whereas Alex worked on the literary section, subbing and writing occasional book reviews. Julia had been brought in as managing editor, and had promptly deleted half the senior members of staff with a single lash of her red pen. Half-admired, half-feared, she was the kind of boss who made grown men cry, according to Alex.

Matthew was tall and broad-shouldered with a broken nose and sandy-coloured hair. He had a face like a boiled ham, and piggy eyes with a devilish, roaming glint. Alex had once told me that he was a legendary womanizer. I'd have to watch what I said, I vowed hastily. I had a bad habit of blurting out bits of office gossip that Alex had told me. We'd had previous evenings of don't mention the bottom photocopying, don't mention the lesbian kiss, don't mention the whisky in the filing cabinet. With Matthew, I had a feeling it was a case of don't mention the nineteen-year-old secretary from Features.

'Sexy Sadie!' he boomed. 'We meet again!'

I smiled politely, accepted his wet kiss on my cheek and tried not to choke at the blast of sickly aftershave that accompanied the lunge of his head. 'We do indeed,' I replied, taking a small step backwards. 'You smell . . . nice. Brut, is it?'

God, the gin was going straight to my head. Luckily, he roared with laughter. 'Brut! You cheeky little minx! What was it he used to say in those ads?'

'Splash it all over!' Henry Cooper – or rather Alex pretending to be Henry Cooper – had materialized at my side and was giving me an odd look. A shut-up kind of look. 'Matthew, did you hear about Hannah's promotion?' he began, steering him away towards the window.

I had another swig of gin. It was going down very well. I turned to Chloe, whose pale fragility was the absolute negative image of her husband's ruddy porkiness. She was a skinny little thing, shivering under her beaded top and spaghetti straps, clutching her wrap around her shoulders like a comfort blanket. She had fine, straw-coloured hair that lay flat against her head in a neat bob.

She took my hand in her bony fingers and gave me a kiss on each cheek, dab, dab. I was reminded of a toy of Molly's where you pull a string and a miniature wooden chicken dips its head down to peck miniature wooden grain.

'Hello, Sadie, what do you do?' she said.

That question again. After a split second's hesitation, I plumped for the mild bullshit option this time. 'I suppose you could call it crisis management,' I replied thoughtfully. 'I'm a . . . Well, I'm basically a diplomat for two . . . clients. It's pretty tough. They're incredibly demanding.'

She leaned in closer to me and I could smell her perfume, light and sweet, and see the flakes of powder on her cheeks. 'Sounds interesting,' she said. 'What do your clients do, exactly?' She had an earnest, librarian-type face, and I suddenly felt mean for teasing her.

'I . . . I'm just making it sound interesting,' I confessed. 'My clients are actually a two-year-old drama queen and a small baby, so . . .'

She blinked. Shit. I had offended her. I'd been rude, taken the piss. Then she laughed. '*That* sort of crisis management,' she said. 'A full-time job with endless overtime, or so I hear.'

'Yes.' I smiled. 'That's the one. How about you?'

God, I was really out of practice at small-talk. I was

bloody rubbish! What was it I'd been hoping for? Sparkling, intellectual debate? Fat chance. I'd spent far too long gossiping with women who would tell you all about their stitches five minutes after you'd met them for the first time, and about how they hadn't had sex with their husbands for six months, and about how they hated their children sometimes. What did normal people talk about? I couldn't remember any more.

What do you do? I hated that question. Why should what you do – or indeed, what you didn't do – have any bearing on anyone? Why did it have to matter so bloody much? You never heard mums asking the 'What do you do?' question. You didn't need to.

Oh, me? I'm the Nappy Control Area Manager, with a bit of Anger Management counselling thrown in. In my spare time, I'm halfway through a diploma in Sleep Training Without Losing Your Marbles.

I listened glumly as Chloe went on about what *she* did – some sort of financial analytical thing that meant absolutely nothing to me. She might as well have been speaking in a foreign language. *Stock market . . . data . . . FTSE 100 . . .* I understood some of the individual words, but put all together, in sentences . . . Hmmm. She had me.

When she finishes banging on about the Dow Jones, I thought to myself, I'll twist the conversation into a more interesting direction. I'll ask her . . . I'll ask her . . . *What* will I ask her?

I'll ask her if she prefers Robbie Williams to Jeremy Paxman, I decided. No, I'll ask what she thinks of Richard Madeley's new haircut. I bit back a giggle and nodded knowledgeably as she told me about the inside info she had on the forthcoming budget. I'll ask her what her favourite book is, I decided in the end, and then wondered what I would reply to the same question. Did *Heat* magazine count?

Mark arrived with a couple of drinks at that moment – good, mine had long been emptied – and so I didn't get the chance.

'Dinner's about ready,' he said. 'Would you like to come through?'

Call me sad or call me a plain old middle-class snob if you want, but I do get a voyeuristic thrill from snooping around other people's homes. Vicarious living, Alex reckons. Nosiness, my mum says disapprovingly. She says she simply can't understand why I get triumphant about seeing a few fat, well-thumbed Jilly Cooper novels stashed away at the top of a bookcase that's otherwise stuffed with the likes of Ian McEwan and Salman Rushdie. 'So what if they like Jilly Cooper?' she asks, looking puzzled. '*I* like Jilly Cooper. What does that say about me?'

'There's nothing wrong with liking Jilly Cooper,' I try to explain. 'I like her too. It's about the pseuds who think they're above reading her, and who try to hide the fact by only putting their Booker nominees on display.'

I was hoping that I could spot the fatal flaw in Julia and Mark's house. The Barbara Cartland in the Martin Amises, if you will, or the tacky Tiffany lampshade. Hey, anything plastic would do, at a pinch. This was completely unfair of me when my own home was about as grubby and fluffy as they came, with plastic toys avalanching out of every cupboard, but that wasn't the point. My game, my rules.

We walked into the dining room, and damn it, there wasn't a single fault visible. In fact, I had to double-check we hadn't walked into the dining display area of Selfridges by mistake. The room was painted a warm plum, which might have ended up looking ghastly elsewhere. As it was, with wall lights softening up the colour, and flickering candles on every shelf of the walnut dresser, the room felt cosy and intimate. The table was laid with a spotless white linen tablecloth, silver cutlery and wine glasses that reflected the candlelight. We even had napkins, for God's sake.

It was about as far removed from dinner *chez nous* as possible. No one at the table was demanding chocolate biscuits and going ballistic with rage when told that they'd mysteriously vanished out of the cupboard. Nobody spat out their food or threw it, or splurged it over their own hair. Nobody had a tantrum about wanting to eat from a pink plate with a pink fork. Nobody . . . OK, enough. Leave it behind, I told myself. *Vive la différence!*

Over plates of sweet chilli noodles wokked to plump perfection, the conversation quickly moved around from the hot gossip at Alex's newspaper to the latest MP to get caught up in a sleaze scandal.

'Did you see him on *Newsnight* last night?' Chloe said, waving her fork animatedly. 'He was so uncomfortable. You could almost smell the sweat coming off him, couldn't you?'

God, *Newsnight*. I hadn't seen it for ages. Way past my usual bedtime. The only reason I ever watched it in the first place was for the Paxman factor.

'He'll brazen it out,' Mark said. 'He would have walked by now if he was going to.'

'The implications are enormous,' Julia put in. 'If it gets to court, there's going to be so much dirt that comes out of the woodwork. Let's just hope we can get the exclusive on his diaries – he's bound to try to cash in on this.'

'Let's hope we DON'T get his diaries,' Alex argued. 'I don't want that toe-rag to make any more money out of this, let alone from our paper. Get him into court and bang him up with the arse-soapers, I say.'

'Innocent until proven guilty, Alex,' Matthew said through a mouthful of noodles. They sprouted out of his blubbery lips in a rather vile maggoty fashion. 'Who's to say it's all true anyway? We know better than anyone how the hacks twist things to suit their own purposes.'

Alex snorted. 'Of course it's true! His political career has been totally built on lies and bribes and pay-offs.' His eyes glittered. 'He's an out-and-out con-man, I can't believe he's been allowed to get away with it all this time.'

Alex could get very passionate about things like this. I envied him for it. The only thing I had the energy to get worked up about was people beating their children or neglecting them or abandoning them. And, every now and then for light relief, how I was never going to be able to afford a Lulu Guinness handbag. Meanwhile, the political arena was passing me by, like a car accelerating past on the motorway. There I was stuck in the slow lane, trapped between the crawler lorries of domesticity and small children, my brain already stuffed to bursting point with other crucial information, like the entire text of *The Gruffalo* and the best way to get Ribena stains out.

I sighed, remembering the political discussions Alex and I had had once upon a time. Him and his Marxist theories, me and my feminist outrage. We'd discuss things that were happening all over the world, not just one small corner of south London where his football socks had vanished and the council tax hadn't been paid.

'What do you think, Sadie?' Chloe asked suddenly, and I jumped.

I hadn't a clue who they were talking about. Not a clue. There was a moment's silence while I put my head on one side and pretended to be considering the matter carefully. Really, I was thinking, Shit, shit, what shall I say? Quick! Something clever. Something meaningful. Something . . .

'He's good-looking, though, isn't he?' I blurted out randomly. 'Bet he's a bit of a sex-pot.'

Julia and Alex were staring at me as if I was mad. Mark spluttered with laughter.

'Joke,' I said quickly. 'Ha ha. This is delicious, by the way. Is there some ginger in it?'

'Yes,' Mark said. 'And lemongrass.'

'Very nice,' I said.

'How old are your children, Sadie?' Julia said as she refilled my glass. 'Two boys, isn't it?'

I looked across at her, wondering if that was her way of putting me in my place. Shut up, Mum, you don't know what you're on about. The adults are trying to *talk*.

Look, sweetheart, I don't give a toss about this MP, I felt like saying. I'm more concerned about whether my mother has been able to talk Molly into wearing her pyjamas rather than her bridesmaid's dress for bed tonight. But since you asked . . .

'Girl and a boy,' I replied. The usual fierce rush of love came the instant I thought of them. 'Molly's nearly two and a half, and Nathan's five months.' And they're both heart-achingly beautiful, I managed to stop myself from adding, voice shaking with pride. Blimey, one more glass of this wine and I'd be getting my baby photos out of my handbag and boring them all senseless.

'Banging them out there, Sade,' Matthew said with a broad wink. 'Going for the hat-trick, are you, eh?'

'Two of them is enough, thanks,' said Alex.

'We haven't decided yet,' I said simultaneously. 'Oh.' I looked across the table at him, feeling rattled. Alex seemed very assured on the subject of No More Children but I wasn't. I hadn't even considered not being pregnant again. Did he really mean that? I didn't know if I could cope with not being able to feel those first wonderful flutters of life in my belly again. Even the blood and grunting of labour for one last time would be worth it if I could plant kisses on a seconds-old pulsing head again.

'Well, *I* haven't decided yet, anyway,' I said, trying to make a joke of it. 'So if anyone's offering . . .'

My noodles suddenly felt squirmingly uncomfortable inside me. And the ginger seemed too hot, now that I thought about it. *Two of them is enough, thanks* – what did he mean by that?

I sighed and drank some more of my wine. I knew exactly what he meant by it, that was the problem. The way he'd been completely unable to comfort Nathan the other night had already flagged that one up. He wouldn't even be able to get past the headlines of the paper, let alone reach the international news pages, if we had a third child.

'Well, if you're serious . . .' Matthew smirked, patting my arm with a damp palm. He was half-drunk already, with a fleck of spittle on his top lip and a moustache of sweat sheening in the candlelight. 'You go for it, Sade. I'm all for big families. Shame Chloe's not so keen, but there you go.'

Ouch. The man was a walking, talking nightmare. Chloe glared at him and a terrible silence crashed down, with a tension that resonated like a vibrato.

'I grew up in a big family,' Mark said quickly. 'They *are* great. Bloody hard work when you're doing the parenting bit, though, I'm sure.'

I smiled at him gratefully and noticed that Julia was frowning. 'Hard work and expensive and messy . . .' she reeled off, through a tight little mouth. You could tell she'd trotted the words out before. 'My sister has children, and honestly, the money she throws at their school fees, you would not believe it.'

I bit my lip. Don't say it, Sadie. Don't mention that most schools are free. Don't get on your socialist high horse and inform her that, in your opinion, private education sucks. Even though I was sliding into drunkenness at an alarming rate, I still managed to cling to the fact that no, I really didn't want to start an argument with Alex's new boss. I didn't. Did I?

Luckily, Mark stepped in again. 'Alex, Julia was telling me that you work on the Review section of the paper,' he said. 'Do you get to do much reviewing as well as editing?'

If Matthew was the nightmare husband, Mark was starting to seem like the dream. He was easy-going and confident, and had a knack of saying the right thing at the right moment. He was what was known as A Good Bloke or, if you thought like Jane Austen's Mrs Bennet, A Good Catch. Actually, I decided, staring at him until my eyes went out of focus, he was pretty tasty, too. Well, if you liked that rich, clean-cut sort of look, anyway. He was wasted on Julia.

Then, quite randomly, I found myself wondering what my life would have been like if I'd married *him* instead of meeting Alex. I bet he would have been up for a third child. He liked big families, didn't he? He wouldn't have spoken to me in that same dismissive tone as Alex.

I stopped myself guiltily before the idea developed any further. What the *hell* was I thinking that for?

'. . . although I started off working on the weekend magazine,' Alex was saying as I snapped back to attention. 'That's where I met Sadie.'

Julia's eyes swivelled across to me, pinning me to my chair, practically. 'You worked on the paper, too, Sadie?'

Yes, once upon a time, Julia, I did. Straight out of university, in my one cheap suit from Topshop, with my non-existent typing skills and CV of lies and exaggerations, yes, I did work on your precious paper. Surprise! I have a brain, too!

'Alex and I were assistants on the magazine,' I said lightly. 'Our eyes met across the filing cabinets—'

'And two weeks later, she'd jacked in the job to go and work in book publishing,' Alex joked. 'Couldn't stand me pestering her to come for a drink any longer. But I won her round in the end.'

'How sweet,' Julia said. 'Goodness, your glass is almost empty, Chloe. Let me top you up.'

There was a moment of silence as we all watched Julia's graceful wrist tilting the bottle over Chloe's wine glass. A trace of lipstick was printed on the rim in an unhappy smile. Suddenly, I felt myself wishing we had gone to the George instead.

'So,' I said brightly. 'What I want to know is, who do you prefer – Jeremy Paxman or Robbie Williams?'

There was frost on the ground as we crunched our way out to the taxi, after one last kiss-kiss and thank you.

'I hope the kids are OK,' I said, checking my mobile to see if there were any new messages. As soon as Julia's front door had closed, so had the evening for me. Now it was time to go back to the real world, where my babies were hopefully both snoring peacefully, and my mum had had an easy night of it, watching *Casualty* with her feet tucked up on the sofa. A doddle, she'd predicted comfortably. I couldn't help but wince at that. How come I never found it a doddle, and they were my children?

'Yeah,' Alex said, opening the cab door for me. Unlike me, he hadn't quite left the dinner table behind. 'Those noodles were good, weren't they? Who do you think did all the cooking? Julia or Mark?'

'Mark,' I said, without a second thought, remembering the warmth of his cheek as we'd kissed hello. A kitchen warmth, I guessed. 'Although Julia might have overseen the process, of course. Given a bit of direction, maybe.'

The taxi pulled away and took us into the night. Alex laughed, his features lit up for a second as we went under a streetlight. 'You didn't like her, did you?'

'Not really,' I replied. 'Too hard. And rude. She's a man's woman.'

'So are you,' Alex said, pulling me across the seat to him. He started nuzzling my neck and his stubble snagged my skin. 'You're *this* man's woman.'

His hot, boozy breath was tickling me. 'You might want to remind Matthew of that,' I said, trying to wrest my chin away from him. 'Matthew of the wandering eye and wandering foot.'

Alex jerked upright. 'Wandering . . .? What, he was playing footsie with you?'

'FTSE? No, that was Chloe. Get it?' He was staring at me as if I was mad. 'She's a financial . . . oh, something. God knows.'

'So was he or wasn't he?'

'What? Oh. Matthew. Footsie. Well, making a pathetic attempt to, yes,' I said. I tried to decipher Alex's expression as we went under another street lamp. Was he jealous or merely bemused?

I was too pissed to tell. Alex was pressing his mouth hard against my ear and saying something dirty.

I wasn't listening, though. 'Could you stop the car a second?' I shouted urgently. 'I think I'm going to be sick.'

That night when we got home and my mum had been taxied away, we had clumsy, half-hearted sex in front of the whisper of the gas fire. I wasn't really in the mood – too knackered and conscious of the forthcoming hangover and night feeds and not wanting to wake the kids up – but it had been a while, and I felt like I owed it to Alex. I stared drunkenly into the fake coals wondering how many women around the world were thinking the same crap, cop-out, completely unsexy thing, and then found myself thinking of Mark's face again, his bright blue eyes, rumpled dark hair, his pink smooth skin.

Like a long-lost memory surfacing in my body, I came sharply and unexpectedly, and I cried out Alex's name, pressing my fingers into his back. It was almost as if I was trying to convince myself of something.

Chapter Three

The next day started like every other day: a wail over the baby monitor, a blur of small people in pyjamas, the smell of Weetabix and a brightly coloured Tweenies video on the box. The difference was that this morning had the added bonus of the most brutal of all hangovers clobbering my senses.

'Oh, Christ,' I moaned, trying not to barf as I poured Molly's warm milk into a cup. I felt utterly shit. My guts churned alarmingly. My head was bound too tightly by my own hot skin. Embarrassing things I'd said the night before kept flashing up in my brain, making me cringe and shudder. Adult conversation? Ha! I was a pleb. I was a philistine. I was never going to be invited anywhere again.

The weak February sun crept up into the sky, casting a faint light across the kitchen floor. The magnolia tree still shivered leaflessly outside in the garden. I pulled my dressing gown tighter around my waist and switched on the radio, skipping quickly through noisy pop stations to find one playing melancholy classical music, in the hope that it would soothe both children and me. Ahh. A dirgy piano piece. Perfect.

I couldn't help thinking about Julia and Mark's kitchen, imagining it full of morning sunlight and silence, in contrast to ours. I'd carried some plates through there last night, ostensibly to help but really so I could have a good old nosey around it and torture myself with comparisons. It was, of course, stunning, with a flagged floor and real oak units. Hand-made, I guessed gloomily, eyeing up the clean lines and clutter-free worktops. And all those gadgets! There was so much chrome, it was like being in a hall of mirrors. (Actually, maybe being mirror-free was best, after all. Seeing fifteen reflections of pasty-faced *moi* this morning wasn't going to do anybody any favours.)

Our kitchen, by contrast, was what you might call cheap and cheerful – all IKEA and B&Q, with a few home-made things chucked into the mix. I looked at it critically through the squinty eyes of a hangover. The lightshade Alex had made looked great – all parchment and copper wire and undulating curves. He'd given it to me for my birthday, soon after we'd met. We had an antique pine dresser, and the shelves were high enough that all my Clarice Cliff crockery remained unsmashed, even if it was rather undusted. I had mosaicked a splashback at the sink – a Celtic, interweaving design in blue and cream. And the room did at least smell good, for once – of coffee and toast and the intoxicating perfume spilling out from the hyacinths on the windowsill.

It was the small-children thing, really, that was what set us apart from the likes of Julia and Mark. The swirling finger-paintings on the fridge door, and the collages largely made up of pink tissue paper and glitter. The lone blue sock on the dresser along with several stray Tweenies jigsaw pieces, two white baby vests, some Playmobil men frozen in uncomfortable-looking contortions and a small wooden banana. Then there were the 30p coupons on the noticeboard, the unloaded washing machine with its red light winking like an accusing eye. And – oh, there was a new one – the small white plastic horse that was poking his nose over one pouch of the oven gloves, for some reason known only to Molly.

My shoulders slumped. It was a bloody tip. I wasn't just an embarrassing old lush; I was a slut on the cleaning front as well. I was a lazy, slovenly, unhygienic . . . Oh, bollocks to it. I didn't even have the energy to think up the adjectives.

We trailed back to the front room, where Fizz and Bella were still skipping around on the telly far too colourfully and loudly for my liking. Very obligingly, Nathan fell asleep in his baby chair within two minutes, and Molly crouched on the floor, half watching, half sorting out her dolls' house. I lay on the sofa, soothed by the high-pitched trills from the TV. I'd just close my eyes, maybe catch a few minutes' sleep . . .

'Mummy, I sit with *you*. Mummy! Wake up!'

*

Three hours later, Alex joined us. The skin on his face was sagging and his eyes were bloodshot. Dark stubble grazed his chin like a bruise. I poured him a coffee without asking, passed him the Nurofen and tried to prise Molly's insistent body away from him without success.

'Daddy read Mr Bear book, Daddy read Mr Bear book,' she chanted, waving one of her library books at him. One corner of the plastic covering scratched a red line on his cheek and I winced on his behalf.

'In a minute,' Alex said feebly. Molly had wrapped both arms around his head and was clinging from it, shrieking like a two-foot banshee.

'Gently, Molls,' I told her, trying not to snigger at Alex's face. 'Daddy looks even more poorly than Mum. In fact, Daddy looks absolutely dog-rough.'

'Yeah, because you're looking so special yourself,' Alex replied sarcastically. 'With your greasy hair and that new spot on your chin.'

I glared at him. Nathan chose that moment to grab a hank of hair and tug experimentally, as if testing its cleanliness for himself.

'Mummy got geesey hair,' Molly shouted. 'Honk honk goosey gander . . .'

'Greasy, not geesey,' Alex said. 'God, how much did we drink, Sade? Do you feel like this? You must do – you were really . . .'

'What?' I put in, trying to unwind Nathan's fingers from my hair. 'I was really what?'

He looked taken aback at the fierceness of my voice. 'Really . . . er . . . talkative. And entertaining.'

My shoulders slumped. 'I was a nightmare, wasn't I?'

'No! You . . .'

I didn't want to think about it. 'I'm going for a bath,' I told him. 'Here's our son. Your turn to look after them for a bit.'

I ran upstairs before he could complain, as I knew he would. I felt slightly mean, leaving him to it when he so obviously felt terrible, but then I remembered just exactly how god-awful *I* felt, actually, and the fact that I'd been up for hours already, and . . .

I sat on the edge of the bath and tried to stop the flood of complaints that were streaming through my mind. Sometimes, I hated the way that the children had turned us into completely different people. Overnight, it seemed, we'd transformed from being adults with careers and social lives into these knackered, shambling grown-ups with . . . whisper it . . . responsibilities.

Once upon a time, Alex and I had had such a romantic relationship. We snogged in public. We held hands when we walked down the street and swung them, like kids. He took me to Florence, I took him to Las Vegas. We had all-day breakfasts in bed with the Sunday papers and Alex's marmalade-coloured cat. We said witty, flirty things to each other and had sex in outrageous places. He made me blush. I made him horny. We discussed for hours how gorgeous we both were, and how great our lives were going to be, and made idyllic roses-round-the-door plans for our wonderful, romantic future.

How come, then, we'd ended up like this?

I turned on the hot tap and poured in my most expensive bubble bath, a present from my older sister, courtesy of her husband's gold Amex card, no doubt. It was so bloody *hard,* this parenting thing. It went on and on being hard, that was the worst part. You couldn't phone in sick and have a day off on the sofa watching crap daytime television if you fancied it. No holiday pay, no sick pay, no praise or promotions, no one letting you go early on a Friday because you'd worked so hard all week . . .

Alex appeared at the door, Nathan tucked under one arm. For a second, I thought he was going to ask me to have him in the bath with me, and my eyebrows were just seizing into a frown, mouth pursing into an automatic 'no', when he passed over the phone instead. 'For you. It's Becca.'

I looked at my watch in surprise. It wasn't even ten o'clock yet. 'What are you doing up so early?' I asked her. Normally she didn't crawl out of her pit until at least midday at the weekend – I should know, she'd bollocked me enough times for calling at earlier hours before now.

'I haven't been to bed yet,' she said. 'Just about to. I had to tell you about my school reunion night though – it was completely mental. You'll never guess who was there.'

'Your what? School reunion? Who?' I wiggled my pyjama bottoms and knickers off with one hand, started unbuttoning my pyjama top.

She laughed. 'Only Gary Taylor. Gorgeous Gary from Mrs Baker's form! Remember? My first love?'

I dredged through my memory and vaguely recalled the wistful look in Becca's eyes as she'd told me about him, and the dodgy photos of a skinny fifteen-year-old with a Clash T-shirt. 'Wow. What was he like?'

'He was *old*,' she wailed. I could hear her suck on a cigarette, as if the disappointment was hitting her all over again. 'Well, obviously not that old, he's the same age as me. But my God, you wouldn't notice him in the street. He was just . . . like someone's dad. Well, he *is* someone's dad. Four kids!' She sounded half-regretful, half-relieved at the thought. 'Beer belly, terrible shoes, bad hair. Cartoon socks! And he wore a jumper to the nightclub – I mean . . . Need I say more? Still, he was loaded, though. Went on and on about golf. Drove an Audi, he said. Big house in Hampstead, blah blah.'

'It could have been you, Bec,' I said, as I stepped into the bath. I was joking but there was a tinge of sadness in her reply.

'It could, couldn't it? Mrs Gary Taylor, with my four kids and Land Rover.'

'Thank your lucky stars it isn't,' I told her firmly. 'So how did this school reunion come about, anyway? How did you all get in touch?'

'Through Friends Reunited. Sukie Clarke organized it – although she was Swotty Susan when I knew her.' She gave a long, stretching yawn. 'God, I'd better go to bed. Just wanted to say hello anyway cos I'm going to crash out for the rest of the day now. Are we still meeting up on Wednesday night?'

'Yeah. Cat's going to come, too, I think. Night night. Sweet dreams of Gary,' I said.

I put the phone down carefully on the floor, trying to keep it out of splashing range. A school reunion – how weird that would be. All those people I hadn't thought about for so many years – what were they up to now? I could still remember the start of our class register all the way through comprehensive school: Jane Bilbie, Alison Bradbury, Robert Butts, Michael Castledine . . . And Danny Cooper – what would he be doing?

Danny Cooper. Now there was a name. If Gary Taylor was the one who did it for Becca, Danny Cooper was my very own fifth-form dynamite. He was so cool, and oh, just so-o-o gorgeous. He'd been a fan of The Jam, like me, and one week we'd both come to school with matching Jam logos painted on our school bags. It was definitely fate.

Of course, we got talking – shyly, first of all, about our favourite songs (mine: 'That's Entertainment', his: 'Going

Underground') and what we were each taking for our O levels, but before long, we moved on to more interesting subjects. We talked about the Falklands War and Thatcher and about how cool Tony Benn was, about our favourite books (mine: *Catcher in the Rye*, his: *On the Road*), about my sisters and his stepdad. We got into the habit of walking to school together because he lived two roads away from me. All of a sudden, we were best friends. We were the centre of each other's universe, the most fascinating people alive.

And then, at the school Christmas disco, we were dancing to New Order and he kissed me.

I rubbed the soap between my hands, remembering. Danny Cooper! We had been so in love it hurt. All the way through sixth form we were inseparable. We bought matching eternity rings from Greenwich Market, and I practised signing 'Mrs Sadie Cooper' all over my exercise books. And then one day – one dank November day that smelled of wet leaves and new gloves – we bunked off school and did it, right there and then, in my mum and dad's bed. It wasn't the greatest introduction to sex, what with having to keep half an ear out for my younger sister Cat skiving off (Lizzie, the eldest, never would have done – she never crossed my mind), or worrying about my parents just happening to pop back from work to get something. And the guilt of smelling my mum's lily-of-the-valley cologne on the pillows, and the horror of thinking, this is what *they* must have done to make the three of us, and trying not to think about *that.*

And his concerned face, asking if it had been OK, and telling me how lovely I was . . .

And stuffing the wet sheet in the washing machine and hoping nobody would notice . . .

It *hadn't* been OK – it had been painful and weird, him lying on top of me, being inside me – but that didn't matter. I loved him even more when I'd seen the fierce ecstasy on his face as he came. I wasn't a virgin any more, anyway. I'd done it. That was something to feel smug about when we sneaked back into school later that afternoon. All the way through my double French lesson, I felt wicked and dirty and grown-up and proud.

Things went on and the sex got much better, thankfully. I was part of a couple, smug and safe and explosively happy.

Then he had dumped me.

I scrubbed between my toes, remembering. It had been a languorously hot day in the post-A-level summer and I was desperately trying to bake myself brown in our square-lawned back garden, when he turned up at my house and told me it was all over. He'd got a place at Manchester University, whereas I was going to Brighton. He didn't want to have any ties. He wanted a clean break.

It had tipped my life upside down.

I squeezed my eyes shut in the bath. I could still feel the

devastating horror of his words. The smell of sun-tan cream, sweet and oily, catching in the back of my throat, my abandoned magazine flapping on the sun lounger in a sudden breeze; every detail had crystallized in my memory. I had heard each solemn, halting word, but I wasn't able to comprehend, to take on board the idea that he didn't want me any more. Surely he didn't mean . . .? Surely he wasn't saying . . .?

I had watched him walk out of my life, the sun dazzling me, and had pulled down my sunglasses with shaking fingers as the tears came skidding over my greased face. There I stood, a small ponytailed figure in a pink halter-neck bikini, with the world crashing in around my sunburned shoulders. The tears had dripped off my chin onto my bare feet.

I touched my face. Even now, I could still remember his teenage fingers on my skin. I could see his soft brown eyes, his longish hair that curled so cutely at the back of his neck.

Danny Cooper. What the hell would he be doing these days?

A loud crash from downstairs shoved Danny to one side in an instant. There was an ear-splitting wail from Molly seconds later, followed by sobs. Oh Christ. I got out of the bath and leaned out of the door, dripping and naked. 'What's happened?'

'She fell off the table,' Alex called up. 'All right, love, come here.'

She fell off the *table*? What the fuck was she doing on the table?

'I want bump cream!' I heard Molly crying. 'BUMP CREAM, DADDY!'

'She means the arnica cream,' I yelled. 'Drawer next to the sink.' I dried myself hurriedly. What was Alex thinking, letting her go up on the table anyway? For God's sake, I couldn't leave him for five minutes without something happening. I just knew he must have been checking the teams for today's football match on teletext, or something. Something completely un-child-related anyway. Why couldn't he just entertain them for a bit so that I could have a break? Was it really too much to ask?

'Let's see if this homeopathic nonsense can work its placebo magic on you, eh?' I heard him saying to Molly. He always spoke to her as if she was fifteen, rather than two and a half.

'Yeah,' Molly gulped, her sobs slowing down and finally stopping.

Crisis over. I looked at my bubbly sanctuary regretfully. The moment was gone, punctured with a single cry. I untied my hair from its tight hairband, and a handful of shining dead strands fell out through my fingers, as usual. This had to be what it was like to go bald for a man, this post-natal hair loss thing. Like traitorous lovers stealing away in the night, my hair was deserting me too, slipping out silently to rest on my pillowcase, clog up the plugholes or sprawl across the carpets. At this rate, I'd have less of the stuff than my baldy five-month-old boy, whose first blond wisps were just tufting out of his scalp.

I looked in the mirror and sighed. The cruelty of the female body is relentless: after the heroic exertion of pregnancy and childbirth, you might expect some relief, but no. Forget it, sweetie! The reward for continuing the human race was nothing more than a roadmap of purple stretchmarks charting the expansion of a formerly bikini-worthy belly, and aching, hot breasts pumped up to bursting point with milk. And then, just as you thought you could rightfully reclaim your body, the hair thing. Mother Nature sure knew how to kick a gal when she was down.

I slapped on some moisturizer, trying not to look too closely at the disturbing wrinkle thing that was going on under each eye, and brushed my teeth hurriedly. I put on underwear – matching, for once – pulled on some old jeans and grabbed a jumper. I wondered what Danny Cooper would say about me now, if he saw me at a school reunion. Would I have been relegated to middle-aged minger status, like the luckless Gary Taylor, or would he still be able to see some last traces of the seventeen-year-old Sadie in my face? My green eyes and dark lashes and snub nose were all still the same. My lips looked a bit thinner and paler than they had once been, admittedly. Teeth weren't bad. All still there, at any rate. It was my tired, aged, sleep-deprived skin that really let the side down . . .

'WAAAAAHHHH!'

And there was Nathan, bellowing for his next feed. Time to return to the front line.

Danny Cooper was forgotten about for a few hours while both children were fed and put down for naps, and then Alex and I sat down with sandwiches and coffees and crackling newspapers in a rare oasis of calm.

Silence. I loved it. It was one of my favourite sounds in the world, after the children's laughter and 'I love you' and the *Coronation Street* music.

'Mind if I have a look at your laptop?' I asked. I still had 'Going Underground' running through my head. *Some people might say my life is in a rut but I'm quite happy with what I got . . .*

'Help yourself.'

I booted it up and searched for the website Becca had mentioned.

Some people might say that I should strive for more but I'm so happy I can't see the point . . .

'What are you looking at?' Alex peered around the 'Sport' section while I typed in the name of my school.

'Hang on,' I said, watching the blue boxes build along the bottom line of the screen as the page whirred itself open. Then a list of names appeared. 'Oh my God!' I cried excitedly. 'Amanda Benson! I'd forgotten all about her!'

'Amanda . . .? Oh, right, Friends Reunited. Is that the first time you've seen it?' He sounded incredulous.

I would have shot him a look, but was too busy staring at the names, all throwing memories at me – Anna Stevenson's amazing ginger freckles, Anthony Woodsley and his reputedly huge willy, Rachael Albright of the pink hair and studded dog collars. 'We don't *all* sit around in offices arsing around on the Internet every day, you know,' I said tartly, and then stopped short. Danny Cooper. There he was.

'All right, all right. I was only saying.'

I ignored him and clicked on Danny's link.

Living and working in Manchester – managing my own record shop. Two dogs, no kids, GSOH.

Yeah, and? I wanted to ask. What else? Wife? Ex-wife? Partner? No one gives a shite about your dogs, Dan – what's the beef on your love-life?

'What's Amanda Benjamin doing with herself, then?' Alex leaned over, trying to look at the screen, and I closed Dan's message at once.

'Amanda Benson,' I corrected him. 'The usual boring stuff.'

'What, married, two kids, six hamsters and a drink problem?'

'Something like that,' I muttered.

Add Your Details, a link was inviting me. I clicked on it and started typing my own message.

> Went to university in Brighton, then travelled for a year. Came back to good old south London and worked in sales before I met my partner Alex and we had our two sprogs – Molly (2) and Nathan (five months) . . .

I stopped. God, it sounded dull. No, *I* sounded dull. What the hell would Danny think when he read that? He'd probably thank his lucky stars he'd got away up the motorway to Manchester when he'd had the chance.

I deleted all of it. Maybe I should just add my name, forget the details. Then I thought back to my conversation with Anna. Maybe I could just . . . embellish a little . . .

> Lived in Brighton for a few years, doing my degree. Then I travelled around the world, stopping in Vietnam to work in an orphanage for two years.

I giggled out loud at the enormity of my lie. The travelling bit was true enough but the only work I'd done had been a few crappy fruit-picking jobs in Australia and New Zealand to raise some extra dollars. Voluntary work in South-East Asia . . . forget it. I'd been too busy bronzing myself, climbing mountains, haggling over sarongs and smoking the mind-bending grass. I sighed nostalgically. It had been such a great time.

'Who have you found now?'

'Nobody. You didn't know her,' I said, typing away again.

Came back and did an MBA before getting a job in finance . . .

No. Too dull – and far too unrealistic.

Came back and retrained at King's. Am now a leading brain surgeon . . .

Even worse. Everyone would know that was a lie. It had to be something at least on the right *side* of credible.

Came back and did three months' work experience on Newsnight, before being offered a permanent place as a researcher.

Yes, good.

Made the jump to Channel 4 two years ago as . . .

I racked my brains. What would everyone have heard of?

. . . a producer of Countdown . . .

Absolutely no way. Terrible idea!

. . . a producer on Big Brother.

Yes! Definitely yes. Then, as a nudge to Danny, I added:

No dogs, but own teeth and GSOH.

There. I sent my details away to the database and a message flashed up, telling me my name and message had been added to our school board. For some weird reason, my hands were trembling.

Chapter Four

I put the laptop away and finished my coffee, trying to imagine Danny's face if he logged on to the site again and saw my name. He'd be impressed, I was sure. Fancy Sadie Morrison working for Channel 4! he'd think. Mind you, she was always creative at school. The paintings she did for her Art A level portfolio – brilliant, they were, especially the portrait of me. Good at English, too. Should have known she'd end up doing something in the media.

I picked up the pile of weekend newspapers that I hadn't so much as glanced at yet, and suddenly felt as if I'd been caught cheating in an exam. First Jack, now Danny. What was I like with my fantasy jobs?

The last job I'd had before I went on maternity leave with Molly had been as a sales manager for a small publishing company. It was fun, sure, and there were lots of perks, and some people – my mum, for example – seemed to think it was terribly glamorous. Which it wasn't. Not as glamorous as being a TV producer by any means. Still, it was something.

A job. I had been an independent working woman, with my Next trouser suits and company car. Needless to say, it all seemed a very long time ago now.

The 'Jobs and Money' section of the paper was on top of the pile, and, on impulse, I grabbed it and started flicking through the ads. Just to see what I could do, you know. Just to remind myself that I could still get an interesting job if I wanted to.

ITN Senior News Correspondent . . .

Cool or what? I couldn't resist imagining myself in sexy little Moschino suits, with horn-rimmed spectacles and a stern interviewing technique. I would frighten those MPs into squealing out their secrets in live interviews or, alternatively, I'd ply them with booze and let them give themselves away. I'd be a TV legend!

I glanced through the details. Nice pay, flexible working hours (good) . . . oh. Keen interest in current affairs. Well, duh. You don't say. I thought back to my outstanding contribution to the political discussion last night and regretfully moved on to the next ad.

Sales Manager for a new publishing company . . .

Now, then. I could definitely get that one, if I wanted to. I was brilliant at sales, wasn't I? I had always met my targets, and was sure that the old magic would still be there. A,B,C my first boss had instructed fervently. Always Be Closing. In my heyday, I could have closed five deals before breakfast!

Well, lunch anyway. It all depended on how hung over I was, really, and how susceptible the booksellers were to my sweet-talking. And, to be quite honest, how short my skirt was.

I read the ad again. Religious books. Oh. That would be a no, then. Even I couldn't be convincing about religious books. I scanned down to the next ad.

That was when I saw it. Talk about coincidence!

Producer required for new chat show. Do you have creative flair, an ability to work on a tight budget, and the organizational skills to juggle a hectic workload?

Yes! I did. I bloody did!

We are an independent television production company in the heart of Soho.

Lovely. All those lunches, and all that shopping . . .

You are an experienced producer with great ideas and a full contacts book.

Well, not quite, but . . .

Interested? Send your details to Emma Tomlinson at . . .

Interested? I was, actually. Apart from the last sentence, the experience bit, it sounded great. A TV producer, just like I'd put on the Friends Reunited website. It really was a coincidence.

My hand hovered over the paper, not quite wanting to turn the page on the ad. I tore it out instead. Maybe it would be fun to apply – not seriously, obviously – but just . . . as a way of proving something to myself. Anyway, it was all good practice. I would have to apply for jobs again in the future, when the kids were older. I had to keep my hand in, didn't I?

I thought back to the lies I'd told to Jack earlier in the week, to Chloe the night before, and now, via a website, to Danny, and everyone else I'd been at school with. I was obviously a good liar, that was without doubt. I could bullshit with the best of them. Was I good enough for the Firestarter TV Company, though?

I switched on the laptop again and started typing.

Dear Ms Tomlinson,

I am writing in application to your advertisement in the Guardian *for the producer's position.*

As you will see from the enclosed CV, I have had many years of experience working on a variety of television programmes, and, in particular, daytime chat shows. After finishing my Media Studies degree, I undertook a voluntary placement on This Morning *where . . .*

I paused for thought. God, I was enjoying this. I was going to flog it for all it was worth, load this letter with bullshit until it reeked of the stuff.

. . . where I learned many aspects of programme-making, both on the studio floor and in the offices.

For me, impeccable organization is the key to a successful live programme like This Morning, *and as a TV producer, good team-working skills are essential.*

Blah, blah, blah, blah, blah. On and on I wrote, turning my CV into a two-page work of art, and my letter into a modest reflection of some of my greater triumphs. Hey, even *I* would have given me the job, I sounded so good. I giggled as I read it back again. Well, even if it wasn't all true, nobody could fault my creative writing skills.

There was a cry from upstairs, and I emailed the thing off without a second thought. Gone. See? Motherhood wasn't the only thing I could do. Lying came as easily as breathing.

The next morning, I dropped in to see my mum. She and my dad still lived in our old family home, a three-bedroom semi in Tooting, with its spotless net curtains and gleaming ornaments arranged neatly on every surface. Everything was just as it had been when I'd grown up there. Same carpets, same curtains, same layout of the furniture. The only difference I noticed whenever I came back, fifteen years after moving out, was the change of soundtrack. No more thumping music from Cat's stereo. No more low giggles from Lizzie, sitting on the stairs, twiddling the phone cord around her fingers as she chatted to her mates. Nowadays I walked in and heard the kettle hissing, the Hoover rumbling or – if my mum was in a frivolous mood – Frank Sinatra.

Molly went to play with the jangly bead curtain and fridge magnets in the kitchen, as always, while I plopped Nathan on the floor to practise rolling, and sipped my scalding tea.

'I take it you've heard about Mrs Green,' Mum said, perching on the edge of an armchair. My mum never seemed to sit comfortably in her own home. She always perched, as if she was ready to fly up and knock together a cauldron of savoury mince at any moment. I knew she'd be thinking of all the things she had to do before going to the school for dinner-lady duty, like ironing my dad's socks or getting out the chicken to defrost for tomorrow's tea. Even in her late fifties, she was every inch the diligent housewife, the domestic goddess of Fernwood Terrace.

'Mrs Green?' I frowned, wondering who the hell Mrs Green was. 'No.'

She clucked her tongue. 'Did Lizzie not tell you? Well!' She put her cup down on the saucer. 'It's lung cancer. They're devastated, of course. Six months, the doctors are giving her.'

'That's terrible,' I said, racking my brains for some memory of the poor woman I was obviously meant to know.

'Isn't it just? With her Leanne almost eight months gone, and the father nowhere to be seen as well.' She shook her head. 'I don't know what the world's coming to, I really don't.'

I saw her looking down fondly at Nathan, who was trying to get over onto his front. ''Course, *you're* all right, aren't you, bubs?' she said. Down went the cup and saucer on a polished side table, and there she was, hoicking him up in the air to nuzzle his hair. 'I said, you're all right, aren't you, eh? Got a smile for your grandma, then?'

Nathan beamed at her and batted a fat hand in her vague direction.

'Isn't he Grandma's little pickle, then? Isn't he Grandma's little darlin'?' Then her tone changed. 'Ooh, is that a tooth he's got coming there?' She squinted into his mouth. 'Is that a toothy-peg, my little chubkin?'

I got to my feet in interest. 'I hadn't noticed anything,' I said. 'Where?'

'Oh, I think it is,' she said, expertly running a finger along his lower gums. 'Right here. My Nathie-wathie got his first little toothy coming, hmmm?'

My hands twitched. 'Can I see?' I asked.

She passed him over. ''Course, you'll want to put some clove oil on that, if it starts bothering him,' she said, pursing her lips. 'Shall I see if I've got some? Your dad uses it on his teeth sometimes.'

'It's all right,' I said. 'I've got some homeopathic stuff for teething back at home.'

She stopped in her tracks. 'Right,' she said doubtfully. There was a pause. 'Because I used clove oil for you three, and it was wonderful. That and a dab of brandy if you were screaming your heads off!'

'I'll see how he goes,' I said. 'He might not be too bothered by it. Molly's teeth came through without too much palaver.'

My mum was still on her feet, poised to make a dash for the clove oil at the slightest sign of encouragement. 'Well, it's here if you want it,' she said in the end. She resumed her perch on the arm of the chair. 'Although I daresay you've got your own brandy.'

I stroked Nathan's back. 'Mmmm,' I replied. I didn't bother telling her that health visitors weren't so encouraging on the babies/alcohol idea these days. In fact, I steered off the subject of babies altogether. Somehow it was easier that way.

Back home, tempted though I was by the tower of washing up and a bout of Hoovering, I couldn't resist making the most of a ten-minute breather. Nathan was dozing and Molly was amusing herself by getting all of the saucepans out of the cupboard, so I got out Alex's laptop again, and booted it up.

I found that my heart was beating fast. My mouth was dry.

This is crazy, I told myself, he won't have replied already. He won't even have *seen* it. But Danny Cooper had been spreading through my subconscious like oil on water ever since my phone call with Becca. Things kept coming into my mind when I wasn't expecting them.

I'd remembered his laugh – his loud, staccato ha!-ha!-ha! that sounded so ridiculous, it always made me giggle.

I'd remembered his handwriting – straight up, girlishly rounded, no curl on his 'g's and 'y's.

I'd remembered how he loved it when I went on top. The wild look of abandon on his face as he'd come.

And what about the quickie we'd sneaked in the boys' toilets one afternoon when school was out? We'd so nearly been caught by the caretaker. Sssshhhh ssssshhhh sssssshhhhh, his broom had gone in the corridor outside. I remembered how desperately we'd tried to stop sniggering as we kissed in the cubicle, smells of pine disinfectant and schoolboy piss all around us.

I tried to ignore the metallic crashes from the kitchen as I waited for the internet connection to start up. It wasn't possible for a child of two to actually *break* a saucepan, was it? Click . . . click . . . whirr . . . the computer went.

Right. Here we go. I went straight to my email account. *Inbox: 0 new messages,* it said.

None. Curses.

I went to the Friends Reunited website again, just to see if I was on there. Maybe there'd been some technical glitch, maybe they hadn't transferred my details yet. Maybe . . . Oh. *Sadie Morrison,* there I was.

I felt deflated. It was ridiculous of me. What had I been expecting? Honestly, I was such an idiot. Had I really thought that . . .?

I pulled back from the path my mind was taking, not sure if I wanted to spell out the hopes that had been stealthily building up since the day before. A first love was just that, after all. The first love before you went on to the second, third, fourth, however many it turned out to be. Just because someone was your first love didn't mean they were your best love. Of course it didn't.

I went back to the website. I would look up *Alex*, I decided, and see how he had portrayed his life to the watching world. After a few clicks, I found his Leeds comprehensive school and quickly scrolled down to his year. Ahh. There it was. And there *he* was. Alex Blake.

It was strange to see such a familiar name in a list of unknown people, some of whom had known him as a teenager, sat in assembly with him, played in the same football team as him, maybe smooched at the Christmas disco with him . . . I clicked on his link.

> Went down south to study at UCL, and never made it back up the M1. Working as a sub-editor now, and loved up with a gorgeous Cockney bird who's kindly given birth to my two beautiful children, so had better stay put for a while. Up the United!

Gorgeous Cockney bird, eh? Was he talking about ME?

I stared at the words. He'd really put that. He'd really described me as a bird. Me, the supposed love of his life. The cheeky bloody sod.

I read it again. My first thought was to hack into his message and rewrite it, make it sound more . . . well, more serious, for starters. More committed to me and the kids. The 'loved up' bit could stay, I supposed, although I would have liked something a *tad* more long-term-sounding, instead of making me sound as if he'd picked me up in a club a few nights before on an E-fuelled bender. *I fell in love six years ago and remain deeply committed to this amazing woman.* That sort of thing. *Oh, and I'm planning to propose to her any day soon.* Yeah. That, too.

The gorgeous bit . . . well, that could stay. That could definitely stay. Had he been pissed when he'd written it? WHEN had he written it? Obviously before the late nights with Nathan had really started kicking in and ravaged my face so cruelly. And the bit about the beautiful children – yes, well, of course I agreed with that wholeheartedly.

It was that 'bird' word . . . it sounded too casual. It sounded like he was laughing at me. And the bit about having to 'stay put for a while', too. For a *while*? Then what was he planning to do, after the 'while' was up? It made him sound such a wanker!

I sat back, considering. It could have been worse, I

supposed. At least I got some kind of a mention, even if it was in a macho, posturing sense. And at least he still thought I was gorgeous – or had he just put that to show off to the other blokes from his school?

I stared at the words until they started jumbling up into nonsense before my eyes. If he was being absolutely truthful, strapped to a lie detector, what would he have written then?

> Am settled down in a tired relationship with Sadie. She was a right minx when I first met her, but she moans a lot these days. Goes on and on about how hard it is to look after our kids – when she was the one who wanted them in the first place! And it's not like she does anything else – I mean, the house is always a pigsty, and nothing ever gets ironed . . .

There were tears in my eyes. Stop it, stop it, I scolded myself. He wouldn't think that, would he? I was just beating myself up after the morning visit to Supermum. Comparing myself with my own mother got me nowhere. She always seemed to win.

I was just about to shut down the connection when a creeping sense of guilt came over me. Hang on a minute, I thought. Here I was, complaining about his terminology but I hadn't even *mentioned* him in my message. I'd pretended he didn't exist. So who was I to make a fuss about being called a gorgeous Cockney bird?

I went back to find my entry, fingers feeling clumsy on the keys. I'd delete it, I vowed. I'd put in the truth. Why on earth had I lied about my life like that? As if I was ashamed of it or something!

'Mummy, I hurt my finger. Mummy!'

Molly's voice from the hall made me jump. God, and now I'd let my child injure herself while I was faffing around spying on my partner. I closed down the connection at once, put the laptop out of trashing range and ran to find her.

Two beautiful children, Alex had said, and a gorgeous Cockney bird. That wasn't so bad, was it?

Was it?

There was nothing from Danny the next day. Still nothing the day after that. By the time Wednesday evening had rolled around and I was frantically trying to pluck some of the werewolfishness out of my eyebrows ready for my night out with the girls, Danny Cooper had started to fade from my mind again. What had I been playing at? It had been a silly mind game. A fantasy. And as for that job . . . it was ridiculous. I must have had too much sun. In February. Either that, or I was losing the plot.

'What you doing, Mummy?'

A little nudie imp had appeared behind me. Alex had come home early so he could bath the children and put them to bed for me, and Molly had obviously spirited herself out of the bathroom, because here she was, all pink and shiny, hair wet and sticking up absurdly, chubby bare legs scrabbling their way up onto my and Alex's bed.

'Hello, lovely,' I said, tears welling in pain as I pulled out a clump of wayward eyebrow hairs. 'Ouch. Do you want to run back and get your pyjamas on?'

'You draw on your eyes now, Mummy?'

She was gazing at me with great interest, head on one side. I barely wore make-up these days, but on the rare occasions she'd seen me putting it on, she had been fascinated by the eyeliner application – indeed, had tried to copy me by putting pink felt-tip along her own eyelids.

'Maybe in a bit,' I said. 'Quick, go and get those jim-jams on with Dad. Quick!'

She bounced a few times on our bed and then scrambled down and vanished as quickly as she'd materialized. I smiled as I rolled on my lippy. I was really looking forward to seeing Becca and Cat. Just a quick pint, we'd all agreed previously, but then, a couple of hours ago, Becca had phoned me to say that she'd booked us a table at some glam new restaurant in Battersea.

'It's been ages since we did something nice. And this is my treat. No arguments,' she'd said.

'Bec, you don't have to do that,' I'd replied automatically, calculating how much money I could reasonably cadge off

Alex. Becca had expensive taste and was used to her men paying for it most of the time.

'I said, no arguments,' she repeated. 'My treat. Call it an early birthday present if it makes you feel better. I'm going to cab it over there, I think. Shall I pick you up about half-seven?'

'Yeah, great. See you later!'

I smacked my lips together and smiled at my reflection. Although I wasn't given to gratuitous shameless boasting, I had to say, I was looking pretty good by my usual bare-faced hasty-ponytailed standards. I was wearing a bell-sleeved powder-blue top that showed a good inch of cleavage, black kick-flare trousers and my favourite old stack-heeled boots. My hair was piled up on my head with just a few loose tendrils curling around my face. My eyebrows were plucked, my skin was looking perkier than it had done for months, thanks to three goodish nights' sleep on the trot, and I had treated myself to a new hazelnut lipstick.

'Phwooarr,' Alex said, running an appreciative hand over my bottom when he saw me. 'Can I come with you?'

I air-kissed him and the kids so as not to smudge my lips. 'No chance. Girls only.'

'Molly a girl,' my daughter said at once. '*I* come, Mummy?'

The taxi beeped and I laughed, checking my face one last

time in the hall mirror. 'Nice try, Molls. Girls over three only. Night night. Bye!'

Becca hugged me when I got into the cab. Her perfume smelled exotic and musky; my own squirt of Green Tea had to struggle not to be smothered by it. She was wearing a grey trouser suit and a shocking-pink shirt. 'Just come from the office,' she explained, seeing me glancing at her briefcase. 'We've been all heads down on this new campaign before it launches next week.'

'Oh, right,' I said, struggling to remember what campaign she was working on. Becca was a creative in advertising. A creative *what,* I had often wondered, but it seemed to be just a one-word job title.

'The new Renault,' she added. 'For men on the move!'

I giggled. 'Is that really the slogan?'

'No, that's just what we call them. Men who wet their pants over big engines, revs, horsepower, all that nonsense. Anyway, I'm not going to talk about that all night. How are you?'

'Well,' I started, planning to launch into my excitement about tracking down Danny on the internet. Then I caught the cabbie's eye in the mirror and changed my mind at the last minute. I didn't feel like talking about it in front of him somehow, so I told her about our night at Julia and Mark's instead.

To be honest, it was quite refreshing to have something to

talk about that Becca might actually be interested in. Before Molly was born, we had sneered about how dull women became when they hit motherhood. 'Promise me you'll tell me if I get like that,' I'd begged her. 'Shoot me if I start telling you about poo or sick or romper suits, like they're remotely interesting.'

'You don't have to ask, babe, of course I will,' she'd agreed. 'That goes for gory details of the birth, too. If I so much as *hear* the word "stitches", our friendship is officially terminated.'

Since I'd crossed the line into parenthood, though, that conversation had never been referred to by either one of us. I didn't know if she was too kind to remind me of it, or if she thought I was in too deep to drag back to sanity. I *did* know that I'd mutated into one of those very women we used to scoff at. I'd moved to the other side, changed teams. While I could talk in encyclopaedic detail about breastfeeding and potty training and language development, Becca still talked about hot dates, nightclub binges, and holidays in Third World countries. We were like different species.

Becca shuddered at my descriptions of Julia and Matthew. 'Ugh! She sounds like some sort of power-dressed ogress,' she grimaced.

'She was,' I said. 'The sort of woman who kisses you on the cheek, then doesn't bother telling you she's left an enormous lipstick print there.'

Becca nodded. 'I know exactly what you mean.' She pulled out a compact mirror and checked her own lipstick. '*He* sounds rather nice, though,' she added.

'Who, Matthew?' I said incredulously. Maybe I'd been too generous when I was describing him. Maybe I should have spelled him out in more obvious terms. Read my lips: *Womanizing, booze-mottled, lecherous old piss-head . . .*

'No, he sounded hideous – Mark. Mark sounded nice.'

I was silent for a second. Mark. 'Yeah. He was, actually. He was lovely.'

'Fifteen pounds forty please, gels,' the cab driver said, pulling up outside a glass-fronted building.

I tried to pay for it, but Becca pushed my pound coins away. 'I'll get it. No, honestly. I'll put it on expenses. Could I have a receipt, please?'

'Now,' she said, as we walked up to the door. Swanks, it was called, and it certainly looked incredibly swanky inside, all immaculate white and bleached wood. 'This is meant to be a bit special, so I hope you've got your celeb-spotting goggles on. Did you see the review it got in *Time Out*?'

I shook my head, not bothering to add that there wasn't really much point in my buying *Time Out* these days.

She made a circle with her thumb and first finger and held it up. 'Top-notch.' She grinned. 'Oh, Cat, hi! We were just about to go in.'

Cat hugged me and kissed Becca on the cheeks. 'Let's do it, then,' she said.

Over our food – top-notch indeed – we got down to the business in hand. Gossip.

'How's your love-life then, Bec?' Cat asked.

A smirk slid over Becca's face. Her mouth twitched. 'Pretty shag-tastic, thanks for asking,' she said.

'Tell us!' Cat demanded.

'Who?' I asked. 'Since when?'

'Star sign, job, sex-factor rating,' Cat added, all in one breath. 'Now.'

Becca spluttered. 'Easy, girls,' she said. 'He's called Nick. He was what you might call a sperm-of-the-moment decision.'

Now it was my turn to choke on my drink. 'Becca!'

Cat's eyes had lit up and she had put down her fork in anticipation. 'Tell. Us. More,' she insisted. 'Where did you meet him?'

'Browns,' Becca said. 'Work leaving do on Monday. I came, I saw, I conquered.'

'And then you came again,' Cat giggled.

'Exactly.' The smugness was practically visible; it was coming off her like steam. 'It was a bit embarrassing, actually. I was quite drunk and eyeing up the talent with my mate Polly. I spotted Nick and said to her, "Right, I'm having him." Only thing was, I said it a bit loudly.'

We rocked with laughter. 'Oh, no!'

She grinned. 'Oh, yes. He winked at me and said, "I heard that," very pointedly. I thought I was going to *die* on the spot, and there's Polly absolutely wetting herself laughing at me. But . . .' She shrugged. 'It worked. I did have him. And he's lovely.' She smirked and twizzled some rocket leaves round with her fork. 'And he's *wadded*.'

'Of course,' Cat nodded. 'Wouldn't expect anything else.'

'So what happens now?' I asked. 'Seeing him again?'

She munched through her leaves. Becca was one of the few people I knew who actually chose to eat salad because she liked it, not just because it wasn't fattening. The freak. '*Seen* him again already,' she said. 'Last night. He took me to Nobu.'

'Ooooh,' we chorused. Blimey, even I'd heard of Nobu.

'Oooh indeed,' Becca said. 'Do you know, I really really like him. He made me laugh. And he's good in bed as well. He makes me feel like . . .' She broke into song. 'Like a natchural wooooman . . .'

Her cheeks were flushed as she waved her microphone fork around. Sparkly eyes. An I've-had-fab-sex-in-the-last-twenty-four-hours glow in her skin.

'Well, I'm very happy for you and not jealous at all,' I said, trying to keep the sigh out of my voice. All that sex and romance and giddiness . . . It had been a long time since I'd felt like that. My cheeks were only flushed from alcohol, and shouting at my children these days.

'I've got some news too,' Cat said. 'Tom and I are going to move in together. A domestic tom-cat, as he put it.'

'Ooooh!' Now it was my and Becca's turn to be the *Trisha*-audience-style chorus.

That *was* good news. Tom was lovely. Cat had been with him for years, but it had been quite on-off, on-off – mainly because they both had feisty firework tempers and the kind of rows where one person stormed out or threw books at the other one's head or said horrible, hurtful things that made the other one cry and say even more horrible, hurtful things back.

Cat had always been charming and lovable in my eyes, though. She was the sweet youngest sister, as opposed to the sensible oldest sister (Lizzie) and the awkward, troublesome middle one (me). Cat was the kind of person that everyone adored. She had long blonde hair, green eyes and freckles and a nose that scrunched up when she laughed. If you strayed into her bad books, though, ouch – you knew about it. That cat could scratch.

'That's brilliant, really brilliant, Cat,' I said warmly, squeezing her hand across the table. 'His place or yours?'

'Neither,' she replied, grinning back. 'We're going to sell up and buy somewhere new. Somewhere that's ours. It's so grown-up it's terrifying. Which is why we're going to have a fuck-off-great, month-long, young-guns holiday first, to cushion the blow.'

'Like it,' Becca nodded. 'Anywhere in mind?'

I poked my cutlery around my plate and tried not to listen *too* hard as Cat started telling us about her plans for India, how she couldn't wait to get back there, how she was desperate for a sunny beach to lie on, Goan fish curries, haggling for rugs in Anjuna market, palm trees, cold beers on the balcony at the Panjim Guest House . . .

I slugged my wine down. 'Shall we get another bottle?' I said, interrupting Cat's *Passage to India* monologue. There was only so much jealousy I could deal with in one evening, after all. Any more of this and I'd be forced to run out of Swanks screaming and crying and checking myself into the nearest loony bin. Or something.

'Have we finished it already?' Becca asked, picking up the bottle and peering through the murky green glass. 'That didn't take long.'

As she waved a hand to the waitress, I noticed somebody staring at me across the room. He looked vaguely familiar but I couldn't place him. Blue eyes, sharp shirt, sexy cheekbones. Was he one of the dads from Molly's playgroup scrubbed up for a night out? Someone Alex played football with? He was smiling and waving, and then he made one hand into a phone shape and held it up to his ear. 'Call me,' he mouthed.

Then I remembered. Jack.

Oh my God, it was Jack from the other night, the one I'd lied to, the one I'd told I was a scriptwriter! I smiled back quickly and nodded and turned around to the table, heart thudding uncomfortably. Shit. I hadn't expected to see him ever again, let alone a week or so later.

Cat kicked me under the table. 'Who is *that* piece of eye candy over there you've just been flirting with?' she hissed. 'Don't tell me you're doing the dirty on Alex?'

'No!' I could feel my ears turning red and the blush sinking down into my neck. 'He's just . . .'

'Go on, Sade, you can tell us. He *is* nice. Out of ten, I'd definitely give him one.'

'Cat, stop it! And stop staring!' I was giggling like a ten-year-old with nerves. 'He's someone I met, that's all. Nothing more than that. Nothing.'

'Well, he keeps looking over here,' Becca said. Then she frowned. Remembered. 'Hang on – isn't he the guy who was in the Prodigal the other night?'

I nodded. 'Yes, he is. Jack.'

Cat's eyes were so wide, I could see the whites around her pupils. 'Oh yeah? So what happened with you and Jack? Why is he telling you to call him?'

Becca leaned forward, elbows on the table, chin resting on her hands. 'Yeah, Sade. Why *is* he telling you to call him?'

I put down my cutlery, cleared my throat. I had to explain, then. There was no way they were going to let me off without giving them every single detail.

'So what's going to happen now?' Cat wanted to know when I'd finished.

'Nothing!' I said hotly. 'Look – his number went through the wash, didn't it? I can't ring even if I wanted to. And, of course, just a small detail, I *don't* want to.'

'Of course,' Becca said, nodding her head, lips pressed together in a smug smile.

'Oh, of course,' Cat agreed. 'Turn down a babe like that? Of course.'

'Stop it,' I groaned. 'Look, I'm a responsible mum, I'm settled down with my long-term partner, I'm . . .'

Then I thought about the alter ego I'd invented on the website. The Sadie who worked at Channel 4, the Sadie who had chosen career over kids, who larged it up every night. Jack was just the kind of man she'd go for, wasn't he?

Sod it.

I stood up. 'Just a minute,' I told them and walked off.

'What's she doing?' I heard Cat saying behind me. Her voice had gone up an octave.

'Is she going over *there*?' Becca asked incredulously.

She was. I was. All the way to Jack's table. It'd be worth it just to see their faces.

'Hi, Jack – oh, sorry to interrupt, everyone,' I said sweetly. I batted my eyelashes, glad of the extra-length mascara I'd whacked on them. 'Jack – I'm so sorry I haven't called. I managed to lose your number. Could you give it to me again, please?'

Someone at the table sniggered. The old 'give it to me' phrase always appealed to someone's juvenile humour. Had I said it deliberately? I wasn't even sure myself.

Jack pulled out a business card and pressed it into my hand. 'Now, don't lose it again,' he ordered, pretending to frown and be stern. 'And ring me!'

'Thanks,' I said, smiling as prettily as I could. 'I will.'

I turned and sashayed back to my table, aware that Jack and all his mates were watching me. So, too, were my mates. With open mouths practically dragging on the linen tablecloth.

'Sadie Morrison, are you going to phone him? For real?' Cat asked, half-giggly, half-disapproving.

'She's messing around,' Becca said, but her voice was uncertain. She caught my eye. 'Aren't you, Sade?'

I shrugged. I was enjoying this. I'd forgotten how much I liked being part of the gossip. The troublesome middle sister seemed to be doing her damnedest to climb out from her confines these days. I'd missed her. 'I'm not sure,' I said in reply to both of them. 'Oh, good, here comes our wine. Cheers!'

I didn't get home until midnight. God, I loved girly nights out. It had been so long since I'd had a proper one. Far too long. When we left the restaurant, around ten, I'd phoned Alex, asking him to give Nathan some formula milk for his last feed. I was having far too good a time to go home now. I didn't want to go home. Ever again. When Alex agreed to the formula idea, I told him he might as well make up a bottle for the morning as well.

'What – you mean, you won't be feeding him yourself tomorrow morning?' he asked.

I sighed, trying not to feel exasperated. 'Alex, I'm pissed. I'm going to be . . . ow!'

I whisked around to see Jack's grin as he sauntered past. He had pinched my bottom. *Jack* had just pinched my bottom. While I'd been on the phone to *Alex*. I sobered up suddenly. What was I doing? I had completely led on this strange man and now he . . . Oh, fuck. Sadie, get a grip.

'What's up?'

'Nothing, nothing,' I said quickly, pulling faces at Cat and Becca to try to stop them laughing as they leaned against the restaurant front. 'Go on, Alex, give me a break. You said you were working at home tomorrow, so please let me have a bit of a lie-in, oh PLEEEEASE . . .'

'Well . . .'

'Look, get up with Nathan for me and you'll be on a promise for the weekend. OK?' I stuck my tongue out at Cat and Becca, who were practically on the floor by now.

'Yeah, OK. It's a deal. Have a good one. And don't do anything stupid.'

'What, me? Stupid?'

Once I'd got that sorted out, we went round to Cat's flat, which was only a short walk away. Cat had lovely taste – a mixture of antique tables and old chests next to funky Habitat sofas and rugs. Her own paintings hung on the walls – seascapes mainly, views of the Suffolk coast where Tom's family lived. She also had a box of tricks under her armchair which contained the smelliest, buddiest grass I had come across for a long time.

Oh, it was good to be back with the girls. Oh, I loved them. Had I told them that? Oh, they were the best. Truly the best. Oh, we had to do this more often. Had I told them how great they were? I was so happy for them. Things were going really well, all that love and lust and oh, I was pleased, really. Because they deserved it. Because they were fab. Had I told them that already?

Chapter Five

My hangover buzzed and grumbled inside me for hours, the next day. I had a hot bath and strong coffee – hey, I'd even had extra sleep – but I still felt terrible. Again. Two hangovers in less than a week. At this rate I'd be an alcoholic by March.

Cat had phoned at ten-ish. 'Tell me you're not going to ring that man,' she had ordered, sounding uncharacteristically strict.

'What? Oh, hi, Cat,' I groaned, still trying to recover from the noise of the telephone ringing. Small drills appeared to be boring into my skull. 'God, I feel dreadful. How about you?'

'Concerned about you, mainly. Sadie, please don't do anything stupid with that Jack guy. Promise me.'

Jack! Jesus, I'd managed to forget all about him in my pain and suffering. What the hell had I done with that business card he'd pressed into my hand? He'd folded my fingers over it, one by one. I'd watched his clean square fingernails as if in a trance. Just remembering it made me feel . . . quivery.

'Sadie! I'll tell Lizzie if you don't promise me.'

'Oh God, don't tell Lizzie,' I said quickly. 'Whatever you do. I'll never hear the end of it. She'll be giving me numbers for Relate and the Samaritans and she'll tell Mum and—'

'Yeah, I know. Exactly. So promise me.'

'Cat, I don't know what you're so worried about. I—'

'Are you going to be long, Sade? Only I need to use the phone.'

Alex had come in. Shit, how much had he heard?

'Listen, Cat, I've got to go. I'll call you later, OK?'

'Sadie, you haven't promised me!' she wailed. 'I feel terrible – we shouldn't have egged you on like that. We—'

'Oh, for God's sake, you didn't egg me on!' Honestly, she was behaving as if I'd rogered him there and then in Swanks, on one of the steam-pressed tablecloths. 'Look, stop fussing. I'll talk to you later, OK? And don't tell Lizzie or I'll kill you. I mean it. Bye.'

Alex gave me a strange look as I put the phone down. 'What was all that about?' he wanted to know. 'Don't tell Lizzie what? Who are you going to kill?'

'Nothing,' I said. 'Cat getting her knickers in a twist about nothing. Too boring to tell you. Right, kids – we're all going to Tesco. Chop chop!'

The day dragged on and on and horribly, drearily, painfully on, as if ten extra hours had been sneakily packed into the clock while I wasn't looking. The Tesco trip was a blur of comfort food in the trolley, forgetting the vegetables and a constant stream of requests from Molly. The drive home was spent worrying that I was still over the limit. At midday, I found myself thinking, only seven hours until they're in bed. I mean, that was how bad it was.

My mum phoned while I was attempting to give the children their lunch. I wedged the phone under one ear as I spooned brown vegetable slop into Nathan's mouth while simultaneously indicating to Molly via sign language that if she didn't finish her scrambled egg there would be trouble.

'What's that noise?' Mum asked suddenly, interrupting a monologue about Mrs Edwards' new dog.

'It's Molly, banging her spoon on the table,' I said wearily. 'Stop that, Molly. I'm trying to talk to Grandma.'

Molly looked me square in the eye and banged even harder.

'I said, *stop that*,' I snapped, turning away from the table. Nathan immediately started grizzling once he realized his food supply had been interrupted. 'Sorry, Mum, what were you saying?'

'Is this a bad time? Shall I call back?' she asked.

'No,' I said through gritted teeth. 'No, it's fine. Molly, I said, *stop banging!*' I wrenched the spoon out of her fingers and she promptly burst into tears.

'Oh dear,' my mum said. I could just about make out her

voice over the howls I now had in stereo. 'I'd better let you go. I'll call you back later.'

As I clicked off the phone with a fierce stab of my finger, Alex came into the kitchen. 'Sadie – I'm trying to work,' he said. 'Do you think you could keep it down a bit?'

It was all I could do not to throw the wretched phone at him, standing there so self-importantly while I was in the middle of the Scrambled Egg War. Did he really not see that?

By the time the kids had had their tea, I'd had enough. We were all sick of the sight of each other and I needed to escape. 'Alex,' I wheedled, going into our bedroom where he was working, with one child in each arm, so that we looked like some kind of three-headed beast. 'I don't suppose you fancy some Daddy-bonding time by giving these two a bath, do you?'

'Yeah, 'course,' he said. He eyed me suspiciously. 'Why? Are you going back to bed?'

'I thought I'd nip out for some fresh air,' I replied.

He stared at me and then out of the window. The street-light outside our bedroom glowed orange. 'But it's dark,' he said, as if I were a simpleton. 'Where are you going?'

'I just want to get out. Be on my own,' I said. 'I think I might go for a quick run.'

'A run? *You?*' He said it as if I had just told him I was going to go fox-hunting or granny-bashing.

'Mum run Mum run Mum run,' Molly babbled helpfully. 'Munrum Munrum RumnumMum.'

Nathan started squeaking fretfully, wanting to be put down. I passed him to Alex and began looking for my track-suit bottoms. Ahh, right at the very bottom of the drawer, not having seen the light of day for a while. I was almost surprised that a formation of indignant moths didn't fly out with them.

'OK. If that's what you want to do.'

'Alex! I'm only going to run round the block a few times. I just want to shake off this bad head, that's all. All right?'

He held his hands up. Submission. Don't blame me if you break your leg. Don't blame me if it makes you feel worse. Don't blame me if you get a stitch at the end of our road. I won't say, 'I told you so,' no, not me.

It was dark outside, just like Alex had warned me, and a cold wind blew around my ears. For two seconds, after the door had banged shut behind me, I wondered if going for a run was a completely insane idea. Why on earth hadn't I just snuggled back into bed for half an hour like Alex had suggested? I hovered on the doorstep for a second, put my key up to the lock.

No. Come on. Just a quick run. Do it. Go.

My trainers bounced along the pavement a few seconds later. I was off. The street lamps were on and windows were lit up all along our street. Run, run, run. I could see people at the bar in the George IV pub as I got to the corner, bright wall lamps shining through the smoky fug, someone's head thrown back, mouth open in a laugh. I ran on past the shops where people were picking up the final edition *Evening Standard*, a pint of milk for the morning, fags and beer for the evening. Run, run, run. A bus pulled up and ten or so people got off, all in their work clothes, some frowning into mobile phones, 'I've just got off the bus. Yeah, I'll be back in five.'

On I went. My breath was starting to feel more laboured now, muscles stretched, but my head felt clear for the first time all day. I imagined my arms to be oiled pistons, powering me along, my legs moved in rhythm, trainers hitting the ground with a satisfying slap. My body was made to do this – to run and hunt and survive. I'm a strong, powerful woman, I reminded myself. Practically Amazonian, all bar the height. I'm a strong, powerful woman. I'm a . . . unfit, red-faced – no! I'm a strong, powerful woman!

I was nearly at the park. I was nearly at the park. Oof. I was nearly at the park. If I could just make it to the park . . . I would just make it to the park and . . .

'Sadie? Is it Sadie?'

I was jolted out of my reverie and stopped abruptly. Only then did I realize how much I was gasping for breath, how my eyes were swimming, how tight my chest felt.

I blinked, but could say nothing.

'It *is* Sadie, isn't it? From the other night?' He was holding out a hand and I blinked again. 'Mark. You came for dinner on Saturday.'

'Mark!' The word heaved out of me in a rush of air. It sounded like a sigh. I shook his hand – such a bloody awful British thing to do – and hoped it was dark enough that he couldn't see how scarlet my cheeks were. How sweaty my hairline was. 'Hello. Oof. Sorry – really out of breath.'

I was expecting him to go on his way – what was he doing round here anyway? He lived miles away! – but disarmingly, he seemed to be waiting for me to catch my breath. Blimey, Mark, I felt like saying, you'll be stood there a while, if that's the case. Got the crossword to do or something?

I rubbed my eyes and noticed he was in running gear too. Well, I say 'running gear *too*' but while I was in baggy old tracksuit bottoms and a fleece so over-washed it had gone bobbly, he was in a spotless white T-shirt and running shorts. I gulped at the sight of his trainers. They had probably cost more than our car.

'Right, I can breathe again. Phew. Sorry about that. How are you? What are you doing round here?' I babbled.

'I work just round the corner. I often have a run before I go home. Where are you going?'

Oh, no. He wanted to run with me. No! No! This was just going to be excruciating.

'I . . . Well, to be honest, this is the first time I've been running in ages. Over a year. As you can probably tell.' I gestured to my red face, my sweaty hair. Good one, Sade – flag up your bad points to the man. Show him how totally unfit and unhealthy you are. 'I was planning to go to the park, but I've just realized it's probably shut by now.'

'Yeah,' he said. 'It is. There's a good path around the outside though if you fancy it?'

I looked at the pavement, scuffed the toe of my trainer along it. I gave him a wry smile.

Oh, bugger it. Be honest.

'Actually,' I confessed, 'if the park gates are shut, I might just make it up to the cafe next door, and then collapse with a hot chocolate instead.'

He smiled back. He really was quite good-looking. 'Mind if I join you as far as the cafe, then?'

'Not at all,' I said. Luckily I was so red-faced he wouldn't have known I was blushing. 'Lead the way.'

There were too many people on the pavement for us to be running next to each other, so he went ahead and I panted after him. I found myself staring at his bottom as he ran, and dragged my eyes away hurriedly. Sadie Morrison, behave yourself! I could hear Cat saying. I seriously hoped she hadn't gone and told Lizzie about Jack. I would never hear the end of it. As the eldest sister and the one who had done everything first, Lizzie liked to think of herself as a bit of an authority.

Run, run, run. The park was in sight. The cafe was in

sight. Come on, Sade. Nearly there. This is helping to burn off that chocolate pudding from last night, I told myself. In fact, I'd probably burned off enough calories by now to warrant having a muffin at the cafe as well as a hot chocolate.

I was fully expecting Mark to wave a hand and keep running along his usual route, but no. He was slowing down as we got to the cafe, stopping. He was bending over, stretching out his hamstrings. I shot another quick look at his bum. Firm and . . . Yes. Very nice. Ding-DONG! Leslie Phillips said inside my head. Purely as one would appreciate a fine piece of art, though, you understand.

Right. So when he'd said, 'Mind if I join you as far as the cafe?' he had meant *to* the cafe as well, not just the running part. Shit. Better forget the idea of the muffin, then. I didn't want him to see me with crumbs all over my chops.

He was looking strangely at me. 'All right?' he asked.

I realized I was frowning. 'Yes. Yes. Fine,' I said quickly. 'Shall we?'

The cafe was one that I sometimes took the kids to if I couldn't face making lunch. It was set back from the road, just before the entrance to the park, and served up perfect toddler food – chips and beans, boiled eggs and soldiers, cheese sandwiches, whatever tickled the little darlings' fancy. It was popular with the local parents and always crammed full of buggies and high chairs in the daytime. Ketchup-smeared kids shouted, grizzled and sang without anyone tutting in annoyance at them. Shell-shocked-looking new mums comforted themselves with sticky cakes while their babies slept or cried.

In the evening, it appeared to be a different place altogether. The box of toys and colouring books was out of sight. The high chairs were stacked up neatly in the corner. There were red tablecloths and flickering tealights on the tables.

My hot chocolate came in a tall glass, with whipped cream and baby marshmallows. Mark had a cappuccino. We sat down at a table in the corner, and suddenly I wasn't sure what to say to him. Then, foolishly, I remembered how I'd thought about his face while Alex and I had had sex the other night and I was struck even dumber. Oh no. I wished I hadn't thought about that. Why had I thought about that now?

Luckily, Mark seemed quite capable of starting the conversation. 'So,' he began cheerfully, stirring his chocolate-dusted froth, 'you live round here, do you?'

'Tennyson Road,' I said.

'Oh, I know,' he said. 'I used to live on Milton Road years ago. Tennyson's the one with the school on, isn't it?'

'That's right,' I replied, sipping my chocolate. Damn. Had I got cream on my nose? I wiped it surreptitiously. Please let me not have any cream on my nose. Please, if there is a God, please let me not have any cream on my nose.

'Handy. For your kids, I mean.'

'Mmmm,' I said, stirring my cream into the chocolate

until it melted away into white streaks. I wasn't taking any more chances. 'Except I hope we'll have moved away by then.'

'Yeah?'

'Yeah. I'm not sure if I want them to go to school round here. I think kids have to grow up really fast in London. I know I did.'

'I'm sure.' His blue eyes were so . . . blue. He was leaning over to me holding something. What was that he had? A napkin? What was he going to do with that napkin? 'Hang on, you've got a blob of cream on your nose. Let me . . .'

'Oh. Oh, thanks.'

AAAARRRGGGHHH. Right. So I had now proved that there *wasn't* a God – or if there was, she wasn't interested in helping me through this one.

I looked at Mark's hands while he wiped my nose. I felt like a grubby little five-year-old. He was actually *wiping my nose*, leaning across the table and wiping my nose. Nice hands though. Not too knuckly. His skin had a tinge of brown and I wondered if it was the last vestiges of a tan. Probably. He and Julia seemed the type who would have winter holidays. A ski chalet somewhere. Or Caribbean sun, maybe.

'I grew up in Dorset,' he went on seamlessly. He hadn't seemed at all bothered by the nose thing, luckily for both of us. 'This tiny village, not even a shop or a pub, just four houses. As a kid it was wonderful – fields and streams and farms to mess around in.'

'Wow,' I said. His words gave me a pang of guilt for my own children. I was denying them this bucolic freedom, us living in London. Oh, no. They would probably grow up asthmatic and pasty-faced and it would be all my fault. Bad mother, Sadie. Evil mother!

''Course, by the time I was a teenager, I thought it was bloody awful,' he laughed. 'Me and my brothers would walk miles to the next village just to go to the pub. And they all knew we were fourteen or whatever because the landlord knew our parents. I couldn't wait to get away.'

'Any plans to move back?' I asked. 'Are your family still down there?'

He looked slightly uncomfortable at my question. 'Ahh. Well, *I* would like to move back sometime. Now, in fact. I'd go like a shot. But . . .'

His voice had trailed away. 'But Julia wouldn't?' I prompted. Aha. Interesting.

He smiled. 'I think I've got this stupid romantic idea of us going back and having a family, dogs, Range Rover, huge garden . . . you know.'

'Sounds great,' I told him. 'What does Julia think?'

'Well, she likes the bit about the Range Rover,' he said, then laughed. 'And she likes the idea of the huge garden and the weekend parties we could have.'

'Just not the dogs and kids bit, then.'

'No.'

There was a pause. I gulped down my chocolate, suddenly feeling awkward. This was all getting rather personal, really, seeing as we barely knew each other. 'I'd better go,' I said. 'I've got to . . .' I was about to say 'put the kids to bed,' but it seemed insensitive after what he'd just told me. 'I've got to get back,' I said instead.

He drained his cappuccino and we both stood up. 'Really nice to see you, Sadie,' he told me, blue eyes holding mine steadily. 'Maybe we could do it again?'

'I'm not sure my heart is up to it,' I said lightly. 'The running, I mean. Not the . . .' Oh, shit. What was I saying? 'Yes, that would be nice. Yes. I need to get fit again.'

'You look all right to me,' he said, eyebrows raised. There was a smile at the corners of his mouth. Was he eyeing me up? He was. I swear his eyes flicked up and down my legs. He was looking at me! What was he doing that for? What was he trying to say?

'Right. Thanks. Lovely to see you. Love to Julia. Bye,' I gabbled. We'd reached the cafe door and I just wanted to get away now. I felt as if I was on dangerous ground all of a sudden. 'Right. I'm going this way. So . . . So I'll see you around. Bye, Mark!'

I turned and ran. I wondered if he was watching my arse

the way I'd watched his. I was glad it was dark. I was glad I was going home.

I went flat-out all the way back to our street. Blood rushed in my ears. I had run away like a lovestruck schoolgirl. No, not lovestruck. Obviously, I wasn't *lovestruck*. I was just . . .

What was I?

Something odd was happening to me. Jack. Danny. Mark. These men that I was flirting with, lying to, playing games with. I kept stepping out of my real life into this pretend one, where I could do that whole flirting thing again. Only, in my real life, I couldn't. Wasn't supposed to.

Nothing has happened. *Nothing has happened,* I told myself as I walked the last few steps to our house, breath groaning out of me. Our house. My and Alex's house. The house where our two babies had been born.

It was more the fact that something *could* happen, if I let it. If I wanted it. Which, of course, I didn't. It was ridiculous to even *think* that, yet . . .

I shivered. Now that I'd stopped running, I could feel how freezing the air was. A few stars were already poking through the smoggy sky. Frost again later, no doubt.

I had to stop all this . . . messing about, I chastised myself. I had to knuckle down to my own, proper life instead of trying to rewrite it as a different story all the time. I had Alex and the kids, after all, and even if it *was* hard work and a bit . . . well, boring at times, and even if I was hankering after my old life of freedom right now, and even if this new life of motherhood and responsibility sometimes didn't feel quite enough, I just had to *make* it enough.

OK. Lecture over.

I panted my way up our front steps, legs heavy. Key in the lock and in. The house was warm and light and I could hear Molly giggling. Home.

It was patronizing of me, I knew, but I was always faintly surprised to come home and find that nothing horrendous had happened in my absence. No one was crying or bleeding. The house hadn't fallen down, wasn't on fire. In fact, not only was everyone all right, they looked positively radiant with model-family-type cosiness.

I walked into the front room to see Nathan and Molly in their pyjamas, both snuggled on Alex's knee as he read them *Five Minutes' Peace,* Molly's current favourite story. For a split-second I was looking at them as an outsider. Curtains drawn, lamps glowing, fire belting out heat. My beautiful children with their fair hair and apple cheeks. And Alex, reading about Mrs Large the elephant struggling to get her longed-for five minutes' peace, making Molly chortle with his silly voices for the elephant children.

Alex looked up and winked. 'Good run?' he asked in his

elephant girl voice. Molly practically fell off his knee with laughter.

I sat down next to them and Nathan immediately started to make hungry little mews. I pulled him over to me for a feed. 'Yeah,' I replied, trying to keep my voice light and casual. I bent over Nathan so Alex couldn't see my face. 'Yeah, I think I'll go more often. I really enjoyed it.'

I paused. Now was the time to tell him about Mark. *Oh, and guess who I saw while I was out there?*

Go on, then. Tell him.

I shut my mouth instead. Fussed over Nathan.

'Nice one,' Alex said, completely unaware of the uneasy feeling that was spreading through me. 'I told you it was a good idea, didn't I?'

I laughed at his cheek. 'No, you bloody didn't.'

He was grinning his most infuriating grin. 'I did, you know I did. Don't forget, Sade, it's me, Alex. The one who's always right about everything.'

I shook my head. 'You've got me there. Don't think I know him.'

'Denial is a terrible thing, Sadie,' he said sorrowfully, then picked up the remote, his fifth limb. 'Right, Molls. Let's have a gander at the news. See if Leeds have signed up Ronaldo.'

Tell him. Tell him you saw Mark. Why don't you just tell him? It's not like anything happened. Just say it!

'I not want news, Daddy, I want elephants again.' She pronounced it 'effalunts'.

'All right. One more time, then it's upstairs to clean those teeth.'

I shut my eyes while Nathan sucked and Alex read and Molly giggled. I didn't tell him. I didn't say a word.

Chapter Six

Next morning, I woke up full of noble intentions. I was going to have a perfect mum day, devoted to my little angels. None of this . . . this parallel life stuff. Just me and the children. Happy families. We were going over to Lizzie's for the morning and I was determined to put on a good show. No tantrums, no fighting, no crying – and that went for the kids, too.

Lizzie hadn't mentioned Jack or Relate or counselling of any description on the phone, so I was pretty sure that Cat hadn't told her anything awful about me. Mind you, I tried to avoid long phone conversations with Lizzie if possible as they were usually about Boring Steve – or her 'hubby' as she called him – and how brilliantly Boring Steve was doing at work and what a massive pay rise Boring Steve had just got, and how Boring Steve was going to take her and Little Felix to Disneyworld next month and . . .

It made me wonder if Steve was in the background listening to all these conversations, sometimes, they were so effusive. Or if he bugged the phone. Surely she didn't really think I was that interested in her dull, balding, businessman hubby, did she?

It was only when I saw Lizzie in person, just us two, that she sometimes cracked and confessed that she was actually quite looking forward to Boring Steve going off for a golfing weekend with his work mates so she and Little Felix could have the house to themselves. Or I'd comment on their new flashily large TV, sleek, silver and gleaming with a remote that could boil the kettle and do the ironing, if you knew what buttons to press – and she'd kind of grit her teeth, and then tell me that, actually, their old TV was perfectly good and she wished Boring Steve wasn't so desperate to have the new model five seconds after it hit the shops every time.

Lizzie lived about twenty minutes' drive away in a terribly nice, terribly middle-class part of Balham with lots of other terribly nice, terribly middle-class families who liked nothing more than to talk about which private school their children would be going to (before they were even born, half the time) and which French classes their three-year-olds attended (*Bonjour, Maman!* was excellent, according to Liz) and how little Matilda and Henry had simply *adored* being down in Whitstable at the weekend, you know, in their little *holiday cottage* down there. Such a sweet place, only three bedrooms (yes, it was *tiny!*) but you know, it was fun roughing it for the weekend, wasn't it? And lovely neighbours there, too!

Lizzie hadn't quite bought into all that bollocks but she was heading that way. Boring Steve earned a fortune, and consequently Lizzie had an eye-poppingly fat allowance every month and seemed to feel obliged to spend the whole lot each time it walloped into her bank account with a hefty thud. Whenever I went round, I had to go through the admiring stage before I could even take the kids' coats off. I would admire the newly plumbed-in bathroom suite or Felix's freshly painted playhouse in the garden or Lizzie's new outfit, shoes, coat, expensive haircut . . . Once, I had poked my nose round their bedroom door after taking Molly to the loo and had seen about ten Selfridges carrier bags piled up by the wardrobe, stuffed with new clothes and shoes that she hadn't even unpacked yet.

As a perfect mum, though, today I simply was not going to envy her for it. After all, I reminded myself, she did have to shag Boring Steve, so she deserved a few treats in her life as compensation.

Molly and Nathan both cried loudly and ceaselessly for the entire car journey. I tried singing 'Ten Green Bottles' to jolly them along but by the time I'd got to seven green bottles hanging on the wall, their cries were louder than ever, so I abandoned it mid-song. Then I tried putting on Molly's tape of Kipper stories. She usually loved Dawn French's honeyed tones describing Kipper's doings but not today. She was wailing so loudly that none of us could hear the story, so

I switched it off and just jammed up the radio instead, in the hope that it would drown them out.

By the time we got to Lizzie's road, I was feeling flustered. Oh, shit. Nowhere to put the car either, as usual. People in Balham seemed to have about three cars each, judging by how impossible to park it always was.

'Right, you two, let Mummy concentrate,' I pleaded. 'How about giving Mummy five minutes' peace like Mrs Large, just while I'm parking the car. OK?'

'I want effalunts story NOW,' Molly wailed instantly. 'I want Mrs Large.'

Ahh. There was a space. A teeny tiny space between a Merc and a Beamer. Oh, good. No pressure to get it right then.

I lined the car up parallel with the Merc. Brand new. Black. Polished to within an inch of its expensive life. Good, good. Even better. If I was going to scrape something, might as well go for the top end of the market.

Clutch. Reverse gear.

'Effalunts, Mummy. EFFALUNTS!'

I gritted my teeth. Perfect mum, perfect mum. What would perfect mum do in this situation? 'Hey, I bet Aunty Lizzie has got the elephants story at her house,' I said in my calm, controlled voice. She'd got just about every other damn kids' book on the market. I would bet my high-heeled fuck-me boots that she had *Five Minutes' Peace*. 'So if you two are really quiet for a minute, just while I park the car, I'll ask Aunty Lizzie if we can read it. OK?'

'I want effalunts, Mummy. I want effalunts NOW!'

'I know you want bloody effa . . . I know you want the elephants story but I don't have it in the car! Now just shush!'

OK. I gripped the wheel. Revs up, wheel round, back back back we went. The kids were still crying. 'Look, shut up, both of you, will you?' I snapped. 'For fuck's sake!'

There was a shocked silence. I made the most of it to swing the wheel round and edge right back into the space. Bit more. Bit more. Bit more. Straighten her up. Yes. Result!

Handbrake on, engine off. We were here. And I hadn't even crashed the car. Well done, Sadie.

'Mummy, I don't like it when you shout at me,' Molly said accusingly.

Nathan started whimpering again as if he agreed, and I had a horrible vision of them both, twenty years on, slagging me off for having been such a neurotic mum and screwing up their childhoods. Alex would be the one they loved best, I thought miserably. I'd be the one they'd bitch about together whenever they met up. Or maybe they'd save all that for their therapists.

I sighed heavily. Something else to beat myself up about. 'Tough shit,' I muttered under my breath. Then I braced myself with a dazzling smile. 'Let's go and see what Felix is up to, shall we?' I said. 'Let's all go and have a fun time at Felix's house!'

'Hi, Sadie. Hello, darlings, come on in.'

Lizzie looked as serene as ever. She was fair, like Cat, only she had a bob and a feathery fringe. Pale skin that burned in the sun. Light brown eyes, elegant hands.

Felix was peeping out from between her legs. He was nine months older than Molly and painfully shy.

'Effalunts, effalunts, effalunts!' Molly bellowed, charging into the front room and completely ignoring Lizzie and Felix.

'What's she saying?' Lizzie frowned. 'Are you all right, Sadie? You look very pink.'

'Oh, just . . .' Oh, I just said 'fuck' in front of the children, that's all, and told them to shut up, and I feel horrible about it. 'Just a parking nightmare, that's all. And grumpy kids.' Nothing to do with me whatsoever. Because I am perfect mum today. Well, almost.

She grimaced sympathetically. 'It's a nightmare, I know. Everyone has such big cars around here, don't they? Let me get you a coffee.'

'Great.'

Lizzie never had any nice biscuits or cakes in the house (Felix wasn't allowed sugar) but she always had delicious blow-your-head-off coffee, which was some consolation.

She showed me her plans for a conservatory at the back. Did I think it would be too much?

No, I didn't. I thought it would be fab, especially in summer.

She told me about Boring Steve's new car. An Audi.

Oh, lovely, I said, trying not to think about the way a new car smelled. Trying not to compare it to our old Peugeot with its plastic toys wedged in the seats, and the crumbs and old pages of the *A to Z* everywhere.

She told me they were thinking of going to Antigua for a spring break and showed me the brochure. Sometimes it was nice to get away from it all, wasn't it?

I looked at the pictures of aquamarine sea and beaming, tanned families and tried to ignore the phrases that were leaping off the page. *All-inclusive. Five-star retreat. Kids' club. Snorkelling. Cocktail hour. Luxury. Sunshine.*

'Listen to me going on, anyway,' Lizzie said brightly. 'How are you?'

'Fine,' I said miserably. 'Alex is doing really well at work and Nathan's sleeping much better these days. Molly's out of nappies. I'm . . . I've taken up running.'

'Good for you.' She cast an eye over her slim, linen-encased flanks and sighed theatrically. 'I could do with going running again. The running machine at our gym is always so busy, I never get to go on it.'

We were all in Lizzie's cream, clean front room by now.

Every cushion plumped up just so, every picture artfully arranged. Even our two children sprawling on the carpet, and the assortment of toys between them (all wooden, all with their original boxes) looked like a scene from a happy families TV programme.

Out of the corner of my eye, I could see that Molly and Felix were both holding on to the same car. I recognized the look of intent on my daughter's face, her don't-mess-with-me expression. She'd done the happy families thing for at least a minute. Now it was time to resort to type.

'Molly, I'm watching you,' I warned. I set Nathan on the floor and started wedging cushions behind him to prop him in a sitting position. 'So, yeah, Liz, we're all fine. I saw Cat the other night – did you hear that she and Tom are going to get a place together?'

'No! That's great. He's—'

'MY car.'

'*I* want it!'

WHACK!

'Molly!' I cried, jumping up and rushing over. 'You mustn't hit people! Say sorry to Felix at once!'

Felix's mouth had opened wider than I'd ever seen it and he howled. His shoulders shook. Tears rolled down his cheeks.

'Oh, darling,' Lizzie said, running over and cuddling him. 'Are you all right? What a bump!'

'I not sorry,' Molly said loudly. 'MY car.'

'It is not your car,' I hissed. What was wrong with her today? She was being a right madam. 'It's Felix's car, isn't it, so if he wants to play with it, he can. Now *say sorry*.'

'I not sorry,' she repeated. God, she was so bloody stubborn. Her mouth was set, and I knew there was no way on earth she was about to cave in and apologize.

'Molly IS sorry,' I lied to Felix. 'She's very sorry and she's going to play on her own for a bit now and think about how horrible it is to hit people.'

'No-o-o-o!' she wailed. I picked her up, her legs bicycling in mid-air as she tried to kick me, and I took her out to the hall. I could hear Nathan bursting into tears as I left the room. Separation anxiety seemed to be starting early at the age of five months. Fantastic.

'Listen to me,' I said as I put my furious daughter down on the carpet. 'I love you very much, but hitting isn't a nice thing to do, and Mummy doesn't like it when you hit people. So you think about that.'

'No-o-o-o-o!' she bellowed, lying down and kicking the row of shoes that had been lined up neatly in the hall.

'And when you feel like saying sorry, you can come back in and play nicely,' I said. I was practically having to shout to make myself heard.

I went back into the front room to see Lizzie trying to cuddle Felix *and* Nathan, both of whom were still crying.

'Thanks, Liz,' I said, taking Nathan off her and rubbing his back. 'God, what a nightmare. What do you reckon – shall we leave them to it and go out to the pub? They start serving in twenty minutes.'

She didn't look at me. 'Come on, Felix, be a big boy,' she was saying. 'Let's dry those tears now.'

'I NOT SORRY!' Molly yelled from the hall.

I was starting to think Lizzie really had the hump with me for Molly's car rage, but then she caught my eye and we both started laughing. 'Sod you, then,' I muttered in the direction of the hall and we laughed even harder.

I always felt a sense of relief driving away from Lizzie's house. Much as I loved her and enjoyed seeing her and cute, basin-haired little Felix, I was always on the edge of my nerves, waiting for Molly to beat Felix up or poo on the carpet or break something expensive.

Still, we were leaving now, and it was her turn to come round to ours next time, where everything that it was possible to break had already been broken, and the carpet was already so knackered that another 'little accident' was easily dismissed with a shrug and the dustpan.

It had been nice to catch up with Lizzie, though. And she had asked me along to a book group she was setting up with some friends, which might be fun – if they weren't too scarily intellectual, of course.

After lunch, when both kids were napping, I tried to pretend I hadn't seen the enormous washing pile, and booted up Alex's laptop instead. After all, I hadn't looked at it for days now. As I waited for the connection to dial through, I thought, *I bet he's written back. No, he won't have written back. Well, he might have, I suppose. Probably not though. Still, you never know.*

'Shut up, moron,' I groaned.

Inbox: (4) new messages.

FOUR! Oh my God. I hardly ever got emails. So there had to be one from him, surely. I knew it. Didn't I say?

I clicked on the inbox, fingers trembling, then scanned down the names as they appeared.

Amazon – a great new offer on some CD I'd never heard of.

Claire Davenport – oh wow, Claire Davenport from school!

Evie Porter – Aussie mate, excellent.

Danny Cooper. *Danny Cooper.*

I clicked on him at once, brain ticking over with the possibilities. My mouth was dry. What, oh what, was he going to say?

Sadie, I made a terrible mistake. I should never have left you.

Sadie, I've been trying to find you for years.

Sadie, I have never been able to get over you.

Shut up, shut up, shut up. My mind was racing – too

much kick-arse coffee at Lizzie's house. The email opened up finally and I read it.

> *Dear Sadie,*
>
> *Good to see your name on the website. I was wondering if you were going to make an appearance. Sounds like things are going really well for you. If you're ever in Manchester, give us a shout. Would be great to meet up after all these years.*
>
> *Cheers,*
>
> *Dan*
>
> *PS I still have your* Hatful of Hollow *album. Do you want me to post it down?*

I stared at the words and read them all again. It was very . . . bland. Disappointingly bland.

Hey, you, I taught you everything about sex, I felt like emailing back. I was your first love, remember! What about that bunk-up in the school toilets, eh? How can you be so cool and polite to me now? Why aren't you begging me to take you back?

I hit the Reply key and gazed at the blank screen for a while.

No. Replying straight away was far too keen, if I was going to keep up my fantasy career story. Career woman Sadie would be too busy and overworked to write back the same day to some no-mark schoolboy she'd once been out with, wouldn't she? I would make him wait. Make him wonder.

I read the message one last time and then switched off the laptop without even bothering to read the others. I had work to be getting on with, after all. OK, so it was a pile of clean washing to hang out and the kitchen floor to sweep and mop, but even so. I was still too busy to drop everything for Danny Cooper. Far too busy.

I went into the kitchen and tried to forget about him. I would give him my address, though, I decided. Just so he could send my album back. I'd loved that album and he had always denied that he had it. Yeah, I'd just get my album back and leave it at that. Closure. OK, so our turntable was broken and had been for well over a year – but that wasn't the point. Danny didn't have to know that. He didn't have to know anything I didn't want him to know.

I pulled the washing into the laundry basket and smiled. Danny Cooper was back in my life. And I was back in his. So pleasing that we could be so mature and adult about these things, wasn't it?

Chapter Seven

Hi Danny,

Nice to hear from you. Sorry it's taken me a while to reply – things have been mad at work. You know how it is. We're all heads down for a new programme that's launching next week called . . .

Hmmm. I flicked through *Heat* magazine for inspiration but couldn't see any new Channel 4 programmes starting soon that I could convincingly put my name to. I didn't want to get too embroiled in details anyway. Probably a very bad idea. Tangled webs, and all that.

Hi Danny,

How's it going? Fancy hearing from you after all these years! Hey, remember that time we sneaked into your brother's room and found his stash of porn mags in the wardrobe? Remember what happened next?

Maybe not. Tempting, but ill-advised, I decided.

Hello Danny,
I'm in Manchester on business next week. How about we meet up and you could give me my record back in person?

Thinking up other-life fantasies seemed to be the only way I was going to get through the afternoon with the children from hell, who seemed to have replaced my own little angels. Molly had refused her usual post-lunch nap and was over-tired and argumentative. I'd taken them out to the playground hoping she'd let off steam, but it had started to rain almost as soon as we'd got there, and we'd had to turn around and come straight back. There'd been tears that the raincover had to go on the buggy, and then furious shouts and small fists banging on the other side of the said hated raincover when it became clear that I wasn't going to allow even one go on the swings.

For a second, I felt like saying, 'OK, you sit in the rain and get drenched and really cold and come down with pneumonia. Fine. If that's what my sweetheart wants, that's what my sweetheart will have. Bollocks to it.'

I didn't, though. I said, 'No, sorry. *I said, no!* Now, that's enough!'

I trudged all the way back through the rain, people

staring at the two wailing infants I was pushing. I tried to assemble my face into an 'Oh, the little scamps!' expression but I was too tired to pretend, and instead found myself glaring and thinking that I hated them. Miserable whining little brats. And why did everyone keep *looking* at us, for goodness' sake? All children cried sometimes, after all. Why did every passer-by seem hell-bent on making me feel like uber-crap parent today?

Back home, rain lashed against the windows all afternoon in long, grey streaks. I had to put the lights on by three o'clock, the sky was so dark. It wasn't just the weather that was miserable, either. Every time I tried to sit Nathan up in a safe cushion ring, he toppled over heavily and cried, face down, sobs muffled. Molly didn't want to do anything. Painting? No. Sticking? No. Play-Doh? No. Drawing? NO.

'What, then?' I snapped, rapidly losing the will to live.

'Video,' she muttered. 'I watch *Monsters*.'

'Fine,' I said. '*Monsters* we can do. Let's all sit down and watch *Monsters* and cheer up and *stop* crying for five minutes.' *Before I do something I regret,* I thought savagely.

I slammed *Monsters, Inc*, Molly's favourite film in the world, into the video and then shut my eyes gratefully as a temporary peace began.

Ten seconds later, the phone rang. 'Oh, hi, Mum,' I said, turning the volume down so she wouldn't hear it. My mum was convinced that children who watched too much television grew up to be psychopaths. 'How are you?'

> *Hi Danny,*
>
> *Sorry not to have replied earlier. I've been in Antigua for a little spring break. Sometimes it's nice to get away from it all, isn't it?*

Alex rang at about five o'clock. 'Sade, you're going to hate me for this, but . . .'

I sighed crossly. Damn right I was. 'You're working late and you can't get out of it,' I finished for him.

'Don't be like that. I'm sorry, but I need to finish something off before I go. Deadlines, Sadie.'

I stared at the TV screen, teeth gritted, bitchy replies forming in my head like poisonous little bubbles.

'Sadie? Don't go all quiet on me. This is what pays the mortgage, remember. Work.'

I could hear someone laughing in the background. A woman's laugh, loud and confident. Julia?

'Alex – it's Friday night. If you're going out for a drink, just tell me. You don't have to give me this work sob story,' I said. And who's that woman tittering away so close to you? I wanted to add. And how close *was* she, anyway? She sounded loud enough to be right next to him.

'It's not a sob story. Look, I'll tell you all about it later. I shouldn't be too long, OK?'

'OK,' I replied. *Whatever,* I said in my head, like a teenager.

As my mum would say, there were two hopes of him coming back before 'too long' – Bob Hope and no hope. It was Friday night. I'd worked in an office, I knew the score. Everyone down the pub as soon as possible. Everyone lagered and in a weekend mood. Who'd get the opening round? Alex! Good old Alex, always first at the bar.

'Bye, then.'

'Bye.'

I put the phone down. We'd had this argument so many times and he always had to throw the *this is what pays the mortgage, remember* line in my face. Like I didn't make any contribution to our home life. Like I was sitting around on my arse all day while he, big, important Alex, went out and grafted for *us.* It made me feel like punching him.

I put a bottle of wine in the fridge instead. The Sancerre that Alex's rich uncle had given him for Christmas, which was, without a doubt, flashily expensive. Sod it. Hadn't I just had a hard day at work, too?

Dear Danny,

OK, here's the truth. I've been with this guy, Alex, for six years but it's all gone a bit pants, and I've decided to leave him for you. I'll be up in Manchester just as soon as I can. Oh, and by the way, I'll be bringing two small children with me. That's all right, isn't it?

Ha.

Huh.

By seven o'clock, I'd already had one glass of wine. By the time I'd got the kids quiet and asleep, I'd had most of another glass. I'd also scoffed my way through all the emergency chocolate buttons (two bags) and biscuits (half a packet) and had dialled out for a curry. I was going to have a girls' night in, all on my own. I had my book to read for Lizzie's book group, a tube of face mask goo at the ready, the rest of the wine in the fridge and a chicken jalfrezi winging its way across south London at that very minute.

Damn it, I was going to have a great time.

I filled up my glass and went into the front room, ignoring the light scattering of toys on the carpet until I trod on a small plastic sheep and nearly woke the children up with furious swearing. Then I tried not to cry.

Dear Dan,

How are you? I'm not quite sure how I am. Swinging between sheer joy and miserable exhaustion seems about the size of it. My kids really got on my nerves today and I'm only starting to like them again now that they're asleep. That makes me sound horrible, doesn't it? Well, it's true. My partner, Alex, is probably boozing and shouting and laughing with all his mates – including women mates – right now. Sometimes he is such a tosser, you know, I can't quite believe I am in a relationship with him. What's more, his boss is very attractive, in a hard-faced-bitch kind of way. I don't think she's Alex's type, but what do I know?

'Sadie? Sadie!'

I stirred and groaned. My arm was numb. I had tight patches of skin on my cheeks where rogue blobs of face mask had escaped being washed off. Mouth wet where I'd been dribbling. 'What? What time is it?'

'It's half-eleven. Come upstairs to bed.'

'What?' I stretched my legs and felt resistance from something soft. I kicked experimentally. A pile of cushions. Oh yeah. I was on the sofa. I sat up. 'Must have fallen asleep,' I muttered.

He crossed the room, crunching over the farmyard animals still on the carpet. I could smell the waves of alcohol that were rolling through the air in front of him before he was even close.

'Get your work done, then?' I asked sarcastically.

'What? Oh, right. Yeah.' He sat down next to me and closed his eyes. 'God, I'm whacked. What a week.'

Oh, here we go, I thought. How tired Alex is, how hard he's been working. I was awake suddenly, remembering our argument. 'Don't tell me. You were kidnapped by *Julia* and she dragged you down to the pub.'

He opened his eyes and looked at me. 'Julia? What are you on about?'

I pursed my lips. Attack was the best form of self-defence, wasn't that right? 'Well, I'll find out sooner or later. You might as well tell me.'

He started laughing. I loved Alex's laugh. It was unashamedly loud and pure and annoyingly infectious. It made me laugh, too, there and then, even though I didn't want to. 'Don't be daft,' he told me, sounding exaggeratedly northern. He always did when he was pissed. 'Julia? Leave it out. She's my boss. And she's really scary. She didn't even come to the pub anyway. Tickets for the opera, darling.'

I believed him. The high-pitched impression alone was enough to convince me. 'Oh, good,' I said. I rubbed my eyes. 'I thought I heard her laughing down the phone when you called, that's all.'

'Julia? No,' he said, taking a swig from my wine glass that was on the coffee table. 'That was Nat, not Julia.'

'Nat?'

'Natasha. She's new in the department.'

Oh, right. Great. New in the department? Needing a bit of looking after? Oh, Alex would do it. Alex was everybody's friend. Alex made everyone laugh. He had made her laugh, anyway. I'd heard her. Nat. Natasha.

He was frowning. Then he patted my leg thoughtfully. 'Actually . . . I've got a bit of bad news about work.'

'What?' My voice was a croak.

He laughed again. 'Don't look like that! It's not *terrible* news. I just know you're going to hate it, and say, "Oh, Alex, do I have to?"'

'What?' I repeated. Then I got it. He was right. 'Oh, Alex, do I have to?' I wailed. Well, I was nothing if not predictable. 'It's another wanky worky do, partners obliged to attend bollocks, isn't it? Oh, no, is it?'

'Sorry,' he said, 'but you guessed right. Another wanky worky do. But it IS at the Laurel Tree. You know, that new bar in Soho? Cutting-edge design and wicked cocktails, according to Steph. She's the one organizing the whole thing.'

'Hmmmph,' I moaned. Inside, I was running through a mental list of pros and cons. I thought: champagne cocktails, swanking around Soho, night out away from the kids. Babysitter. *New dress.*

'And you'll get to meet lots of interesting people,' he added coaxingly.

'Hmmmph,' I said again. Not so appealing. I thought: Sloanie babes, Botoxed career women, dull, drunk men, air-kissing.

'And at least you'll know some other people this time – Matthew and Chloe, Julia and Mark.'

My mouth opened and then closed. I thought: Mark.

'All right,' I said. 'When did you say it was?'

I struck a deal with Alex over the weekend. If I took the kids out on Sunday and gave him time to watch the Leeds match in peace, I could go out *on my own* for lunch with Becca and Nick on Saturday. It sounded good to me. I was pretty much game on for anything that involved the words *on my own*.

Cleaning? No. Cleaning on my own? Ooh, yes, please. How relaxing!

Supermarket shopping? No. Supermarket shopping on my own? God, yeah, great. Bring it on!

I was just about to leave the house *on my own*, though, when I felt a sudden ache that made me stop and clutch the hall radiator. Oh, no. It couldn't be.

Ouch. Yes. I would recognize that kick anywhere.

I ran upstairs.

'What are you doing?' Alex shouted. Fair enough question, seeing as I'd only just said goodbye to him and the kids.

I was rummaging through my chest of drawers like a maniac. Where on earth were they? It had been so long since I'd needed them . . . Ahh. Tampons. Welcome back into my life, little white friends. Not.

'Nothing,' I yelled back. I didn't want to start shouting

about periods down the stairs. Mrs Wilkes next door was bound to be listening as usual. I wasn't sure that she needed to know the ins and outs of my menstrual cycle as well as everything else about our family.

God, my body had it in for me, it really did. Traitor. I'd only squeezed Nathan out a paltry five months ago, and boom! I was fertile all over again already, everything geared up inside me to house another baby for another nine months. Ha! Not likely.

'Right, bye again,' I shouted, rushing downstairs and out of the hall. My legs were still aching from running the other night. My bottom felt as if someone had been whacking it repeatedly with an oar. But I'd enjoyed it, at the same time. I was definitely going to go again.

What was it Mark had said? *Let's do it again.*

Yeah, right, Mark. How was that supposed to happen, then? London was massive. It wasn't like we were going to bump into each other again, just like that.

I thought about his face. How good his arse looked in running shorts . . . Ding-DONG! Maybe it was better if we didn't meet again after all, if it was going to turn me into a bottom-staring lech.

I smiled and swung my bag as I walked down the road to the bus stop. I'd bumped into Mark once, hadn't I? Maybe it would happen again. Fate would bring us together, and . . .

And what?

And nothing, I told myself firmly, as the bus pulled up. God, absolutely nothing, you stupid cow. Earth calling deluded woman on faraway planet: you have a long-term partner and two children! Mark is a happily married man. Remember?

Oh yeah.

Enough about him, anyway. I was actually out on my own, going for lunch with Becca and her new man! That was enough to think about right now. I was dying to know what Nick was going to be like. Becca had eclectic taste in men, to put it politely. She'd fallen in love with whey-faced poets and fake-tanned businessmen alike, would go on a date to a cutting-edge art 'event' or, just as happily, to a company golf day depending on who she was with. She'd date a slick, groomed Notting Hill lad one month and then be seen with a Burberry mac and wellies type the next. Becca just had two main criteria when it came to her men: good sex and fat wallets. Anything else – sense of humour, attractiveness, political preference – seemed to be optional extras from where I was standing.

Nick had actually sounded quite promising the other night. What had it been? Six foot, six-pack, and sexy, or something similar. The package was good enough in those terms, but I wasn't fooled. I'd learned the hard way, after years of being friends with Becca, that there still might be a shock in store for me when it came to actually meeting a new man.

I hoped Nick wasn't religious. Or depressed. Or really, really old.

I jumped off the bus at the Common and strolled up to the tapas bar Becca had suggested, smiling and blinking at the unfamiliar sensation of sun on my face. I would have to dig out my sunglasses soon, I thought happily. And track down all my summer dresses, too. I'd missed out on a summer, clothes-wise. I'd sweated my way through the heat the year before, Nath budding and then blooming in my belly, and had lived in enormous maternity vest tops and stretchy skirts for months on end.

But this year, I deserved some new clothes. And shoes. Oh boy, did I need some new shoes! I'd make an afternoon of it – drag the girls out to dither enjoyably over which type of heel to choose. Oh, I would be urban and hip and effortlessly stylish this summer. A chic London babe. Sequinned flip-flops and cool floaty dresses . . . Cropped trousers and wedge-heeled mules . . .

'Hiya! Over here!'

As I pushed open the restaurant door, I heard Becca's voice above the low rumble of chatter and turned to see her waving and smiling in the far corner. I threaded my way through the lines of wooden tables, breathing in the scent of frying potatoes, bacon, rosemary. The walls were white-washed and hung with kitschy Spanish souvenirs – grinning plastic donkeys with stuffed panniers, raffia sombreros, miniature guitars. No doubt it had been lauded in all the reviews as some kind of ironic celebration of tack, but it looked pretty naff to me. Like my nan's old front room, but worse.

'Hello,' I said, finally making it across to their table. She stood up and grabbed my hands, then kissed me on both cheeks.

'Hi, babe,' she grinned, squeezing my fingers. 'This is Nick.'

He stood up, too, and held out a hand. 'Nice to meet you,' he said.

'And you,' I replied.

Good first impression, anyway. Open, friendly face. Seemed to have all his teeth, which was always a bonus. Sparkly eyes. Short, blond hair. Wide mouth, just the right shade of pink.

I sat down hurriedly, aware that I was staring. Poor bloke, leave him alone. 'So!' I said brightly. 'How are you two?'

'Great. Just got up actually.' There was a look between them. A secret lovers-only look. 'We've only just got here ourselves so we haven't ordered anything yet. Have a menu.' Becca slid one across the table.

'Lovely. Thanks.'

She and Nick were holding hands and beaming at each other across the table. Bless. I scanned the menu, feeling hungrier by the second. It had been hours since my six-thirty breakfast with the *bambinos.*

Patatas bravas

Tortilla Española

Jalapeños

Chorizo a los Pimientos

Pollo al Chilindrón

'What does *Chilindrón* mean?' I muttered, trying to dredge up some phrases from my stint in Mexico.

'*Chilindrón*? Cooked with tomatoes, fresh peppers, chilli and aromatic spices,' Nick told me.

I raised my eyebrows, impressed. He was good. 'Blimey. Are you fluent?' I asked.

He laughed. 'No. The translation is underneath. There.' He leaned over me to point at the menu and I caught a whiff of his aftershave, sharp and clean.

I blushed chilli-red. I was so dim. How on earth had I managed to miss that?

'He's a fluent bullshitter, that's what he is,' Becca said affectionately, stroking his fingers. Her eyes didn't leave him for a second.

His face was a picture of feigned outrage. Who, me? 'I think you'd better take that back, darlin',' he growled.

I laughed. First impressions were definitely thumbs up. He was cheeky; I liked that in a man. Actually, I liked it in anyone. 'What are we having, then?' I asked. 'Anyone made any decisions?'

It wasn't until Nick got up to go to the loo, midway through our feast of chorizo, tiger prawns, salad, garlic mushrooms and the rest of it, that Becca and I got a few minutes to ourselves.

'So, what do you think?' she asked, leaning over conspiratorially the nanosecond that Nick was out of earshot.

'I like him,' I said at once. It was such a relief that I was able to be honest about my opinion, after all the times I'd been forced to lie about Becca's other weirdo boyfriends, that I started gushing effusively. 'He's great. Easy to talk to, funny, good-looking . . .'

'Yeah, I know,' she smirked. 'Oh, Sadie, it's going really, *really* well. We have such a laugh – and it's all just so . . . easy.' Her lips shone with butter. 'And hey, guess what, we've been talking about going away already. Rome!'

'*Rome?*' I echoed. I nearly choked on a mussel. 'God, how utterly fantastic.' I was thinking Vespas, ice creams, Trevi fountain. I was thinking Peroni beer, Colosseum, spaghetti. Alex and I had been to Rome one hot, dusty weekend years and years ago. Now I was back there like a shot. Scorchio!

'I know!' She was beaming again. Her face was animated, eyes bright as the words bubbled out of her. 'I can't wait. Just a dirty weekend, but I've gotta say, I like his style. I mean, dirty weekend in Britain or dirty weekend in Italy. Hmmm . . . Now, let me think . . .'

'What, are you saying that Rome was *his* idea?' I asked, eyes boggling. This man got better by the second. In fact, I was half starting to fall in love with him myself.

'Yeah!' She tipped her beer bottle up and drank. 'It was totally his idea.'

'Wow,' I said.

She nodded. 'I know. That's what I thought. I hadn't even dared go near the "weekend away" thing – thought I'd leave that for a couple of months at least. But he was planning to see some friends over there anyway so he said, come along. Just like that! All those shoe shops and bars. Imagine!'

'I'm imagining,' I replied. Oh boy, I was imagining. Remembering. Alex had had a promotion and pay rise at work, and had booked us plane tickets as a surprise. We'd stayed in a fourth-floor apartment near the Spanish Steps. If I closed my eyes, I knew I'd be straight back in there again – antique iron bed, white sheets, the whirr of the ceiling fan. And me and Alex, post-coital, giggling and cuddling. 'You lucky cow,' I said feelingly. 'You lucky, lucky, *lucky* . . .'

Nick came back at that moment. 'So. Finished talking about me yet, ladies, or should I loiter outside the gents for a bit longer?' he asked.

'Talk about you? Don't flatter yourself!' Becca snorted, but her eyes were soft.

He kissed her as he sat back on his chair, and I looked away quickly, eyes down at my plate. Rare and wonderful as it was to see my best friend so happy and loved up, I was starting to get a bad case of that green, hairy gooseberry feeling.

I drank the last of my juice. 'I'd better make a move,' I said, pushing my chair back.

'Already?' Becca's head jerked round towards me in surprise. 'You've only been here about two minutes!'

'I know but . . .' I fished under the table for my bag. 'I should get on, really.'

Nick put his knife and fork down, an awkward smile hovering around his mouth. 'I hope it's not because you're thinking three's a crowd?'

'No! I bloody hope you're not!' Becca put in. 'That's not why you're going, is it? Three's company, just as much as two's company.' She was gabbling. 'Anyway, you haven't even told us what's happening with Jack yet.'

I had tracked down my purse by then, and was sorting through it. 'If I leave you a tenner . . .' I started saying. Then I stopped. I could feel my nose wrinkling in surprise at the mention of his name. 'Jack? Nothing. I told you last week.'

'*Jack?* I thought your husband was called Alex.' Nick frowned in confusion. 'Or is that another Sadie?'

'No, that's me. Alex *is* my h— Well, we're not married but, you know—'

'Same difference,' Becca said quickly. She knew how I felt about the marrying thing. 'Come on, Sade, you're stalling. Out with it.' She turned to Nick. 'Jack is Sadie's *bit on the side*.'

I flushed. 'No, he is *not*,' I said, feeling hot and flustered under Nick's gaze. Actually, I felt out-and-out indignant. It was all very well laughing about this harmless, *meaningless* Jack flirtation with Cat and Becca, but it sounded awful, said out loud in this tapas bar to Nick. Awful and completely untrue, more to the point.

'He is definitely *not* my bit on the side,' I said firmly. I stood up, with some difficulty. The chairs and tables were packed so tightly into the room, I could hardly get out without elbowing someone in the back. 'Look, here's some money,' I said. Nick started to say something about him paying for lunch, but I put a pile on the table before he could finish his sentence. I was sick of other people paying for me all the time. I did have money, even if I didn't have a sodding job. My fingers were shaking for some reason, and the coins started bouncing and rolling everywhere.

Becca grabbed my hand. 'Sadie – I was only joking,' she said. 'About Jack, I mean. I was just teasing you. What's wrong?'

'Nothing. Look – I'll talk to you soon. Lovely to meet you, Nick. Bye.' I grabbed my bag and jacket. 'And enjoy Rome,' I said over my shoulder, trying to sound as if I meant it, rather than spitting the words out.

Becca shot me a puzzled look but let me go. When I went past the window seconds later, their heads were huddled together, low over the table, food ignored as they resumed their mutual love-in.

I walked quickly down the high street. What was wrong with me? Why couldn't I be pleased for her that she and Nick were going to Rome? After all, I'd been there, done it, once upon a time. Why should I begrudge her the same happiness?

I was jealous. I was a horrible, bitter, jealous best friend. I was . . . I was going to go home.

Chapter Eight

Back at the ranch, I greeted the kids and Alex loudly and over-enthusiastically, as if I'd been away for a week instead of just two hours.

'That was quick,' Alex said. He'd been painting with them, and the kitchen was covered in streaks of red, yellow and blue. 'I thought you'd be hours yet. Everything all right?'

'Fine,' I said, not quite meeting him in the eye. I busied myself by wiping a smudge of yellow paint from under his nose. 'He's nice. Nick. They seem really happy.'

'And?'

'And what?'

He shrugged. 'You seem a bit weird. Twitchy.'

'They're going to Rome,' I said, by way of explanation. I carried Molly at arm's length to the sink and started scrubbing her fingers with washing-up liquid. She squealed and wriggled at the coldness of the water.

'Ahh.' He was silent. I knew that he, too, would be thinking of us holding hands as we strolled through the streets, pointing up at the beautiful buildings, pausing for a cappuccino here, stopping for a beer there . . . 'Bastards,' he said.

I smiled at him gratefully. He understood. 'I *know*,' I said. My words fell out in a rush. 'I was so jealous, Alex. I practically ran out of there because I couldn't bear it.' I patted Molly's hands dry and put her down. 'I feel a bit of an idiot, actually. I mean, I did go off quite abruptly. Nick probably thinks I'm a right nutter.'

Alex came over and put his arms around me. 'Well, he was going to find that out sometime, I suppose,' he said, and then kissed the top of my head. 'Only joking. Anyway, if it makes you feel any better – and I swear I'm not just saying this because of Becca and Nick – I was thinking of taking you away somewhere for your birthday this year. Not quite Rome, but—'

'Where? Where?'

'And I know we'd have to take the kids with us—'

'Where?'

'Maybe Cambridge. Or Brighton. It's not exactly Rome, but . . .'

I rested my cheek against him. 'That would be lovely. Either. Good idea. Let's get out of London for a bit.'

'Exactly.' He ruffled my hair in an annoying kind of way. 'Let's face it, we both know I'm right about—'

'Everything, yes,' I finished. 'Well, whatever boosts your confidence, sweetheart. If you want me to go along with that, then I will. I'll humour you for the sake of love. And also because you're taking me out of south London.'

Molly ran over at that moment, and butted our legs like a little goat. 'Fuffuxy!' she shouted. 'Mummy say *fuffuxy!*'

Alex pulled away and crouched down to her level. 'What's that, love? Mummy say what?' he asked.

'Fuffuxy!' she yelled and started dancing around the room.

Fuffuxy? Oh God . . . I started to laugh. 'I have the horrible feeling,' I groaned, 'that our darling little daughter is trying to say, "For fuck's sake".'

That night, while Alex was immersed in some awful sci-fi film on ITV, I borrowed his laptop and took it up to the bedroom. Once I was online, I went straight to the Friends Reunited website and deleted my details, just left my name. There. No more lying, I decided. No more Channel 4 nonsense. I hadn't heard a word back from the TV production company and that was also good. I was going to end all that bollocks.

I was just about to put on the rather less exciting truth instead – *living with my partner, Alex, I'm a full-time mum to two children* – when something stopped me.

What was it Danny had said all those years ago?

I think we're too young to settle down, Sadie.

Things have changed, Sadie.

My fingers hovered over the keys as I remembered. My

shoulders shaking with sobs. The drip, drip of tears onto my bare feet in the garden. The pain in my chest that stayed there for weeks, as if something had broken inside me. Feeling like I wanted to die with misery. The git.

Things have changed? Not with me, they hadn't. I'd have done anything for him. Stayed faithful all those miles south of him while we were doing our degrees. Oh, I would have done, given half a chance.

Maybe . . . Maybe I'd tell just one or two more lies. To Danny. Just to Danny, to keep up appearances. He deserved it, anyway.

Dear Dan,

Nice to hear from you. Sorry it's taken me a while to get back to you – work has been mad lately. I'm doing two different programmes and they're both being wrapped up this month so it's been all heads down while we get them in the can.

(Did telly people say 'in the can' or was that just in the film industry?)

How about you, how's the shop?

(Ha. My job's more glamorous than *your* job.)

Next time I'm in Manchester I'll definitely look you up. I travel about on business quite a bit. I wonder if we would recognize each other?!

(Oh, I'd know him anywhere, though. Even now. Anywhere.)

Same goes for you – if you're ever back in London, let me know. Maybe we could do lunch?

(Yes, lunch. I'd be far too busy in the evenings, love. I've moved on.)

Sadie
PS Don't worry about the album. Keep it. Or sell it!

I hit the Send button before I could change my mind. There. I'd done it. Friendly but not too friendly. Cool and adult. I was starting to enjoy this, I realized. I found myself hoping he would write back, so that I could keep the story going a little bit longer, spin out the shelf-life of my alter ego for just another few emails. Why not? It was only a bit of harmless fun, after all.

Alex usually got home in time to help with the end-of-bath-time chaos, the wrestling of small people into pyjamas, the reading of stories and the drawn-out saga of bedtime. It was always the hardest part of the day and I was pretty much ready to faint with relief when I heard his key in the front door each evening. Hurrah! The cavalry back from the news front line at last.

This week, though, he worked late on Monday and Tuesday so I had to get through the whole thing on my own each time – which was enough to send me straight to the wine in the fridge the very minute after I'd said my final night-nights. Then on Wednesday, I was up in the bathroom, drying Nathan and trying to get his vest back on without making him cry while simultaneously having an argument with my stroppy daughter about why she had to pull the plug out and put the bath toys away right *now*, when I heard that familiar clicking sound of key turning in lock downstairs. About bloody time.

'Great, Dad's home,' I said to Molly. 'Quick – let's surprise him by having you all dry and dressed by the time he gets up here!'

'No,' she said, kicking her feet murderously through the bubbles. 'Not dry and dressed.'

'Yes, dry and dressed,' I replied, struggling with Nathan's poppers. 'All right, baby, just a second . . .'

'No, no, NOT dry and dressed!' she yelled doggedly.

My ears were straining hopefully for the sound of Alex's footsteps on the stairs, but no footsteps came. What was he doing down there? Couldn't he hear that Bathroom War No. 278 was breaking out up here?

Clearly not. I heard the low mumble of Radio 4 start up in the kitchen. Ahh! Maybe he was pouring me a glass of red and he was going to bring it up here. Medicinal, and all that. He was practically a mind-reader.

I leaned over and pulled the plug out.

'No!' screamed Molly, trying to wrest it out of my hands again. 'No, Mummy!'

'Yes, Molly,' I said wearily, hauling her out of the water. God, that wine was going to taste good. I could practically smell it already. Fruity . . . velvety . . . rich . . .

'NO! Bad Mummy!' she wailed, lunging at me with two wet fists. Water ran down my neck and splashed all over Nathan, who promptly started crying again.

'Hey!' I said sharply. 'That's enough!'

Where was Alex? Where was my damn wine?

'Alex! Can you give me a hand?' I yelled through the door, as I threw a towel around Molly. She was clinging to the side of the bath, trying to swing her leg up and over the top of it like a monkey. 'Oh, no, you don't,' I said, drying her as fast as possible, prising her fingers off the bath as best I could.

Now they were both crying. Oh God! This had all gone totally pear-shaped now. I leaned against the radiator, feeling like crying myself. 'Let's just get you dressed . . .' I muttered through gritted teeth, jamming her vest over her head, even though she was shaking her head so wildly her wet hair was slapping my hands. 'Oh, come on, Molls . . . Don't be difficult . . .' I said pathetically. 'All right, Nath, hang on just a second . . .'

Jesus! Who was it who'd decided that bathtime was a relaxing end to the day? Somebody with a full-time nanny and a vivid imagination, that was who. I'm sure bathtime *was* very relaxing, if you didn't have to be present every bloody evening.

At last we were tumbling out of the bathroom door together, two of us still blubbing. At last we were down the stairs and in front of CBeebies in time for *Fimbles*. And there was Alex, sitting on the sofa, reading the newspaper – with a single glass of wine by his side!

'All right?' I asked crossly. My raised eyebrows clearly added the subtext, 'Are you deaf? Did you not hear all that?', but he chose to ignore the latter questions.

'Knackered,' he replied, not making eye contact.

I couldn't help feeling a little pleased when Molly scrambled onto his lap accidentally kneeing him in the groin. 'Me too,' I said pointedly, then dumped Nathan on him, crumpling the very bit of newspaper he'd been reading. 'Right – if you don't mind, I think I'll head out for another run before it gets too cold,' I said. The words were out of my mouth before I'd even thought the idea through.

'What, now – before they're in bed?' he asked, sounding appalled.

'Yeah, now,' I replied shortly, 'before they're in bed.' I turned to leave the room, just about managing to hang on to my self-respect enough to stop myself flicking him the Vs. Ha! You do it for a change, Alex, and see how much you like it on *your* own, I thought. I am outta here.

I heard him make a noise of protest but I was already racing up the stairs to get changed. Tough shit, *partner.* I needed head space.

I threw on some tracksuit bottoms and my trainers before he could come and wheedle me out of it, then headed outside. As I shut the door behind me, I could hear Nathan yelling, and I sprinted off like a maniac, trying to throw the sound from my ears.

I was out. I had escaped. Sadie Morrison had left the building.

It had stopped raining, thank God. It had poured down all day. I'd spent the afternoon at my friend Rose's, with Anna and all of our kids, and the three of us had polished off a whole Entemann's carrot cake while the older children had played upstairs.

Rose had told us about her new job. 'Three days a week, project management,' she said happily. 'Three days a week, boys in nursery. Fan-bloody-tastic.'

'Project-managing what?' I asked. No fretting for Rose

over the whole childcare issue. She'd done two and a half years as a full-time mum and that, she reckoned, was her lot. Fair play to her. I wasn't sure if I could have managed her demon twin boys single-handedly for that long.

'All sorts of things. It's a TV production company. I'm going to be overseeing their children's strand.' She was looking more contented than I'd seen her for years. 'I know it sounds awful, but I can't wait. I think it's going to be like three days off, every week.'

'It doesn't sound awful at all,' Anna said. 'It sounds great. Which nursery have you put the boys into?'

'Which TV company is it?' I asked. Surely it would be too much of a coincidence. 'Not . . .' I coughed. 'It's not Firestarter, is it?'

'Firestarter? No. They're called Jewel Productions. They do that DIY programme with Alan Brisket. And *Snowy the Snowman* for kids.' She stuck her tongue out. 'Which is crap, I know, but don't worry, I've got loads of better ideas.' Then she looked at me. 'Why, do you know someone at Firestarter?' Her eyes narrowed. 'Who was it I used to work with who went there? Bridget someone, I think . . .'

I could feel myself blushing. 'No, I don't know anyone there. I . . .' I hesitated, swirled the last of my tea around in its cup. 'Actually, I applied for a job at Firestarter the other week.'

They probably didn't mean to, but both Rose and Anna

swivelled their eyes down to Nathan, then looked up at me. Meaning, *But your baby is so young! And you're thinking of* leaving *him? Already?*

'It was kind of a . . . joke,' I said, but it sounded so lame, I felt I had to explain myself. 'Well, all right then, it was more to see if I still had it. Had what it takes to get a job, I mean. An interesting one, not just bag-packing in Tesco.'

They were still looking doubtful. 'I didn't know you'd worked in telly,' Rose said.

'Did you actually apply?' Anna asked.

I licked my lips. I felt such a prat. 'Yes, I did apply. And no, I haven't worked in telly.'

Rose seemed reassured at that. 'Oh, well, you won't get the job anyway,' she said heartlessly. 'Unless you've got contacts, forget it.'

Anna was still wearing a confused expression. I could tell she didn't get why I had wasted my time writing an application for a job I wasn't going to take, even if it was offered to me, which it wouldn't be.

Mind you, when it was put like that, I didn't really get why I had done it either.

'Oh, didn't I say?' I exclaimed. 'I didn't tell the truth on the application – I made everything up!'

I grinned to myself as I thudded through the street-lamp-lit gloom, trainers squeaking on the wet pavement. I was just so utterly tragic. Rose and Anna obviously thought so too, from their humouring expressions. And now, even more tragically, here I was, pounding the streets and wondering if I might see Mark again. What a saddo! Like that was going to happen! Just because he'd given me the eye once, I thought that . . .

I frowned. Oh, what did I think?

I slowed to a fast walk. I'd overdone it, started too quickly. My heart thudded painfully inside me, my cheeks were flame hot.

It was just . . . nice to be flirted with. If I'd read the signs right, anyway. It was refreshing – and bloody unusual, more to the point. And he was a good-looking man, too. Not necessarily any better looking than Alex, but . . . He was someone different. Someone who seemed interested in me, the real me, not the Channel 4 scriptwriting Sadie I'd invented and not the old thigh-booted party animal I once had been. He hadn't seen the day-to-day me, the bum-wiping, sick-splattered, baggy-eyed, temper-snapping me like most people had. He hadn't seen the bellowing, grunting me of childbirth like Alex had, which, although he denied it, I was sure had knocked hundreds of points off my sex-kitten rating. He was just a new friend. A man who hadn't pissed me off with his crapness and selfishness and uselessness. A man who happened to have given me the eye. And it wasn't like I was actually going to *do* anything!

Right. That was that, then. Harmless friendship. Sorted.

My breath was smoother now, less raggedy and urgent. Time to pick up the pace again. But then, just as I was easing back into my stride, I heard my name, carried on the wind, from across the road.

'Sadie!'

Mark. Unbelievable.

My face split into a village-idiot-type beam. I couldn't help it. I was delighted to see him again. My body tingled as I waved at him. The lights changed to green, engines revved, and then he was gone, hidden behind a blue van, an MPV, a grumbling bus . . .

I stood there motionless, waiting for the traffic to clear. When the line of cars had at last all gone on their way towards the A3 and the motorway and their own light-filled homes, there he was again, grinning back at me.

The green man was winking. Go, girl.

I was over the crossing in giant strides, full of energy once more.

'Fancy seeing you here!' I said, trying to sound casual. Really, though, my skin was prickling all over just at being near him again.

'Come here often?' he asked at the same time.

'No, hardly ever,' I laughed. 'Such a beautiful part of the world, I can't think why not.'

His eyes were fixed upon me as we stood there under a street lamp, traffic roaring and belching all around us. 'Very beautiful,' he said, still gazing at me, and I shivered. There was just something about him, I couldn't put my finger on it. He was . . . bewitching. Magnetic. I felt as if all my senses were charged up, whenever I was near him.

We were standing inches apart, just smiling at each other. The done thing, obviously, would be for me to say how nice it was to see him again, and carry on with my run now. 'Well . . .' I began reluctantly. 'Nice to . . .'

'Coffee?' he suggested, before I could get any further. 'Same place as before?' Then he leaned in conspiratorially. 'Or maybe a beer?'

Beer. That raised the stakes somewhat, didn't it?

An image flashed into my head of Alex, boozing it up after work. Whereas I hadn't been to a pub for ages. At least a week. 'OK,' I said slowly. I couldn't help myself. 'Don't mind if I do.'

We walked towards the Prince Albert together. My heart was thudding for different reasons now. Beer meant more than coffee, didn't it? Going for a beer was way different to casually bumping into someone and happening to have an innocent coffee together. Dangerously different.

'Glad you came along just then,' he said. 'I'd been stood there waiting for you for ages.'

'Had you really?' I glanced sideways at him in shock.

He turned to meet me in the eye, and laughed at the look on my face. 'No, I was joking,' he said. 'Well, joking about waiting there for you anyway. I meant the bit about being glad you came along.'

'Oh,' I said, fiddling with the zip on my top. 'Thank you. I'm . . . Well, I'm glad I saw you, too.'

We'd reached the Albert. It was a pub I'd met Alex in, many times before, back in the days before we were living together. It was a proper pub, still untouched by developers. Real fire, good choice of beers, sticky carpet, pork scratchings behind the bar.

'What are you having?'

I checked my watch. Only six-thirty, but . . . 'I'll have a vodka and tonic, please,' I said. Then at least my breath wouldn't smell, I was thinking.

The thought gave me a jolt. God! I was acting as if I was doing something deceitful, when all that was happening was a quick drink with a new friend.

Was that all that was happening?

I could feel Mark's presence beside me, heard him joking with the barmaid as he ordered the drinks.

I wouldn't tell Alex, though. He'd just get the wrong idea. It would just make life easier all round if I didn't tell Alex.

'There's a table over in the corner, look,' Mark said a moment later, sliding my vodka along the bar to me. Tall glass, clinking ice, yellow-labelled bottle at the side.

I stared at the wet trail my glass had left along the bar. Deceit. It didn't have to mean betrayal though, did it? It didn't have to mean actually hurting anybody. One little drink. One little lie. That was it. It wasn't as if Alex told me every single time *he* went to the pub anyway. It wasn't as if . . .

I followed Mark through the clusters of tables. Friends were laughing together. Music blared from the jukebox. Pool balls cracked and rolled on the pool table. Someone was applauding the shot.

I sat down and peeled off my jacket, realizing too late what a clingy T-shirt I had on underneath it. As I turned sideways to hang it on the back of my chair, I was aware of my breasts moving beneath the material. I wondered if Mark was aware of them too.

My nipples were hardening, puckering. The T-shirt was thin. I knew he could see them.

'Cheers,' I said, lifting my glass. My bare arm brushed against my chest. Goose pimples prickled over my skin at the sensation.

'Cheers,' he replied.

Chapter Nine

'So,' he said, drumming his fingers on the table.

'So,' I said, at the same moment. Then we both laughed.

'How have you been?' I asked, after a moment's pause. 'Good week?'

'Not bad,' he said. 'You?'

'Yeah, fine,' I said. I ducked my head suddenly, uncomfortable under his blue gaze. I fiddled with the beer mat. What was I doing here anyway? With this man?

'Are you going to this thing at the Laurel Tree, then?' he asked.

'Yeah,' I said. I took a sip of vodka, waited for the kick. 'God, I hate going to Alex's office dos. He seems to work with so many wankers.'

I broke off hurriedly. Shit. Good one, Sade – don't forget Alex works with *Julia*. Slag off the man's wife, why don't you?

Luckily, Mark seemed to agree. 'I know. Media darlings, Jesus.' He swigged his pint, banged the glass back on the table. 'Other people's office parties are hideous, aren't they? You don't know anyone except the person you came with, you have to behave yourself all night for fear of embarrassing your partner . . .'

'You don't know the in-jokes, the leches, the bores,' I added, with feeling. 'You don't know who you have to be polite to and who you can afford to piss off.'

'And then you have to pretend you don't know any of the gossip you've heard about them,' Mark said. 'That Matthew guy who was round for dinner at ours the other week – apparently, he's this incredible philanderer who—'

'Oh, I know,' I laughed. 'The secretary from Features, wasn't it?'

It was his turn to laugh. 'I don't know about her. I was told about some new assistant in the post room.'

I rolled my eyes and took another mouthful of vodka. I could feel it hitting the spot already, burning its way stealthily through my body. I was starting to relax now. Enjoy myself. I would tell Alex I'd bumped into one of the mums, I decided quickly. No rush to get back.

'He's such a creep, that Matthew,' I said. 'Do you know, at your dinner party, he was trying to play footsie with me all night. With poor Chloe sat just the other side of him!'

Mark feigned outrage. 'He wasn't!'

I nodded my head, indignant. 'He was!'

Mark held my eye for a second. Then he asked, 'What, playing footsie like this?'

Under the table, his foot started sliding gently up my leg.

I jolted as I felt it, stared at him in shock. I tried not to let out the gasp that rushed up through me.

He was smiling at me, his mouth crooked, blue eyes steady.

Alex, I thought guiltily. Then I remembered him slumped on our sofa reading the paper and not helping me bath the children. And I thought about hearing that woman – Nat – laughing down the phone with him the other night.

Two can play that game, I thought to myself. And I took a deep breath, held Mark's gaze. 'It was a bit . . . higher actually,' I said.

'What, more like . . . up here?'

He moved closer towards me. Under the table, his knee pressed hard against my thigh, and I gulped. His eyes never left mine. Teasing, challenging. He was so close, I could see the lines on his skin. What looked like a scar on his cheek. I could smell him. That spicy scent again.

A surge of lust powered right through me, obliterating Alex and everything else from my mind. I gripped the table. Took another breath. 'Yeah,' I said, trying to keep my voice casual. 'Yeah, just there.'

'Dirty old bastard,' Mark said, looking amused. Then he slid his hand under the table to rest lightly on my knee.

'Did he do this, as well?' he asked. His mouth twitched.

I wanted to touch it, suddenly. Press my finger between his lips. Just to see what it felt like. Just to see what he did.

I watched my knuckles turn white as they gripped the table tighter. My knee trembled where Mark's hand lay on it. What was he going to do? Oh God, why did I have to be wearing these wretched tracksuit bottoms? Why couldn't I be wearing something sexier, like . . . like a skirt and no knickers?

'No,' I said, after what seemed like hours. My mouth was dry. I raised my glass to it and gulped a mouthful, to hide my face as much as anything.

My fingers were shaking. The pit of my stomach felt hollow.

'Better hope he's sitting at another table at the Laurel Tree on Saturday, eh?' Mark went on. His thumb was tracing slow, deliberate circles on my knee now, yet his face was impassive.

'Let's hope so,' I said. My heart was banging around under my ribs. What was he doing? What was *I* doing, sitting here, letting him do it? Tell him to stop, tell him to stop, part of my brain was ordering my mouth. Tell him you've got to leave right now. Right now!

I didn't say a thing. Couldn't. I wanted him to go on touching me.

His fingers slid further up my leg. They were on my thigh. My skin felt clammy under the Adidas stripes. My knickers felt damp. My nipples were starting to ache from wanting him to touch them, run his fingers around them, take them into his mouth . . .

His watch bleeped under the table, a quiet, nothingy sound, but I almost jumped out of my skin. I was on the edge of my nerves, I realized, strung out as taut as piano wire.

'I'm going to have to go,' I said. My eyes locked with his. *Talk me out of it,* I was thinking. *Don't let me go.*

'That's a shame,' he said. He took his hand away and rested it on the table. I wanted to snatch it back. No, no, carry on! Carry on with that stroking thing. Don't stop now!

The skin on my thigh was warm where he had touched it. I looked on helplessly as he drained his pint. His throat was exposed. I saw him gulp down his lager, watched him put down the empty glass.

'You've got froth on your lip,' I lied, reaching over to touch his face. I pretended to wipe it off, brushing my thumb along his mouth. His lips moved beneath my touch; they felt soft, different to Alex's.

'I really had better go now,' I said, abruptly pulling away and standing up. 'Before . . .'

'Before something happens?' he said. He stood up, came over to me. We were about two inches apart. 'Something you might regret?'

I bit my lip. 'Yes,' I said hoarsely. I didn't dare touch him again. I couldn't let myself.

He lifted his hand, hesitated for a second, then ran a

finger down my cheek. 'I reckon it's too late to stop, Sadie. It's already started.'

'Yes,' I said again, frozen to the spot.

There was a pause where I wanted him to grab me and stop me going. He didn't.

He cleared his throat. 'So I'll see you at the Laurel Tree, then,' he said after a few moments, sounding strangely formal. 'Saturday.'

'Yes, you will.' I nodded and started edging back towards the door. 'Saturday. Bye.'

I walked quickly out of the pub, not looking back. Shock tremors were coursing through me. My heart was still thudding hard. Once I was out of the door, I ran for home as fast as I could.

Oh my God!

What had just happened? What had I done?

I had let him do that. I had let him touch me like that. Loving, faithful partners didn't do that sort of thing, did they? Loving, faithful partners stayed well clear of men like Mark. I was a slut, a slapper. I was a bad person to have let him done that.

I wanted to cry suddenly, in shame. I wanted to wind back the hands of the pub clock, to when we first entered. What had I been thinking? Why had I gone along with it? I should have walked away as soon as he put his hand on me. Sorry, no, I don't do that kind of thing. I think you've got the wrong person . . .

But I had done it.

Alex, I thought helplessly, with an ache of guilt. Alex, Alex, Alex. If Alex had sat there letting some woman run her hand all over his leg, I would have been really, shoutily pissed off. I would have gone completely tonto about it. And God, I hardly dared imagine Alex's reaction if he'd seen me sitting there in my clingy T-shirt, doing nothing to stop Mark's wandering hand.

I remembered the conversation I'd had with Anna the other week. The one where I was moaning that I wanted to feel like a sex kitten again. Well, I *had* felt like that again. I'd got what I'd wished for, hadn't I? *Was* that what I had wished for?

Too late to stop, Mark had said in the pub, like that made everything OK. Like that was our excuse. *We couldn't help ourselves. It just happened.* Pathetic, I'd always thought, whenever I'd read magazine articles where other people used those words. Pathetic! Of course you could have stopped yourselves! Yet now I knew how they felt. And it wasn't as simple as that.

The worst thing was how much I'd liked it. How much I'd wanted him to carry on. My cheeks flamed. I'd seen the lust in his eyes. He'd been imagining taking me out the back, fucking me up against the steel barrels and beer crates, no doubt.

I wrapped my arms around myself suddenly. I'd been imagining that too.

Too late to stop, he'd said, and blood roared in my ears as I heard him say it again, in my mind. I found that I was shaking my head. No. It wasn't too late at all. Because of course I was going to stop it. Damn right I was going to stop it! Like I'd throw away my life with Alex and the children, and for what? A bit on the side? Housewife's pleasure? No way.

I slowed to a jog. I had done a bad thing, but I wasn't going to do it again. *See you Saturday,* he'd said, but he wouldn't. I'd make some excuse, bottle it so that I didn't have to see him at Alex's work do. And that would be that. I never had to see him again.

I glanced at my watch as I ran and was shocked when I realized it was still early. I had only been out of the house for forty minutes. I couldn't believe it. Time seemed to have been stretched out in the Albert. I felt as if we'd been there the whole evening, it had been so intense. So lust-driven. The very air between us had felt charged.

I raced back home and up the front steps, as if I was running away from *him*.

'Only me,' I yelled, bursting through the front door, kicking my trainers off in the hall. I ran straight upstairs, stripped off and got in the shower, washing the pub smoke from my hair as well as the treacherous scarlet flush from my cheeks.

Mark. I ran a soapy hand across my breasts and shuddered

at the hardness of my nipples. A hand on my knee and I was a quivering mess. I had physically ached for him.

The thought made me feel sick now that I was back in my own home. It seemed like a dream, a weird kind of dream. Me and Mark – yeah, right. Time to wake up now, back in the real world.

The next evening, Cat and Tom came over for dinner, full of happy plans for moving in together and their India trip.

I put together an Indian-themed banquet for their benefit. Poppadoms and pickles, jasmine rice, a gloopy mustard-coloured dal, sag aloo, bhindi bhajis and a dodgy-looking vegetarian dhansak, plus as much beer as it was possible to cram into our fridge.

We clinked bottles of Kingfisher across the table. 'Hey, you know that Molly was conceived in Goa, don't you?' I said conversationally. 'So watch out. Must be something in the water.'

'Probably just that I'm incredibly fertile though,' Alex said, raising an eyebrow at me.

'Oh, so are you saying Tom's *not* incredibly fertile?' Cat joked, arching an eyebrow in imitation.

I had been feeling antsy all day over the Mark thing, avoiding Alex's eye and trying to act as if nothing untoward had happened. Now, for the first time all evening, I found myself smiling over at Alex, trying not to get teary-eyed at the thought of Molly as a little bud inside my belly. We hadn't been able to take our hands off each other on that holiday, Alex and I. He had woken me up with his hard-on every morning and we'd panted and bucked and gasped under the thrumming ceiling fan each time. Then he'd untangled himself from the sheets and gone to shower while I lay there with my legs in the air, willing his sperm to do their thing. He would come back after a while, water dripping off his tanned body, and then we'd start all over again. We never once made it down in time for breakfast.

I forked some curry into my mouth. 'Started house-hunting yet?' I asked.

Cat and Tom exchanged glances, and she pulled a face. 'We're going to do that when we get back,' she said. 'We've got to decide what area to look in first, though.' She rolled her eyes theatrically. 'Which is taking a bit of time to negotiate, shall we say.'

'Ahh,' said Alex. He caught Tom's eye. 'I see.'

'Let me guess,' I said. 'You want to stay in Battersea, Cat, and Tom wants to stay in Hammersmith.'

'Correct,' Cat said. 'But I hate Hammersmith. I hate driving around it. The shops aren't very good—'

'What, and the shops in Battersea *are*?' Tom put in at once. You could tell this was well-worn territory.

'Why not compromise?' I said, wiping a naan around my plate. 'Putney is nice.'

'Can't afford it,' Tom said at once.

'The Bush, then,' Alex said.

'The Bush is a dump,' Cat growled.

There was a momentary silence as everyone busily forked in another mouthful and avoided eye contact.

The CD ended and the room felt even more silent. Alex got up. 'What does everyone fancy listening to?' he asked, flipping through the CD rack. 'Ahh, this'll do.'

He pushed the CD tray into the machine and some familiar notes started up. Air, *Moon Safari*.

'I love this album,' Cat said at once.

I had gone off on another nostalgia trip. I loved this album too. It was the one that had been playing when I'd given birth to Nathan, upstairs, on my and Alex's bed. It had been one of those glorious late September days, sun low in a perfect blue sky, leaves glowing russet and yellow on the trees. The student midwife had been rubbing my lower back. 'Good choice,' she'd said approvingly as the first song had started. 'Saw them at Glastonbury once. So-o-o fab.'

I found myself getting tearful all over again, thinking of the moment just before Nathan had been born, when he'd been poised on the very edge of me. I could feel him there, perfectly balanced on the verge of coming into our lives, and had shut my eyes, breathed in more gas and air, braced for the final push. He had rushed out of me in a bloody slither. *It's a boy!* I had cried, choking with happiness, clutching his wet, slippery limbs to me. *Alex, it's a boy!*

'You all right, Sadie?' Cat asked, noticing my glassy eyes.

I pulled myself up quickly. 'Yeah, fine,' I said. 'This curry's a bit on the hot side, that's all. Making my eyes water.'

What was *wrong* with me? All this emotional reminiscing. It was as if my subconscious was trying to flag up all the best shared memories between Alex and me. All right, all right, I felt like telling it. I know. Mark was just a stupid mistake. A vodka-on-an-empty-stomach mistake, one not to be repeated. OK?

When we'd all finished eating, Cat helped me carry the plates and dishes into the kitchen.

'Sadie,' she said, and then stopped.

I turned to look at her. She was standing against the worktop, her arms still full of plates, green eyes anxious. 'What?' I asked.

'Sadie, has anything happened with that guy?' she went on. Her eyebrows were at ten to two, cheeks pink from the beer.

I nearly dropped my serving dishes in shock. 'What do you mean?' I asked, turning away from her to the sink. I put the taps on, squirted washing-up liquid into the bowl, busy, busy. How did she know? *What* did she know? Had one of her friends seen us in the Albert? My fingers shook under the bubbly water. Reflected light winked up at me from the cutlery.

'That guy in the bar the other week. The one we saw with Becca.'

With *Becca*? Oh. Oh! Jack. She meant Jack.

I almost laughed out loud in relief. 'No way!' I said. 'Absolutely not. Nothing has happened with him!' I was careful to put my emphasis on the 'nothing' rather than on the 'him'.

Cat put the plates down on the side and came over to me. 'Really?' she asked, looking into my face. 'Really and truly? Only you're acting a bit strangely. And I couldn't help wondering . . .'

I looked straight back at her. 'Cat, I don't even know what happened to that number he gave me,' I said. The truth felt like a luxury. She could bang on about Jack until she was hoarse, and I could honestly answer everything without guilt, for the simple reason that there was nothing whatsoever to tell. I laughed. 'Anyway, he's hardly my type, is he?'

'Good,' she said. The words rushed out of her; I could see her transparent relief. 'Good. I'm really glad. Because you and Alex are just so great together and I would hate anything to mess it up.'

The smile tightened on my face like an uncomfortable mask. 'Well . . .' I started. Then I got stuck. 'I wouldn't go that far,' I said. I looked over at the door guiltily and lowered my voice. 'I mean, I wouldn't say that we're that "great together" at the moment. Yeah, we get on, obviously, and we still have a laugh, but . . .' I shrugged. 'It's all so bloody domestic. We don't do much any more. We don't go anywhere. We've been out together *once* since Nathan was born. I mean, look at you and Tom, off to India, making plans—'

She interrupted, shaking her head. 'Look at you and Alex, with your house and two gorgeous children!' she countered.

I pulled a face. 'Exactly,' I said. 'Look at me right now with my hands in the kitchen sink, where they are every single bloody day.' I closed my mouth abruptly. My voice sounded shrill and bitter.

Cat hesitated. 'Are you sure you're OK?' she asked.

'Yes, fine,' I said, not looking her in the eye. 'Why wouldn't I be?'

I put the pile of plates into the foamy water and dried my hands. I would finish those in the morning. Right now, I needed to drink some more beer.

'No reason,' she replied awkwardly. 'I'm just glad you're all right. I mean, I'm glad that the Jack thing was . . . well, that it was just a bit of a laugh. Nothing serious.'

'Yeah,' I said briskly. 'Another drink?'

Friday went by slowly and exhaustingly in the usual whirl of deeply trivial yet deeply passionate battles over which socks Molly was going to wear, what she didn't want to eat for lunch, how she didn't want a nap, and all the rest of it.

Nathan and I weren't the happiest of souls either. I had started phasing out breastfeeding, which meant reproachful glances from him every time I produced a bottle instead of my own boob (or so I interpreted it anyway) and hot, full, uncomfortably lumpy breasts for me, with milk inadvertently dribbling out if I so much as heard him snivel.

Who would be a woman? I thought miserably as I discarded another drenched breast pad. All this leaking and bleeding, and all the rest of it. I had been chatting to a heavily pregnant mum, Nicki, down at the park that afternoon, who had started coughing, only to wet herself all down the front of her khaki maternity trousers. I mean . . . Was there no end to the lack of dignity?

'Oh, *bollocks*, not again,' she'd moaned, trying and failing to gather up the wet material over her enormous mound of bump to inspect the damage. 'Does it show?'

'Ye-e-eah,' I'd replied carefully. 'Only a bit, though.'

'Fucking fuck shit bollocks,' she'd growled, low enough that her two-year-old wouldn't hear. Then, with a resigned shrug, she'd carried on where we'd left off in our conversation, moments before. 'And then he suggested Octavia if it's a girl! Octavia! I said, Liam, remind me what kind of car we've got again.'

I grinned. 'You haven't.'

'We have! A Skoda fucking Octavia!'

'Mummy, what she saying?' Molly had asked loudly.

Nicki had clamped a hand to her mouth. 'Sorry. Bad case of pregnancy Tourette's. I think it's my repressed rage at being a woman, you know. Having to do all . . .' She'd waved a hand over her seam-straining bump. 'Having to do all this.'

I knew exactly how she felt. *Having to do all this,* indeed.

On Saturday morning, I woke up feeling shivery inside with apprehension. Alex's work do was that evening and I desperately didn't want to go. I needed a good excuse to get me out of it.

'Oh-h-h,' I moaned at the breakfast table. 'I think I'm coming down with something. I feel really ropy.'

'What sort of ropy?' Alex asked from behind the newspaper.

'Just a bit fluey,' I said, improvising rapidly as I glimpsed a packet of Lemsip in the open kitchen cupboard. 'Um . . . Headache, aching joints, blocked nose,' I said, reading aloud from the box. 'That sort of thing.'

'Mmmm,' he replied, as if he wasn't really very interested. 'Lot of it going around at the moment.'

'Yes,' I said, then played my trump card. 'I just hope I'm up to going out later on. Because right now' – I coughed pathetically – 'I don't feel like going anywhere other than bed.'

That made him put the newspaper down. 'What – you're backing out of the do tonight?' he asked. 'Sade – I know you don't like these things, but . . .'

'And I like them even less when I feel ill,' I said as weakly as I could. 'But hopefully if I just take it easy today . . .'

Alex looked at me disbelievingly. 'Sade, you're such a crap actress,' he said. He actually sounded exasperated. 'If you don't want to go, just say so. Don't give me all this I'm-so-ill stuff.'

I stared at him, open-mouthed. 'That's a bit rich, coming from Brixton's biggest hypochondriac,' I said accusingly. 'Oh, I've got a twinge in my back – ooh, I must be practically paralysed. Get me to a consultant at once!'

Alex smirked at me and picked up the newspaper. 'Sounds like you're feeling better already,' he said lightly.

Smug git, I thought crossly, and made a big show of mixing myself a disgusting honey and lemon drink, knowing I'd only pour it down the toilet as soon as I had a chance.

'Still,' he went on, from behind his paper battlements, 'if you're going to duck out on me at the last minute, then at least I won't feel really bad about getting hammered with everyone else, I suppose.'

I stared at his newspaper, quite tempted to punch a fist through it. Right. So that was the score then, was it? Either I came with him – which I so didn't want to do – or, by not going, I gave him licence to . . . Well, to do absolutely anything he wanted, by the sound of it. And what exactly did he have in mind? Something with new-girl Nat, she of the loud laugh?

'Like I said, I'll see how I feel later,' I said through gritted teeth. Curses. I'd handled that really badly. So . . . what to do? Go, and risk bumping into Mark? Or stay, and torture myself imagining what drunken Alex was up to all night?

I flounced out of the room with my horrible honey drink. I'd have to go, I decided – but I'd just stick by Alex's side all night. After all, there was no way on earth that Mark was going to try anything on with me while Alex was in the same room, was there? No way on earth.

By the time the evening rolled around, I was starting to get a bit trembly with nerves. I felt really odd about seeing Mark again after that strange, intense encounter in the pub – how would I be able to look him in the face after that? I also hated going to these work parties, where they all knew each other and I knew almost no one.

'It'll be fine,' Cat, who'd come to babysit, said cheeringly, slapping on my make-up for me. 'Look, I'm making you look utterly ravishing here, so *everyone* will want to talk to you. You'll be the belle of the ball.'

'Ding-dong,' I said glumly.

'There,' she said, spinning me round so that I could see my reflection. 'Whaddya think?'

I gulped at the sophisticated-looking woman who was staring back at me. Cat had really done the business. She'd put my hair up in a neat twist at the back with an elaborate cross-over pattern on the top of my head – the sort of thing that I would need five hands in order to accomplish. Then she'd given me smouldering Catherine-Zeta-type eyes, shimmering cheeks and a perfect coral pout.

'Wow,' the glamorous stranger said in the mirror. 'Is that really me?' I giggled in a most unsophisticated way. 'God!'

'Fucking hell,' Alex gulped when I swished down the stairs and into the kitchen, two minutes later.

It wasn't just the make-up he was ogling, it was also Cat's black Chanel dress she'd lent me. 'Fifteen quid from Portobello,' she'd said, 'and it'll look great on you.'

'I've changed my mind,' Alex said, coming over to run a hand over my bottom. 'Let's stay in instead. Cat – you're dismissed.'

'Really?' I asked in delight.

He laughed. 'No, you idiot, I was only joking.' He looked at his watch. 'Taxi should be here any minute,' he said. 'Get your coat, love – you've pulled.'

I hugged Cat goodbye, feeling even more twitchy inside. I really didn't want to go, especially now I was looking so dolled up. Mark might think I'd done that for him – and of course I hadn't. 'Come on, then,' I said to Alex, hearing a faint beep from outside. 'Let's go.'

The taxi roared up Acre Lane and towards Chelsea Bridge and town. As we crossed the river, I looked at the black water, sparkling with reflected headlights, and shivered. No going back, Sadie. Uncharted waters straight ahead.

The Laurel Tree was everything Becca had excitedly told me. Slippery leather sofas, Philippe Starck bar stools, beautiful androgynous staff with Prozac smiles and hundred-pound haircuts, and, most impressively, designer toilets that had probably cost more than our house.

The place was buzzing with people when we arrived. It was the leaving do for Bob Saville, some legend or other from the sports desk, and there was a display of his best articles up on one wall. I recognized a picture of Gazza crying, and one of David Beckham being sent off against Argentina, but that was about it.

Alex whisked me into a group of people and started introducing me to some of them. Jenny, one of the international writers – bad perm and no chin. Paul, political affairs columnist – sharp suit and fox-coloured hair. David, Westminster diarist – jowly and heavy-set. I smiled and nodded blankly at them, and tried not to sigh.

'Right,' Alex said. 'I'll just get us something from the bar. Back in a tick.'

The git. Was he seriously expecting me to make idle chit-chat about Bush's current fiscal policy with these political boffins? Not likely.

I glared at him. 'I'll join you,' I said, treading on his toe with a carefully placed spike heel. 'Nice to meet you all. Bye.'

The bar was heaving with women in expensive, plunging dresses and men in their best shirts, some that had even been ironed. I couldn't see Mark anywhere but it was hardly surprising, with the current body count. The bar was three deep – something to do with the free-drinks element, at a wild guess. I suddenly felt tired and old and past it. My feet were killing me in my heels and it was only half-eight. And my bloody G-string was wedged right up my arse – it was all I could do to stop myself hoicking it out.

'Christ, we're going to be here all night,' Alex said. 'Tell you what. You carry on queuing here; I'll go to the downstairs bar, see if that's less hectic.'

'No,' I said quickly, not wanting us to be separated, but his back was already turned, and seconds later he'd been swallowed up in the crowd.

I sighed. Typical. We'd only been here two minutes and I'd lost him already. This is what happened every time, at these work dos of his. We arrived together but then seemed to get instantly separated until the end of the evening. Still, it had been far, far worse all those times when I was pregnant and not drinking, I comforted myself. At least there was a free bar here and I could get lashed without remorse.

Someone elbowed my side, and I whipped round with a glare. A skinny blonde in a black trouser suit, jacket buttoned in the middle, no shirt underneath. She didn't even notice me.

The bar staff were busily pouring champagne, pulling beer bottles from the fridge, uncorking wine, lining up tequila shots. I watched one of them, a girl with glossy hair so black it shone blue under the neon lights, like a raven's wing. She was wiggling to the music, laughing, singing as she shook a cocktail, looking for all the world as if it was her private party she was hostessing.

Then, I felt someone pressing up behind me. A familiar spicy tang made my breath catch in my throat. A hand brushed the side of my leg lightly before the fingers started sliding around to my bottom.

Mark.

'No,' I said stiffly, trying to sidestep him. There was nowhere to go, though. The crowd was all packed together like sardines. Oh no, you don't! I thought. Not here. Not *here!*

'Hello again,' he said in my ear, his voice low and gruff, his breath hot on my neck.

I shook my head, hoping he would get the message. But oh . . . feeling him so close behind me was making me giddy. His hand was still on me. It was all I could think about. His fingers on my dress, sending shock waves right through me, radiating out from each finger, like ripples on a lake.

My mouth was dry. I needed to break away. I had to get

out of this crowd right now, and find Alex in the downstairs bar. Right now.

I didn't move. I stood in the middle of the bar throng, people around me on all sides, and shivered with anticipation, my heart missing several beats as his fingers lightly roamed my black dress.

What should I do? What should I do?

Go – quickly! Just go! Find Alex!

But . . . oh, the way his hand was slipping forward, up, onto my waist, his fingers harder on me.

I took a deep breath. I wanted him. That was the problem.

I put my hand over his. I touched his skin, ran my fingers over his knuckles and felt a throb of excitement.

He was pressed right into me. I could feel his hard-on through my dress. Oh my God. This was really happening.

There was still time to go. Still time to say, sorry, no, I think you've misunderstood. I'm not that kind of . . .

But I was hypnotized. Bewitched all over again. Without any permission from my brain, my own hand was stretching slowly, slowly back behind me, over his trouser leg, to stroke an experimental finger over his groin. His whole body stiffened. I heard him gasp.

Now he was running his hand down the front of my legs, pulling up the material, gathering it between his finger and thumb. One swoop and he was underneath, discovering my stockings, moving up, up . . .

'Sadie! Over here!'

My head spun round as if it were on a string being pulled. Alex. Oh Christ, Alex, at the side of the crowd, triumphantly holding up two glasses of something or other, and beaming.

I smiled and waved back. Still I didn't look behind me. I walked over to my partner, to the father of my children, the man I had loved for years, with my knickers made wet by someone else's touch. 'Excuse me, excuse me,' I said as I made my way through the crowd of thirsty hacks. 'Can I just . . .? Thanks. Cheers.'

I could feel Mark's eyes on me all the while. I didn't dare turn round to look at him. Fucking hell. Fucking hell!

'It's stuffy in here, isn't it?' I said when I reached Alex's side. 'Phew.' I fanned my hot cheeks – mentally thanking Cat for slapping on so much foundation – and drank my drink. Champagne cocktail. Delicious. I couldn't look Alex in the eye. Betraying him under his nose, with all his colleagues in the room. What sort of a bitch did that to her man?

We went and stood with a load of the news hacks and I did the dutiful partner thing, smiling in the right places, polite and friendly, not saying anything offensive. I couldn't concentrate on a word anyone said, though, just kept pouring booze into myself. All I could think about was Mark's hands on my body. I wondered where he was, if he was still watching me. And where was Julia, anyway? Presumably not at the bar with Mark when I'd been there. I prayed she was with him right now, whisking him away to introduce him to some important people who'd keep him busy for the rest of the party.

A tall bespectacled journalist in the middle of our group was saying something about a scandal concerning the Department of Health, and hospital waiting lists.

'And of course, that's exactly what they promised *wouldn't* happen, according to their election manifesto,' he was droning.

Christ on a bike, did they all have to talk shop? It was meant to be an office party. Why weren't people discussing who fancied who, and *EastEnders,* and where they bought their outfits? Wasn't anyone going to get pissed and get a conga going?

I drained my cocktail in a gulp, felt it fizz through me. 'Back in a minute,' I said to Alex.

He nodded absent-mindedly, listening to and nodding at a middle-aged woman with a sparkly shawl who was quoting NHS statistics as if she'd been up all night revising them.

'Up twenty-eight per cent on last year, whichever way you look at it . . .' she wittered.

I made my escape, struck out in the direction of the loos. I was feeling quite drunk now and wobbled precariously on my heels. Oops! I just knocked somebody's drink with my elbow. Oops! I just bumped against one of the whitewashed pillars. Bloody hell! Get yourself in the loos fast before you go flying arse over tit, I told myself sternly.

I had a great time in the ladies', working out how to use the flush, admiring the stand-alone sinks and mosaic tiles, then helped myself to all the free hairspray and other cosmetic goodies on offer. I smiled at my flushed reflection in the enormous mirror, checked for lipstick on my teeth and tried to repair the damage to my Catherine Zeta Jones eyes, which were looking rather smudged by now.

I walked out of the toilets and there was Mark, waiting for me by a pillar, blue eyes fixed upon me. Just like I had known he would be.

Shit. This is serious, I told myself. Time to get a grip. Should I stop to talk to him? Or should I keep on walking, back to Alex?

'Hello again,' I said, feeling my pulse quicken at the sight of him. He had a dark blue shirt on, well-cut black trousers. I stopped for a second, and found myself rocking back on my heels. Bloody *hell!* Why had I let myself get so drunk?

'Here, I've got you a drink,' he said. 'Champagne.'

'Thanks,' I said, taking it. Our fingers touched and I looked up at him. He had felt it too, the electric shock of contact.

'You look amazing,' he said.

I tried to be flippant. 'Well, I *was* going to wear my running gear, you seemed to like me in that, but . . .'

Oh, no. That sounded really flirtatious. And I shouldn't be flirting with him. I should not be flirting with . . .

'I like you better in Chanel,' he said. That crooked smile again. And how did he know it was Chanel? Did that mean Julia had the same dress? I bet hers hadn't come from Portobello Market, I thought drunkenly. 'Actually, I think I'd like you with anything on, Sadie,' he said. He took a step closer to me and the space between us became an intimate one, our heads bent towards each other. 'Better still, with nothing at all.'

I felt as if I couldn't breathe in. The music seemed to have stopped. I couldn't see anyone else in the bar, only him. Everything else was a blur.

I knew I had two distinct options ahead of me, lying like two long paths stretching out into the distance. In one, I walked away from Mark and his hard-on, went back to Alex and lived happily ever after. Hopefully. In the other, I abandoned myself to some glorious sex – and it *would* be glorious, I could just tell – with Mark, and . . . And what? Then what happened?

I swallowed, almost dropping my champagne glass. 'Where can we go?' I asked. I couldn't help myself. The words just came out of me – and at that moment, I didn't regret them.

'Follow me,' he said. He grabbed my hand and pulled me after him, towards the far end of the room. There was a door marked 'Private – Staff Only' on the back wall. He pushed it open, led me in, and slammed the door behind us again.

We were in a brightly lit, white-painted corridor that stank of cigarettes. Music thudded from the other side of the wall. I gulped, suddenly uncertain, but as he slotted his arms around my waist, and bent his head down to kiss me, I breathed him in, felt his mouth upon mine and it was right, so right.

His hands were on me, pushing up my breasts, squeezing them hard, running his fingers down to my waist and then up again, back up to my breasts and pulling the shoulders of my dress down so that he could . . . oh, so that he could slip a hand in, around the side of my bra, searching for my nipple. There. Oh yes.

I was gasping, eyes squeezed shut, mouth on his, one hand in his hair, the other trying to undo his flies.

Now he'd discovered my suspenders and was running a finger around the top of my stocking, letting it snap back against my thigh. Up his hand went, and up, now pressing a palm into the black satin triangle of G-string, sliding a finger along the top, now moving his hands out to grip my bare bottom and groan into my neck.

I fumbled with the zip, feeling how stiff he was inside his trousers. Oh God, I just wanted to do it there and then under the strip lights, back to the wall, legs curled up around him . . .

'Excuse me – this is a staff corridor. Excuse me – you'll have to go back into the bar. You're not meant to be in here.'

I turned my head away from the voice – young, nervous and male – not wanting to see. My heart thumped hard. Mark's hands had stopped moving on me.

'Right. Sorry, mate. Just give us a minute,' he was saying.

I waited until our intruder had gone, then looked up at Mark. Colour flooded my face. Oh God. We'd practically had sex in the corridor. 'We'd better get back,' I said, suddenly stricken with guilt at being there, away from the party.

He was shaking his head, eyes dazed-looking. 'Christ, I can't bear it. I just want to . . .'

'I know,' I said. 'Me too. But we can't. We mustn't.'

'We can,' he said. He put both hands on my breasts, pushed me into the wall, kissed me again. My hair clip dug into the back of my head and tears started to my eyes, tears of sudden pain and of something else I couldn't quite name.

'Monday night,' he said. 'Outside the Albert. Sixish.'

He was rubbing circles around my nipples and it was too much; I had to pull away. 'Yes,' I said.

Chapter Ten

Dear Sadie,

Sounds like you're really busy with work. Did you get your programmes finished on time? What are they, anyway? Let me know so I can look out for them.

Life in the shop is going well. It's an independent record shop I set up with a mate, Vic. We specialize in dodgy old punk, your favourite. If you're serious about me selling your album, I will. How long do you reckon it'll take me to shift it? I give it two weeks, tops. Still lots of Smiths fans in Manchester.

I'm going to be down in London for my mum's 60th soon (last week in March). You suggested 'doing lunch' but I was wondering how you felt about a pint instead. What do you reckon?

Love Dan x

Oh, Danny boy. From being a mad moment of escapism, he was becoming a complication. There was a brief ten seconds or so while I wondered if Vic was male or female before realizing I didn't actually care. And now he wanted to go out for a pint with me . . . Hmmm. Could I really carry my bluff off, in person? Did I even want to? After all, there were other irons in the fire right now. In fact, the fire was liable to burn my hands if I wasn't careful.

It was the Monday after the Saturday before, and the secrets of Saturday night had beaten their wings inside my chest like caged birds for the whole of Sunday.

I hadn't seen Mark for the rest of the evening. It was as if he had been spirited away by Julia, or the whole thing had been a mere delusion, a wildly erotic dream I'd had that seemed more and more fantastical every time I thought about it.

I had spent a good ten minutes sitting on one of the loos, my mind in utter turmoil. Drunken slut, I chastised myself. Drunken idiot! So much for sticking to Alex's side all night! I'd all but had sex behind the scenes at Alex's work do – I mean, what sort of a person did that? How could that have happened?

I'd been pissed, sure, but I hadn't been comatose. I still could have pushed him off me, click-clacked away from him as fast as my heels would carry me. And I should have done.

But . . . God! It had been electrifying! It had been utterly primitive – an animal lust. Just his touch had bewitched me. I'd been completely under his spell. And when I was with him, it felt incredible. It was only when I was apart from him that the thump of guilt kicked in. And boy, what a kicking I'd taken ever since.

Alex hadn't noticed my prolonged absence or my dishevelled appearance when I had rejoined him. Hadn't smelled desire on me, or noticed the nervous fiddling guilt of my hands. He had smiled at me, and then gone straight on with his story about bumping into John Prescott by the lifts the other day. At least the conversation had moved on to celeb spotting anyway, even if it was only John Prescott. That was some small thing to be grateful for.

We had gone home after a couple more hours of free booze and polite chit-chat. I'd packed Cat off in a taxi with drunken, stumbling hugs, and then, for the first time in, well, ages – I literally couldn't remember when – I had instigated sex with Alex, had pushed him flat on the bed, climbed on top of him, and eased his trousers down. He had looked dazzled, as if Christmas had come ten months early, when really it was only guilt walking the walk.

'I'll have to take you out to more swanky bars if this is what it does to you,' he'd said afterwards, smirking all over his face.

'You do that,' I'd said, rolling off him and lying on my back, panting. I stared up into the darkness of our bedroom. Mark. Had he done the same thing, gone home and demanded sex from Julia? Or was he going to wait until Monday night . . . and me?

Monday morning was sunny and warm. Once the kids had been fed and watered, I got straight on the phone to Anna and arranged to meet her in the playground down the road. I felt as if I was about to explode with the weight of my guilty secret; I couldn't think of anyone else to tell. Becca was too loved up with Nick to listen to anything I had to say, and my sisters were just a bit too close for comfort. They would be disapproving, tell me what a terrible mistake I was making in full sisterly honesty. As for my mum, yeah right. She and Dad had been together since the dark ages; she had absolutely no truck with broken marriages. Even if they weren't actually marriages as such. 'People don't work enough at their relationships these days,' she'd sniffed disapprovingly, more times than I could remember.

Anna, on the other hand, had never met Alex, so I wouldn't be putting her in a position where she'd have to lie to him, or deceive him in any way, on my behalf. I just wanted ears to hear me spill out those secret words.

It was a gorgeous day, T-shirt weather when the wind dropped. The clouds had melted away to nothing for once, leaving seamless blue sky stretched out underneath. The snowdrops were all out now in the gardens, daffodils too, pushed right up through the bare earth. Leaves were budding on the trees. It was the beginning of March, and new life was bursting out all over the place.

The playground was heaving. Every mum in the area seemed to have had the same idea as us because the sandpit was packed with digging toddlers, there was a queue for the swings, and babies crawled on the warm grass in wonder – the first time they had ever felt it under their hands and knees for some of them. I looked at one who was on all fours, stroking the blades, pulling at a green tuft, with a look of amazement on his face. The beauty of babyhood – the endless discoveries to be made.

Anna was already there, camped out on the edge of the sandpit. Theo was sound asleep in the buggy; Ella was making sandcastles, her small tongue sticking out with concentration.

I parked up beside her, unclipped my boy and then sat down next to Anna, wiggling my shoes off and burrowing my toes into the damp, cool sand. I propped Nathan in a sitting position against my shins and he patted the sand in front of him wonderingly.

I looked around. None of the local gossips were visible. Molly was already engrossed in a chasing game with a boy she'd just palled up with, and was squealing with practised coquettishness.

'Anna,' I said, 'have you ever thought about having an affair?'

She laughed. 'Oh yeah, right in between changing nappies and toddler music club,' she joked. 'In fact, I'm due a secret rendezvous by the swings in ten minutes' time . . .' Her voice trailed away as she saw the edgy look on my face. 'Sade?' she asked, frowning. She leaned in towards me. 'Have you got something to tell me?'

'Yeah,' I replied. 'Actually . . . yeah.' I coughed. 'Guess what?' I said. 'I think . . . I think I'm about to have an affair.' The words, when they finally came out, shocked me. Because I hadn't actually meant to say that. I'd meant to say, *I've done a really awful thing,* then launch into my whole guilt routine. I hadn't meant to sound quite so . . . certain about it. I tried to backtrack. 'I mean . . .'

Her mouth fell open. 'You're what? An affair?' She was gaping. 'For real?'

I nodded. The conversation was definitely straying from the way I'd intended it to. It *was* real now. I had said it. 'Yeah,' I replied.

She was staring with wide eyes, mouth still open, half-shocked, half-intrigued. 'Wow. Where did that come from? Who is he?'

'He's called Mark.' Just saying his name made me want to squeeze my eyes shut so that I could conjure up his image in my mind. If I tried hard enough, I might even be able to smell his scent. 'I met him at that dinner party we went to the other weekend. Then I bumped into him out running, and—'

'Running?'

I laughed at her face. She seemed more incredulous that I had been running than at the news of the affair. 'Yeah, I know, astonishing, eh?'

Theo chose that moment to wake up, and Anna fumbled with his straps before releasing him. She held him on her knee, both arms around his small body, chin in his straw-blond hair.

'I'm . . . Blimey, Sadie, I'm really shocked,' she said. There was a slight look of alarm in her eyes. 'How come? I thought you and Alex were getting on OK? Well, I mean, you've never said . . .'

I shrugged. It felt awkward to mention Alex's name, here in the sunny playground as small children shrieked and shouted around us. 'It's not . . . It's not really about Alex,' I said. I pulled a face. 'Well, all right, it is a bit, I suppose. He's been pretty crap lately. It's been getting on my nerves.' I stopped. That sounded a pathetic excuse, even to me. 'It's more about me,' I went on. 'You know what I was saying the other week, about wondering if there was more to life? Well, there is. I've rediscovered the meaning of it.'

She put a hand over her mouth. Classic body language, Anna, I thought. Hug your child to your chest away from adulterous Sadie. Cover up what you really want to say.

'Be careful,' she said doubtfully.

'I'm not going to leave Alex or anything,' I assured her. 'It's just . . . *him*. I can't explain it. I find him so attractive, I've just got to . . .'

'Shag him,' she finished for me. 'What, and then that'll be that? End of?'

I paused. 'I don't know,' I confessed. 'Yes, probably,' I said, warming to the idea. 'Just to get it out of my system. Then I can carry on like it never happened.'

She raised her eyebrows at me. 'Like it's ever that easy . . .' she said. 'Sadie – are you sure this is what you want to do?'

I nodded. 'Do you think I'm awful?' I asked, but didn't wait for a reply. 'It's just that he makes me feel like I've got a parallel life,' I went on, 'like somebody's released me from my boring everyday existence and let me be something else for a change. Someone else.' I shrugged. 'Someone who does more outrageous things than me, if that doesn't sound completely mad.'

She was raising her eyebrows again, grinning. A tightness inside me started to relax. I had been right to tell her. She understood.

'A parallel life. Nice.' Her eyes flicked over to Ella. 'Gently with that, darling. Spades are for digging, not hitting people.' She turned back to me, face alight with vicarious expectation. 'So what's he like, then, Mr Loverman?' she asked. 'Mark, did you say? Tell me all about these outrageous things you've been doing with him.'

She broke off, squinting across to the far side of the playground, where the path went towards the duckpond. 'Sadie,' she said. 'That's not him, is it? Over by the fence? There's a man there staring right at you.'

My heart pounded at the thought; my whole body started to ache at the very idea he could be here, in the park. I stared around blankly at where she was pointing, eyes yearning for a glimpse of Mark's dark hair, his square shoulders. Already I was thinking of ways I could somehow leave the kids with Anna for two minutes, and maybe vanish into the undergrowth with him . . .

'Him, the guy in the suit,' Anna said. 'There!'

My gaze finally landed upon the man she was pointing at, and I gasped. I really did, a full-blown, dramatic, comedy gasp, as if I were an actress in a sitcom. My God. What was *he* doing here? Was he following me?

It was Jack. Again! Bloody hell, Jack. He'd followed me from one world I occasionally inhabited to this one, my usual one, thousands of miles away. He was staring at me, and scowled as our eyes met. He shook his head at me, mouth pursed in an angry line, and then stalked away. He'd just needed a wagging finger to complete the look of disapproval.

Ah. I guessed he didn't want me to ring him any more. Not now he'd seen me in my natural habitat, small baby at my ankles, scruffy old jeans and no make-up. Not now he knew who I really was.

I started to giggle. I leaned against Anna's shoulder and laughed, loud enough so that Jack would be able to hear me over all the playground ruckus, if he was listening hard enough. I watched him striding away, out of my life, in his long black coat and shiny shoes. The other side of the fence.

'*Was* that him? Why are you laughing?'

'If I tell you, you'll think I'm the biggest slut out,' I gurgled, looking at the empty space where Jack had stood on the path.

'Sadie! You haven't!' Now she really was shocked. I had obviously broken all the rules of the order with that remark. I would be banished from the sisterhood in a matter of seconds.

'No, I haven't,' I said. 'I—'

'Nathan – don't eat that, love,' Anna said suddenly, leaning forwards to fish something out of his mouth. She held it up. A stone – black and shining from his saliva.

I felt cold. Nathan. For a minute, it was as if I had forgotten he was there at all, propped against my legs. I hadn't even been looking at him, let alone making sure he wasn't eating stones or sand or . . .

'Shit,' I said. '*Shit*. Thanks, Anna.' I looked around anxiously. 'Where are the girls?'

'They're on the little climbing frame,' Anna said, pointing.

I hadn't even seen them go. Too busy with my stories and my deception. Bad mother. *Bad* mother. Molly waved at me from the top of the slide and then pushed off, squealing all the way to the bottom.

'God,' I said, waving back, trying to smile. 'I wasn't even looking.'

Anna gave me a sideways glance. 'Don't worry,' she said. 'I was.'

Hiya Dan,
I reckon it'll go in a week. Quality album, that. Any longer and you've priced it too high.

A pint at the end of March sounds great. I've got a lot on with work again this month, but hopefully I'll be able to get out of some of it, and meet you. Give my love and happy returns to your mum.

Sadie x

Danny's mum had always adored me. She had ambushed me on the High Street one day, not long after Danny had dumped me, clasped me to her hard, high bosom with a squeezing hug, and told me, 'My son is an idiot, and I've told him as much, Sadie. I am so sorry.'

I had dissolved into tears and we'd stood there, clasped together outside Marks and Spencer, as I dripped snot and tears on her flowered polyester chest. That had been the last time I had seen her.

Still, I wasn't quite sure she would love me so much if she

could see me now, nursing a vodka in the Albert, waiting to meet Mark. The other man. Wouldn't have liked that one bit.

I shoved Mrs Cooper out of my head, ordered her to leave the pub at once. No point getting the guilts now. I was here, same table as last time, watching for the door to swing open and Mark to appear. Mark. Who, as of this evening, was going to be my lover. Maybe. Probably. The thought made me feel sick with nerves, half-frightened, half-euphoric. What I was doing was wrong. I knew that. But it was like the man had said himself – it was too late to stop.

My heart started to thud as I saw the door pushed open. And then he was there, eyes straight over to the table and me, mouth curling in satisfaction. He strode over. My hands were trembling.

'You came,' he said.

He bent down and kissed my mouth, steadied himself with a hand on my back.

I kissed him back, eyes closed blindly against the rest of the pub, ears deaf to the jukebox. My nerves vanished as my pulse quickened. This was right. Sod everyone else. This was right, me and Mark. This was good.

He pulled away eventually, looked at me. Grinned. 'Do you always wear that to go running?'

I looked down at my clothes. It had been like being fourteen again, dressing in secretly tarty clothes and covering myself up with something baggy and unsexy to sneak out in.

Alex hadn't given me a second look as I'd swished by him in my tracksuit. Yet, once in the pub, I had unzipped and discarded my tracksuit top to reveal a low-cut black top, with a black satin bra underneath. And although my tracksuit bottoms were still on, underneath them were matching black satin knickers, tiny enough to be practically indecent. Just in case Mark happened to find his way there.

'The Chanel was in the wash,' I said, pretending to shrug.

'Same again?' he asked, indicating my glass on the table.

I nodded. 'Better make it a double,' I told him.

Ten minutes later, we had left the pub. 'Where?' I asked.

'This way,' he said. He took my hand and we walked towards the park in silence. Stupid questions kept popping into my head. By the way, Mark, what's your second name? I feel like I ought to know. And what do you do again? I think I was too drunk to take it in when we first met. And, most important of all, what star sign are you, anyway?

I said nothing. Thought about the warmth of his hand in mine instead. Wondered where he was taking me.

We were on a side-street behind the pub. Industrial-sized waste bins, high brick walls, unlit office buildings. As he opened the door of one red-brick, two-storey unit, I was hit by a flood of irrational fears. What if he was a serial killer? What if this was all a trick to lure me in and chop me up? My children would never see me again. Nathan would have no memory of me whatsoever but Molly would cry every night, 'Where's my mummy? I want my mummy!' And Alex would have to say . . .

He flicked a light on. 'Come in,' he said. 'This is my studio.'

Then he was pulling me through the doorway and up a flight of stairs. I followed, blindly, consumed with excitement. He kissed me hard in the stairwell, and then he was taking me up to a dark corridor, flicking on another light, pushing open a solid pine door, leading me into a dark office with open Venetian blinds. The A3 rumbled below us, streetlights twinkled through the slats.

Before I could take in anything else, he was kissing me again, moving me gently across to a sofa. It was as if we were slow-dancing across the room, locked in each other's arms. I kicked off my trainers, lips never leaving his, then fumbled with his belt, pulling it through the loops, finding his button and fly. He was yanking down my tracksuit bottoms, his body stiffening in pleasure as his fingers slid across my satin knickers, and then he was undoing my jacket, pulling it off my shoulders, hands under my top, ripping it over my head.

Then we were lying down and he was on top of me, hands inside my bra, cupping my breasts in their silky casing, his breath hot and raggedy in my ear.

My fingers travelled down his chest, jammed their way into his waistband, forced it down over his hips and then I was into his boxers, I had his cock in my hand and he was groaning again.

Somehow we were both naked. He pulled back from my neck, lifted his head to look at me in the half-light. A police siren wailed somewhere below us.

'You are so gorgeous,' he said, and, without further warning, plunged into me.

Condoms, I thought fleetingly, but was hypnotized by Mark's slow smile, the light in his eyes, the weight of him on top of me, the way he had slid right into me. He was a perfect fit.

It was quick; no endless changes of position, no tantric climaxes. His fingers felt foreign after Alex, he was in the wrong place, he didn't know which spot to hit. And then, before I could show him, he was breathing harder, teeth clenched, his head was rearing up and . . .

'OHHHHHHH.'

The noise was a roar, loud against the mumble of traffic outside. He slumped heavily on top of me and then, as an afterthought, withdrew quickly and wetly.

I stared at the sticky trail across my leg, sent up a silent prayer. It was probably safe enough.

He was smiling at me, his eyes soft.

'Phew,' I said jokily. 'What was your name again?'

He sat up, stroked my hot cheek. 'Sorry. That was a bit fast and furious,' he said. 'Next time, I'll be more patient.'

'Next time?' I echoed, arching my eyebrows.

He smiled. Kissed my neck. Collarbone. Shoulder. Then he ran a finger between my breasts so lightly I could hardly tell it was there. 'Next time you go for a run,' he said. 'Which is . . .'

'Wednesday?' I suggested at once, conveniently forgetting my original plan for once and once only. I stretched my arms behind my head, knowing it made my boobs look good, thanking my lucky stars that I'd shaved my pits that morning.

'How about tomorrow?' he asked, tracing a circle around my nipple. We both watched, fascinated, as it quivered.

I shook my head. 'I'm busy tomorrow night,' I said, half-regretfully. Lizzie's book group. I'd been looking forward to it for ages, actually read the book and everything, and now I was on the verge of bailing out.

'Wednesday it is, then,' Mark said. 'Tell you what. Why don't you come straight here? Save time.'

'What, less vodka, more shagging?' I said, paraphrasing.

He laughed, and suddenly squeezed my breast hard, on the very edge of too hard. 'If you want to put it like that, yes,' he said lazily, watching my face as I tried not to gasp out loud. 'What do you say?'

I reached over for my bra. 'Sounds good to me.'

There was an awkward couple of moments when we pulled our clothes back on. We were somewhere between the lust-fuelled shagging scenario and the goodbye ceremony.

Suddenly I could hardly bear to look at him. He flipped a side light on and I looked around his studio instead.

Large windows at one end. Wooden plan chest along one side of the room; a long shelf of books and files above it. White tilted drawing board in front of the window, with a couple of papers attached. The top one showed an intricately mapped-out floor plan.

Aha. Flashing light bulb. He was an architect. Now I remembered.

'Got everything?' he said. He took a step towards the door.

I would have liked to look around for a while longer in the hope of picking up more clues about Mark, this man I'd just had electrifying sex with on his office sofa, but he was obviously keen to leave. Shagged her, time to go. Was that what he was thinking?

'Yeah. Yeah, I reckon,' I said, fiddling with the zip on my tracksuit top. There was a knot of something – disappointment? anticlimax? – inside me as well as the routine guilt, but I couldn't identify it. I wasn't exactly wanting him to shower me with romantic compliments, but all the same . . .

This is an affair, a fling, I reminded myself as I followed him silently down the stairs and outside. *It's just sex. Nothing else. You don't get the hearts and flowers thing when it's just sex.*

'Right, bye then,' I said in a too-loud voice, as he locked up. I watched the back of his head bent over the lock, and scuffed my trainer along the ground, feeling rather cheap. Used. Yet how could I possibly complain about that when I was using him too, just as much?

He stuffed the keys back in his trouser pocket and pulled me in to him; it took me by surprise and I clung to his arms to stop myself losing my balance. He kissed me, slowly, and the tingling feeling started again inside me.

So what if he was using me, anyway? It felt great to be used by Mark, thank you very much.

'I am so glad this is happening,' he said thickly, muttering the words into my hair.

I squeezed his hands. 'I'd better go,' I said.

'One last . . .' he said, sliding his hands under my top.

'Mark!' I giggled as he reached my bra.

'You just have the most amazing breasts, Sadie,' he said. 'I can't help myself. I can't bear to look at them without touching them.'

I looked away, suddenly embarrassed. 'Stop it. Get your hands off them at once,' I said sternly. If he didn't, we would be back on that sofa all over again and I'd never get home.

'Goodbye, Sadie,' he said. 'Roll on Wednesday.'

There couldn't have been more of a contrast between Monday and Tuesday evening. From the sublime of an illicit lust-shag to the ridiculous of Lizzie's book group – ten thirty-something women in a bland suburban front room, drinking herbal tea and earnestly discussing Sarah Waters. Was I the only person in the world who had thought that book groups were more about drinking wine and gossiping, with a few token minutes spent discussing the book in question? I had turned up with a bottle, which the hostess, Celia, had duly fridged, but everyone else had opted for camomile tea, making me feel like the biggest lush in south London.

The absence of calorific snacks was something of a letdown, too. I had been banking on a plate of gooey cakes, or a bowl of Kettle Chips at the very least, but all I could see, food-wise, was a nutritionally stacked fruit bowl up on the sideboard, which was no doubt intended for Celia's kids. My stomach rumbled in disappointment, and the very faint hope I'd had of someone producing a spliff went out of the window immediately.

Lizzie, resplendent in a fawn cashmere jumper and cream trousers that made her blend in with the magnolia walls, like pale, don't-look-at-me camouflage, introduced me around Balham's answer to *The Late Review*.

Skinny, anxious-looking Amanda, who was clutching her beaded evening bag as if she thought someone might do a runner with it.

Dreamy-eyed, Pre-Raphaelite-haired Sara, who talked so slowly I wondered if she was on Mogadon.

Fast-talking Fee, who needed some Mogadon. Or maybe a good slap.

Caroline, with cropped dark hair and an intense stare, who was having problems with her nanny.

Gwen, in a Prada suit, who was having problems at work.

Margaret, with the MG keys prominently placed on the coffee table, who wanted everyone to know how well read she was.

Gail, who wanted everyone to know she was gay.

Lily, who showed me her diamond engagement ring within approximately eight seconds. I caught Margaret rolling her eyes at Gwen in the background.

Once the camomile had been served – and a solitary glass of wine for li'l old alcoholic me – we got down to business.

'I love all the literary allusions Waters makes,' Margaret began. 'Dickens is the obvious reference, of course, but when Sue is at Briar, there are definite echoes of Brontë there. Even Poe.'

Po? I nearly giggled. What about Tinky-Winky?

Lizzie was nodding earnestly, and opened her mouth to speak the second after Margaret had finished. 'All the twists and turns were done brilliantly,' she said quickly. Her cheeks flushed as everyone looked at her. 'Just as you thought you knew where you were and you had everyone sussed, the whole thing turned upside down again.' She leaned back, taking a sip of camomile in what looked like relief. I had the feeling she had rehearsed that line all week and, now that she had made a contribution, could relax.

'I agree,' I said. Sisterly support and all that. 'It really—'

Gwen's mobile was ringing. 'What? What?' Her voice rose in irritation. 'Look, tell the little fuckwit I'll . . . Yes. I'll be back in at eight tomorrow. Well, he'll have to wait.' She sucked her lips into her mouth and shook her head. 'You'll have to stay and do it, otherwise. You decide.'

No one seemed perturbed by the interruption but I felt a creeping horror for the person on the other end of the line, still at work at eight-thirty, only to be barked at by Prada Gwen. Poor sod.

'Sorry,' Gwen said, with a tight white smile that must have cost thousands. She slid her phone back into her bag and clasped her hands. 'I thought the novel was very dark, personally.'

'Yes,' said Lily, nodding sagely. 'Very dark. Actually, Celia, I'll have a glass of that wine. If that's OK with you, Sadie?'

''Course!' I said, grateful that I had a drinking partner at last. 'Tuck on in! Anyone else?'

'I'm only going to have the one,' she said, pouting in a naughty-me way that might have looked cute on a four-year-old but didn't suit a grown woman. 'I've got to lose half a stone before the wedding, you know!'

Again, that look between Margaret and Gwen. It was a mix of shut-the-fuck-up-about-your-wedding crossed with she's-so-o-o-naive-it'll-end-in-tears.

'They were both very incomplete, weren't they, Maud and

Sue?' drawled Sara. It took her about a minute to get the question out. 'Sue has never learned to write. Maud can't dress herself. They are both victims of confinement in their own way.'

I stared at her hard, while other people congratulated her on this insight. I was sure I had read that comment myself on the internet, when I had swotted up on clever things to say earlier that afternoon. In fact, I'd been waiting for a moment when I could drop it in myself.

'And what about Mrs Sucksby?' Caroline asked. 'Fascinating character. What did everyone make of her?'

Everyone had something to say about Mrs Sucksby. The conversation was so heated, Celia started to make shush-shush gestures and motioned upstairs. 'Can we just keep it down a bit?' she pleaded. 'Jeremy is such a light sleeper.'

Lizzie looked sympathetic. Time for a mum moment. 'Felix is, too! I just have to walk outside his room sometimes and he wakes up,' she said. 'I don't—'

'I thought every character had darkness and light,' Gail said, with a determined glint in her eye.

'The theme of madness was incredibly well handled,' someone else said.

'Weren't the asylum scenes terrifying?' another person droned in agreement.

I had tuned out. I was wondering what Mark was doing, and planning what to wear tomorrow, for our next assignation. Maybe my lilac push-up bra. He would love that. I shivered, remembering the way he had shoved his hands up my top as we had parted.

You just have the most amazing breasts, Sadie, he had said. *I can't bear to look at them without touching them.*

Lizzie was elbowing me. 'Still here?' she asked in a low voice.

I nodded. 'This is great,' I told her. 'Really interesting.'

The book discussion seemed to be over. Margaret had launched into a story about her day at work, and Lily was telling Amanda and Sara about her wedding plans. I found myself included in a conversation with Lizzie, Caroline and Celia about our children, and tried not to groan. Please! I'd had years of mum discussions – I'd come here hoping for a break.

After another mouthful of wine – now distinctly warmish – I managed to break away from the school league tables debate, and escaped to the conversation on my other side. Surely Fee, Gwen and Gail could manage to talk about something interesting?

'So I told the imbecile, that's it, you're sacked. I want you out!' Gwen was saying.

The others were nodding sympathetically.

'Trouble at work?' I asked.

'Work?' she sniffed. 'No, that was my husband. Just found out he's been having an affair. Prick.'

Ouch. Looked like I'd invited myself into a personal one. 'I'm . . . I'm sorry to hear that,' I replied awkwardly.

She didn't seem to care who knew about it, though. In fact, give her two more minutes at that volume, and Jeremy upstairs would know the whole story, I thought. Her face was granite-hard; not a flinch of emotion. Small lines around her mouth rose and fell in bitterness as she spoke. 'It's been going on for six months, he said. Him and this slag. He said I was too busy with work for him.'

'Diddums,' Gail put in sarcastically.

'Exactly. So I said . . .'

I made my excuses and left. I didn't want to hear about slaggy mistresses and the ensuing fall-out. I didn't want any of that to spoil my own fun.

I drove away from the quiet closed-curtains Balham streets, where good little children were sleeping and their good little parents were watching the news, and back to the narrower terraces of home, where music blared from cars and the corner shops were all still open and lit.

It goes on everywhere, I thought, wherever you live. Adultery and treachery and lying. Everyone does it. Stripped of our Prada suits and cashmere camouflage, we were all just animals who liked fucking, and who lied about it, simple as that. Put like that, it was quite a liberating revelation.

Chapter Eleven

Wednesday evening turned out to be a veritable feast of fucking and lying about it, in fact. Mark was waiting for me in his office, as arranged. He buzzed me in through the intercom and I all but ran up the stairs to meet him. After Monday, I had expected more frantic sofa sex – in fact, I was half expecting him to be lying there, kit off, wearing nothing but a large smile – but he surprised me again.

He had turned the lamps down low. The blinds were closed, shutting out the rest of the world. A blues CD was playing; Ella Fitzgerald, it sounded like, throaty and seductive. There were white roses in a vase on a side table.

'Wine?' he asked. He looked pleased with himself.

'Great,' I said. I had been propelled upstairs by the momentum of seeing him again. Now that I was here, I found myself standing still, arms by my sides, waiting in delicious anticipation to see what he was going to do next.

He poured out a glass for me, put it on the table next to

his, then pulled me into him. 'Let's dance,' he said, his hand on the small of my back.

I put my arms around him, leaned my head on his chest. I listened to the steady bump of his heart, traced around his shirt buttons with my fingers. I am here, in Mark's studio, dancing with him, I thought. I reached up behind him and stroked the back of his neck, where his short hair became its shortest, that soft, vulnerable line above the shirt collar. I felt myself ticking inside with excitement, a time-bomb waiting to explode.

We swayed to the music, and his hands slid down, slowly, slowly to my bottom. 'Two ripe peaches,' he said, nuzzling the top of my head.

I snorted. 'Peaches? I don't know about that.'

'Watermelons, then,' he said. 'Two firm watermelons . . .'

I giggled. 'Oi,' I said. 'That's a bit much. One watermelon, I can just about live with. TWO watermelons, and you're getting insulting.'

'Am I?'

'Yeah, stick to the nice stuff.'

He stroked my hair, pulled gently at the end of it. 'Take your clothes off,' he said.

'You take them off.'

'I thought you'd never ask.'

It was slower, this time. Peeling, rather than pulling off my clothes. Sliding his hands over the material, then under the material, nothing hurried about it. Somehow, it was even sexier because I could hardly wait to get out of them. Now it was my turn to be impatient.

'Hell-o, matron,' he said. He'd reached my bra – the lilac push-up one. 'This can definitely stay on for a while.'

I started tugging at his clothes, wanting to speed things up. Dammit, I'd stopped caring about the hearts-and-flowers thing, now I just wanted him to be inside me again. I just wanted the sharp shock of sex with him, this man I barely knew.

'Slowly,' he said. He pushed my hands away, held them behind my back for a second. As soon as he let go of them, though, I attacked his buttons once more, tried to pull down his trousers.

He stepped back from me. 'You've asked for it now,' he said. 'I warned you.'

A delicious thrill ran through me. What did he mean by that?

I soon found out. A pale blue silk tie, from his suit, hanging up on the door. My wrists tied behind my back as I stood there, in just my bra and knickers. For a split-second, I felt nervous again. He seemed to have this hard, sexual edge to him, a flash of cruelty in his eyes. He stepped behind me and I suddenly felt terrified he was going to leave the office and go home, with me left standing there.

Then he pressed up close behind me and started kissing me. 'You are so gorgeous,' he whispered into my neck.

I closed my eyes. I could hardly bear not being able to touch him. My hands flapped uselessly behind my back as he kissed between my shoulder blades and down, down my back. Goose pimples prickled up all over me.

'I should keep you here, locked away,' he teased. 'My little prisoner.'

Now he was kissing my thighs, parting them slightly with a hand. I could feel a flush of heat spreading across my face, down my throat. His finger slid into my knickers, and I groaned.

He pushed me forwards so that I was in front of the desk, started bending me over it.

'No, wait,' I said, turning round, 'I want to see you. I want to look at you.'

Then somehow or other, we were both on his desk, sending files flying to the floor and pens scattering to the side. Something fell over with a crash, but neither of us looked or cared.

'Come on,' I panted. I was on my side, with something hard, the edge of a folder it felt like, digging into my waist. 'Keep going. Keep going. Keep . . . Ohhh . . .'

And then he was in me and his weight on me was almost unbearable, and then his face contorted, and he seemed to stop breathing and . . . It was over. He sank down, limbs relaxed.

We lay there for a few seconds in silence, and then he pulled out of me. Bloody hell. No contraception again.

I moved my head and felt something sharp. 'Ouch,' I said. 'Alex, what's . . .'

I froze at such a terrible gaffe. 'Oh, shit. Sorry, Mark.'

'It's all right. Call me what you like,' he replied jokily. It was too dark to see his eyes properly, though; I couldn't tell if I had hurt him.

'Sorry. I was going to say, Is something in my hair?' With my hands still behind me, it was difficult to tell. I levered myself upright.

'Stop – careful,' he said, suddenly. His fingers were combing my hair. 'Look.'

I looked. A piece of broken glass, coming to a sharp point. 'We broke this,' Mark said, picking up a framed photo. A tanned Julia, in shades and a duck-egg-blue bikini, beamed out at me from underneath her cracked covering. 'That's symbolism for you.'

'Yes,' I said, looking away. I thought of Gwen and the bitter set of her mouth, the angry tone in which she'd spoken about her husband's affair. *That slaggy mistress . . .*

He held the shard of glass up to the light. 'Could have

killed you if it had gone in your neck,' he said thoughtfully. 'What a way to go.'

I struggled to get my hands free. 'Thanks for that, Mark. Very cheery. Can you untie this, please? I'd better make a move.'

'Already? You haven't finished your wine.' He had found my glass, was holding it up to my mouth. I started giggling and the glass shook between my lips. Red wine dribbled down my chin and into my cleavage. 'Mark! Stop it! Untie my hands!'

'What's it worth?'

I pulled my head away from the glass. 'Fifty pence,' I said, still giggling.

He shook his head. 'You'll have to do better than that, Sadie,' he said, sounding sorrowful. 'Come on, drink up.'

I spluttered as the glass was put to my lips again, gagged on the wine he poured into my mouth. I pressed my lips shut, and there were more dribbles down my chest. I swallowed quickly. 'Hey, you'd better not ruin this bra,' I said, ducking away again.

'Come on, what's it worth, me untying you?' he said. He sat down on his sofa, watching me with amusement.

'Oh, *Mark*,' I groaned, frenziedly trying to loosen the knots. My chin was wet; my legs were sticky. 'Don't be mean. Much as I'd love to be your prisoner up here in your ivory tower, I . . .'

Ah. I'd done it! I held my hands up in triumph and stuck my tongue out at him. 'Ha! Should have settled for fifty pence, shouldn't you?'

He grabbed me around the waist and pulled me over to sit on his knee. 'I'm going to be thinking about that for days, you know. You and that fantastic bra, boobs almost bursting out of it as you struggle to get free, red wine dripping from your chin—'

'Stop it, you pervert,' I told him, swinging a leg round so that I was astride him.

He put his hands over my breasts. '*Have I* ruined this bra?' he asked. 'I'll get you another one.'

'Yeah, yeah,' I said. 'Whatever you say, Mark.'

'No, I will. I'll get you the works. I'll get you anything you want. Red crotchless knickers, peephole bra with two-inch tassels . . .'

'Very funny,' I said, poking his chest. I put my head on one side, considering him. He took me by surprise every time I saw him. I'd thought him the mild-mannered gent the first night I'd met him – A Good Catch, I'd said to myself, hadn't I? Polite and charming. The perfect host. And now here I was, sitting on his lap, while he promised me the tackiest underwear money could buy.

'What are you thinking about?' he asked.

'You. What a funny mixture you are,' I replied.

'Isn't everyone?'

'I suppose so, but . . .' I shrugged. 'You're unpredictable. I never know what you're going to say next.'

He put his arms around me, hugged me in so that I slid all the way down his legs and we were crotch to crotch. 'Good,' he said.

There was a silence again.

'OK, your turn,' I said. 'What are you thinking about?'

He ran a finger under the strap of my bra. 'You. How much I fancied you. As soon as I saw you.'

'Really?' I tried to hide my astonished delight but failed abysmally. 'Did you really?'

'Of course I did! We all did! You in that low-cut top, making everyone laugh, being so bubbly and funny and . . .'

'Pissed,' I reminded him.

'Yeah, that as well, but . . . phhwooarrr. I could hardly get to sleep thinking about you that night. Thinking about how much I wished—'

I kissed his nose. 'How much you wished what?'

His voice had been wistful; now he laughed it off. 'Oh, just how much I wished you'd given me a blow job under the dinner table. I could tell from your dirty mouth it would have been good.'

'You . . .!' I gave him a push and tried to sound stern, rather than shocked. 'No, what did you really wish?'

He took my hands in his, and looked serious for the first

time all evening, so serious in fact that I regretted asking. 'I wished that we could have met each other before – well, before we both settled down with different people,' he said.

There was a silence while I tried to make sense of this. Hang on a minute, I was thinking, wasn't this supposed to be a bit of no-strings, no-feelings sex on the side? I didn't think that people involved in no-strings, no-feelings sex on the side were meant to start talking about wishes like that. Because I thought everyone knew that wishes didn't come true, however much you wanted them to. And some wishes just *couldn't* come true, end of story.

'Right,' I said, stalling for time. I didn't like the way the conversation was going. He was looking too serious, too much like he wanted me to reciprocate. But I didn't want any falling-in-love stuff from him. No way! I knew where falling in love got you. I'd been there, done that, had the children.

'That's . . . sweet,' I said eventually. I climbed off his knee and turned away, hunting for my clothes. 'Listen, I'd better go.'

He stayed put on the sofa; I could feel him watching me dress. 'What's up?' he asked.

'Nothing,' I told him.

'Have I said something wrong?' he asked.

'No, but . . .' I pulled on my trainers, wondering how best to phrase it. 'Let's not get all heavy, yeah?'

He shrugged, then leaned back against the sofa. 'What,

you mean let's stick to joking about tasselled bras and blow jobs?'

'Yeah,' I said. 'That's exactly what I mean.'

He stood up and drank the rest of his wine. 'All right,' he said. 'We'll stick to that. For now.'

I ran home with my mind in turmoil. I had been gone for ages. I felt sick with guilt for what I'd done with Mark, but at the same time, I felt I was rushing with the sweetest, purest drug, on the best high I'd had for years. How was it possible to feel so dreadful and so exultant in the same second?

I kept my eyes straight ahead as I ran. I was a bad, bad person. I was cheating on Alex. Not just a one-off either; I'd done it twice now. Three times if you counted the near-miss at the Laurel Tree. I was the type of slaggy mistress that women like Gwen hated. I kind of hated myself for it too.

The wind was buffeting me along the road, sending a beer can skittering and bouncing down the pavement ahead of me. The branches of the trees were groaning. Oh, and how I had groaned with *Mark*. He made me feel so . . . desired. So horny. He made me feel like sex kitten Sadie again. I hadn't felt like that for a long time.

So that was all skin-tinglingly marvellous and breath-stoppingly exciting but . . .

I ducked my head. I wasn't sure if I was ready to confront the 'but'. The 'but' was so enormous and terrifying, I couldn't quite bring myself to look it in the eye. I knew that once I started thinking about the consequences, they would snowball out of proportion. Because it wasn't just Alex I would be hurting. It was the kids, too, and I'd rather flay myself alive than have to hurt them.

Plus there was Julia. She struck me as the kind of woman who would want to flay me alive as well. We could both do it, take turns, maybe.

Anyway, I wasn't going to think about her. I would see Mark maybe once or twice more, get him *completely* out of my system, then nip the whole thing in the bud before anyone got hurt. And before anyone found out, more to the point.

I felt myself fill with virtuous intentions, like a balloon, puffed up with its own hot air. I would renounce Mark, and the secret would go with me to the grave. I would renounce my inner slut too, send her packing, and instead would become a devoted partner and mother to Alex and the kids. I would cook proper meals for them rather than opening packets of Alphabites and fishfingers all the time. I would read Molly's story books all the way through, instead of editing them down to two lines per page in the hope of an early bedtime. And as for Alex, I would make more of an effort. I'd be super-partner. I'd be dirty in the bedroom and clean around the house. Yes, I'd do the whole domestic goddess thing – perhaps even trying out some of Nigella's recipes in the book Alex had given me, rather than leaving it on our shelf like some kind of upmarket ornament.

Then I spoiled all my good work by thinking, *Mark* would never have given me a cookbook. A rotating-head vibrator maybe, or that tasselled bra he seemed to know all about perhaps, but cookery? I doubted it.

I was home. 'I'm back!' I yelled, poking my head around the sitting-room door. James the little red engine was falling off a bridge again on the telly, but there was no one watching.

Alex called back an echoey hello and I looked upstairs in alarm. Oh no. The kids were still in the bath. I'd been planning to leap in the shower like last time, wash away my guilt and the smell of sex before I could be seen. But with Molly and Nathan still splashing around up there, what was I going to do?

I was dithering horribly. 'Mummy, come see me!' Molly was yelling from upstairs. 'I got a bubbly beard!'

I couldn't go in there. Alex would know at once. I smelled of Mark. He was all over my skin.

'Just a sec,' I yelled back. Then I stripped off in front of the washing machine and bundled everything in. Everything – knickers, bra, the lot. I grabbed a large towel from the washing pile on the dresser and wrapped it around me.

'Room for me in there?' I asked jokingly as I went into the bathroom.

Oh God, I was so horrible. I was a whore, a slut. I was . . . Oh, I hated myself as I slid into the water between my pink beaming children. Molly wrapped her slippery arms around me and decorated my hair with bubbles, and Nathan stretched out his fat hands for a cuddle, and oh, they were so innocent and unknowing, and I was so deceitful and full of shit and evil.

Alex was strangely quiet. No banter tonight. In fact, he barely said hello. 'You were ages,' he said. It was a statement and a question at the same time. I couldn't read his eyes; his face was impassive.

'Yeah, sorry,' I said. 'I bumped into Nicki on the way back and stopped for a chat.'

'Nicki?' he repeated. His eyes never left my face.

I grabbed the Teletubbies flannel and draped it over my head, making the kids giggle. 'Blub, blub, blub,' I said to them, reaching out to tickle Molly in her most ticklish spot, under the knees. 'It's the flannel monster! Yeah, Nicki,' I added in a normal voice. 'Why?'

'Just wondering.'

I didn't answer. I felt sick with paranoia. He knew. He must know. He never 'just wondered' about anything I did usually. He barely listened to what I told him, let alone wonder about it for any length of time. Oh God. The game was up. Someone had told him something. Or he had followed me, seen me going to Mark's studio . . .

I gasped inadvertently under the flannel. Act normal, I thought, and put the flannel on Nathan's head to make him laugh, then busied myself soaping Molly's hair and sculpting it into a bubbly Mohican.

'Good day? See anyone interesting?' he asked.

I stared hard at Molly's hair. Making sure her Mohican was bang in the centre of her head was suddenly crucial. 'It was OK. Met up with a couple of the mums. You?'

'Same old, same old.' He stood up and rolled down his shirt sleeves. 'Now you're back, could you finish off in here? I've got a few emails to send.'

Before I could reply, he was gone. 'Wait, I . . .' I began, but I could already hear his footsteps tramping down the stairs.

'Mummy, you be flannel monster again,' Molly said insistently, leaning over me to try to pull it off Nathan.

'Careful, love – gently!' I said, as Nathan lost his balance and almost fell. Now that I could drop my air of forced gaiety, I felt exhausted. I didn't have the energy to be the entertaining flannel monster any more. It was all I could do to be corrupt Sadie, she who had gone so terribly astray.

It wasn't until the kids were in bed that he finally confronted me. Large whisky in one hand, eyes unwavering, he sat forward on the edge of the sofa, with his elbows on his knees.

'Who's Jack?' he said.

'*What?*' I replied.

'I said, "Who's Jack?"' he repeated grimly. 'I found this in our bedroom. Who is he?'

He was holding Jack's business card – where the hell had he found that? – and I tried to take it off him but he snatched it away.

'Jack,' I began haltingly, 'is some guy I met in the pub. When I went out with Becca a few weeks ago.'

'And?'

'And nothing! He chatted me up, gave me that card, then *you* phoned, my boobs started leaking everywhere, and I came home. That's it. End of story.'

'Sadie, just tell me. If something's happening, just tell me. Seriously.'

Thank God he doesn't know the truth, I thought, as adrenaline pumped around me. It was like a premonition of another conversation – an infinitely worse conversation – we could be having if he ever found out about Mark.

I sat down next to him. 'Nothing is happening with Jack,' I said evenly. 'I promise. I *swear!* He was just some wideboy, that's all. You can chuck that away. I didn't even know I still had it.'

'Why did you take his card, then, if he's just some wide-boy? Have you phoned him?' His eyes were glittering. He looked as if he wanted a fight – with me, or preferably with Jack for daring to speak to me and press his number on me in the first place. For all his left-wing, right-on, new-man behaviour, there still lurked a slice of caveman in Alex's personality. *You looking at my bird? I'll kill yeh!*

I shrugged. 'I don't know. Politeness, I suppose.' His face hadn't changed. 'Phone him if you want. Ask him yourself if you don't believe me.'

Don't phone him. Don't ask him. Please believe me. After Jack had seen me in the park the other day, the last thing I wanted was for Alex to start ringing him up, harassing him for looking at 'his bird'.

There was a silence. 'Anyway,' I said, trying to sound hurt. 'If you don't want to marry me, what am I supposed to think?'

His eyes swivelled round. He looked incredulous. 'Run that by me again,' he said coldly. 'You think that because I don't want to get married – not just to you, to anyone – it means that . . . what? That our relationship doesn't mean anything to me?'

Damn. That had not been the best thing to say. 'No, I didn't mean—'

'So the fact that we've got two kids and a house, and we've been together donkey's years doesn't count for anything, is that what you're saying?' He was on a roll now. Oh, Christ. I could write off the rest of the evening, then. It would be lecture, lecture, lecture until dawn, if he had his way. 'And you take that as meaning you can go off and chat up the likes of *Jack* with your single mates, yeah?'

'No! I—'

'Because that is bollocks, Sadie. That's a piss-poor excuse, and you know it.'

'All right, I . . .'

'Why do you have to keep going on and on about getting married anyway? I don't want to. I just don't want to. It's not you or us or anything, I just think it's all a load of cobblers. And we can't afford it anyway. Not unless you want a second mortgage or—'

'All *right!*' I shouted. 'You've made your point! I am sorry I spoke to a strange man when I went out. I am sorry I mentioned the dreaded, forbidden M-word that is obviously so traumatic for you to hear. I'm sorry I . . .' I'd run out of things to be sorry about. Well, things he knew about anyway. No, wait, I'd just thought of another one. 'I'm sorry you can't *trust* me to go out with my friend – well, to *try* and go out with her anyway – only to be called back because you can't cope with two children for one evening, even though I have to do it every single bloody day, and—'

'All right, all right. Stop shouting, will you?'

'I'm going to bed,' I said, and walked out before he could see the tears gathering in my eyes.

It's hard to sleep next to somebody you've just had an argument with, so I lay under the duvet, trying to nod off as fast as possible before Alex came up to bed. Instead, though, my mind kept running through our argument in an annoying, spot-picking kind of way. Even when I was trying to be scrupulously fair about what had been said, I found it impossible to decide who should be madder with whom. Both of us were in the wrong somewhere or other in the argument, but both of us, equally, could claim the moral high ground for different reasons. Moreover, I was nursing my Mark secret and feeling guilty enough to start with, so I didn't feel I could blame Alex for everything. Although, after a bit of effort, I eventually managed to.

I was still awake when he came to bed a few hours later.

'Are you awake?' he whispered.

I shut my eyes hurriedly and tried to breathe as slowly and evenly as possible.

'Oh, right, you are. Not farting and snoring like you usually do.'

I rolled over indignantly. 'Fuck off. I don't fart and snore. I think you'll find that's you.'

He climbed into bed and put an arm across me. He was drunk, I could tell by the clumsiness of his arm. That and his breath, which smelled of pure Laphroaig.

'Sadie, Sadie, Sadie,' he slurred.

I was hoping he'd fall into an alcoholic comatose sleep. That often happened. Although when it didn't happen . . .

'I don't suppose you fancy giving me a hand-job, do you?'

he asked, fumbling around with the old T-shirt I was sleeping in.

'No, I bloody don't. You stink,' I told him. 'And get off me.'

'Come on, Sade. It's been hours. It's been days! Come on. Let me show you where I am. Let me *introduce* you to an old friend.'

He took my hand and tried to drag it down to his boxers, but I snatched it away. 'Sod *off*,' I said. 'First you wake me up, crashing around like a tanked-up wart hog, then you start insulting me, then you start on the sexual harassment front . . .'

His hand had found a way underneath my T-shirt. 'Oh, Alex,' I moaned. 'I'm too tired.'

'You just go back to sleep then,' he slurred boozily. 'Pretend it's a dream. I won't be long.'

I laughed, despite myself. 'You are so romantic, it's untrue,' I said sarcastically.

'I know. The Yorkshire Casanova,' he said, rolling on top of me and nearly toppling off the other side of the bed.

'God, careful, you moron!' I cried, dragging him back.

His hand had found my breast now. 'Good evening,' he said reverently. 'Nice to be back here, at Sadie's left breast. My particular favourite.'

'Since when?' Oh, no. Now I was getting drawn into his

booze-soaked bullshit. Even worse, I was starting to feel turned on by the breast-stroking thing he was doing.

'Or is it the right?' He'd managed to roll on top of me now and I could feel his stiffy against my leg.

He was kissing my neck. Jesus, he stank. He absolutely reeked. 'You are such a pig,' I grumbled, not trying to stop him any more. Sod it, a guilt shag would ease my conscience a tad, I reckoned. 'You are such an animal. Such a bloody oaf.'

'I love it when you talk dirty to me. Keep going.'

He was in me, his breath panting out heavily.

'You're a dirty, stinking, caveman sex maniac,' I told him, warming to my theme. 'A—'

'UHHHHHHHH!'

He collapsed on top of me. After a moment or two of silence, I tentatively pushed at him, only to hear a grumbling snore start up in his nose. Oh, great. And now, having ravished my love, I will . . . fall asleep on her. Before even rolling off!

I shoved him away from me. He weighed a bloody ton.

'We've got to get some condoms,' I said to the darkness. '*Must* get some condoms tomorrow.'

The Yorkshire Casanova snored throatily in reply, a satisfied smile across his face. So that was that.

Chapter Twelve

Dear Ms Morrison,

Thank you for your letter regarding our Producer vacancy. I'm delighted to invite you for an interview on 29th March at our Soho office, and would be grateful if you could contact me to arrange a convenient time . . .

It was the morning after the night before and I practically choked on my mouthful of toast as I read my letter from Firestarter.

Nathan, smeared in Weetabix, tried to grab it from my fingers. 'Oh, no, you don't,' I told him, snatching it away quickly. 'Mummy's going to frame this and put it on the wall. Mummy is so desirable and talented that she—'

'What's that?' Alex said, walking into the kitchen. He jammed two slices of bread down the toaster and rubbed his eyes. 'Have you seen my blue shirt anywhere?'

I stared at the letter again as Molly swarmed up my legs. Yes, I'd read it correctly. No, I hadn't been delusional.

Shit. SHIT!! They'd believed it. Ha! They'd really believed it, all those outrageous bullshit lies I'd so enjoyed concocting! And now they wanted to interview me!

I laughed out loud in delight. 'Oh, nothing.' I stuffed it into my dressing-gown pocket before he caught sight of the red embossed flame logo. 'Molly, be careful, love. Blue shirt is probably in the clean washing pile, Alex, if you can remember where that is. Nurofen in the usual place if you just so happen to need a handful.'

He stared at me, his eyes bloodshot and gritty-looking. 'A handful? What, you're encouraging me to top myself now? Are you going to book me in this afternoon for a stomach pump as well?'

I raised my eyebrows in the no-hangover-here smug kind of way that he hated. 'Bit tetchy this morning, are we, darling?' I cooed. 'Is the Yorkshire Casanova a teensy-weensy bit tired after all his molestation activities last night?'

His expression was that of a man who feared he might have overstepped the mark but wasn't exactly sure how. 'Sadie, I'm not in the mood,' he muttered, pouring himself a coffee.

'Yeah, I think that's what I told you last night too, only for you to completely ignore me,' I added.

Funnily enough, he completely ignored that, too. Alex tended to descend into the depths of primitive beast whenever he was soaked in a hangover. His speech regressed to grunts, his actions became clumsy and ham-fisted. He practically swung his arms in front of him when he walked.

The letter crackled in my pocket as I stood up to clean Nathan's goo-splurged face, hair, hands and vest. So the big question of the morning was, what the hell was I going to do about this interview?

Well, I phoned up a few hours later, and arranged a convenient time for it, of course. In for a penny, in for a pound, as my nan would have said. Keep your options open, as my school careers officer would have advised. Keep on lying until they catch you with your pants down, as . . . Who had said that? Oh yeah, it was me, wasn't it?

March 29th, 2.30, Michelle McKean. I wrote it in my diary triumphantly. I would persuade Alex to skive off work – it never took that much persuading, let's face it – and he could look after the kids, while I . . . Well. While I did whatever.

I stared into space. Or, of course, slightly more realistically, I could always bail out of the whole thing. I mean, obviously, I *would* bail out of the whole thing. There would be absolutely no point in going for an interview for a job I couldn't possibly do, on the basis of a CV full of lies, would there?

I doodled a string of hearts along the edge of my diary page. *Michelle McKean, 2.30.* It did look nice there on my blank week. It looked important, businesslike. No, I wasn't ready to cross her out just yet. I would phone up and break the news to her nearer the time. Yes, that was what I would do.

Time seemed to have become crystallized for me into Mark time and non-Mark time. Somehow I'd become an addict. Thursday was the worst day. It was painful to think about how long it would be before I could see him again. I even made a detour around to his office on the way back from a friend's house in the hope of catching a glimpse of him. The kids were conveniently napping in the double buggy so it would have been safe to say hello, at least, and I was light-headed as I pushed them down the alley to his building. I rang the buzzer and felt quite desolate when nobody answered.

And then we were into the weekend, which from first glance at Friday teatime seemed to be stretching out boringly for ever. Alex did his usual working-late-oh-accidentally-fell-into-a-pub-on-the-way-home routine on Friday night, which was intensely irritating until the phone went again at nine o'clock, and then, all I could feel was sheer joy, plus relief that Alex *wasn't* there.

A voice, low and teasing, said, 'Hello, sexy.'

There was a warm rush inside me, and I grinned broadly. 'Is that that architect again? The one with the gorgeous arse?'

His chuckle sounded intimate against my ear. 'I think I

might put that on my business card, you know. See if it gets me more work.'

I stretched full out on the sofa. My whole body was tingling blissfully at the unexpected sound of his voice. 'Oh, it would. If I was going through the Yellow Pages, I'd definitely pick out an architect if he was claiming to have a nice bottom. Sod your qualifications. How do you look bent over a plan chest? That's what it comes down to.'

'Bent over a plan chest, that sounds interesting,' he said. I could hear the smile in his voice. 'I think you should show me *exactly* what you mean by that next time you're in the office.'

'Oh, I will,' I assured him. 'I will have great pleasure in showing you.'

'Believe me, sweetheart,' he said, 'the pleasure will be all mine.'

There was a pause and then I said, 'Hey, how did you get my number anyway?'

'There are lots of things I know about you, Sadie Morrison,' he told me.

'Oh yeah?' I said. 'So what else do you know about me, Mystic Mark?'

He coughed. 'Let's see now. You smell of vanilla. You buy your knickers from M&S. Your throat turns an amazing shade of pink when you're turned on. You—'

'Astounding,' I interrupted sarcastically. 'Practically clairvoyant!'

'And you're sitting there all on your own tonight,' he finished. 'All on your own, watching *Sex and the City* or something, maybe doing your nails, or tidying up the kids' toys . . .'

I paused, not able to resist flicking a glance at the telly, where a re-run of *Sex and the City* was indeed starting. 'Well, yeah, obviously I am on my own, otherwise I wouldn't be shit-talking with you,' I said. 'It doesn't take a genius to work that out.'

'It's Natasha's birthday do in Covent Garden tonight, isn't it?' His voice was breezy. 'So Alex will be gone for ages yet. You know what that lot are like when they're unleashed at the weekend. Trashed is not the word.'

'Well . . .' His words had taken me by surprise. Alex hadn't mentioned Natasha having a birthday do tonight. Nothing about Covent Garden, either. *Why* hadn't Alex mentioned Natasha having a birthday do? 'I . . .'

'And while my wife and your partner are out celebrating the lovely Natasha's birthday, you're stuck inside and I'm still at work,' he went on. 'Now, that's not right on a Friday night, is it?'

I hit the mute button on the remote. The house felt very still. 'Mark,' I said carefully, 'where are you going with this conversation?'

'I thought you might like some company,' he said innocently.

'No,' I told him at once. It pained me to turn him away, but no. Not here. I couldn't let him come here.

'I'm very near your house, Sadie. Tennyson Road, isn't it? I can be there in ten minutes.'

'No,' I repeated. 'Honestly, I can't. The kids are upstairs.' And Nathan was unpredictable enough to wake at any moment between now and six, and Molly had only finished bossing Fizz around in her bed an hour ago. No, no, no. Definitely no.

'Come on, Sadie,' he coaxed. His voice was teasing, persuasive. I held the phone closer to my ear and shut my eyes, drinking in the sound of him. He was so . . . so delicious. I physically ached at the thought of seeing him again. 'Take a risk, Sadie. Take control. Anyway, what do you think Alex is doing? We both know what he's like.'

Alex. The man had a point. I knew exactly what he was like. Alex would be drunk and shouting and making everyone around the table laugh, I would lay my last pound on it. Alex would be getting the next round in and taking the piss out of new-girl Natasha, so that her cheeks flushed prettily with alcohol plus all that attention . . . Oh God. Why hadn't he told me it was Natasha's birthday do? He could have told me. He hadn't said anything about going into the West End. I'd assumed it was just a few pints in the office local.

I sighed and glanced down at my paint-splattered jeans, my T-shirt with a faint smear of milk puke over one boob. I absolutely couldn't let Mark come here. I wouldn't. It was too dangerous. It was too scary. Yet my treacherous body was twitching with excitement at the very sound of him. My mouth felt dry, my pulse raced.

'OK,' I said.

There was a soft knock at the door ten minutes later. I walked towards it on cotton-wool legs. 'Come in,' I said, checking quickly that no one had seen him on the doorstep. I was jittery with nerves. 'We'll have to be quick,' I said. 'Alex could be back any—'

'Sssshhh,' he said, shaking his head. He put a finger to my lips to stop me. 'No, he won't.'

He closed the front door and my heart stepped up a beat as I watched him do it – Mark, here, in my own hallway, closing my and Alex's front door. I caught a glimpse of Molly's pink wellies on the shoe rack and looked away as if my face had been slapped. No. Don't think about that now. Bad idea.

He had turned back and was looking at me questioningly.

'This way,' I said, leading him into the front room. I was trembling with excitement, but also prickling with guilt. It was so wrong bringing him in here, Alex's territory, while our yellow-haired babies slept upstairs, Molly cuddled up to Fizz, no doubt, and Nathan, with his arms stretched out above his head . . . The thought of them was almost enough to stop me breathing.

'Sadie,' he said gently. He came round to face me, put his hands on my shoulders. A car zoomed by outside and I stiffened. 'Relax. It's OK. Everything will be OK.'

I breathed in his scent, looked into his eyes, and the fear started to melt. I stared at his beautiful, sensuous mouth, and desire surged through me in its place. I leaned against him. 'Sorry,' I said. 'I'm a bit jumpy. I'm not used to doing this.'

He ran his fingers lightly down my back. 'What, not used to a strange man arriving on your doorstep to seduce you?'

'Oh yeah, I'm used to *that*,' I joked. 'Just not on a Friday usually, that's all.' I was starting to feel better. 'And actually, I'm used to seducing the strange men who arrive, not the other way around, if you must know.'

'Really?' I knew from his voice that he was smiling. He rested his hands lightly on my bottom. 'So tell me . . . how do you go about doing that, then?'

'Well,' I said, 'I generally start by kissing them about . . . Let's see . . . About here.' I brushed my lips against his neck.

'And then what do you do?' he asked, moving his hands up to my waist.

'A bit more kissing here,' I murmured, returning to his neck, 'and perhaps a little bit here.' I stretched up to kiss his ear, and he closed his eyes. 'Then, I usually move around to the throat.' I could feel his breath quickening. His hands gripped me a fraction harder.

'Then what?' he asked thickly.

I ran a hand down his chest and felt him shudder beneath my touch. 'Then,' I said, 'I undo his buttons, one by one, just like this. One . . . by . . . one. And I kiss all the way down his belly, just like this.' My kisses were light, butterfly kisses; I traced a finger lazily around his nipples. 'I undo his belt,' I said. 'I undo his trousers. I ease them down his thighs,' I said.

I stopped, knowing it would drive him wild.

'Keep going,' he said.

'Tell you what,' I said thoughtfully, 'I'll just show you.'

An hour or so later, I lay in bed, listening to the sounds of the night. A couple of cats scrapping and yowling. A motorbike. A gang of pissed-up lads on their way to a club, no doubt, or a party. I lay quite still, the duvet pulled up under my chin, elbows bent, hands behind my head, trying to examine how I felt.

Mark had gone, and I had just raced through an orgy of cushion plumping, air-freshener spraying, wine-glass rinsing after his departure in an attempt to conceal the evidence. The children slept on upstairs, unaware that an intruder had been in their home and, even worse, in their mother.

Car headlights swung across the ceiling; a wavering fan of yellow, then darkness again. The curtain fluttered at the window. So how did I feel?

I felt addicted. Hooked by the thrill of him. Numb with shock that he had been here, in my house. I felt deceitful and traitorous and tangled up inside with questions to which I had no answers. I felt as if I was spinning out of control into outer space. I was fizzing with excitement, a bottle of champagne that had been shaken up.

I heard a key scratching in the lock downstairs. It went on for quite a few seconds, a useful gauge of just how pissed Alex was (moderately – but not so much so that he wasn't able eventually to open the door). The door banged shut and I jumped, and tensed in the darkness, straining my ears for sounds of small people waking up. But the heavy blanket of silence never twitched.

I rolled over away from Alex's side of the bed as I heard him blunder his way through to the kitchen. Let me guess: a bacon sandwich and the last can of Stella in the fridge. He'd be there ages. Quick – if I was lucky I would just be able to doze off without having to suffer his clumsy advances again. I shut my eyes, pulled the quilt over my head and tried to fall asleep. I hoped I would dream about Mark.

'What do you think, Jamie Oliver or Nigel Slater?'

Alex pursed his lips. 'I don't fancy either of them, love,' he replied.

I threw the dishcloth at him. 'No, you moron, I'm trying to decide what to cook. Any suggestions?'

'Those fishfingers you did for the kids tonight were good.'

I went back to the cookbook shelf and stared at it glumly,

hoping for inspiration. I couldn't help noticing how dusty it was looking. Shit, one more thing to clean. Great.

Lizzie and Boring Steve were coming over for dinner. We tended to take turns once a month or so, and it always seemed like a good idea whenever we arranged a date over the phone. Yet, as the night in question grew nearer, I had a creeping dread every time, and it became something to get through as painlessly as possible, rather than an evening I actually enjoyed. I couldn't decide which was harder: having to go to their house and watch Alex's visible jealousy at Steve's new expensive boy toys, or have them come to us and spend the week beforehand agonizing about what to cook, and trying to get the house smelling as clean and hygienic as Lizzie's always did.

It was stupid; she was my sister, I had no idea why I always got worked up into such a competitive lather whenever she was due to come round. After all, I never did when Cat and Tom were here; in fact I barely bothered to Hoover the front room properly, such was their easy acceptance of Alex and me. Yet the run-up to Lizzie and Steve's visit would see me dusting the mantelpiece, scrubbing the bathroom until everything gleamed like something from a Flash advert, mopping the kitchen floor, putting all the washing away etc. This time, I even started cleaning the windows, until Alex pointed out that it would be dark by the time they came round and they wouldn't notice anyway. At which point I immediately stopped, obviously, and sat down, pulling the bowl of olives across the table towards me so that I could sample a few.

Lizzie was something of a dinner-party queen, so a further complication was that it was always difficult to come up with food that she wouldn't already have cooked herself. For this meal, after much deliberation and no help from my uninterested partner, I settled on Jamie Oliver's beef with pak-choi and ginger in the end, on the premise that Lizzie loathed the boy Jamie with a passion bordering on the psychopathic, and was therefore unlikely to possess any of his books. That was the reasoning I gave to Alex, who promptly looked at me as if I were a halfwit.

'Who cares if she has cooked it before anyway? You're weird. Just get loads of red wine in, that's the main thing. Let's get Steve pissed and wind him up about politics again. Trust me. Didn't I tell you I'm always right about everything?'

I rolled my eyes at him. 'If she's cooked it before, she'll know what it's meant to *taste* like,' I explained patiently. 'She'll know if I've missed an ingredient or ballsed it up, or . . .'

Alex didn't reply, just opened our booze cupboard and slid two more bottles of white into the fridge. 'Be like the wine, Sadie,' he instructed me, in the solemn manner of a culinary guru. Or maybe it was his Yoda impression, I wasn't sure. 'Chill, babe. Just chill.'

'Make me a gin and tonic,' I ordered, 'and then I just might.'

Lizzie and Steve were never too early and they wouldn't dream of coming too late. They always brought good wine with them plus a little extra – a bunch of flowers, or some yummy truffles. In many ways, they were the perfect dinner guests. In many other ways, they were not.

'So, Steve,' Alex said ritualistically, once we were all sitting at the table, tucking into our starter of stuffed mushrooms. 'How's work?'

Unfortunately, Alex always asked this question while Steve was sober enough to be very coherent and earnest about his boring, boring IT job. I had asked Alex repeatedly – no, actually, I had *begged* him repeatedly – to wait until Steve was at least half-cut before trotting out the work question so that he wouldn't notice how little I gave a shit about what he was saying. But did Alex heed my pleas? Did he buggery. I was starting to think it was his running joke, to wind me up.

On and on droned Steve every time, about how many new staff he had had to take on, and how his profits were quadrupling every day, and similar height-of-tediousness conversation points. Every single time we had had dinner together, there had been Steve's fifteen-minute brain-combustingly dull work lecture to endure, during which I raised my eyebrows approximately three times, said, 'Mmm, how interesting,' on average seven times, and had to hold myself back from stabbing my fork repeatedly into his windpipe approximately 588 times.

Steve's stuffed mushroom sat on his plate, getting cold. Butter congealed around it while the melted cheese cooled and hardened to a crisp. Eat your sodding starter, you ignorant bloody dullard, I wanted to yell at him as he launched into a monologue of new Bill Gates jokes.

I looked over at Lizzie to see how she was enjoying Steve's witterings. For once, she wasn't nodding enthusiastically at key moments, laughing along obediently as he mistimed the punchline to another of his 'gags'. She stared dully at her mushroom as she cut it up – sawed it, actually; had I overcooked hers? – and on a closer look that was just short of leaning across the table to peer at her, I noticed how red her eyes were. Had she been crying?

I kicked her gently under the table and she jerked in her seat. I lowered my eyebrows in a 'You all right?' kind of frown. Wordlessly, she shook her head. A tiny movement, side to side, then down again to her mushroom with the same miserable expression. God, surely the mushroom wasn't *that* bad? My cooking wasn't exactly Michelin starred, but it had never caused anyone to look quite so pained before.

'Right!' I said, interrupting Steve mid-flow. Sod it. My sister was upset and the twat hadn't even noticed. It was time to shut him right up, I decided. 'Who's ready for their beef? Oh – Steve, you haven't started on your mushroom yet!'

'It's delicious,' said Lizzie, bravely swallowing a huge lump of it.

Steve opened his mouth to carry on his droning, but Alex moved in quickly before he could speak.

'Lizzie, Sadie was telling me all about your book group,' he said randomly. 'Sounds like it's an interesting mix of people.'

Steve closed his mouth with a snap and then looked down at his mushroom with barely concealed dismay. I turned my head away swiftly for fear of the fork-windpipe urge coming upon me too strongly.

'Yes, it is,' Lizzie said. 'Actually, Sadie, I forgot to tell you. I've got details of the book for next month. *Boardroom Bitch,* it's called, by—'

'Gwen?' I sniggered.

'Sounds more like Jackie Collins,' Alex put in.

Lizzie gave me a strange look and I wished I'd kept my mouth shut. 'No, it's this American feminist, I can't think of her name offhand. Margaret knows her.'

'Uh-huh,' I said. That figured.

'I know who you mean. Sandra somebody. A copy came into the office the other week,' Alex said. Mr Literary Know-All. At least I wouldn't have to buy a copy of the book though, I thought. 'It looked incredibly earnest and tedious,' he went on. '*Do* let me borrow it when you've finished it, Sadie. It looked *so* my sort of read. I hope it's got lots of bits slagging off men and saying how much better women are.'

I pointed my knife at him, in as threatening a way as I could muster. 'Shut it, Blake. You just stick to reading Calvin and Hobbes. Leave the serious stuff to us birds.'

I turned to Lizzie, hoping for some support, at least a 'Yeah, shut your face, Alex, you tosser' or something similar, but she had that pained, strained look on her face again. Oh God, what was *wrong* with her?

She stayed glued to her seat for the entire meal, not even helping me take the dishes out as usual. I knew it was because she didn't want me bombarding her with what's-up questions. And then afterwards, when we moved to the sofas, she sat and talked to Alex about books, while I got lumbered with Boring Steve, who was, by now, Boring and Very Drunk Steve.

'So, Sadie, how's your pension?' he said, his eyes bulgy and moist-looking in their sockets.

I had to try very hard not to laugh. Or cry. It seemed there was one predictable question for every era of your life, from 'How's school?' to 'How's your love-life?' to 'How's work?' to the one I considered myself to still be on, 'How are the kids?' Trust Steve to make me feel about ninety.

'Oh, brilliant,' I said breezily. 'Hey, did you see *Corrie* last night?'

That shut him up pretty fast. I decided to wreak my

revenge and bore him senseless with my very own monologue about the latest happenings in Weatherfield, while trying to make subtle eye contact with Lizzie for the ninety-fifth time. I didn't get a thing back from her. She didn't want to tell me, whatever it was.

It was only as they were leaving and I was hugging her goodbye that I managed to whisper, 'What's happening?'

She squeezed me hard, rested her cheek against mine, and let a sigh escape into my hair. 'I'll phone you,' was all she said in reply.

I watched her packing Steve into the taxi and then wave a pale hand as they drove off. I hoped it was something minor, like Felix failing his *Bonjour Maman!* entrance exam, or her gym being closed for a week, but deep down I knew it was something far more serious. What if . . .

A crash in the kitchen stopped my line of thought as I spun round to see what Alex was breaking. 'Uh-oh,' I heard him mutter.

'Don't say that,' I told him. 'You sound like a Teletubby. Just leave all that anyway. Come on.'

He smiled and looked almost pathetically grateful. 'Cheers,' he said.

'Yeah, you can do it all in the morning instead,' I told him. 'Let's go to bed.'

*

The following Monday night, I saw Mark again. In a post-coital embrace, squashed along his sofa together, we started chatting, and I happened to mention the forthcoming Brighton trip for my birthday weekend.

He stroked my hair and looked wistful.

'What?' I asked.

'I would love to spend a night with you,' he said. 'Can you imagine? I'd love to wake up with you.'

'Nice bit of morning glory,' I joked, raising my eyebrows comically. 'Followed by some room servicing.'

He didn't smile back. 'I'm serious,' he said. 'How can we arrange it?'

'Arrange what? A night away together?' I asked. I frowned. 'With great difficulty, that's how – i.e., not at all.'

'Well, an evening, then. A proper evening. That would be a start.' His mouth was turned down petulantly. He looked like Molly did when I refused to produce the chocolate button packet.

I sighed. 'Mark . . .' I started. I pulled away from him and sat up. 'Mark, let's just enjoy what we're doing now, yeah?'

'What, forty minutes of sex twice a week?' A muscle in his cheek twitched. He leaned forward and tucked a strand of my hair behind my ear. 'It's not enough for me, Sadie. I want more. I have to have more.'

I shook my head. 'I . . . I can't give you any more,' I told him. 'I know what you're saying – and you're right, it would be brilliant to have a night away somewhere together, but I can't do that. You know I can't. I can't give you that.'

There was a silence. 'I'm sorry,' I said in the end, feeling obliged to speak.

His eyes narrowed. 'Sadie, you can't keep people in pigeon-holes. You can't slot them into convenient sections of your life,' he said tightly. 'I want to be with you. I think about you all the time. I—'

I shook my head again, not wanting to hear it. 'Stop,' I said. 'Don't. Don't say it. No strings, remember.'

'No strings, no feelings, just sex, yeah, I remember,' he said. His voice was bitter. 'But I want more, Sadie.'

'Well, I can't give you more,' I told him again. 'Mark, I mean it. I can't give you more.'

His hand closed on my breast. For a second I was scared that he was going to hurt me, but then his features softened. 'Yeah, OK,' he said. 'I know. You've just put a spell on me, that's all.'

'I put a spell on you . . .' I sang, without thinking.

He finished off the line for me. 'Because I'm yours.' His gaze was intense, and I had to look away.

'No,' I said. 'You're not. You're Julia's.'

'I'm not Julia's,' he said flatly. 'Haven't been for a long time. Being with you has made me see that. She's a habit. You're the real thing.'

It was all getting too full-on again. I desperately wanted

to lighten the tone. 'You're just too, too kind,' I said breezily, tweaking his nose. 'Now, it's time for me to go. I'll see you on Wednesday.'

The next morning, I phoned Lizzie. 'Are you doing anything? Can I come over?' I asked.

She started protesting immediately. 'Oh God, the house is a complete state, I'm not sure I'm up to a visit . . .'

'Liz, it's *me*. I don't care what your house looks like,' I said. 'I want to see you.' There was a pause, so I added, 'I know something's wrong.'

She sniffed down the phone. 'Something *is* wrong,' she admitted. 'I won't be able to talk about it in front of Felix, though.'

I glanced outside. It wasn't exactly a joys-of-spring sunshiny day but it wasn't raining at least. 'We'll pack the kids off into the garden. Keep an eye on them and talk discreetly, out of earshot.' There was another pause. 'I'll take that as a yes, then. And I'll bring some biscuits with me.'

'Great,' she said, and I blinked in surprise. Bloody hell, it had to be something major if she was willing to accept a packet of previously embargoed HobNobs across the threshold.

'I mean, we can be subtle about eating them, I won't let Molly or Felix see we've got them . . .' I burbled anxiously, then stopped myself. This was *ridiculous*! I thought. It was only a few biscuits, not Class A drugs that had been prohibited until this particular morning.

'Honestly, Sade, it doesn't matter. I've probably been a bit uptight about the biscuits thing anyway,' Lizzie said.

I stared at the wall in shock, vacantly taking in the fact that it needed painting again. *I've probably been a bit uptight about the biscuits thing*. God. Admission of the year. 'Right. OK. Shall I just come over?' I asked.

'Come over whenever,' she said. 'And don't forget the contraband, whatever you do.'

'Don't worry,' I reassured her. 'They're top of my list.'

Once we'd got to Lizzie's house, and the kids had been packed outside regardless of their complaints ('Don't want to play in garden, Mummy.' 'Oh dear, that's a shame. Bye!'), we relocated to the kitchen for caffeine and HobNob partaking. Lizzie took a deep breath.

'Tell me,' I urged.

'Sadie,' she began, then it all came out in a rush. 'Did Steve seem *normal* to you last night?'

'Er . . .' I was flummoxed. Normal? He'd never seemed normal to me, no. Not ever. But normal in a Steve kind of way . . . yes. 'What do you mean?'

'Did you think he seemed at all . . . different?' she asked.

'No,' I replied truthfully. 'He seemed just the same as he always is.'

She sighed. 'I think he's having an affair,' she said flatly.

I spluttered, and a crumb lodged itself in my throat. 'What?' I yelped. Steve having an affair I had *not* anticipated. Money problems, house problems, wallpaper problems, yes, but Steve? An *affair*? Was there another person in the world who could find Steve attractive?

'God,' I said, once I'd finished coughing. 'What on earth makes you think that?'

'He's been going out loads after work,' she said. She wasn't *quite* wringing her hands, but she might as well have been. 'There's this woman who started at the firm a couple of months ago, Jessica. She's really attractive and bubbly and—'

'But what makes you think she's after Steve?' I asked, trying to keep the note of incredulity out of my voice. Was it her guide dog, or the white stick? Or did she get turned on by Bill Gates jokes too?

Lizzie shrugged miserably and ate another biscuit. Her fourth. 'Just a sixth sense. He mentions her all the time. Jessica says this, Jessica did that today, it's Jessie's birthday do tonight . . .'

'And have you said anything about all this Jessica stuff?' I asked.

She sighed. 'Well, I wouldn't have taken that much notice if it hadn't been for the phone calls.'

'Phone calls? From Jessica?'

Lizzie looked out of the window, her eyes resting on the

kids. Molly was chasing Felix around the garden, and they were both laughing their heads off. 'I don't know who they're from,' she said sadly. 'Every time I answer, the connection is cut. I dial 1471 and it says the caller has withheld the number. I mentioned it to Steve and he went all awkward about it. He blushed. He actually blushed!'

'Hmmm,' I said. Blushing was not good. I couldn't even imagine a blush on Steve's pasty, jowly face; he looked like he didn't even have the circulation to be able to turn any colour other than white.

Lizzie put her head in her hands. 'I don't know, Sade,' she said. 'Maybe I'm just inventing it all. Making something out of nothing. Maybe I'm just looking for an excuse to fall out with Steve.'

I tried to stop my eyes from boggling at her words. I moved chairs so that I was next to her at the table, and patted her back. 'Liz . . . you seem so unhappy. Is it just this Steve thing, or is something else bothering you?'

She shook her head dumbly and, to my horror, two tears fell from her eyes and plopped onto the table.

'Oh God, what is it?' I asked in alarm. Lizzie didn't go in for crying. She was way too private a person. Her emotions were kept as tightly under control as her paint schemes. Cat and I were the ones who were always bawling about something one minute, then laughing uproariously the next. Lizzie was the ship who sailed on an even keel, stately and upright, always in a straight line.

'It's . . .' She couldn't speak for sobs. 'It's everything. We've been trying for another baby. I feel *obliged* to. Everyone knows that lots of only children end up in therapy. Everyone I know keeps asking me when we're having another one. And so we've . . .' She hiccuped and shook. 'We've been trying, but I've started to think . . . My heart's not in it. I don't *want* another baby. I can't bear the thought of going through it all again – being so big and unwieldy and hot, and then all that breast-feeding and puke and shit and mess everywhere. I just hated all that. I hated it.'

The savageness of her tone was enough to make me flinch. I'd still been in my clubbing-partying-working whirl when she'd had Felix, and I hadn't really taken on board the momentous shift in her life. I hadn't looked past the 'Ooh, cute baby clothes' thing to see what was in Lizzie's eyes. Now that I was also on Planet Motherhood, I could kind of see how it must have been for her. The ultimate control freak having to relinquish said control to an eight-pound screamer. Gutted.

'Don't do it, then,' I said bluntly. 'Jesus, Liz, don't do it. You don't have to. Felix won't end up in therapy, that's rubbish. Felix is absolutely fine.' I hugged her and put the biscuit packet squarely in front of her. 'And if you and Steve have hit a rocky patch, that's even more of a reason for sticking at one child for now.'

She sighed and plunged her hand in for another HobNob. 'You know, I thought I'd be good at being a mum,' she said. Both our heads flicked to the kitchen window to check on the kids again. Amazingly, neither of them had hurt the other one yet. 'I'm organized and tidy and practical . . .'

'You are,' I agreed. 'Far more organized and tidy and practical than I'll ever be. And you *are* good at being a mum anyway. You're really patient with Felix and do loads of interesting things with him.'

She sniffed. She'd stopped crying now at least. 'D'you know,' she said quietly, 'I wish I could be more like you. So competent and fun and—'

Hold on a minute. 'Competent? Me? Ha!' I laughed loud enough to wake Nathan, who had been dozing in his car seat under the table. 'Liz, I wish I could be more like *you*, with your house always so clean, and—'

She shook her head. 'A clean house isn't everything,' she said. The tears shone in her eyes under the bright kitchen spotlights. 'I'd swap it like a shot for a happy marriage.'

The smile fell abruptly off my face. Ahh yes. I'd forgotten how all of this had started. 'So what are you going to do about Steve?' I asked.

She fiddled with her wedding ring. 'I suppose I'll have to ask him about it.'

I stood up, having just seen my daughter push poor old Felix off the plastic truck he'd been riding on. 'Molly! I'm watching you!' I bellowed through the window, making Nathan jump and then wail, holding his arms up to be released from his car seat imprisonment. I turned back to my sister, the sister I'd always envied for her perfect life.

'I suppose you will,' I said gently.

On Wednesday, I buzzed Mark's office door as usual and waited for the lock to click open. My hand was on the door, ready to push it and walk through as soon as the click came. But there was no click. There was no reply.

I took a step back and looked up at the windows. Total darkness. I pushed against the door impatiently, buzzed again.

The wind blew a couple of fag ends around my ankles and I wedged my hands into my pockets, leaned in to the building again for shelter. Come on, Mark. What was he doing? I buzzed a third time, but a sick feeling was spreading through me. He wasn't there. He had gone.

'MARK!' I yelled through cupped hands, leaning my head back. A pigeon flapped over my head and made me jump.

I shivered. It was freezing. The weatherman had predicted a ground frost that would no doubt stunt or kill off everything in the garden. And Mark wasn't there. He wasn't there. I felt like crying.

After a few minutes' not wanting to believe it was true, I finally admitted defeat. I bowed my head and sunk my chin into my zipped-up jacket. Then I started trudging back the way I'd come. What was I going to do now? I couldn't face actually going running, I was too stunned with the shock of Mark's absence. Oh God, I must have upset him. He must have felt pushed away by me. What if I never saw him again?

Suddenly, all my plans for nipping our fling in the bud seemed ridiculous. I couldn't bear not seeing him again. How could I even have thought of telling him I wasn't going to see him again? It was unthinkable. It was unbearable.

I walked along the road, mind spinning as I tried to take in the enormity of the situation. Did this mean it was over? Didn't he want to see me any more?

The thoughts swam around my brain. No more wild passion with Mark. No more sex kitten Sadie antics. No more . . .

A car was purring along behind me and I stepped up my pace. Oh, typical. Tonight of all nights to be harassed by a sodding kerb-crawler. Didn't he know there were police cameras all over this area now? All the prostitutes had moved out to the Clapham Park estate, Anna reckoned. So why didn't this sad old punter just fuck off over there with them?

Then I heard his voice. 'Sadie.'

I turned round and it was his car, Mark's car. He was leaning out of the window, an unreadable expression on his face.

'Mark!' I cried. I ran over and wrenched the passenger door open, and threw myself into his arms. I found I was sobbing with relief, clutching folds of his T-shirt to my face, tears spilling all over his chest. 'I thought . . . I thought . . .'

He pulled up the handbrake. 'It's all right,' he said, holding me. 'Put your seat belt on and shut the door.'

'Where are we going?' I asked in a small voice, doing what he told me. I choked on the words as another sob hiccuped out of me.

He passed me a tissue, then put the car in gear. 'It's all right, sweetheart,' he told me. 'I just wanted to go somewhere else for a change, that's all.'

I dried my eyes and he drove off. I was passive, didn't ask any more questions. I suddenly realized I didn't care where we were going, that was why. As long as I was with him . . .

He pulled up outside a smart, white-painted Victorian semi in Clapham. Wisteria sprawled over its front, and I could smell winter jasmine as we walked up the drive. I didn't ask a thing, just held his hand as he led me.

He opened the door. The house was dark inside. 'It's a friend's place,' he said. 'She's away and lent me the keys. I thought we could spend the evening on neutral ground.'

I blew my nose. 'Yeah,' I said. I didn't have the energy to speak; I was still reeling from the shock of what had happened. I had thought it was over.

He switched the living-room light on. 'There's a phone

there,' he said, pointing to the corner. 'Why don't you ring Alex, tell him you've bumped into a mate and you're going to have a few drinks in the pub with her?'

'OK,' I said. I had thought the worst, that I would never see him again. Never touch him or hold him.

'I'll run a bath,' he said. 'Leave you to it.'

'OK,' I said again, nodding. I couldn't take my eyes off him. I wanted to look at him every moment I possibly could.

'And when you've finished on the phone,' he said, 'I want you to take off every single one of your clothes, and come upstairs to find me.'

I nodded dumbly. 'OK,' I said for a third time. I watched him until he had left the room, and then I picked up the phone and dialled.

Chapter Thirteen

After I'd phoned Alex and lied into the receiver, I sat down on one of the squashy, honey-coloured sofas, and took off my shoes. Then I took off my clothes. I folded everything up very neatly and left it in a pile on the sofa. Then I went to find Mark.

The house was mostly in darkness. A boiler was wheezing and rattling somewhere further down the hall, and I could hear the faint sound of running water and gurgling pipes coming from above me. I padded back towards the front door, stark naked. The seagrass matting was scratchy under my bare feet as I headed for the stairs.

Mark had lit a couple of tea lights on the stairs. The bright little flames swayed perilously on their wicks as a draught slipped under the front door, but there was just enough light for me to find my way. I held on to the banister, feeling a thrill spreading through me as I walked up, naked, to find Mark. My love.

At the top of the stairs, I glanced up and down the

landing, my pupils as wide as a cat's, as I tried to get my bearings. There was a room straight ahead of me with the door open, a bedroom, I guessed. Then there was another shut door – a cupboard? a loo? – and then, even further along, a door that was also shut, but outlined in a faint light. I breathed in and smelled lavender, heard the noise of the running water. Aha. The bathroom, I deduced.

I started walking along the hall towards it, my heart quickening at the thought of Mark waiting for me – naked, wet, bubbly – when there was a noise behind me. A floorboard creaking, it sounded like. I stopped at once and spun round in the darkness. 'Mark?' I whispered. 'Is that you?'

I couldn't see a thing. My eyes strained uselessly to make out something, anything in the gloom, but all that was in front of me was blackness. The silence felt deafening. I turned back towards the bathroom and started walking to it again, hand on the banister for guidance.

The noise came from behind me a second time. 'Mark,' I said. 'I know that's you. Stop it.'

I took another step and then almost fell over in shock as a hand slipped around my waist. He was behind me, kissing my neck, his fingers moving up to my breasts. 'Not a stitch on,' he was saying in a pleased sort of way. 'Not a stitch on.'

'There's a name for men like you,' I said, leaning back against him, my heart beating hard in relief. 'Pervert. Hanging around in dark corners, jumping out on innocent, naked women . . .'

'Sounds good to me,' he muttered, his hand sliding across my belly.

I turned round and we stood there kissing. It was cold; I could hear the wind gusting around the house, branches batting at the windows.

I shivered, and he held me tightly. 'Come on, let's have that bath,' he said. 'It must be full by now.'

I clasped my arms around him as we walked to the bathroom, a strange four-legged beast shuffling awkwardly along the landing. I was vaguely aware of my own children probably in their bath right about now, far, far away, in a galaxy many miles from here, but the thought didn't seem quite real. I was tuning their faces out, fading their voices so that they were muffled and distant. And Alex, soaping them, drying them, putting them in pyjamas . . . he was muffled and distant, too. He was hardly there at all.

We were in the bathroom and I glanced around curiously as Mark turned the taps off. The room was lit by candlelight; the claw-footed bath was full of bubbles. There was a large, shell-edged mirror above the sink. A French-style showerhead, the size of a dinner plate. No toys. No suckered safety mat. This was a room strictly for adults.

I gazed at the drifts of steam rising to the ceiling and

Mark passed me a glass of wine. 'I'll have the tap end,' he said. 'See? I know how to treat a bird proper, like.'

'You're pure class, you,' I replied, stepping into the water. 'Cheers.'

'Cheers to us,' he said.

I was falling in love with him, I realized. I was under his spell, just in the way that he claimed to be under mine. I was hopelessly, utterly hooked.

Dear Sadie,

How's it going? Hope London is sunny. I don't think Manchester knows that it's meant to be spring yet – grey drizzle here day after day. God, it's tough up north, you know. You southerners don't know you're born etc etc.

Anyway – enough about the weather, and on to the thrilling news of my mum's 60th. She's having a banging hard-house session at the . . . Oh, no. Hang on. Wrong party. My mum's having a knees-up with all her old muckers at the community centre on Jacobs Street. Sausages on sticks and warm wine all round. It's going to be bloody awful – in fact it's going to be the kind of thing that Channel 4 make sneering documentaries about – but we can always sneak off for a pint elsewhere if Frank Sinatra and Elvis ain't your bag. Anyway, it's on the 27th, Saturday, eight till late. Let me know what you think. It's the only night I'm around to catch up with you while I'm in London, but if it all seems too unbearable for words then we can sort something else out for another time.

Love Dan

Danny's email gave me a warm, cosy feeling. At least he was writing properly now, not just terse sentences about The Smiths or what have you. And the promise of sausages on sticks and twirling around a sticky parquet dancefloor to Frank Sinatra sounded quite a laugh actually. It would also be a useful way of getting out of too much Channel 4 talk as well. I closed the internet connection thoughtfully, and shut down the computer. Yes, that could work, couldn't it? Every time he asked me a tricky question about my so-called job, I would jump up, assume an ecstatic expression – 'Oh, "Viva Las Vegas", I *love* this!' – and sprint off to the dancefloor.

I smiled, and put the laptop away. I would email back when I had more time and accept the invitation gracefully.

It was Tuesday, and I'd just put the kids in bed. Nathan was asleep already, clutching his blue bear with a look of sheer contentment, hair fluffing up around his head like a golden halo. Molly was chatting away to her dolls in bed with the light off. I'd just heard her saying, 'No messing around tonight, Fizz. I told you lots of times,' in a stern voice, so hopefully she was up for an early night, too.

Alex was late. I had resisted making any digs about Natasha when he'd phoned, just sighed with enough exasperation to let him know that being late was not a good option. 'Sorry, Sade,' he'd said. He actually sounded like he meant it for once. 'I've just got one last thing to finish, then I'll be on my way, promise. And don't cook – I've already ordered a takeaway from the Taj Mahal. It should be ready just in time for me to pick it up on my way back.'

'Oh.' The wind was rather taken out of my sails. 'OK. Great. See you in a bit, then.'

Alex in thoughtful man shock! Alex in 'Don't cook' shock! Alex in apology shock!

What the *hell* was going on?

If anything was going to make me suspicious, this was. Perhaps he was nobbing Natasha and feeling really, really, curry-buyingly guilty about it. Or perhaps he had broken or lost something of mine, and was going to work his way up to a grovelling confession later that evening. Something was definitely up, that was for sure.

It was even more obvious something peculiar was happening when Alex arrived home. Swinging from the handlebars of his bike was a white plastic bag crammed with steaming silver-foil cartons, plus a Threshers' bag that was clinking in a most pleasing way. And then, from out of the back of his rucksack, he pulled a bunch of flowers.

'Thank you,' I said, slightly dazed. Creamy-white narcissi,

sulphur-coloured anemones, long sticks of forsythia with yolk-yellow petals like cheerful flags. 'Lovely,' I said, clutching the wet paper wrapping in shock. I just about let him take his boots and jacket off before I asked, 'So what's all this about then?'

'What's all what about?' He was grinning as he leaned forward to kiss me. Not just a customary peck either, a full smooch of a kiss.

I wrestled the flowers out from between us, worried they would be crushed between our combined smooching weight. 'Blimey,' I said, when he finally pulled away. 'You're being very . . . er . . . romantic. Any particular reason?'

He unhooked the bags of curry and booze and took them through to the kitchen. 'Does there have to be a reason?' he mused. 'Other than I'm in love with the most gorgeous woman in south London?'

I stared at him. He looked like Alex. He sounded like Alex too. But the things he was saying . . . Was there a secret long-lost twin his mum had never told me about? Or just a body double?

He was unpacking the curry, lifting the foil boxes from the bag and peeling the tops off. Wafts of coriander and cumin and meat were sent up into the air with every new box. 'There's a madras and a rogan josh here,' he said over his shoulder. 'I thought we could share both of them.'

'Great,' I said, getting some plates out. I threw him

another glance. Yes, it definitely was Alex. A thought struck me. It was Alex on his best behaviour, that was all. Something I hadn't seen since our second date, or thereabouts. God. I almost felt scared at this unexpected turn of events.

'Let's eat in here for a change, rather than in front of the TV,' he said, pulling the cutlery drawer open and fishing out a couple of forks. 'Then we can talk.'

Talk? *Talk?* Now I *was* scared. He was totally freaking me out. All this niceness just made me feel uneasy. Not to mention suspicious.

Once I'd cleared the table of pink and silver glitter, the latest washing pile and an interesting assortment of crumbs, we sat down to eat. Curry and red wine and candlelight. Good Lord. No expense spared. I could hardly *wait* to hear what he was going to say.

After a mouthful of curry, a slurp of wine and a couple of appreciative noises, he put down his fork and cleared his throat. 'Sadie,' he began.

OK. Here he goes, I thought.

From the look on his face, I couldn't decide whether it was going to be the nobbing-Natasha scenario or an announcement that he'd been sacked, or perhaps even the jubilant news that he'd moved into first place in the office fantasy football league. 'Yes?' I replied guardedly.

'I want to say sorry,' he said. His eyes were fixed on me, his gaze so solemn that I had to fight the urge to giggle.

'*Sorry?*' I repeated. I hadn't been expecting that one. 'Sorry for what?'

'Sorry for having a go at you about that Jack bloke. And for coming in so late last Friday. And I'm really sorry if I upset Lizzie on Saturday. I've been a bit of a prat lately.'

I frowned. 'Remind me how you upset Lizzie again,' I said, not having the faintest idea what he was on about.

He looked a little shame-faced. It wasn't a natural expression for Alex to wear; he suddenly seemed five years younger, awkward and shifty. 'Well, when I kept going on about how I was going to get Felix a toy gun for his birthday,' he said, dropping his gaze for the first time. 'I think I pissed her off, big-time. She looked dead upset.'

'She was upset anyway. I don't think it was you,' I told him. Lizzie. I wondered if she'd confronted Steve yet about Jessica.

'Oh. Oh, good.' He took a large gulp of wine in what looked like relief. 'Well, the other stuff, then. I don't know what's happened lately between us, if something's gone wrong or what, but we've both been drinking loads and not getting on very well, and . . .' He shrugged. 'I just wanted to do something nice, that's all. Make an effort for a change. Tell you that I really love you after all these years and all these children—'

'There's only two of them!' I objected.

'And all these days and nights we've spent together.' He was on a roll now. It was sounding rather scripted, to be honest. 'I think it's easy to forget to tell someone you love them when your lives are so . . . so . . .' He was struggling for words; perhaps this was an inpromptu bit.

'Boring?' I suggested.

He looked startled. 'I was going to say meshed together, actually,' he said. 'Anyway, what I'm trying to tell you is, I'm sorry I've been a bit crap lately. I know I haven't been pulling my weight. And I know that you know that. And you deserve better. And I'm going to make things better.'

He finished abruptly and leaned back in his chair, as if waiting for a round of applause or, at the very least, an 'I love you *too!*' kind of declaration.

I was working my way through a particularly chewy mouthful of naan bread so he had to watch me masticating and gurning in an extremely bovine and unattractive way instead. 'Thanks,' I said when I'd eventually swallowed the last bit. 'Um . . . That's really lovely. And I know what you mean. We've let things drift a bit, haven't we?'

'We have,' he said earnestly. My God. Alex was never earnest. Even when our children had been born he'd been cracking jokes and making dodgy comments about pointy-headed alien babies only seconds later. 'We only seem to have sex when we're drunk,' he went on.

I looked down at my plate guiltily.

'We're both knackered and working hard, and everyone says having kids is the biggest test a relationship can face,' he said. 'But I don't want to lose "us". You know, I want us to come through the other side, still loving each other and making plans for our future and . . .' He shrugged and scuffed a fork around his plate, suddenly seeming embarrassed. 'You know what I mean.'

Oh, Alex. Why hadn't he said all this a month ago? I felt consumed by guilt. The chicken in my mouth felt dry and rubbery. The smell of my wine suddenly made me feel sick. I stretched an arm across the table and held his hand. I found that my eyes had filled with tears.

'Sadie,' he said gently. 'Don't cry. Why are you crying?'

I shook my head, shiny-eyed, terrified that I was going to start a torrent of blubbing and be unable to stop. There were so many emotions inside that I didn't dare let out.

He pushed his chair back, got up and came round to my side of the table. He put his arms around me and I rested my head against his shirt, his comforting smell making me feel even more wretched.

'Come on,' he said. 'What's wrong? What's wrong?'

'I don't know,' I lied. My voice was barely more than a whisper. 'You're right. We've been taking each other for granted.' He was so close, I could feel his breath on my cheek. Alex, the person who knew me best in the world. The person with whom I shared two children and a home. The person whose pants and socks I washed every day, whose tea I cooked every evening, who slept next to me in our bed every night. I pulled away and steeled myself to look him in the eye. 'You know, I thought this was going to be something about Natasha.'

He blinked and stared, as if I'd spoken in a foreign language. 'Natasha?' he repeated. 'What, Natasha that I work with?'

I nodded. From the way he'd said her name, I realized my suspicions were probably wrong. 'Yeah,' I said, then forced a shrug in the hope of seeming casual about it all. 'I thought you two were . . . you know.'

'What? Me and Natasha, having it away?' He laughed, his mouth so wide that I could see rice on his back teeth. Then his jaw closed with a snap and he looked back at me with a strange expression on his face. 'You're joking, aren't you?'

'Kind of,' I told him. I was trying to step back delicately from the confession now, ease my way back into the conversation we'd had minutes earlier. 'It's just you've been working late a lot and you went to her birthday do the other night without telling me, and—'

'Her birthday do? What are you talking about?'

Ahh. How could I explain this, when it had been Mark who had told me about the birthday do?

'I thought you said you went out to Covent Garden for her birthday last Friday?' I said. I watched his face carefully. Hang on a minute, I was thinking. If he *didn't* go to Covent Garden last Friday . . .

'Covent *Garden*? No. Where did you get that from? We were in the local, just like we always are.'

Then why had Mark told me that?

I bent my head over my curry. You fool, Sadie. You utter fool.

'I must have got muddled up with someone else,' I said. 'It was probably Becca, now I think about it.'

'Right.' I could feel him watching me. Why had Mark lied to me? 'Well, I *didn't* go to Covent Garden, and Natasha wasn't even out on Friday. She went out with Paul, I think.'

'Paul?'

'Yeah, Paul. Paul Brookes? Her husband. He works in the Sports section with Matthew.' I looked up to see him grinning. 'You nana. Did you really think me and Mrs Brookes were gettin' it on?'

I had lost track of the conversation. My mind felt as if it had been blown apart with shock. Mark had lied to me. Why had he lied to me?

'Well, you know,' I said, trying to sound jokey. 'You're a good-looking guy. You're a bit of a catch . . .'

'I am, I am,' the catch said proudly. 'It's all true.'

'But anyway,' I said, making a heroic effort to banish Mark from my head. The liar! The manipulative liar! He had wanted me to think that . . . 'Forget Natasha. Going back to what you were saying before, we'll both have to make more of an effort from now on. And it's not just down to you. I will, too.'

He kissed the top of my head and gave me a last squeeze. Crisis over – time to get back to the rogan josh before it cooled down too much.

'I tell you what set me off thinking,' he said, sitting back down. 'It was seeing you come in last night after seeing your mate. You were all sparkly eyed and happy. It made me wish that *I* could make you so happy, all the time. So—'

'You *do* make me happy,' I put in quickly. It was just that I'd been shagged senseless in a bubble bath by Mark and had about twenty orgasms, that was all.

I didn't tell him that bit, obviously. Pushed Mark out of my mind again before the anger started rising up inside me.

'So,' he went on, ignoring me, 'I've booked us a table at Humbugs on Saturday night. I've already asked your mum, who said she would babysit, no problem. And then there's Cat and Tom's leaving do the Friday after that. And then it's your birthday weekend and I've booked us in at a hotel in Brighton, on the seafront.' His voice was gruff with pride. 'We'll just have to keep arranging lots of things to look forward to, Sade. I know money's a bit tight, but . . .'

I leaned across the table and kissed him, trying not to get curry all over my front. 'You are a lovely, lovely man,' I told him. 'And I love you very, very much. And I'm very lucky to have caught the catch. Thank you.'

''S all right,' he said magnanimously. He forked a mouthful of lamb into his mouth and then raised his glass. 'Cheers to us,' he said.

'Cheers to us,' I said, raising mine. That was twice in two evenings now that I had toasted my relationships with two different men. I felt about as hypocritical as it was possible to feel.

Dear Dan,

The 27th sounds great. Looking forward to strutting my stuff to 'New York, New York' in between cheese and pineapple on sticks. Oh, and looking forward to seeing you as well. Shall I meet you there?

Love Sadie x

The new, improved, making-an-effort Alex was turning out to be pretty bloody good actually. On Saturday afternoon, he looked after the kids so I could go and get my hair cut for the first time since Nathan had been born. On Saturday night, he took me to Humbugs, the nicest vegetarian restaurant in the world, and made me laugh all night, then took me home and made sweet, sweet love to me. On Sunday morning, he got up with the kids so I could have a lie-in.

By Monday evening, I was feeling like the most ungrateful woman on the planet as I put on my faux running gear to meet Mark. I was also feeling confused about the lying issue.

I had decided, in the end, after many hours feeling angry and then bruised and then plain old curious about the reasons for the lie, that *Julia* must have misled Mark about the staff whereabouts last Friday. Maybe she'd been in Covent Garden with someone who sounded a bit like Natasha. Sasha, say. Or Natalie. And Mark had told me that and I'd just heard Natasha because . . .

Well, something like that anyway. It could have happened. It sounded plausible to me.

Alex gave my bottom a friendly squeeze as I passed him on my way out. 'You know, all this running is really paying off,' he said. 'Your legs definitely look leaner.'

'Do you think so?' I asked, feeling a rush of guilt. Running didn't get a look in any more. If anything was making my legs lean, it was the contortions Mark bent me into. The frantic sex, the nervous energy and bucketloads of adrenaline.

'Definitely,' he said. 'Didn't I always say I was right about—?'

'Yes,' I said. 'You might have mentioned it. Listen, I'm going to meet up with Anna again afterwards so I'll probably be a bit late, OK?'

He kissed me and I wanted to push him away. No, don't believe me, I'm an evil lying slut, Alex, I felt like shouting. Walk away from me while you can. You deserve better.

'Have a good one,' he said.

'Thanks,' I said miserably. 'I will.'

I started running down our road towards Mark's office as usual, but then a car pulled up alongside me a few hundred yards from our house.

'Jump in,' he said.

'Hello,' I said. 'Where are we going tonight?'

'Just a pub,' he told me, kissing my mouth tenderly. 'The Duke of Devonshire. Do you know it?'

'No,' I said happily, doing up my seat belt. I loved going to new places. Especially with the prospect of sex with Mark at the end of it.

He was driving a familiar route. 'Hey,' I said after a while. 'We're in Balham.'

'Yeah, and . . . ?' He sounded amused. 'Is that a problem?'

Lizzie. With my luck, I'd probably bump into her, right here on her home turf. 'Well, one of my sisters lives here,' I said. He parked the car in a side street, and I looked around uneasily as if she was about to jump up at my window any second, a frown under that fair fringe as she took in who I was with. *A man? Who isn't Alex? What IS she doing?*

He was unclipping his seat belt, sliding the keys from the ignition. Then he looked across at me. 'What, you want to go somewhere else?'

'No-o-o,' I said. I thought quickly. 'No. She won't be out on a Monday night. She's got a little boy. No, this'll be fine.'

The Duke of Devonshire was the kind of pub I liked: not

too flashy or cool or chintzy. Not full of drug dealers and over-friendly alkies either. Just a normal pub with a good jukebox and big pine tables and benches. Perfect.

'What do you want to drink?' I asked, pulling my purse out.

'Better make it a half, as I'm driving,' he said. 'Half of bitter. I thought we could have a quick drink here then go and find somewhere unusual to have amazing sex. What do you reckon?'

I blushed. 'Mark, have we ever done it somewhere that *isn't* unusual?' I joked. He was having his knicker-melting-lust effect on me, as always. One look at that amazing mouth was enough to start me off.

'You've got a point,' he said, his eyes crinkling with amusement.

I went to the bar. For once, I didn't want something alcoholic. I'd been up half the night with Nathan, whose first tooth was indeed coming through, and I was feeling light-headed with tiredness. Plus, Alex had been right about how much we'd both been drinking. I felt the need for some time off the booze. So grapefruit juice it was going to be.

While I was waiting to be served, I had the distinct feeling I was being watched. Well, I knew Mark would be watching me; I was already leaning slightly forward, elbows on the bar, bottom sticking out just a fraction, as I knew it would be tormenting him. He seemed to have a thing about me bending over, but anyway . . . No, I knew that *he* was looking at me, but I sensed that someone else was, too, from a different direction.

I cast my eyes stealthily about. Nobody on my right had noticed me. And on the left . . .

There. I saw her. Brown eyes looking inquiringly across from the left, where the bar turned a corner. I knew that face. How did I know that face?

She lifted a hand in acknowledgement, smiled a brief smile. And then I knew. Oh fuck, then I knew, all right. It was Caroline from Lizzie's sodding book group. Bollocking bollock shit fuck. Caroline, of the cropped hair and freckles. Caroline who was bound to report back to Lizzie, 'Oh, I saw your sister in the Duke the other night. Sadie, is it?' The cat was so going to be out of the bag now. I was toast.

I waved back, a frozen grin on my face. Don't come over, I thought. Don't come over. *Please* don't come over.

She was coming over.

'Hiya,' she said. 'I thought it was you. How are things?'

'Fine, just fine,' I gabbled. 'You?'

'So-so,' she said, then sighed, a pained expression on her face. 'Stressing about Claudia's birthday party actually. You know how it is. I've got a face painter and a clown coming, plus I've hired a load of fairy costumes for her friends to wear, and . . .' She pulled a face. 'It's a nightmare, isn't it? Now I've just got to sort out a caterer. I don't suppose you know any, do you?'

'No, sorry,' I said. 'How old is she going to be?'

'One.' She was looking wistful. 'My little baby's going to be one. I can hardly believe it. It's gone so fast. Simply whizzed by. Only seems a few minutes ago that I was holding her for the first time.'

'I know what you mean,' I said, automatically tuning into mum mode, although I was still trying not to giggle at the thought of a one-year-old having a catered fairy party complete with face painter and clown. Such a shame that she would have absolutely no memory of it whatsoever. 'My youngest is six months now and I don't know *where* the time has gone.'

'Hello there.'

I turned to see Mark behind me. He was smiling at Caroline. 'I should have known she'd be chatting to somebody,' he was saying to her. 'Sadie manages to make friends with everyone. I'm Mark, by the way.'

'Caroline,' she told him, smiling back at him, holding out a hand.

I felt a twinge of something – fear? irritation? – that Mark had invited himself into the conversation and, even worse, told her his name. 'Mark is an old friend,' I said quickly. *Don't tell Lizzie about Mark,* I willed Caroline. *Whatever you do, don't tell Lizzie!*

'Oh, right,' she said. 'I thought you two were . . .'

Mark had put an arm around me. 'What, you think we

make a good couple?' His voice was light but his grip felt uncomfortable.

I faked a laugh and stepped out of his embrace. What was he playing at now?

Caroline looked at me, unsure of the right thing to say.

'Mark, don't be daft,' I said. Bloody hell. Why had we come to bloody Balham of all places? 'Anyway, nice to see you again, Caroline,' I said firmly. Enough was enough. 'Are you going to the next book group meeting?'

'Yes, I should think so. The book looks rather . . .' She lowered her voice, obviously concerned that Margaret's spies would be out in the pub too. 'Rather dull, but I'll give it a go.'

'See you then, then,' I smiled, as brightly as I could. Now push off and forget we ever had this conversation, I thought, through gritted teeth.

She pushed off obediently and I gave Mark a hard look. 'What was all that for?' I asked.

'What?'

'You know. All that "Do you think we make a good couple?" stuff. It just made you look really weird, you know. Suspicious.'

He seemed amused rather than repentant. 'I was just being friendly,' he replied.

I kept staring at him with my best Paddington Bear stare until he looked away. There was friendly, yeah, and there was trying to screw things up for me. I was starting to think he was bent on the latter. 'Let's go,' I said. 'I don't really want to stay here any more. Can we go now?'

'OK,' he said, still with that amused, unruffled air. 'If you want to. I don't think she thought anything of it, us being here, two friends meeting in a pub, but . . .' He shrugged. *It's your problem, Sadie.* 'I don't mind going straight to the main course tonight, if that's what you want.' He leaned in closer to me. 'I've got a whole box of condoms with your name on it, Ms Morrison.'

He seemed so unmoved by the whole episode that I was starting to feel a little foolish. Had I made too much out of it? Maybe it wasn't such a big deal. Caroline would have better things to talk to Lizzie about, after all, than bumping into me. She'd been so fixated by her baby's Beckham-style party plans that I was small potatoes.

'Come on, then,' I said, pulling him along in an attempt at jollity. 'I'll show you my etchings and you can show me your condoms.'

By the middle of the week, I was starting to glow with smugness. 'Blimey, look at you,' Anna said when she came round for lunch with her kids. 'You look absolutely amazing. You've lost weight. And you practically reek of wonderful sex.'

I smirked and put the kettle on. The girls had gone upstairs to play shops, and we were in the kitchen with the boys. 'I've got wonderful sex coming out of my ears,' I said, then giggled. 'Oops, that sounds a tad dodgy. What I mean is, I'm having wonderful sex with Mark *and* Alex. I've kind of fallen in love with both of them.'

Anna shook her head. 'I'm trying not to look envious but . . .' she said. Then she leaned in curiously. 'I've got to ask . . . Aren't you knackered, though? Honestly, Jamie thinks his luck's in if we have sex once a week at the moment. I just don't have the energy for it other than that. And until Theo starts sleeping better, I can't see me having a rampant sex-life ever again. Let alone with a bit on the side as well.'

'Yeah, I have to say, I could do with a week of sleep,' I admitted. 'Oh, a week of sleep, I would kill for it. I think I'm coasting along on adrenaline. Any day now, there'll be a crash and I'll collapse.' I spooned coffee into the cafetière. 'But I'm loving it. It's such a kick. Everything is balanced so brilliantly at the moment. Alex is being a darling, dead sweet and thoughtful. Mark surprises me every time I see him by being so sexy and outrageous. We ended up having a bit of alfresco on Clapham Common the other night.'

Anna snorted in amusement. 'What, with all the MPs and rent boys?' she sniggered. 'Very tasteful, Sadie. It's every housewife's dream.'

'You may scoff,' I told her, pointing a teaspoon at her, 'but it was bloody exciting.'

'And cold and draughty and . . .' She laughed at the look

on my face. 'Sorry. Ignore me. I'm jealous. I feel like a chaste old spinster next to you.'

I pushed down the plunger on the cafetière and then bent down to rescue Nathan. He'd been sitting up brilliantly for ten minutes or so, examining a particularly fascinating rattle, but had just collapsed sideways unexpectedly on the lino, and was now complaining loudly. 'All right, babe,' I said, kissing his hot head. 'Come and help me make the coffee.'

'So who will you choose then?' Anna asked. 'At the end of it all, who are you going to choose?'

I stared at her and leaned against the side. Now she'd mentioned it, I did feel exhausted. My whole body ached to lie down. 'Who am I going to *choose*?' I repeated. 'What, between Mark and Alex, you mean?'

'Yeah,' she said. 'I mean, you can't carry on with both of them for ever. Sooner or later, something's got to give. One of them will have to go.'

Her words seemed incredibly callous; I practically flinched. 'Oh God,' I said, pulling a face. 'What an awful question. I can't bear to think of either of them going. Can't I choose both of them?'

Anna's eyes were cool and amused. 'I doubt it,' she said. 'It doesn't usually work like that, does it?'

Who would I choose? Once Anna had asked the question, it played over and over in my head like a jumping CD. Who would I *choose*? I kept asking myself, but the answer continued to elude me. I had absolutely no idea. People kept on with affairs for years and years, though, didn't they? I certainly didn't have to make any choices right now.

'It'll have to be a quick one,' I announced, arriving at Mark's office later that evening. 'Much as I'd like to be ravished by you for hours on end, I really must say goodnight to the kids tonight. They were a bit upset I wasn't there on Monday apparently.'

'Sure that's not just Alex trying to make you feel bad about going out?' Mark asked.

'No,' I said. 'Look, don't get all funny on me, I—'

'How *are* the kids?' Mark asked, interrupting me. 'Nathan got that tooth through yet?'

We were both sitting fully dressed on his sofa. Suddenly, he felt too close for comfort and I had to inch away. 'Well, no, not yet,' I said. 'Why?'

'Just taking an interest,' he replied. 'Your kids are a big thing in your life, I know, and I'm interested, that's all.'

'Right,' I said slowly.

'So how's Molly?' he went on chattily. 'Is she like you? Who does she look like? I'd love to meet her. Well, both of them obviously.'

I shook my head. 'I don't think so,' I said. 'I don't think that's a good idea.'

'Why not?'

'Because . . . Because the thing we've got going is about me and you and fantastic sex and fancying each other's pants off,' I said, as gently as I could. 'It's not about my kids.'

'No, but . . .' He looked dismayed. He reached out to put an arm around me. 'Sorry,' he said. 'I didn't mean to upset you. I just want to know everything about you, that's all, and—'

I shut him up with a kiss, full on the mouth. It was time to distract him. I didn't like the way the conversation was heading. My kids were definitely out of bounds as far as Mark was concerned and that was non-negotiable.

'Now then,' I said, in my best businesslike manner. 'Would you like to see what I've got on under this?'

I took his hand and started pulling down the zip of my top.

I leaned forward.

'Not a stitch,' I whispered into his ear. 'Not a fucking stitch.'

Chapter Fourteen

The next morning Lizzie came by unannounced. This was absolutely unheard of. Normally, Lizzie's weeks were planned so meticulously, with Felix booked in to a vast curriculum of different activities – music, gymnastics, swimming, art club, Spanish, pre-primary football etc – every hour of every day that there simply wasn't any available window of time for spontaneous trips out.

I had been putting the kids' coats on ready for a spontaneous trip to the park – my own week being slightly more haphazard – but when I opened the door and saw Lizzie's face, I took them straight off again.

'Come in. What's happened?' I said in alarm.

She stood frozen on the doorstep, not even watching Felix as he crept shyly past me into the front room.

I took her by the arm and led her inside. 'Come on, Liz,' I said. 'Come and sit down. Is this about Steve?'

She nodded, and a single tear rolled down her cheek.

Oh, *no.*

'Molly, why don't you take Felix upstairs to play in your bedroom?' I said in my falsest, brightest voice. 'You could get the farm set out.'

Molly wasn't fooled for a second. 'No. Not go upstairs,' she said. 'We play here.'

'Molly,' I said, my voice edging over into a warning tone. 'Go and play upstairs with the farm.' Seeing her shake her head with such mute doggedness, I caved in pathetically, and added, 'For a chocolate button.'

Felix turned to his mum with a thrilled expression, just as I remembered, too late, the no-sugar rule.

'Oops,' I said apologetically. Oh God, what was I like? Something awful had happened to my sister and I was making a complete mess of her son's healthy, chocolate-button-free diet, just to put the sugar-free icing on the cake. So to speak.

She waved a hand, her eyes numb. 'It's fine. He can have one.'

I gave them a chocolate button each, feeling sick inside. Something truly terrible must have gone on. They'd split up. Steve had left her for Jessica. Jessica was up the duff with his baby. 'Right, off you go then, you two,' I said, shooing our children away. 'And play nicely.'

I put Nathan on the floor at our feet where he rolled over onto his front at once and heaved his bottom in the air in an attempt to move. Oh, great. An early crawler, just what I didn't want.

'So,' I said, grabbing Lizzie's hand. 'Tell me. Did you ask him about Jessica? Is that what's happened?'

'Yes,' she said. Her eyes were red-rimmed and bruised-looking. *Bloody Steve,* I thought furiously. *How dare he do this to her?*

She took a deep breath. 'I asked him about Jessica. He said I was right. He said he was in love with her. He . . .' She swallowed hard, as if the words were too painful to get out. 'He said he doesn't think he's in love with me any more.' Her voice broke as she was saying it. More tears slid down her cheeks, and I put my arms around her. 'He said I'm . . . boring. Our relationship is boring.'

The nerve of the man! 'He said *you're* boring?' I repeated incredulously. '*He* said that about *you*? What an arse!'

She wiped her eyes. 'Apparently Jessica makes him feel like he's twenty-one again,' she went on. *I bet she bloody does,* I thought. 'Whereas he says I make him feel middle-aged.'

This was too much. 'He *is* sodding well middle-aged!' I shouted indignantly. 'For God's sake! He's the most middle-aged person I've ever met!'

She was silent for a moment and I shut my mouth hurriedly. Better not slag the man off too much, I thought. Now was not the best time for complete character assassination.

'So . . . what happens now?' I asked. 'How did you leave

things? Is it . . .' I could hardly bring myself to say the word. 'Over?'

She fiddled with her hands and I noticed her nails were bitten down to the quick. I hadn't seen them like that since we were schoolgirls. Pigtails, acne and bitten nails had been the order of the day. Such ugliness looked all wrong on Lizzie's elegantly shaped hands now. 'We're going to get counselling,' she said wearily. She bowed her head. 'I can't believe it's come to this. It's going to scar Felix for life, I know it is. I've ruined my son's life, Sadie. How can I live with myself, knowing that?'

I rubbed her back. I was starting to feel numb myself. How quickly a perfect life unravels, I was thinking. How fast it all falls apart. 'You have not ruined anybody's life,' I said firmly. 'Get that out of your head at once. You mustn't blame yourself for what Steve is doing. He's the one having a mid-life crisis and getting sweaty hands over Jessica.' She was silent so I went on. 'And Felix is only three. You can keep any horrible stuff well away from him. Children are very resilient.'

She was crying again. 'I don't *want* him to have to be resilient, though,' she wailed. 'That's the thing. He shouldn't have to be! I thought I could protect him from having to be tough at three years old. I don't want him to worry about *anything*, other than which story to choose at bedtime.'

'Oh, *Liz*,' I said sympathetically. 'Felix is going to be fine. It's you I'm worried about.'

'I just don't get it,' she cried. 'I thought we were happy, me and Steve. I've given him everything. I'm a good wife. I look nice, I keep the house clean, I'm bringing up Felix, I . . .' She broke off to blow her nose. 'I've tried so hard to make things work, you know. And he goes and has an affair. I still can't get my head round it, Sadie. What's so bad about his life with me that he has to go and do that?'

I was glad she couldn't see my expression. I've never had much of a poker face and I knew guilt was spreading right across it at her words.

I swallowed hard. 'I don't know, Liz,' I said. 'I really don't know.'

After an hour or so, Lizzie happened to glance up at the clock on the mantelpiece, and a look of panic swept across her face. 'Oh no, we're going to be late for Felix's pottery class,' she gulped, jumping to her feet. She ran to check her reflection in the mirror, whipped out a powder compact and dabbed away all the red blotches around her eyes and nose. 'Felix!' she called up the stairs. 'Time to go, darling.'

I was gawping at her. 'Liz – why don't you stay here this morning?' I asked. 'Stay for lunch. I don't think you should be—'

She shook her head briskly and twizzled up her lipstick.

'No,' she said. 'Thanks, but no. I don't want to upset his routine any more than I have to.'

'Are you sure you feel up to it?' I asked, feeling uncomfortable about letting her leave the house still in a state. To be honest, I didn't want her to even drive when she was still so wobbly and distracted. 'Go on. I've got some pittas we can have for lunch. And cold chicken. And—'

She wasn't listening, just went to the foot of the stairs. 'Felix, come and get your shoes!' she called.

I went after her, desperate to change her mind. 'Or you could leave him here with me for a bit, if you want,' I said. 'Why don't you crash out on our bed for a couple of hours? You look . . .' bloody awful, I thought '. . . so tired,' I finished.

'I'm fine,' she said. 'Honestly.'

I knew there was no budging her. Stubborn old Taurean Lizzie. 'Well, if you change your mind,' I said, conceding the battle. 'You know where we are. Any time. And if you need a babysitter while you go to counselling, then—'

'Thanks,' she said. She forced a smile at her son, who was tramping down the stairs in Molly's princess dress. 'There you are. Don't you look lovely, darling?'

Molly, Nathan and I waved them off. Lizzie was the most careful, sensible driver of the family, and even now, when her life had been tipped upside down, she steered the wheel of their midnight-blue people carrier with the care and precision of a brain surgeon.

'I'll call you tomorrow,' I yelled helplessly, as the car slid away at a safe twenty miles an hour. Then I looked down at my own children's fair innocent heads and shivered. I had the feeling someone was trying to tell me something.

'Let's go to the park before lunch,' I said.

Five minutes or so later, I was still rushing around trying to get everything ready to go when the doorbell rang. Jehovah's Witnesses, rather than the postman with an exciting parcel, I assumed pessimistically, hauling up Nathan and taking him to the front door with me.

'Mummy, Mummy, I come too,' Molly yelled, hurtling after me and all but tripping me up as she flung herself at my legs.

'Well, mind out the way of the door, then,' I said. 'Molly, mind your toes or the door will go right over them . . .'

There was a laugh from the other side of the door, and I froze.

No way, I thought. No *way*. He'd better not have . . .

I opened the front door. He had.

'Hello,' said Mark.

I stared at him, momentarily stunned to see him there on my doorstep in broad daylight, smiling as if this were an everyday call. My mouth opened to speak, then closed. 'I thought I said . . .' I began, my throat feeling dry. 'I thought I . . .'

He was bending down. 'You must be Molly,' he said. 'Hello, sweetie.'

Molly slunk behind my legs. She wasn't a shy child but I knew she'd picked up on my displeasure at our visitor. 'Mummy, who that man?' she asked.

'That man has made a mistake,' I said tightly. 'He's got the wrong house. He's going to go away now.'

'And this must be Nathan,' Mark went on blithely. 'Hello there, fella. Don't you look like your mummy?' He stroked Nathan's pudgy forearm, and my son beamed unknowingly back at him. Hey, kids, this is the man who might just wreck things with Mummy and Daddy, I thought, as my stomach twisted itself into knots. That's who he is! Say hello nicely, now!

Mark straightened up and smiled at me. 'Can I come in?' he asked.

'No, you can't,' I said irritably. Either he just didn't get it, in which case he had to be completely insensitive, or he was trying to wind me up. Neither of which scenarios was at all good. 'We're just about to go out.'

'Can I give you a lift anywhere?' He gestured, and I could see his car parked on the street behind him.

I laughed a hard little laugh. 'I doubt it,' I said, 'unless you've got two new car seats in there.' I patted Molly's head. 'Molls, can you go and get the bag of bread for the ducks, love?'

Of course, being my obedient child, she didn't move a muscle. 'What that man SAYING, Mummy?' she asked, creeping out from behind my legs to get a closer look.

Mark turned his gaze upon her. 'He's saying sorry to your mummy and that maybe he could come round another time?'

I stiffened. 'Don't talk to me through my daughter,' I said. I was clutching Nathan so tightly, he let out a yell and tried to wrestle himself out of my arms. 'Mark, I don't want to discuss this now, in front of my kids. Don't fuck me about,' I said, mouthing the 'fuck' so Molly wouldn't yell it out later at an inopportune moment.

'I thought you liked it when I did that?' he smirked. 'The . . .' He mouthed 'fucking' right back at me.

I glared at him. Shook my head. This was so not the time or the place to talk dirty to me. Did he really not get that?

'I'll ring you later, shall I?' he said.

'No, don't,' I told him. The dog over the road started barking frenziedly, and within about five barks, I had the start of a headache, a tight, pinching band across my forehead.

'What are you saying? That it's over?' he asked.

'Mummy, cuddle me. I want a cuddle, Mummy.'

I picked Molly up so that I had a child in each arm. She pressed her face into my neck. 'I not like that man,' she said loudly.

'I don't want to talk about this on my doorstep,' I said.

'My kids are out of bounds. I thought I'd said as much the other night.'

His eyes glittered with some emotion or other, I couldn't tell what. He didn't reply or move.

'Look,' I said in a kinder tone, 'everything gets too complicated otherwise.' Nathan wedged three fingers into my mouth and beamed at me. I pretended to eat his hand and he giggled.

'Right,' Mark said stiffly. 'I'll go, then. Have a nice birthday. Hope Brighton is sunny for you.' He reached into his pocket. 'Here – I got you this. Open it when you're on your own.'

He held out a small wrapped box. He had to press it right into my fingers, as I was carrying the kids. 'Thanks,' I said. That headache was really kicking in now. I suddenly felt like lying down and falling asleep right there and then, on the hall carpet. 'Listen, I'm sorry I had a go,' I said. 'I just—'

'Don't worry about it,' he replied. 'See you around.'

'See you,' I said. The flood of relief as I shut the door on him left me momentarily speechless. Then I felt nothing but fury.

How dare he come here? How dare he, when I'd said I didn't want him to? The cheek of him! The downright fucking *nerve* of him!

I sat down on the floor and put my arms around the children, leaning my back against the front door. I shoved the present in my pocket. I didn't want to open it. It looked too suspiciously jewellery-box-shaped. I hadn't wanted him to get me anything, hadn't expected it. Why was he so bent on upping the stakes? Why did he have to try to turn this into a relationship, when all I wanted was fun?

Oh, everything's so wonderfully balanced, I had said, smug as anything, to Anna just the day before. *I'm loving it. It's such a kick!*

And yes, things *had* been so wonderfully balanced when they'd stayed in their own separate compartments of my life. But all it took was for Mark to stray over the boundary, and I was left feeling shell-shocked and rattled, and fearful that my house of cards was about to crash down to the ground at any second.

On Friday night, it was Cat and Tom's leaving do. I phoned Lizzie at lunchtime to see whether Steve was going to come with her, or if she wanted to come with Alex and me.

'How are you feeling?' I asked. 'Any new developments?'

She sighed down the phone. 'He was out all last night. Crashed into bed about midnight, stinking of booze. So no, no developments other than I'm feeling really pissed off with him.'

'I'm not surprised,' I told her, shuddering at the thought of scarlet-faced drunk Steve coming anywhere near a bed while I was in it. Talk about a waking nightmare. 'What about tonight, though? You are going to come, aren't you?'

'Of course I am,' she said. 'I've told Steve he can babysit Felix. I don't want him there. Not while all this is going on. And I don't want Cat to know at the moment. I don't want it to spoil her big send-off. And I definitely don't want Mum in the know. You won't say a word to her, will you?'

'God, no, of course not,' I said. Like I would let our mother loose with her marital advice on anyone! Sure, she'd take Lizzie's side in it, but she'd probably track Steve down and attempt to castrate the man. Which, although Steve wasn't in my top ten of fab friends, I wouldn't even wish upon him. 'Right, well, in that case, we'll pick you up about eight, OK?'

Cat and Tom had booked the upstairs room of Tom's local in Hammersmith for the night, and had invited everyone they knew – family, friends, neighbours, work colleagues – to come and say goodbye. There were balloons and streamers everywhere, a twirling glitter ball above the dancefloor and a cheesy DJ who seemed to be stuck in an Eighties time-warp. He was playing 'Kajagoogoo' as we walked in, and Lizzie and I immediately caught each other's eye and burst out laughing. We'd both spent hours working out a dance routine to this song in the bedroom we'd once shared. There was a lot of bum-wiggling and arm-waving as I recalled.

'What do you say, us two on the dancefloor for old times' sake?' I said, nudging her.

She looked over to the empty dancefloor and grimaced. 'I think I'd better have a drink first,' she said. 'Or five.'

Cat came over while we were waiting at the bar. She looked flushed and radiant in a black jersey dress, with a flattering scoop neck showing her ample cleavage, and clingy long sleeves that made her arms look slim and shapely. I felt a bit tearful just to see her. She and Tom were only going away for a month but I was so going to miss her.

'You look gorgeous,' I told her. 'All ready for the off?'

'Just about,' she said. 'Let me get this round. What are you having, all of you?'

'A pint of Stella for Alex,' I said, watching him stroll over to say hello to my dad. He was wearing the stone-coloured crinkly shirt I'd bought him for Christmas, and all of a sudden, it was like watching a stranger. A good-looking stranger, I mused thoughtfully, eyeing up his dark-jeaned bottom.

I dragged my eyes away. 'And . . . er . . . what are we drinking, Liz?'

Lizzie took a deep breath. 'I think, as it's our last night out together for a while, it had better be something special,' she said, trying her hardest to smile.

Cat elbowed her. 'Oi, you, when I said it was my round, I didn't mean . . .'

We all laughed, and Lizzie pulled out a credit card. Steve's gold Amex card. 'My treat,' she said. 'Or rather, my husband's. How about some bubbly?'

'Lovely,' I said.

Cat looked around as if she was only just remembering something. 'What about Steve? What's he having?' she said. 'Let me at least buy the man a pint.'

Lizzie deliberately kept her head towards the bar as she tried to attract the barmaid's attention. 'Oh, sorry, Cat. I meant to say, the babysitter let us down at the last minute, so he's looking after Felix.' She gave the barmaid a dazzling smile and ordered the champers. 'He sends his love, though,' she added to Cat. 'And says . . . er . . . don't forget the postcard.'

'Postcard?' Cat snorted. 'Emails, that's what you'll be getting. If you're lucky.'

She was doing well, Lizzie, I thought as I watched her for a few moments. She looked great, too, in a rose-patterned dress and matching shoes that would have done for Ascot, let alone a grotty west London pub. I couldn't help but wonder if the Amex card had taken an extra beating in the last few days as some form of therapy. Or revenge.

'Cheers,' she said lightly, passing me a champagne glass full of bubbles. 'And cheers to you, Cat. Happy travels.'

'Happy travels,' I echoed, chinking glasses carefully.

Cat's beam was right across her face. 'Here's to us three. Happy days for all of us.'

'Happy days,' Lizzie and I repeated. Her voice was a whisper and I reached down and squeezed her hand. Here's hoping, I thought.

*

Saturday was my birthday. At nine o'clock I was woken up by a beaming face at the side of my bed, tunelessly intoning,

'Happy BURRday to you,
Happy BURRday to you,
Happy BURRday to you,
Happy BURRday to you . . .'

'Happy birthday, gorgeous Sadie, also known as Mummy, happy birthday to you,' Alex finished quickly, obviously fearful that Molly's own song was going to prove to be a never-ending loop.

I blinked and smiled. 'Thank you, sweetheart,' I croaked. 'And you, too, Molly. Ha ha.'

Alex plonked a breakfast tray on the bed, and Molly scrambled up to assist me with it. 'That your toast, Mummy,' she said helpfully, pushing a finger through the middle of it and wearing the top slice like a ring. 'There your cup-a-tea. That your egg. I have your bacon?'

'Go on, then, cheeky.' I laughed, unable to resist the hopeful smile.

Alex was looking incredibly bleary. He'd managed to spend most of the night before embroiled in a heated debate about football with my dad and Nick, which involved lots of drinking and shouting, I recalled.

'Cat and Tom will be heading off to the airport in an

hour,' I said, watching him rub his eyes and sit down heavily on the bed.

'A month in India,' he said wistfully.

'A month in India,' I echoed. Our eyes met. I knew he was thinking about our own time there. He winked at me and I smiled in return.

'Tom-Cat productions go global,' Alex joked. 'Talking of going . . . I was thinking we could head off at eleven or so. Get to Brighton in time for lunch. What do you think?'

'I think that sounds fabulous,' I said, kissing him. 'Now, where are my presents?'

Perhaps I should have guessed, after hearing about Lizzie's relationship problems and then the fact that Becca and Nick's relationship seemed to have turned a touch frosty ('How was Rome?' 'Don't ask'), that there was something in the air that seemed to be wrecking previously harmonious arrangements.

It was either that or sheer old-fashioned bad luck that saw us walking into the Crab and Crayfish restaurant on Brighton seafront, that Saturday lunchtime. We'd taken Molly to the pier and had a few goes at the slot machines, then had wandered down past the arches and the fairground in search of somewhere to eat.

'This is new,' I said, stopping outside one place and peering at their specials board. *Fresh lobster, fresh red snapper, fresh octopus,* the loopy chalk writing read. 'Or rather, it's changed hands since I lived down here. What do you think?'

'I want chips,' Molly said immediately. 'And Ribena. And crisps.'

'How about octopus?' I joked. 'Would you like to eat an octopus?'

'It's your birthday,' Alex said to me. He picked up Molly so she could have a look through the open door. 'You choose.'

'Where the octopus?' Molly asked, searching the restaurant for it.

'I'll choose here, then,' I said, smiling up at him. 'It looks great.'

Suddenly Molly's arm was pointing straight out like a ramrod. 'There that man,' she said excitedly, pointing into the restaurant. 'Mummy not like him. Mummy say, "Don't talk a *me,* man."'

'What's that, darling?' Alex said. I could tell he wasn't really listening, but I was. I had heard. I knew exactly what she was saying and my mouth had fallen open in dismay.

'Mummy shut door. Say, "Go away, man." He say, "Hello sweetie," like that, Daddy.'

'Mmmm.' Luckily for me, Alex was scanning the room for a free table and not really paying attention. I was also scanning the room, but for different reasons. Praying Molly had got muddled up and . . .

'Alex? Alex!'

A slim arm waved above the table like an elegant reed in the wind. Light glinted from the silver bangle watch around the wrist.

Oh, shit.

Shit, shit, shit, shit, shit. Molly hadn't got muddled up. Eagle-eyed Molly had just seen . . .

'Julia!' Alex's voice was a gasp of surprise. 'What are you doing here? Look, Sadie. Look who's here! Hello again, Mark.'

We stepped into the restaurant and it felt like a very bad dream. Surely it couldn't be a coincidence that Mark and Julia happened to be in Brighton, too. What the *hell* were they doing here? For a split second I thought that Alex must have somehow set us up. He'd got wind of it. He'd . . .

But no. I knew what the truth was, really. I knew *exactly* what they were doing here. Mark's idea, no doubt. *Darling, why don't we pop down to the coast for the day*? he'd have said this morning, as if the thought had just materialized in his head.

What was he playing at now?

'Look, Mummy, it's that man. You say, don't talk a *me*, man.'

'Let's get you a high chair,' I said on automatic pilot. Shock waves thudded through me, one after another, after another.

Oh. My. God.

SHIT.

'Come and join us,' Julia said at once. 'How funny! Typical, isn't it – you get out of London and London comes with you. How are you both?'

'Fine,' I said quietly. I didn't look at Mark. Couldn't bring myself to. I felt so fucking . . . angry with him. No, not just angry. Angry didn't come anywhere near describing it. I was *incandescent*. He was playing with me. Trying to throw me by putting me in this awful, ridiculous, downright *farcical* situation.

Alex was wheeling the buggy over to their table. No, I thought, panicking, no, no, no. I couldn't do it. I couldn't sit across the table from Mark and chit-chat, and pretend that we were polite strangers, with Molly piping up every five minutes about 'that man'.

Actually, forget 'couldn't'. I just wouldn't. It was my birthday after all. Sod it.

'I hope you don't mind, but this is a bit of a family occasion,' I said sweetly. 'There's a table over there by the window, look, Alex. Sorry, Julia. I'm not being rude. It's my birthday and—'

'Oh.' From her expression, she obviously thought I *was* being rude. Not good enough to sit with your husband's – sorry, your *partner's* – boss now, are you? 'Oh, right. Well. Happy birthday,' she said insincerely.

'Happy birthday,' echoed Mark.

I still refused to look at him. Wanker. Idiot. It was all a

big game to him, wasn't it? A big, funny, fucking game. He had nothing to lose except his crappy, stuck-up wife – big deal – whereas I had everything to lose. Everything.

'Thanks,' I said dully, turning away. I remembered the present he'd given me, which was still unopened back at our house. Stupid bloody idiot. I would throw it away. I wasn't interested.

'Hey, we were just saying the other day, weren't we, Sadie, that we'll have to sort a date out for you two to come over to us,' Alex said gamely, trying to repair the damage.

I pretended I hadn't heard and started fussing around at our table, getting a high chair for Molly and suchlike. The smell of frying fish was starting to make me feel nauseous. I wished and wished we had walked past the Crab and Crayfish. Wished we were somewhere else so that I could have stayed in my jolly birthday day tripper mood. Instead, I just felt like launching myself off the pier in despair.

I had my back to Julia and Mark's table and so I didn't have to look at them throughout our meal. I made sure Molly couldn't see them either. The less she said about 'that man', the better. It was only when I saw Alex raise a hand in goodbye that I turned and waved and smiled as enthusiastically as I could at Julia – she was Alex's boss after all. It was only then, when I knew they'd gone, that I could start to relax.

'What do you want to do for the rest of the day, then, birthday girl?' Alex asked. 'Sunbathing and swimming, yeah?'

It was dull and cloudy outside, so patently *not* sunbathing weather that I laughed. It was good to laugh again. 'How about a stroll around the shops and coffee bars before you show me which little love-nest hotel we're booked in to?' I said, patting his hand affectionately.

He pulled himself up proudly. For a moment, I thought he was going to burp, but it turned out he just had an announcement to make. 'Actually, I've got a surprise about our hotel,' he said.

I couldn't help smiling at him. He was so bloody delighted with himself, whatever he'd arranged. 'And what's that, then?'

'Call me thoughtful,' he started grandly, 'call me considerate—'

'I'll call you a cab home in a minute, if you don't tell me,' I interrupted.

'I call you DADDY,' Molly told him, and we both laughed.

'Whatever you want to call me, ladies,' he went on, 'I'd just like it to be known that—'

I groaned. 'What?! Get to the point!'

'That I've booked us *two* rooms at the hotel,' he said. He paused, enjoying my frown. 'One room just for us, Alex and

Sadie. One room for the kids . . . and your mum. Our babysitter.'

I gaped at him. One room just for . . .

'Say that again,' I ordered. 'My mum's down here?'

He nodded. 'Yep. We're meeting her at the station in . . .' He looked at his watch. 'In half an hour. It was partly her idea,' he admitted. 'So we can have a night out together tonight – and a lie-in together tomorrow morning.' He grinned. 'So what do you say to that, Ms Morrison?'

'Oh, Alex!' It was the best birthday present he could have given me. 'You are such a superstar. Thank you. Thank you!'

It's Alex, I thought joyfully, throwing my arms around his neck. *I'm going to choose Alex. Of course I'm going to choose Alex. How could I have ever doubted that choice?*

It was as if the clouds had cleared right away and the sun was shining straight into my face, dazzling me with its light.

Chapter Fifteen

The rest of the weekend passed relatively smoothly and happily. Still, I suppose after trying to eat lunch while both my long-term partner and my lover were under the same roof, with my daughter valiantly trying to grass me up at any opportunity, anything would have seemed smooth and happy. Re-sitting my finals without a moment's revision would have seemed a doddle in comparison.

We met my mum at the station, before checking into our hotel – four-poster bed with sea views for Alex and me. I was unable to switch off my looking-for-Mark radar as we walked there, which meant me twitching my head from side to side repeatedly in a nervous kind of way, but so far, there had been no further sightings. From being the person I had physically ached to see again, he had metamorphosed into a character of almost pantomime-villain-type sinisterness.

Mark, you've blown it, I kept thinking. You tried to be too clever and get too close, and now you've blown it. First there had been the story about Covent Garden. Then that whole thing with Caroline in the pub. Now this. It was too much.

Having said which, although the rational part of me was starting to think that enough was enough, the emotional side of me felt like I was being stabbed in the guts every time I even considered ending things with Mark. If I so much as imagined myself saying the words to his face, I wanted to collapse with pain and weep.

What was it Anna had said? *You can't carry on with both of them for ever. Sooner or later, something's got to give. One of them will have to go.* So it seemed. I couldn't carry on with the lies. They were starting to wear me down.

After leaving our bags at the hotel, Alex took the kids off down to the beach while Mum and I hit the shops. Alex had bravely volunteered to come shopping with me, but I knew that would involve him sitting *outside* the actual shops, reading the paper and complaining that I was taking ages. Or, if by some miracle I actually managed to drag him into a shop, he would say that he liked absolutely every garment I picked up with a single cursory glance over it in the vain hope that I would hurry up and buy something, oh, and could we pop into a bookie's now to check the half-time football scores?

Sadly, these were not qualities that I looked for in a shopping companion. In fact, shopping alone was way, way preferable to shopping with bored, complaining Alex.

My mum, on the other hand, had more stamina than a

Sherpa when it came to battling through a mall. She had excellent taste and could spot a bargain from twenty paces, plus she'd just received a new credit card that she was dying to whack some purchases on to.

Two hours and mucho purchasing later, we both needed a skinny latte and a sit-down. Mum had just bought a new handbag from a rather swanky boutique we'd stumbled upon, and was already fretting about the price.

'So if your dad asks, it was twenty pounds in the sale, all right?' she instructed me. She leaned back in her chair and stretched her legs out. 'Oh, I just know what he's going to say when he sees it. He won't notice its lovely shape, or how glossy it is, or how well cut the leather is. He'll say, "Mary, you've already *got* a bag. Why in God's name do you need another one?"'

I shook my head and sipped my coffee. 'They don't get it, do they?' I said, patting my carrier bags happily. 'They just have no idea.'

'"Mary, you've already *got* a pair of shoes,"' she went on, warming to her theme, and imitating Dad's Belfast accent to a T. '"Why in God's name do you need another pair?"'

I slipped into broad Leeds to mimic Alex. 'Sadie, you've already got a T-shirt. Why the fook do you need another?'

We were both giggling by now. 'Next time he says it – tomorrow, I bet you – I'm going to remind him, Ted, you've already seen one football match. "Why in God's name do you need to watch another one?"' she joked.

I sniggered. 'Yeah, and I'll say, Alex, you've already *got* one newspaper. Why the fook do you need to read another one?'

'Exactly,' Mum said. Then, as a cheerful, green-eyed waitress laughed about something at the next table, her expression turned wistful. 'I wonder what Catherine's doing now,' she said. 'Will they have landed yet, do you think?'

I checked my watch. 'Probably not,' I said. 'I can't believe she's gone, Mum. I know it's not for very long, but . . .'

'I know. I feel the same,' Mum said before I could get the sentence out. 'My little baby girl, half the way around the world.'

I fiddled with my cup and saucer. Should I say something about Lizzie? Or should I keep schtum? The waitress was laughing about something else now, and the memory of Lizzie's pale-faced misery opened my mouth for me. 'Actually, Mum, I think Lizzie could do with getting away from it all too, you know,' I confided. 'Have you spoken to her lately?'

'A quick chat last night at Catherine's party, but not properly. Why? What's wrong?'

There was a difficult line to tread when it came to Mum and passing on sisterly gossip. I wouldn't tell her everything – she'd be too worried, for starters, not to mention the fact that she would also be inclined to go straight over to Balham and wallop Boring Steve in the nads with her handbag, before she'd even got to the truth of the matter. Yet, at the same time, as a parent myself, I couldn't bear the idea of one of my children being miserable and my not knowing about it. I felt duty-bound to at least point her in the right direction.

'She seems a bit down at the moment, that's all,' I said in the end. 'You know what she's like, though – she never says much.'

'No.' Mum pursed her lips thoughtfully. 'Tell you what, I'll pop round in the week and take Felix off her hands for a while, so she can go and do something nice. Or perhaps she can tell me what's bothering her.'

I grinned at her. 'That's a good idea. She'd love that. In fact, I'll drop my two off as well – you can set up a crèche, Mum.'

'I'd have them like a shot, Sadie – seriously! Any time, you know that. I love being with them. They're so *good*, your two, aren't they?'

As she squeezed my hand across the table, the thought that leaped unbidden into my head was: Mark. I could leave the kids with Mum and sneak out to . . .

Then, the stab in the guts again. No, I couldn't. Absolutely not! Hadn't I just been thinking that I would choose Alex? How could I have forgotten what had just happened?

I had to break the habit of Mark. Had to get him out of my head. I was horrified that I had even gone along that thought path in the first place.

The ringing tone of my mobile jerked me out of my turmoil.

'Where are you now? We've thrown just about all the pebbles on the beach into the sea now, and Molly's had three goes on the little train. How's the shopping?'

'We're having a break in Daniella's,' I said. 'Come and meet us; you can admire all the things we've bought.' I winked at my mum, and started giving Alex directions.

After Alex had rung off, I noticed I had a new text message. From Mark.

I opened it up, my mouth suddenly dry.

Sorry, Sadie, I read. **So very sorry. I love you. Mark xxx**

'What did he say?' my mum wanted to know.

'What?' I replied, dragging my eyes away from the words. 'Who?'

She was smiling across the table at me. No. She didn't mean Mark. Calm down.

Sorry, Sadie. So very sorry. I love you.

How could he even say that? How could he say that he loved me when he'd just put me through that whole charade in the restaurant?

'Alex, you great nelly.' She laughed. 'Remember him?'

I deleted Mark's message and stuffed the mobile back in my bag. 'He's coming to meet us,' I said, trying to cast my mind back to the phone conversation we'd had. Somehow it seemed hours ago. 'He sounds absolutely knackered.'

She caught my eye and we both laughed. 'Bless him,' she said fondly. 'You've got a good one there, Sadie. Wasn't it lovely of him to sort all this out?' She waved a hand across the coffee bar, obviously intending to take in the whole of Brighton, plus her, plus our hotel. 'You've got a good one there,' she repeated. 'Of the three of you girls – I probably shouldn't say this, but bugger it,' she said, in a confidential manner. 'Of the three of you girls, I feel happiest with the relationship you and Alex have got. Two equals, that's what you are. You're a good team.'

Sorry, Sadie. So very sorry. I love you.

'Oh, thanks, Mum, that's a lovely thing to say,' I told her, finishing the rest of my coffee so I didn't have to look her in the eye. If only she knew. Or rather, thank God she didn't know. If she knew, it would probably be me on the receiving end of the handbag walloping. And that would be just for starters.

There was another text message that evening. Then another. Alex had taken me to dinner at Edward's, which was, according to someone he worked with, the coolest place to be seen in Brighton. It was hidden away in a row of Georgian terraces the far side of Kemp Town and, unless you were in the know, you wouldn't have looked twice at the outside.

Inside, the bar was cosy and intimate. It was the front room of the house, so perhaps had once been a drawing room or a dining room for the family that had lived here one hundred or more years before. Now, there were large painted canvases on the walls and a long, high, chocolate-brown sofa that ran around the entire left side of the room as you walked in, with small square tables and caramel-coloured suede cubes lined up in front.

The bar itself had an enormous mirror behind it, glass shelves, and subtle back-lighting. The whole effect was like something from *Sex and the City*. Of course, to sit there without ordering a Cosmopolitan would have been unthinkable.

I'd taken my phone along for Mum's benefit, with the promise that if she had any problem getting the kids off to sleep, she just had to ring, and I would jump in a taxi and sort them out, pronto. Alex and I had just settled into a good people-watching spot in front of the bay window, when there was a familiar-sounding bleep.

'Is that your mobile?' Alex asked. He sniffed suspiciously at the lurid purple cocktail he'd randomly selected from the menu.

'Yeah, hang on,' I said.

I am so sorry, I read. **I made a mistake.**

'Is it your mum? Should I go back?' Alex wanted to know.

'No,' I said, deleting it quickly before he could lean over

my shoulder and have a look. Go away, Mark. 'It's just a text from Becca to say happy birthday,' I lied.

Hey, slick. I shoved the phone back in my bag. 'What were we talking about? Weren't you saying something about how great my new top looked?'

He smirked and looked straight at my tits. 'It looks very, very great,' he said.

'Very, very great?' I repeated. 'Call yourself a sub-editor? What sort of a compliment is that?'

He sniggered. 'Sorry,' he said. 'You're absolutely right. I was so transfixed by the elegance and beauty of the stitching that—'

I elbowed him. 'No, you weren't. You were looking at my tits.'

He held up his hands. A fair cop, guv. 'All right, all right. But show me a straight man who wouldn't. They look absolutely spectacular. In fact . . .'

His hand hovered dangerously close to my chest, and I squeaked and ducked back quickly. Overt boob-grabbing was probably not the thing to do in Edward's. 'Oi,' I said. 'Save that for later.'

'Go on,' he teased. 'Just a quick squeeze. No one will notice.'

'They bloody will,' I told him primly, edging back even further. 'Keep both hands on the table, please. And one foot on the floor at all times.'

'Sorry,' he said, taking a tentative swig of his cocktail. 'Bloody hell. Think I'll stick to lager next time. Now, going back to your breasts. It's just that no-bra thing, that's all. Somehow they look bigger than usual. And it's the way that they . . . move when you walk. Or when you laugh. Actually, they move when you do anything, now that I come to think about it.'

'What, and you seriously expect me to believe that you weren't thinking about it before?' I folded my hands across my chest and did my best to look stern. He was practically dribbling at the way the conversation was going.

He sighed melodramatically, one hand clapped to his forehead. 'God, I tell you what, Sade,' he said, 'we're going to have to stop talking about your boobs, or I'll have to drag you down to the beach for a quick how's-your-father before we've even ordered our starter.'

'Let's talk about Mrs Thatcher instead,' I put in quickly. 'That should cool your ardour.'

'Is that your phone going again?' he said.

'God, it is as well,' I grumbled. 'Anyone would think it was my birthday or something.' I felt a quick flip of panic as I pulled it out of my bag. Was Mark going to keep this up all night? I wouldn't even be able to switch the wretched thing off, as I needed to keep the line open for Mum.

Sadie, I'm going mad. Pls tell me u forgive me.

'Lizzie this time, saying happy birthday blah blah,' I lied, feeling my cheeks flush with the mixture of deceit and alcohol.

Alex stood up, rather awkwardly, I couldn't help noticing. 'Just going to the gents,' he said.

I was so relieved to have a minute to myself that I refrained from making any jokes about him going for an Armitage Shank.

'OK,' I said. I watched him go, then frantically started texting Mark back.

OK. C U Monday. Don't txt again.

I glanced at the message. Shit, the 'C U Monday' looked horribly like 'CUM on' at first glance. I deleted the whole thing, started again.

OK. It's cool. Don't txt again.

I pressed Send just as Alex came back, and then slid the phone back into my bag.

'Alex and Sadie? Your table's ready,' said a man who looked so art-house and trendy it was hard to believe he was actually a waiter.

Alex took my arm and in we went.

Brighton had been so fresh and lively and fun – birthday lunches aside – that I was gutted to pack up our things and go home on the Sunday. The meal had been delicious: carefully stacked towers of treats on enormous white plates, circled perfectly by hard-to-pronounce sauces. The four-poster had been sexy: my wrists were still chafed and red-ringed from some over-enthusiastic tying up. Hell, the kids had even been well behaved for my mum. The whole weekend had been a blast of sea air into our London-choked lungs.

Leaving was a wrench. The smell of the car was enough to make me feel physically sick before Alex had even started up the engine. There was something about returning to London that I always found vaguely depressing. Perhaps it was the volume of traffic, even on a Sunday, the long, slow haul through the Croydon stretch of the A23 and all the stressed-out Sunday IKEA shoppers queuing up for miles. Perhaps it was the way that litter blew across the road in front of us whenever we stopped at traffic lights, the way that people leaned in doorways clutching their cans of Special Brew with nowhere else to go. Perhaps it was the narrowing of the streets, the dirt on the pavements, the gangs of hard-faced kids scowling out from under their hooded tops as we drove to our road after dropping off Mum. Suddenly Brighton, with its wide, far-reaching skies, the slow ssshhh of the grey waves onto the pebbled beach, and the bright lights on the pier, seemed very far away.

'Back to reality,' Alex commented, parking the car.

'Mmmm,' I said, glancing up at the front of our house and noticing just how grimy the windows were. 'You can say that again.'

The phone started ringing almost as soon as we'd got in and I made a run for it, still holding Nathan. I was worried that it would be Mark again. After the last couple of days, nothing would have surprised me. In fact, it was rather a relief to see he wasn't camped out on our front doorstep.

'Hiya, Sadie – happy birthday for yesterday!'

'Cat!' I glanced at the photo of her on our mantelpiece in surprised delight. It was a picture that had been taken a couple of Christmases ago of me, Lizzie and Cat all wearing party hats and looking pink-cheeked and tipsy. 'It's so fab to hear your voice! I wasn't expecting you to ring. Where are you?'

'We're here, we're in Goa. Got in last night, Indian time. The hotel's so sweet. I wasn't going to ring for a few days, but I've got some news and I just couldn't wait to tell you.'

'What? What's the news?' I hoisted Nathan higher on my shoulder, pressing my face against him. I knew. I already knew from the way her words were bubbling excitedly down the phone line. My face was splitting into a smile before she'd even told me.

'I'm pregnant! I can't believe it, Sadie – it was a bit of an accident to be honest – I found out in the ladies' toilets at bloody Heathrow airport, can you believe? Bought a test kit from Boots and . . . I was late, you see, you know me, never late. And anyway, I did that whole weeing on the white stick thing, and yeah, I'm pregnant! We're going to have a baby!'

'Oh, *Cat*.' I could hardly speak, I felt so choked up with emotion. 'I'm so pleased for you. So very brilliantly pleased! That is such amazing news! How are you feeling?'

'Fine.' The phone crackled and I missed her next words. '. . . massive, swollen boobs, I can hardly bear to have a shower because even the water splashing on them feels so sore.'

'Yeah, I remember that one. Ouch.'

'And Tom is so excited, and we've just told our parents – I mean, Mum and Dad and his parents and . . . God. I can't believe I'm going to be a mum. Me! Aaargh!' She laughed, thousands and thousands of miles away. 'And I can't even get plastered on the cheap booze out here now!'

'What a nightmare,' I joked. 'Oh, that is so fab. I'm just made up for you, Cat. Wow. So you must be due . . .'

'November, I think. I'm not sure. Too stunned to work it out. Oh – listen, better go. Running out of time.'

'Take care of yourself then. Thanks so much for ringing. I'll—'

The phone went dead then and I held it to my ear for just a few more seconds, in case there was a sudden reconnection before I put the receiver down. Wow. Cat and Tom having a baby. It was enough to get me clucky all over again, with Nathan barely six months old. I smelled his hair, rubbed his cheek against mine. 'Lovely, lovely boy,' I murmured, before striding out to the hall to find Alex. 'Hey, guess what?'

It wasn't until later that evening, when I was lying in a bath feeling increasingly irritated by the awful bitch-in the-boardroom rant of a book I was supposed to be reading for Lizzie's book group, that several pennies started to drop.

Clatter, clatter, clatter.

I had been absent-mindedly thinking about Cat's baby news when I remembered what she'd said about her boobs. What was it? Something about them being massive and swollen and sore.

Then I thought about Alex's comment about how big my own boobs had looked in my new top.

Clatter.

I remembered the achey cramp I'd had last week, that I'd put down to period pain. Yet my period still hadn't started.

Clatter.

I remembered how the smell of fish at the Crab and Crayfish restaurant had made me want to heave, and how sick I'd felt that morning. And then, with a horrible thudding feeling inside, I remembered all those times I'd had sex without contraception. Not just with Alex. With Mark, too.

Clunk.

CLUNK.

I threw the dreary book onto the bathroom floor and tried to weigh my breasts with my hands. Did they feel heavier? Were they bigger? Did they look at all swollen? Fuck. *FUCK.* How did they feel normally? I couldn't even think, my brain was buzzing away so frenziedly, speeding off at different tangents every second.

I took a deep breath and tried the weighing thing again. It was hard to tell in the water so then I sat up, one boob in each hand, and tried to gauge their feel.

Of course, at that very moment, Alex walked into the bathroom. 'Wa-hey,' he said, his eyes bulging in lusting delight at the sight of me wet and naked with a hand under each breast.

'Can't you knock?' I asked crossly, plunging under the water again.

'Sorry,' he said. He was still grinning. He held out the phone. 'For you. If it's not a bad time, obviously. Shall I give you a few minutes to finish yourself off?'

Alarm at who was on the end of the line just about stopped me from slapping him and telling him to piss off. I grabbed the phone instead and made 'Get lost' motions with my other hand.

'Hello?'

There was a sniff from the other end of the phone.

'Lizzie, is that you?' I asked. Oh, no. She'd given Boring Steve his marching orders. She was a single parent, having pushed him out of the house and straight into Jessica's arms. She . . .

'No, it's me. Becca.' She sounded so doleful I hardly recognized her voice.

'Becca! Have you got a cold? I was going to ring you

tonight,' I said. There was a pause. 'What's up? Are you all right?'

She sighed heavily. 'Me and Nick have split up,' she said. 'It's all over. After one bloody month.' She sniffed again. 'Why are men such a nightmare? Why can't I find one I want to be with for longer than a bloody month? It's the same old thing every time. What am I doing wrong?'

Of course. I remembered now. The 'Don't ask' Rome trip hadn't sounded terribly promising. 'Oh, darlin',' I said sympathetically. 'What happened?'

She told me about the bickering and how tight-fisted he was and how he was always eyeing up other women and it drove her crazy and . . . well, about twenty minutes' worth of other stuff, with a thesaurus-worthy list of damning adjectives about him.

'So anyway, enough moaning,' she said in the end, when my ear was hot with having the phone pressed against it. I heard her inhaling a deep yogic breath. 'Time to forget all about Nobby Nick.'

'Absolutely,' I said, as cheeringly as I knew how. 'You can do better than that.'

'Yeah. I can,' she agreed. 'You know, I am really desperate for a good girls' night out on the town,' she went on. 'Desperate. When can we do it?'

The hand that wasn't holding the phone to my ear slid

across my belly. The belly that was still a bit on the saggy side from being pregnant with Nathan. The belly that . . .

'Um . . . I'll check with Alex,' I said. 'Can I ring you back tomorrow?'

'Yeah, great,' she said. 'I'll ring around a couple of others, try and get some more of the old crowd out. We can have a bit of a girly reunion, doll ourselves up to the nines, drink dodgy spirits all night and go and dance round our handbags somewhere.'

'Look forward to it,' I said loyally, my eyes fixed on my belly all the while. Oh God. 'Talk to you tomorrow. And sorry to hear about Nick. Go round to the offy and get yourself some wine and chocolate at once.'

She sighed. 'Yeah. The old stand-bys.' She sounded sad again. 'We'll always have wine and chocolate. Anyway. Thanks for listening, Sadie. Bye.'

I pressed the button to switch the phone off and lay there in the water, quite, quite still, trying to ignore the doubt that was creeping through my mind. Listen, I told myself firmly, your period is only a day or so late. Big deal. And besides, it's bound to be a bit skewed at first, starting up after pregnancy and birth, isn't it? Now that I thought about it, I was sure that things had been a bit irregular after Molly, too. Yeah. Actually, I was *convinced* my periods had been irregular for a while afterwards. Same as now. Why was I even expecting them to fall back into a routine, like clockwork?

I was imagining it all, just because of Cat's news. A kind of sympathetic pregnancy, if you like. I was worse than a man!

Besides, it was far too soon to be . . .

No, it would just be unfair if I was . . .

I absolutely couldn't even think about being . . .

I pulled the plug out of the bath, stood up and dried myself roughly. I would stop thinking about it. I would pull on my dressing gown, go downstairs and sterilize all of Nathan's bottles for tomorrow, clean the kitchen, watch drossy Sunday night TV, flick through the *Observer* and forget that the thought had even crossed my mind.

What thought? Exactly.

For the whole of the next week, I tried to go through the motions without dwelling on the thought that was too terrible to be named. I saw Mark on Monday, which I had been alternately dreading and planning to bottle out of. On the evening itself, I decided that the no-show option was just too cowardly, and that instead, I should go round and tell him exactly how I felt. Which is what I did. Well, what I tried to do, anyway.

The thing was, before I could launch into my carefully rehearsed 'I am so-o-o mad with you, what the hell were you playing at?' speech, he got in first and apologized. Profusely. I then gave him a toned-down version of the 'I am so-o-o mad with you etc' speech, and he said he'd never pull a stunt like that again. Actually, he promised, hand on heart, the works. There's nothing like a man with a sincere look in his come-to-bed eyes to make me waver.

That was the point at which I had planned to tell him, kindly but firmly, that things weren't working out and we should probably stop seeing each other. Yet somehow or other, we had a kiss and a cuddle instead, just to make friends. And then, somehow or other, the kiss and cuddle swiftly turned into passionate, gasping sex on his office floor.

As he held me afterwards, he whispered, 'I love you so much,' into my ear, and even though I tried my damnedest not to listen – I did try, I really did – the words made my blood sing around my body. At least I didn't say it back to him. I hadn't quite forgiven him enough to say it back to him. Those three little words were still for Alex's ears only.

I had brought along the as-yet-unwrapped present he'd given me, originally intending to coolly return it to him without even opening it, but the passionate, gasping, I-love-you-so-much sex had changed my mind somewhat and I opened it, half-dressed, sitting on his knee. It was such a gorgeous silver bangle with such an elegant curve to it that I felt I simply had to show him my appreciation all over again.

After that, I decided to forget about the whole 'choosing Alex or choosing Mark' decision for the time being. Yeah, Mark had been out of order. I had been angry with him, furious even, but the problem was, I couldn't bear to say goodbye to him. He still made me feel so dizzy and euphoric. And anyway, he'd apologized *and* promised never to play games with me ever again. Hopefully the status quo was about to return.

It was a similar story on Wednesday. We just stayed safely in his office and had a quick burst of rude and satisfying sex and a laugh about something stupid or other, before I went back home to my children and Alex, and he went back to his wife. It was OK again. In fact, it was more than OK again. We both knew where we stood. Or knelt. Or lay. Or . . . Well, whatever.

I was feeling so much better about being able to juggle both men successfully without dropping either of them, and so happy that Mark had dropped his pantomime-villain stalker tendencies, that I even arranged for my mum to look after the kids on Thursday afternoon. Then I called Mark and persuaded him to skive work and take me to Richmond Park for a spontaneous date. It was exhilarating to be holding hands with him in the park, in the fresh air and sunshine, and I quite forgot I had a single care in the world.

It wasn't until Friday, when my period was a whole week late, that reality slammed up against me. Much as I was loath to do so, it was time to face facts. Actually, for the first time since the weekend, I felt confident about it. I had had a crampy feeling all morning and was sure that the late arrival was at last on its way. So I would do a test, just to confirm the happy news, and then, once I knew I was in the clear, I would devote myself to being the most careful contraceptive user in the world. This would never have to happen again.

I took the kids shopping in the morning and, when I was sure that nobody I knew was within a half-mile radius of the chemist, or at least within view, I picked up a home pregnancy test kit and paid for it, with all the fake casualness of a virgin buying condoms for the first time. Hey. It was no big deal. I was probably going to get my period any moment now and I would have wasted a tenner. I'd be laughing about it with Anna in a couple of days' time.

For all that, though, the pregnancy test kit felt like a lead weight in my handbag; I was aware of its presence with every single step I took home. I rushed through making the kids' lunch. Baked beans for Molly, bunged straight in the microwave – there you go, sweetheart. Defrosted veggie mush I'd made for Nathan the week before – spoonful, spoonful, spoonful, wipe faces and hands, time for a nap. Off you pop!

When at last the house was quiet and all that I could hear was the sound of my own fast breathing, I walked quickly to my bag, took the test kit from it, stealthily, like a thief, and went straight up to the bathroom with it. No going back now. Oh God. This was the moment of reckoning, all right. Pregnancy test. Two of the most monumental words that had ever related to me. Apart from, perhaps, 'Tena Lady'.

Cat's words echoed around my head, taunting me.

Bought a test kit from Boots and . . . I was late, you see, you know me, never late. And anyway, I did that whole weeing on the white stick thing, and yeah, I'm pregnant! We're going to have a baby!

OK. Do it. Just do it. I opened the box and ripped off the foil wrapper, my fingers shaking so much I could hardly pull the stick out. I read the instructions. Like I didn't know what I had to do.

WITH THE TIP POINTING DOWNWARDS, HOLD THE ABSORBENT SAMPLER IN YOUR URINE STREAM FOR 5 SECONDS ONLY.

Oh, bloody *hell.* I couldn't believe I was doing this again. It had only been just over a year since the last time I'd had to do it. Why hadn't I *insisted* on using condoms? Why had I been so half-arsed about the whole thing?

I did what the instructions told me to do and waited for the result.

CHECKING THAT THE TEST HAS WORKED:
A BLUE LINE SHOULD APPEAR IN THE **SMALL** WINDOW, AS SHOWN IN PICTURE ONE. THIS INDICATES THAT THE TEST IS COMPLETE AND HAS WORKED CORRECTLY.
IF THERE IS A BLUE LINE IN THE **LARGE** WINDOW,

AS SHOWN IN PICTURE TWO, YOU ARE PREGNANT.
EVEN IF THIS LINE IS FAINTER THAN THE ONE IN THE SMALL WINDOW, IT STILL MEANS THAT YOU ARE PREGNANT.
IF THERE IS NO BLUE LINE IN THE **LARGE** WINDOW, AS SHOWN IN PICTURE THREE, YOU ARE NOT PREGNANT.

I stared at the stick and watched a blue line appear in the small window. OK. Blue line in the small window was fine. That just meant the test had worked. Don't panic.

Then I stared and stared at the large window until my eyes ached in their sockets. Please don't let a blue line appear. Oh please, God, please, *please* don't let there be a blue line.

I sat there on the edge of the bath and watched as, slowly but surely, a blue line appeared in the large window, pale and hardly there at first, so that I blinked and thought it was a trick of the light. I held my breath and watched as it darkened and thickened until there was absolutely no doubt left in my mind whatsoever.

Chapter Sixteen

I was five weeks pregnant. Things were happening inside me that were completely out of my control. Cells were splitting and multiplying, my uterus was thickening, extra blood was coursing around me as my body revved up to set the whole process in motion, all over again.

A third baby.

A mother of three.

With every heartbeat, the secret hidden inside me was growing bigger and stronger. Bigger and stronger.

I sat on the edge of the bath for a long time, trying not to cry. This was so, so wrong. It was so badly, painfully wrong for so many different reasons, I couldn't even begin to think about them. Alex, Mark, me . . . The eternal triangle had become an eternal *quadrilateral* now that there was an extra character in the picture. The lines between us all had blurred and tangled without a chance of repair now. I had fucked everything up beyond all recognition, as somebody had once said.

I stared at the white tester stick again. Could there be a mistake? Could there be something wrong with the test? I twisted the stick this way and that, hoping it was an optical illusion, but no. All I could see were the twin blue lines, accusing me in their symmetry. Pregnant, pregnant, pregnant.

It was horribly ironic. I'd loved the discovery of both of my previous pregnancies, had rushed straight to consult the books by Miriam Stoppard and Sheila Kitzinger, and all the other childbirth gurus, as soon as I'd found out the wonderful news each time. I had devoured great volumes of information, charted my (our) development week by week, month by month, monitored everything I ate or drank or did with the solemnity of a religion. I revised for it harder than I had done for my A levels, thought of nothing else.

Oh, and I'd simply sailed through the nine months confidently and easily both times, with none of the morning sickness or backache or diabetes that my friends complained of. It had made me feel important – quick, pregnant woman, get her a chair, let her sit down, can we get you anything, pet? – oh, I'd just loved all that. Loved the strangers coming up to me predicting the sex of my hidden babe, wanting to pat my proudly blooming belly.

The difference was, they had been wanted pregnancies. Yearned-for, hoped-for, planned pregnancies.

This one was a cuckoo in the wrong nest. The changeling in the womb. The child I wasn't ready to bear, the child whose father's identity I couldn't even name with any certainty. Oh, God. It sounded so awful when I thought of it like that. It made me feel like someone from *Trisha. Who's the daddy?* the strapline would read across the screen. *Sadie's pregnant – but who's the daddy?*

Alex was going to *kill* me when I told him I was up the stick again. Or, if he managed not to kill me, he'd leave me. He was going to be totally and utterly pissed off when he heard the news. I could picture the look of horror that would spread across his face, could almost hear him blurting out, 'Oh, *no*,' when I told him. He had said, plain and simple, *Two is enough for me, thanks,* hadn't he? I mean, how unequivocal could you get? He might even try to talk me into having an abortion, flushing the thing out of me before it had a chance to develop its vital organs.

I shut my eyes and crossed my arms around myself protectively at the thought. No. Whatever the complications, I knew that I didn't want that. But how the hell was I going to break the news to him?

As for Mark . . . he would know, he would just *know* if I told him I was pregnant. He wasn't stupid, he could work out dates. And let's face it, Mark was longing to have a child, wasn't he? It was his great sorrow that Julia didn't seem interested in starting a family. If I told Mark he was going to be a father, that we were going to have a baby, he would . . .

I put my head in my hands. He would be over the moon.

The most wonderful gift I could have given him. He would probably leave Julia for it, and . . .

Hold on. Stop.

Stop, stop, stop, stop, STOP.

I didn't want to get into thinking about that stuff. That was another thought for another day. I didn't have to tell anybody anything just yet; I would work out what to do later. In the meantime, I would sit on my secret and wait for it to hatch. Right now, though, I needed lunch. Eating for two again, eh? No wonder I had been so hungry all the time lately.

I went downstairs and made three rounds of thickly buttered toast. Then I sat down at the kitchen table and sobbed as if my heart was broken.

Come Saturday, the thought of meeting up with Danny at his mum's birthday party seemed just about the worst night out it was possible to have, short of a date with Jim Davidson.

Incredibly, it was Alex who talked me into going. This was largely because I'd told him a teeny-weeny lie and said that it was my best school friend that I was meeting, rather than my first boyfriend. Which was kind of true, but also kind of deceptive. 'Come on, Sade, if it's been arranged for ages, it would be a bit crap of you to pull out now,' he said.

'But I'm so tired,' I moaned. 'Look at me. I look like something next door's cat might have sicked up after a big night on the Whiskas.'

'Put some make-up on, then,' he ordered me heartlessly. 'And wash your hair. Go on, you haven't been out on the lash for ages. You know I'm right. I'm right about everything, remember? Did I mention that I was right about everything?'

I looked away, ignoring his rambling. I was hardly going to be on the lash in my condition, as Miriam Stoppard might have said. Pickling a foetus, whether it was wanted or unwanted, was not my style.

I turned back to Alex, my eyes narrowing accusingly as I thought of something. 'Hang on a second. Why are you so keen for me to go out anyway? What have you got planned?'

He did have the grace to look slightly shifty at the question. 'Not a lot. Watch a bit of telly, you know,' he blustered.

'Anything else? Anything that you're not telling me, perhaps?'

He faltered under the fierceness of my gaze. I had my hands on my hips, head on one side, the lot. 'Well, all right, I've asked a couple of the lads round for a bit of poker.'

'Oh, ri-i-i-ight,' I said, working at least four syllables into the word. I folded my arms across my chest. 'And were you planning to tell me about this before I went out, or was I just going to wake up tomorrow morning to be told you'd betted our house away?'

He rolled his eyes. 'Don't be daft. You'll be waking up to wads of money at the end of the bed, that's what.'

'Mmm, well, I'll look forward to that, then,' I said sarcastically, 'when I see it.'

He pulled a face. 'Go on, chop-chop,' he said. 'What are you waiting for? Get in the shower and I'll get the kids their milk. Go!'

My mind had been such a blur of unanswered questions, ever since Friday and the pregnancy test of doom, that I hadn't had the time or energy to formulate a watertight gameplan for Mrs Cooper's party. Whether it was all psychological or not, I felt as if I had already plunged into no-brainer pregnancy mode where thinking about anything more taxing than *Hollyoaks* was instantly out of the window. The idea of having to concoct a whole wedge of lies about my job, lifestyle and home, and then carry them off plausibly to the entire Cooper clan all evening, seemed an acute impossibility.

The alternative, though, wasn't particularly appealing either: coming clean, telling Danny the truth, confessing that every email I'd sent him had been a pack of lies. But why? he would ask. I don't get it. Why didn't you tell me what you were really doing?

And what the hell would I say to that? Oh, well, you see, Danny, I wanted to impress you. I was so bored with the real world that I escaped to a cosy little fantasy life. I invented this alter ego to dazzle you, make you wish you hadn't dumped me. I was punishing you.

It had been years and years since I had clapped eyes on him, but I could imagine exactly his response. *Punishing* me? *Kidding yourself, you mean. You loser!*

My eyes stung with half-formed tears at the thought. I put my make-up on in front of the bedroom mirror, feeling panicky. Oh God, what was I going to say? And, more pressingly, what was I going to wear?

The door creaked and Molly came in, just as I'd flung open the wardrobe doors. She was wearing her pyjamas and clutching Fizz. 'Mummy, we singing "Pump Up" downstairs,' she confided, walking over and cuddling my bare legs.

'"Pump Up?" What's that, darling?' I asked distractedly. Gap black trousers or French Connection black trousers or Next black trousers? I was thinking.

Molly started pogoing around the room like a badly co-ordinated, gambolling chimp. '"Pump up! You feel it! Pump up!"' she started yelling.

The words sounded vaguely familiar, but her yells were so tuneless, I couldn't put my finger on precisely what she was meant to be singing. 'Is it one of Daddy's songs?' I asked, skimming through the clothes for another look. Ahh. Perhaps these black trousers from Warehouse. They were a bit more forgiving on the waist. Even though the cells in my womb were still only microscopically tiny, my belly seemed to have slumped outwards already, admitted defeat before the growth thing had even started.

'Yeah, Daddy sing it downstairs,' Molly said. 'Daddy sing, "Pump up! You feel it! Pump up!"'

'Ahh, right,' I said, nodding.

Alex was on a mission to musically educate our children whenever possible, which meant scornfully tossing aside their Nursery Collection CDs and their 'Wheels on the Bus' tape for car journeys, and playing them his favourite albums instead. He had proudly informed me that Molly was into ska before she was even crawling, with The Beat being her particular favourites, he reckoned. He was also convinced she was well into The Specials and The Pogues for dancing purposes, plus Massive Attack and Portishead for chilled-out pre-bedtime moods.

The music from downstairs suddenly got louder – no doubt he was trying to educate Nathan now – and a snatch of the bass line made everything click. 'Pump It Up' by Elvis Costello. Of course.

'Mummy, you wear THIS.'

Pogoing temporarily on hold, Molly had come to inspect the contents of my wardrobe. Of course, being Molly, she had ignored the swathe of blackness that was my usual going-out wear and had pulled out a plum-coloured, halterneck, knee-length, office-Christmas-party-type dress instead.

'What, this?' I hadn't worn it for years. Not since the Christmas party just before I'd conceived Molly, in fact. It belonged to a different age and, with it, a different, carefree me.

'This. I like this one.' She clutched it adamantly, swung it on the hanger.

I touched the satiny material myself, pulled it out for a closer look. 'I don't know, Molls. I'm not sure it'll fit any more.'

The look on her face was so beseeching and keen that I relented. Oh, whatever. I'd put it on just to show her, then I'd get back to choosing which pair of black trousers was the right one to wear for a sixty-year-old's birthday party.

I pulled the dress over my arms and shoulders; the material was silky-smooth and slipped down over me in one flowing movement. Good God, it still fitted. A little tight on the chest maybe, but fine on the hips. I'd forgotten the way that the skirt flipped out if I twirled around, how weightless the material was, and how it shone almost two-tone under the light.

'Mummy, you PRETTY. That your party dress.'

I hugged my fashion critic daughter. Who needed Trinny and Susannah when you had the complimentary Molly advising you on your outfits? 'Thanks, sweetpea.' I had danced all night in this dress, arsed around with Jo and Bernadette from the marketing department, necking free drinks and trying to resist boss-eyed Matt from the post room's drunken advances. God, it was like a lifetime ago.

Satisfied that she'd made the right choice for me, Molly trotted back downstairs. 'Daddy! I want you dance again!' I could hear her instructing.

I eyed my reflection critically. Was it going to be too much for Mrs Cooper's party? Would I turn up to see everyone else in jeans and trainers?

I twirled around, watching the flippy skirt fan out around my knees. Yet if I didn't wear it tonight, when would I ever put it on again? The dress was loose on my tummy now, but give it a couple of months and it could be gathering dust on its hanger again when I . . . if I . . .

Sod it. Where were my strappy sandals? This might be my last chance to be the belle of the ball for a while. So belle of the ball I would be, for one final night only.

I had arranged to meet Danny in a pub just off Streatham High Road. As I pushed the doors open, I realized with a jolt that the last time I had been in there was when I was eighteen years old. Jesus! Everything still looked exactly the same, right down to the dour-faced landlady slouching meatily over her beer pumps.

I scanned the pub slowly as I walked up to the bar. The thin straps of my shoes were already cutting into my feet, and

I felt ridiculously over-dressed as I swanned in there with my slinky party dress and beaded wrap, plus a dinky little handbag to round the outfit off. An old man who was sitting alone, nursing a pint of Guinness at so leisurely a pace that the froth had yellowed and was crusting around his glass, stared openly at me as if I were a different species.

And then I saw him at the bar: Danny, with his smile just as wide and friendly as it had been all those years ago, and suddenly everything turned to slow motion as I walked the last few steps up to him. Daniel Patrick Cooper. The man himself.

'Hello, Sadie,' he said. He sounded as London as ever. 'You look magic.'

'Hiya, Dan,' I said, feeling shy and delighted all in the same moment. 'It's great to see you.' I couldn't stop smiling. Me and Danny Cooper, in the Nag's Head again! It was like a bizarre dream where different parts of my life were mixed up with each other. Any minute now, my old primary school teacher would come in juggling grapefruit on a unicycle, followed by Nathan, walking on his hands.

We stood there, rather awkwardly, just grinning at each other for a second, then he grabbed me and hugged me. 'Come here,' he said. 'Sadie Morrison. Isn't this weird?'

'*Isn't* it?' I echoed, breathing in the scent of him: soap, and a faintly scorched smell from his shirt where it had been ironed a second too long, and a light, refreshing cologne. Still the boy around town. His hair, untamed as it always had been, with that wayward curl to it, brushed against my cheek.

'What are you drinking?' he asked. He had an almost full pint of lager by his elbow.

I was sorely tempted by a glass of wine for Dutch courage, or a gin – oh God, a gin and tonic, I so desperately wanted one – but . . . 'Better just have an orange juice,' I said, breezily. 'I'm detoxing this week.'

'Oh, right.' If he was surprised, he didn't show it. 'Been overdoing it, have we?'

'You could say,' I replied.

We made small-talk – how his mum was feeling, how the party preparations had all gone amusingly pear-shaped, how rainy it had been in the week, his journey down from Manchester – and then moved to a corner table where we could talk more privately.

'So, how's work going?' I said. 'How's the shop?'

The minute the words were out, I wanted to kick myself with my own pointy-heeled shoe. Stupid, stupid question! Stupid, stupid woman! Because once he'd answered me, *his* next question was bound to be, how's *your* work going? Fantastic. I had walked right into that one, hadn't I?

He paused and took a mouthful of his beer. I watched the lager tilt down the glass towards his mouth, and licked my own lips in envy. I suddenly felt very thirsty at the sight of the cold, gold liquid, the glass frosted up with its chill.

'Actually, I er . . .' He was coughing, and fiddling around with his pack of cigarettes. When I finally dragged my eyes away from his delicious-looking Stella, I noticed how uncomfortable he seemed to be with the subject.

Then he sighed, as if something had been resolved in his mind. 'Actually, Sadie,' he started again, 'you're going to think I'm the biggest prick in the northern hemisphere, but there *is* no shop. I made it all up. My record shop doesn't exist.' I was staring at him, but he ploughed through the words anyway. 'I'm a recruitment consultant. That's what I really do. Work in an office. The record shop thing was . . .' He shrugged. 'It was my little pipe dream.'

I was still staring. 'So you're saying that . . .' I frowned. 'So you're saying that all that stuff on the website—'

'Is a load of bollocks, yeah,' he said. 'I'm sorry. I don't know why I did it. I just wanted to sound good, I suppose.' He forced out an unhappy laugh. 'What a wanker, eh?'

'No,' I said. 'Not at all. In fact . . .'

'I mean, I know there's nothing wrong with being a recruitment consultant. It pays the rent anyway, and it's quite a laugh sometimes, but . . . You know. That website, everyone seems to be doing wonderful things with their lives, and I just . . .' He took another swig of his pint. 'I don't know. It was a bit of fun, that's all. Then I got carried away, and didn't want to stop.'

A bit of fun. Hadn't I said the exact same thing about my own lies?

'Don't tell my mum, will you?' he added, leaning forward with such a sweet expression of anxiety that I wanted to cuddle him.

'What, that you're a recruitment consultant?'

'No, that I lied to you. She'd go apeshit. She'd think I'm even more of a tosser than you must do.'

I shook my head. 'Danny,' I said gently, 'I don't think you're a tosser. I think it's funny. And actually . . .'

His shoulders sagged with relief. 'Really? You think it's funny? You're not pissed off about it?'

'No,' I told him. 'Because I know why you did it.'

He was visibly relaxing into his chair, leaning back and spreading his arms out expansively so that his hands dangled over the sides. 'You know, I reckon loads of people must do it. That temptation of, Oh, who cares? Might as well have a bit of a laugh, put down a few fibs . . .'

'Yeah,' I said, 'I'm sure loads of people exaggerate, or tell porkies. Which is funny, because—'

'Of course, the likes of Ms Sadie Morrison would have no truck with that, though,' he teased. 'The media princess, stalking the corridors of power at Channel 4, eh?'

I shook my head.

'Oh, sorry, is it the BBC? I thought it was—'

'No,' I said. Bloody hell, was I going to have to spell it out to him?

He was looking blankly back at me; I was.

'Look,' I started, 'it's funny that you made up a fantasy career, because I did too.'

His lower jaw swung open, like a trap-door. 'You what?'

'I don't work at Channel 4, same as you don't have a record shop,' I said. 'I'm not even a recruitment consultant. In fact, I don't have a job at all.'

'You're on the dole?'

'No, I'm a mum. I'm a housewife. Except for the "wife" bit.'

'You're a mum? You've got a kid?' His eyes were wide with shock.

'Kids. Plural. Yeah.'

'Oh my . . . Sadie! That's great!' A second later, he had enveloped me in a hug. 'God, how brilliant! How old are they? What are they called?'

I laughed, partly in surprise at how well he was taking this, and partly at his genuine enthusiasm and interest. So many people I'd worked with or known had dismissed me as a non-contributor once I'd stepped off the career ship into the choppy waters of motherhood. I'd been slapped by the incredulous 'You don't *work*?' response so many times that it was wholly unexpected to hear someone other than a family member sound excited about my children.

And so it was that I told him everything – 'All About Me', by Sadie Morrison. Not everything, obviously – I didn't go near the subject of Mark, or indeed the fact that I was carrying a secret changeling baby deep inside me – but pretty much everything else. It didn't take long, but he was interested. Well, he managed not to slump over the table into a deep sleep anyway, which I took as interest.

When I'd finished the edited but truthful version of my life story, he shook his head. 'But what I don't get,' he said, frowning, 'is why you had to lie about *that*? I would be dead proud if I had what you've got.'

There was a pause. 'I thought it sounded boring,' I admitted in the end.

His nose wrinkled as he frowned; I'd forgotten the way it did that. 'Boring to who?' he asked.

I shrugged, feeling like an idiot. 'Well, everyone. All the class boffins who are mega-successful, you know.' I swallowed. 'And you, as well, I suppose. I thought you would find it boring.'

'Sadie.' He practically groaned out my name. 'You daft cow. Come on, let's drink up and go. Wait till we tell my mum. She's going to be made up for you.'

She was, as well. Of course she was. This was the woman who had raised four children within five years and who'd run her house like a military boot camp. She clutched me to that bolster of a bosom again with a squeal of joy, followed by a barrage of questions and demands to see baby photos. Only then did she confide drunkenly to me that she'd hoped Danny and I would have a bit of a reunion kiss and make up. 'What *am* I going to do with that boy, Sadie?' she grumbled. 'I'm half expecting him to turn round one day and announce that he's gay. I'm telling you, there have been no decent girlfriends like you for a long old year. Oh, no. Standards have fallen since you, Sadie, sweetheart, believe you me.'

You can imagine how much Danny liked that. Although, judging by the good-natured eye-rolling he did at me, he'd heard it all before many, many times.

At the end of the night, he asked me to dance.

'What, to this? "Seasons in the Sun"?' I snorted. 'The Danny Cooper I once knew would have spat upon Terry Jacks.'

'You're right,' he said. He was pretty pissed, I realized. 'Come outside with me instead.'

'No chance,' I laughed. 'Not while you've got that lecherous glint in your eye.'

'Come on,' he said, grabbing my arm. 'For old times' sake. Come on, Sadie, we're quits now, aren't we? We both told each other lies so . . .'

'Sorry, mate. I'm sober, remember? Not about to forget I've got a man at home.' The hypocrisy of my words was like a thorn in my flesh, but Danny was too drunk to notice me wincing.

He grinned. 'Oh well. You've got to try. My mum would have kicked my arse for not trying.'

'Do you always do everything your mum tells you to?' I said archly, but I didn't really mind. It was a neat kind of closure in many ways. It was what I had wanted all those weeks ago, wasn't it, Danny Cooper back in my life, trying to get his hands in my knickers again? And now he had tried, and I'd turned him down, and it was probably time to go home.

I was feeling decidedly out of place by now anyway. A fish out of water, or rather, judging by the bloodshot eyes and lurching staggers of everyone else in the room, the only fish in the party who wasn't completely inebriated. And then I was reminded sharply of the reason *why* I wasn't completely inebriated when I saw two little girls, not much older than Molly, in their best pink party dresses skipping nimbly around the dancefloor far faster than Terry Jacks had originally intended. I saw them and smiled and felt my hand creep around to my belly. Oh, little one. What was I going to do about you?

Danny saw my hand on my belly, and the half-wistful look in my eye, and then I saw his gaze rise to the glass of orange juice in my hand. PING! Connection being made. 'Sadie. Are you . . .?'

It was *definitely* time to go. I did not want to tell him any more of my secrets. I grabbed my shawl and bag quickly and kissed him on the cheek. 'So lovely to see you again, Dan. Let's keep in touch, yeah? And no more bullshit.'

'No more bullshit,' he repeated, but his eyes were decidedly thoughtful beneath the alcoholic fog. His hand closed around mine. 'See you around, Sadie. Take care.'

Chapter Seventeen

The next week, everything fell out of its usual place. On Monday morning, Alex departed for a two-day training course in Wolverhampton. Normally I'd have gone into a 'How am I supposed to manage everything on my own?' type strop about it, but in the light of the pregnancy shock horror, it was actually quite good timing. At least I would have another few days to grind it out in my head before I had to actually inform him of the news.

The phone rang at ten-ish, just as I was about to take the kids out for the usual Tumble Tots endurance session.

'Hello, sexy.'

There was only one person in the world who would start a phone conversation with me like that.

'Hello,' I said in reply, feeling the usual warm flutter start up inside me at his voice. 'Listen, can I call you back? I'm just on my way out.'

'I'll make it quick then,' he said. 'Tonight, I thought—'

'Oh,' I interrupted, realizing. 'I should have called you. I won't be able to come out tonight. Alex is—'

'Away, yeah. I know,' he said, interrupting me right back. 'Alex is away. So is Julia. So I was wondering how you felt about me staying over?'

'Eh?' I looked dumbly towards the hall where I could hear Molly kicking the radiator with impatience. 'We go NOW,' she was shouting.

'Staying the night. In your bed. Waking up together. Hard-on at four o'clock, turning into a half-awake shag.'

'Yeah, yeah, I get your drift,' I said. I bit my lip, glanced down at my boobs which seemed even more obviously inflated than ever. He would guess. Surely he knew my body so well he would notice? How would I get away with it, once I had my clothes off?

'Great. So shall we say eight o'clock? I'll bring some wine. We can get a takeaway.'

'Well . . .' My resolve faltered. It wasn't like he was inviting himself round when the kids would be awake or anything. They wouldn't have to know he was there. I'd chuck him out early, sneak him out secretly before the sun was up and the neighbours could nosey . . . 'I suppose so,' I said doubtfully.

'I'll see you later then. Can't wait. Have a nice day.'

'You too,' I said.

I put the receiver back, feeling shaken, and wished I'd had more time to think about the idea before agreeing to it.

I couldn't decide if Mark staying over was a sexy, saucy thing to do, or just shady and a bit dirty. Mark in Alex's bed . . . There was something very seedy about it all. There would definitely be a thorough washing of sheets and pillow cases and everything else on Tuesday morning, put it like that.

The feelings of doubt stayed with me all the way through Tumble Tots and lunch at Anna's and the walk home. And then, later that afternoon, when I was sorting out the milk for Nathan's feed, the phone rang again.

I ran to answer it, feeling flustered at the thought that it could be either Alex or Mark. Actually, it was neither.

'Is that Sadie? Sadie Morrison?'

'Yes,' I replied, trying to work out if the voice was familiar or not.

'This is Paige Kozinski, Michelle McKean's assistant.'

Paige Kozinski? Michelle McKean? 'Er . . . yes?' I prompted hesitantly.

There was a pause. 'Michelle McKean from Firestarter?' she added.

Michelle McKean from . . . Oh, no. Was it really the end of the month already? 'Oh,' I said. I sat heavily on a chair. 'Oh dear. This is about the interview, isn't it?'

'Yes.' Paige was starting to sound irritated by my slowness. 'Yes, it is. We had you booked in for two-thirty, and I was just ringing to try to find out what had happened to you.'

I rubbed my forehead wearily. It seemed like five years had passed since I'd stupidly written my blagging, lie-stuffed CV and sent it off so light-heartedly. Five years, and a million twists and turns.

'Ms Morrison?' Paige said. 'Are you there? I said—'

'Yes, I'm here,' I said. Rude little upstart. 'I'm sorry. Something has . . . happened. I should have phoned but . . .' To my horror, I started to cry. 'I'm not . . . I won't be able to apply for the job any more.'

Paige, mercifully, was silent for a few seconds. 'O-K,' she said finally. The sharpness had left her voice; so had the authority. She'd probably never had a job applicant blub down the phone at her. 'And you'd like me to tell Michelle . . . what, exactly?'

'That I'm pregnant,' I sobbed. The relief at actually saying the words to somebody, even if it was just a voice down a phone line, was immense. Unfortunately, it was such a relief, I couldn't then rein myself back once I'd started. 'I'm pregnant and it's not a very good time for it to happen.' My body was shaking with the cries; I could hardly get the words out. 'I don't know what to do. Everything's gone wrong. I—'

'OK, well, I'll pass that on to Michelle,' Paige said hurriedly. *Hey, lady, agony aunt is so not in my job description*. 'And . . . er . . . good luck with everything.'

'Thanks, Paige,' I said, but the line was already dead. I put my head in my hands and rocked and wept.

'Mummy?'

There was a small hand tentatively placed on my back. Oh, no. Now I would traumatize my daughter by being a weeping misery in front of her, when everybody knew that mums were meant to be the ones in control of the world.

I couldn't speak for a few seconds, just reached out an arm and hugged her.

'Mummy, you crying? You had a bump?' she said, voice full of concern. 'Want a chocolate button?'

I tried to pull myself together. 'Mummy's fine, sweetheart,' I told her, my voice breaking on every word. 'I'm just a bit sad about something but I'll be all right again in a minute.'

She was kissing my leg. 'I lub you VERY much,' she said. 'I get you Fizz to cuddle. Yeah? Make you all better?'

She skipped off to find her doll while I wiped my eyes and blew my nose. Come on, I told myself. It'll be OK. I don't know how yet, but everything will be OK. Then I broke into fresh sobs at the thought of my own daughter comforting me with Fizz and chocolate buttons. What sort of a mother was I?

I heaved my shoulders back. Enough, now. Nathan needs his milk, remember?

Then I glanced back at the phone. There was still one person who I could talk to, tell everything to. I flipped through my address book quickly and dialled. 'Jemima?' I said, feeling another burst of relief as her sweet voice answered. 'Is that you? Have you got a minute?'

'For you, babe, I've got all day,' she said. 'What's up?'

An hour or so later, we were in the car and heading out of London. I had left a message on Alex's voicemail saying that I had decided to visit Jemima, and to call me there if he needed me. Then, I had phoned Mark and told him there had been a change of plan and not to come round that evening after all. He'd been miffed – and had let me know so in no uncertain terms – but I didn't have the energy to listen or care any more. It was high time I wrested back some control in the Mark thing, I reckoned. I had been letting him call too many of the shots for too long.

Jemima was an old college friend who lived near Chichester with her ten-year-old son, Noah. She was kind and funny and sensible, and the very second that she'd heard the wobble in my voice, she had ordered me to pack some things and come to stay. I hadn't needed telling twice. Jemima was the most sorted person I knew. She would know exactly what was the right thing to do and say. She would help me.

Molly and I sang along to 'Snap! Snap! Crocodile' and 'Two Red Hens' and all the other greats from her animal songs tape as we powered down the A3. It seemed a luxury to sing again, after spending the last few days in a haze of self-flagellating guilt and despair.

Snap! Snap! Crocodile
We can see your toothy smile . . .

'Mummy, you not cry any more,' Molly said suddenly, breaking off from the rousing chorus. 'You happy now?'

'Of course I am,' I lied as gaily as I knew how. 'Mummy's very happy again, and everything's going to be just fine.'

I wasn't sure who I was trying to kid more – my two-year-old, or me. She seemed to fall for it anyway. That was the main thing. Now I just had to go about convincing myself.

Jemima lived in a picturesque, straight-from-Beatrix-Potter cottage near a long, sandy beach, a few miles outside Chichester. She had an enviably idyllic lifestyle, which included honeysuckle sprawling around the front door, a vegetable patch and herb garden, and several profit-turning sidelines of pottery, jewellery-making and watercolour-painting. She was tall and willowy, with long, tousled blonde hair, blue eyes and a button nose. When I'd first met Jemima, I'd spent a whole term wishing I could look more like her. Now I just wished I *was* her.

'Come in,' she said, hugging me on the threshold. 'Hi, kids. Love those tights, Molly. And look at that bruiser of a boy! Isn't he ginormous?'

'I got my snowflake tights on,' Molly said proudly, sticking a leg out so that Jemima could have a closer look.

'You have! Aren't they fab? I wish I had some like that. Now then. Tea, coffee, beer, gin?'

'Tea,' I said.

'Beer,' Molly said.

Jemima laughed and chucked her under the chin. 'You're your daddy's daughter, aren't you, pet?' she said. 'Let's see what we can find.'

Jemima and I hadn't seen each other since she'd come to visit just after Nathan had been born. It had been the usual 'Isn't he gorgeous? How was the birth? Well done!' kind of conversation, punctuated by breastfeeds and photos of the birth and adoring looks galore. Luckily, she was the kind of friend that I could pick up with exactly where I left off straight away, even though it had been months since we'd been in the same room.

After a pot of ratatouille and some green salad and cous-cous, we persuaded Molly to sleep in the box room, unpacked the travel cot for Nathan, and then Jemima started to open a bottle of wine.

'Not for me,' I said quickly. Then, as she gave me a quizzical look, I relented. 'Go on, then. I'll have half a glass, please.'

She said nothing, just poured the wine and dug out a tin of shortbread. Then she bribed Noah to stay upstairs with a promise of a PlayStation all-dayer, just the two of them, at the weekend. From the way he cheered and ran upstairs to his room at once, I gathered this was a rare and much pestered-for treat indeed.

'So,' she said cheerfully, stirring the fire until sparks flew up the chimney, 'are you going to tell me, then?'

Talking to Jemima was like being in the best kind of therapy. I leaned back on the saggy sofa and told her everything. Everything. How smitten I had been with Mark. How alive and desirable he made me feel. How the sex had been in another league.

Then I took a deep breath and told her about the bad side of him, too. All the things that had been niggling away inside me as being not quite right: the mind games, the lie about Natasha, the way he had been with Caroline. Oh yeah, and while I was at it: my birthday lunch, appearing on my doorstep the other day, inviting himself round to stay the night. There was quite a list of wrongdoings when I dared to think about them all at once.

'No offence, Sade, but he sounds horrible,' Jemima said bluntly, lighting a fag. She blew the smoke up towards the ceiling. 'He sounds really controlling. What do you see in him? Is it just the sex?'

I stared at the fire. 'He is quite horrible,' I admitted, 'but the horribleness is just a part of *him*, if you know what I mean. It makes him exciting somehow. More dangerous. And the sex *is* amazing.'

'Well, great, if that's what you want, carry on,' Jemima said. 'I'm pleased for you.'

My head whipped round. That was not the answer I had been expecting. 'I thought you were going to say, "Stop seeing him, you must stop seeing him,"' I told her.

She raised her eyebrows at me. 'Is that what you wanted me to say?'

'I don't know. I suppose so.' I shrugged, feeling confused. This wasn't going quite the way I had expected.

She laughed. 'God, don't ask me! I'm hardly someone to call on for relationship advice, Jemima the single mother, queen of failed romances. What do you want to do? You're obviously still madly attracted to him, even though you can see how manipulative and . . . well, horrible he is to you.' She blew a smoke ring and we both watched it widen and disappear into the air.

'That's not the only problem, though,' I said. It felt as if there was a stone in my mouth, I couldn't get the words out without a struggle. 'I'm pregnant.'

She didn't look terribly surprised. 'Is it Mark's?' she asked, hastily fanning her smoke away from my direction.

I fiddled with my hair. 'Well, that's the thing. I don't know,' I said. I grimaced. 'I am so white trash, Jemima. I'm up the stick and I don't even know whose baby it is. Can you believe how awful I am?'

She stubbed out her fag and put her arms around me. I was

crying again. 'Oh, babe,' she said. She stroked my hair and it felt wonderful. 'Oh, babe. Come on. Have a good cry. You're not awful. You're lovely. You're so bloody lovely, it's no wonder men are queuing up to impregnate you.'

I giggled and snorted through my tears, then started sobbing again. 'Don't,' I said. 'Don't be nice. I don't deserve it.'

'Of course you do,' Jemima said, hugging me tighter. 'Now more than ever, by the look of it. I've never seen you so skinny before – your face has practically caved in. And you look exhausted.' She gave me another squeeze. 'Now, listen. This is what you're going to do. You're going to stay here for as long as you want. I'll take the kids off down to the beach every day so you can rest, and I'll fatten you up with lots of yummy, home-cooked food. Then, when you've had loads of sleep and sea air, and feel human again, you can start thinking about what you want to do. How does that sound?'

I leaned my head against her. 'It sounds great. You're great. You're like a fairy godmother,' I told her. 'Thank you.'

She was as good as her word. Actually, she was even better than that. She got up with Molly and Nathan to give them breakfast every morning, and then she literally disappeared with them into the wilds of Sussex. I woke up after a full ten hours' sleep each morning to the blissful sound of silence, with the occasional snatch of birdsong thrown in, just to remind me that life was carrying on outside the walls of the cottage.

I spent three days largely by myself. I showered and dressed, then had breakfast in Jemima's tiny kitchen, with its glorious sea view. I couldn't believe how calming it was to watch boats and seagulls while eating a plate of toast. The rest of my life seemed far away from here, where the waves rolled and smashed, rolled and smashed under the screeches of the gulls above.

After breakfast, I took long walks along the coastal path, or curled up on the sofa to read, or ate my way through the contents of the fridge. One afternoon, Noah came back from school before Jemima and my two had returned, so we spent an hour playing Scrabble and Cluedo, sprawled out on the living-room floor. For the first time in months, I felt at peace.

I'd given Alex Jemima's number but had kept my mobile switched off, not wanting to hear from Mark, or anyone else for that matter. It felt safer that way, more relaxing. I was taking a complete break, clearing my head of everything and everyone.

Alex phoned every night for a chat. He was as funny and down to earth as ever, but on the third night, he sounded sad. 'When are you coming home? It's so quiet here on my own,' he moaned.

I laughed at the little-boy-ness of his voice, and suddenly

felt a great yearning to see him. 'We'll come back tomorrow. I've missed you,' I told him.

'I've missed you, too,' he said. 'Tomorrow, did you say? Great. I'd better get in a quick night down the pub tonight then, hadn't I?'

'You had,' I said sternly. 'Because there'll be none of that going-out malarkey when I'm back, let me tell you.'

'I'm looking forward to a bit of staying-in malarkey with you,' he said.

'So am I,' I replied. 'I really am, Alex.'

The next morning, I had enough energy to get up with the kids and then, once Noah had left for school, we all went down to the beach for a last paddle. Molly was an old hand by now, kicking her football along the hard ribbed sand, building moats and sandcastles, screaming with delight as she splashed her toes in the freezing sea. I watched her run with Jemima, hand in hand along the sand, their blonde hair blowing wildly in the wind, and felt a fierce urge of protection. 'I will never hurt you,' I told Nathan, cuddling him into my jacket to keep him warm. 'Or Molly. I'd never do anything to hurt you because I love you both so much.'

For a second, I thought I was about to cry, then I realized that what I was actually feeling was a rush of joy. 'That goes for you, too.' I said the words aloud but meant them for the little prawn-shaped stranger inside me. The odd-looking ball of cells that now had a beating heart, the start of a spinal cord, a rudimentary circulation system. 'You're staying put, sunshine. Whatever happens, I'm going to love you, too.'

The wind snatched my words and took them out to sea. I watched the waves rise and crash upon the shore and felt happier than I had done for a long time. I could taste salt on my lips, could feel the warmth of my boy's body against mine. And I was keeping my baby. It felt the right thing to do.

The trip to Jemima's had cleared my head and given me strength and a new sense of calm. I had come to several decisions.

I would tell Mark that our affair was over. It didn't feel like fun any more. It had become something else.

I would persuade Alex that we really needed to move down to the sea, get out of London.

And I would tell him that I was pregnant, already, for a third time.

The idea of living by the sea had grown on me like seaweed on a rock. I had already convinced myself that it would be the best thing for everyone. Hey, Alex had a laptop, he could easily work from home sometimes, couldn't he? We would start again, in a stone cottage with a walled garden, away from Mark. We would have our third child; yes, of course it would be hard work but we'd manage. We'd slog it out together, as a family. And I'd plant hollyhocks and delphiniums in the garden, sweet-peas and lilies and roses. We'd grow vegetables and have a cat – hey, even a dog – and we'd all live happily ever after. It was all going to be just fine.

'You can do it,' Jemima had assured me, clasping my hands as we said goodbye. 'The anticipation will be the worst bit. You might be surprised at how well they take the news.'

'Mmmm,' I had said noncommittally. Inside I was thinking, you don't know them like I do, though, darling.

I wasn't sure which of the three things on my to-do list was going to be the hardest. Telling Alex about the baby would be awful. I could hardly bear to think about the dismay that would undoubtedly spread across his face when the information registered. Yet cooling things with Mark was definitely the scariest option. He was so unpredictable, I was half expecting him to hit me. Or hurt me. Or print posters of my face and the word SLUT and stick them up all over town. He wouldn't let go without a fight, I knew that much. The eight messages on my voicemail were testament to that.

Over the weekend, I planned everything out thoroughly. I would go round to Mark's office as usual on Monday and tell him then. This time I wouldn't cave in so pathetically, the way I'd done after my birthday weekend. I wouldn't bang on and on about the reasons why, I'd just say it and then get the hell out of there before the storm broke.

I figured I'd soften up Alex over the following weekend. He'd loved it in Brighton, hadn't he? Perhaps I would suggest another trip to the coast – either down to Brighton again, or somewhere prettier like Rye or Hayling Island – and then, once there, I'd guide him gently to some estate agent windows and say, 'Gosh, look what we could get for our money down here, darling!'

And, if he really baulked at the thought of being even further south than we already were, I'd play my trump card and suggest a move north instead. Yorkshire. I knew exactly how much he would love to move back there. Hell, if it meant escaping London, I'd do it, even if it did mean our children would grow up talking like him.

Then, once he was really softened up and excited about moving, a week or so later, I'd drop in the pregnancy news. And, with a bit of luck, he'd be pleased.

I was starting to feel happier about being pregnant. I'd even sneaked a couple of looks at my Miriam Stoppard book to see exactly what was happening inside me. It was just as magical and awe-inspiring reading about the process for a third time. I looked at the amazing photos of six-week-old foetuses, and their bumps and nodules that would eventually turn into a face, arms and legs, with a throb of excitement.

My secret third baby that only Jemima and I knew about. Well, and Paige Kozinski, too, I supposed, but she didn't count. Was this one going to be a girl or a boy? I wondered. Blonde again or dark-haired this time? Would they be mercurial and entertaining, like Molly, or placid and calm, like

Nathan? I had worked out that the baby would be due on 27 November. A Sagittarian. I circled the date in my diary but wrote nothing next to it. It wasn't like I was about to forget that in a hurry, anyway.

On Monday, I woke up feeling determined. It was D-Day. Dumping Day. Out with the old and in with the new. Nothing would stop me this time.

But then something terrible happened.

Anna was round for lunch, and I was just bending to get a pizza out of the oven when there was an agonizing cramp in my side.

'Oh my God,' I groaned, clutching my belly. The pain was so violent, I dropped the baking tray, which crashed against the floor, pizza landing the wrong side up. I was bent double, gasping, vaguely aware of Anna's open mouth saying something to me, yet I couldn't hear her.

'The baby,' I managed to say. I could feel something wet in my knickers. Blood, rolling out of me, along with all those precious, precious cells. 'I'm losing the baby.'

'I'll phone an ambulance,' I heard Anna say, and I started to cry.

Don't go, I wanted to shout to my baby. Don't leave me yet, little prawn. I want you. I always wanted you, really. Please hang on. Please stay with me. Please, please, please . . .

I was on the floor with the pain, crying and shouting. Molly and Ella had run into the kitchen at the sound of the crash and were hovering nervously a few feet away, staring at me with frightened expressions.

'Mummy, what you doing?' Molly asked, her face pale.

I couldn't even pretend to be all right this time. Anna was kneeling next to me, stroking my hair. 'They're on their way,' she said, over and over again. 'I'll look after the kids. What's Alex's number?'

I had never believed much in the idea of divine retribution, but I did now. I knew that this was utterly my fault. If I'd only been keener about the pregnancy from the word go, the baby wouldn't have felt unwanted. If only I'd been happier! It must have known I hadn't planned for it to come along. I must have driven it out of me somehow with all my bad thoughts and stress.

My kitchen was suddenly a blur of activity. Two male paramedics, kind and concerned, asking me questions as I lay on the floor. Molly's wail of incomprehension as one of them lifted me up and took me to the ambulance. 'I want my mummy! Mummy, come back!'

Her cries rang around my ears the entire way to the A&E department.

I was wheeled in for an ultrasound scan, which confirmed the worst. As the most horrible kind of foil to the scans I'd had of Molly and Nathan where I'd seen their wriggling fish-like bodies on the screen, and counted off their limbs and organs with joyous relief, this time the screen was black and empty. Too late. My baby had gone before I'd even seen it.

I felt just as empty as I looked. I lay on the hard trolley, my stomach cold and wet from the jelly they'd squirted on it, and wept as if I'd never stop. Then the door burst open and Alex was there, kissing my face and hair, hugging me, holding my hand. And then he looked at the screen, too, and cried with me.

'Did you know?' he asked.

'Yes,' I told him. This one was too important to lie about. 'Yes, I knew. I was scared to tell you,' I whispered, breaking down into sobs again. 'I didn't think you'd want it.' I swallowed hard. '*I* didn't want it at first. But now that it's gone, I want it back. Oh, I so want it back, Alex.'

'I know you do,' he said, stroking my face. 'I know, sweetheart. I know.'

'I feel so sad,' I cried. 'I'm so, so sad, Alex. I can't bear to think about what's just happened.'

He hugged me tightly, his broad arms around me so that he ended up covered with the ultrasound jelly. I was half expecting him to make a joke about it, but for once, he didn't. 'I'm sad, too,' he said, with a catch in his voice. 'I'm really sad, too, sweetheart. But we'll get through this, Sadie.' He was squeezing me so tight, his fingers were digging into my back. 'You and me. Good times ahead, I promise you.'

'Do you mean it? Do you really promise?' I was like a kid,

desperate for reassurance, clinging to his words as if they could save me.

'I promise.' He kissed the top of my head. 'I promise.'

Chapter Eighteen

Alex stayed with me and held my hand while I had the D&C. Every last bit of baby had been taken from me now. Each cell and fibre and feature. Gone. Flushed away. Irretrievable.

Everybody around me seemed desperate to say the right thing, yet there were no words in any dictionary that could make me feel any less devastated.

'You have to remember, this wasn't your fault,' a well-meaning nurse told me kindly. 'It's very common to miscarry so early on in pregnancy.'

That only made me cry harder. How could she say it wasn't my fault? She knew nothing! Of course it was my fault! And now she'd made me think about all those other women who were going through this, day in, day out, as a frequent occurrence. It was unbearable.

'Maybe your body just wasn't ready to be pregnant again so soon,' Alex said, squeezing my hand tentatively.

I turned my face away from him and wailed into the pillow. My own body had failed me. I had been a traitor to my unborn child, let him or her slip from me so carelessly. How could I have done that? I hated myself for it.

'You know, there could have been something wrong with the baby,' Mum said when we were back home later that night. 'It might be for the best. One of those things.'

I didn't reply, just snivelled into a tissue, but inside I was raging. For the *best*? One of those things? How could this possibly have been for the best? I'd just lost a baby! How the hell did that equate to 'one of those things'?

It seemed as though I had been away a long time, when we finally made it back to Tennyson Road. Everything had changed. *I* had changed. I had left the house, clinging to faint shreds of hope that my baby would survive. I had returned empty. Cleaned out.

The hospital staff had wanted me to stay in overnight, as I was still bleeding and in pain, but I refused point-blank. I had just lost one child; I didn't want to throw the lives of my other two into upheaval by not being there when they woke up in the morning. So, dosed up on painkillers and numb with grief and shock, here I was. I had industrial-strength sanitary towels between my thighs, so thick I could barely walk, and a swirling sensation in my head from the drugs. And there was a dead space inside me where my baby had once budded and floated.

The kids were in bed, and I crept in to see them, trying not to cry too loudly and wetly over them. My beautiful, darling children, stretched out in slumber, breathing deeply, cheeks warm under my touch. How lucky I was to have them in my life. I was so, so grateful. I would never take them for granted again.

The house was spotless, all traces of dropped pizza removed from the kitchen floor, carpets Hoovered, everything washed up and put away. Someone had even cleaned Nathan's high chair, which had had disgusting dried-on Weetabix splashes on it for so long I had started to think they were part of the design. Mum had obviously been thrown into a cleaning frenzy in a must-do-something-to-help response to the news. She rocked me on the sofa while Alex went to make everyone coffee, and it was like being five again, and having her comfort me for a skinned knee or a hair-pulling scrap with Lizzie.

'It'll be OK,' she crooned, stroking my hair. 'Don't cry, pet. It'll all be OK.'

The phone rang and Mum stiffened in annoyance. 'It's been doing that all night,' she said. 'Whoever it is won't talk to me though. I answer it, say hello, and the line goes dead. Bloomin' kids.'

RING RING. A chill crept down my back. No, not kids. It wasn't kids. I knew who it was, all right. Who else would it be? The very person I'd been planning to see this evening until the unthinkable had happened.

RING RING.

I went over and wrenched the phone line out of the wall socket and the noise stopped abruptly, mid-trill. 'I don't want to talk to anyone tonight, anyway,' I muttered.

I sat down again next to Mum, feeling light-headed and woozy. Sod it. Bring on complete annihilation. Tonight, I needed it. 'Alex,' I called through to the kitchen, 'could you make mine a large brandy instead?'

The next morning, I awoke with an eyeball-drying, brain-shrivelling, gut-churning hangover, and the nagging feeling that something unusual had happened. Then I remembered, and promptly burst into tears all over again. My baby. My little prawn.

Alex brought me breakfast in bed with the rest of the hospital painkillers, and Nathan to cuddle, but Molly hung back at the bedroom door, with the same anxious expression she'd worn the day before.

I dried my tears quickly, choked back the sobs and held out my arms for her. She shook her head mutely, her eyes fixed upon mine.

'Come on, Molls, come and give Mum a kiss,' Alex said, rolling Nathan up and down the bed to make him chortle.

Molly was still looking at me warily. 'You lie on kitchen floor, Mummy. You cry,' she said in a small voice. 'Mans take you away.'

'I know, darling. I was poorly,' I told her. 'The men took

me to hospital to make me better. I'm really sorry if you felt frightened.'

Then she was over at my side in a rush, scrambling up on the bed, one knee in the toast in her haste. And she was clinging to me and kissing me and pressing herself right into me, bony arms squeezing around my neck.

Alex looked at me above her head. 'We've got these two,' he said, and his eyes were soft.

I was glad he hadn't said 'at least'. I was sick to the back teeth of hearing 'at least', and how I should count my blessings. Counting blessings and 'at least' didn't change a damn thing.

'I know,' I said. I rubbed Molly's back, feeling every knobble of her spine through her thin cow-print pyjamas. 'We have.'

Alex had already called in to the office to say he would be off work all week, for which I was grateful and relieved. I felt as if my stuffing had leaked out of me along with the baby, plus every ounce of energy and sparkle, too. There was nothing left of me now, just bones and skin and a face. Yeah, so I was breathing in and out. My pulse was ticking along, same as ever. For all that, though, I felt utterly lifeless. I could scarcely drag myself out of bed to the toilet, let alone carry on as normal with the kids and our usual day.

Alex brought the TV up to our bedroom and switched on

Lorraine Kelly for me. 'I'm going to the shops,' he said. 'I'll get you some magazines and oranges and chocolate biscuits and . . . stuff. Anything else you fancy?'

I shook my head and lay back on the pillows, watching with the very feeblest of interest as Lorraine interviewed a new family that were going to be appearing on *Emmerdale*. Everything was suddenly so . . . unimportant. So trivial. I listened to the front door slam and Molly's high, cheerful voice as it floated up to the window outside, and then their footsteps faded away down the road.

My teeth were chattering. I was cold. Then, once the quilt was up to my neck, I felt hot. I smelled of hospital; I could feel it coming out of my pores, along with all the brandy fumes. I knew, without checking the mirror, that I'd look as if I'd been in a punch-up – red, swollen eyes, puffed-up cheeks. My baby had died. My baby had died. My baby had *died*.

Someone was knocking at the front door but I ignored them. Go away. Forget it. Not interested, whoever you are. Probably someone trying to sell me badly made oven gloves or pegs or some other household product that I always bought out of soft-heartedness and never used. Or it might be God-botherers trying to convert me. One glimpse of my slumped shoulders and they'd know I was easy prey. Alex would come home from the shops to find me signed up to choir practice and canvassing, with enough spare copies of *The True Light* to paper our bedroom.

More knocking, louder this time. Go a-bloody-way. My baby is dead, go away. I pulled the quilt over my head. Nobody is in. Get it?

Then a voice. 'SADIE! Open up!'

My eyelids jerked up and I yanked the quilt away from me. Was I hallucinating with too many painkillers now? That had sounded like . . .

'SADIE! Answer the door!'

It was. Mark. Oh, no. Bad timing, Mark. I wasn't fit for seeing him right now. I was so not up for this.

'SADIE! I know you're there!'

I swung my legs out of the bed. *Fuffuxy*, as Molly would have said. I knew he wouldn't go away if I ignored him. He would bang on that door until his knuckles had been ripped apart to cartilage and blood and bone. Oh, and then cue Alex returning from the shops, of course. *All right, mate? What are you doing here?*

And Mark would say . . .

I pulled on my dressing gown and managed to get down the stairs somehow, although my legs were so wobbly they didn't seem to belong to me any more.

I opened the door, and his mouth literally fell open as he saw me. 'Jesus Christ. What happened to you?'

I was finding it hard to meet him in the eye. Those blue

eyes that the prawn might have inherited. Or not. 'It's a bad time, OK? I don't really want to talk about it.' I swallowed, feeling out of breath with the effort of speaking to him. I gripped the door frame for support. My baby was dead. 'Mark, I don't want to see you any more.'

He took a step towards me and I cringed away from him. 'But . . . but why?' he asked. He sounded incredulous. 'Has Alex found out? Is that why you look so . . .'

I shut my eyes. Go on, check out those swollen eyelids as well, I thought wretchedly. See me at my ugliest and weakest, Mark. That should be enough to put you off having sex with me ever again. 'Listen, I just . . . I'm not well,' I said feebly.

'I saw Alex going off with the kids a few minutes ago,' he said. 'And you two were back late last night. What was all that about?'

I pulled my dressing gown tighter around me and frowned as my brain tried to make sense of his words. 'What do you mean, we were back late last night?' I asked. 'How do you know that?'

He was leaning against the door jamb. Somehow he'd managed to get even nearer to the threshold without me noticing. 'When you didn't turn up last night, I drove over,' he said. 'I was watching the house. I kept phoning and phoning and this woman kept answering. Who was that? A babysitter?'

'You were watching the house?' I repeated. My fingers were trembling. I was starting to feel sick. Why had I ever got into this whole mess? This was my punishment now for bad behaviour. First the miscarriage, and now . . .

I didn't get to think all the way to the end of the sentence, though. Just the word *miscarriage* flashing up in my head again was enough to bring tears to my eyes. Miscarriage. Miscarriage. Miscarriage. My baby had died before it had even had fingers and toes. I was never going to cuddle it, sing to it, pull stupid hats on its head . . .

'Look, Mark,' I said, trying not to cry in front of him. I didn't want him to think I was crying about our relationship when I couldn't give a stuff about that any more. It was nothing. 'Please go. If you want, we can meet up when I'm better, and we can talk things through. I owe you that much.' My teeth were chattering again; I was shivering and light-headed, swaying on my bare feet.

His eyes were savage. 'You little bitch,' he said softly.

I reeled as if he'd slapped my face.

'Do you really think you can end things here and now, on your fucking *doorstep*?' He spat out the word as if it were poison. 'I mean so little to you that—'

I flinched away from him, half expecting him to slap me for real. 'Please. Stop.' I covered my face with my hands; my fingers were shaking. 'I can't do this.' My baby just died, Mark, don't you realize my baby just—

He grabbed one of my wrists, pulled me roughly over to him. I stumbled on the step, stubbed my toe, fell painfully against him. 'Don't give me that,' he said. 'Don't fob me off with that.'

I was crying, trying to drag my hand away from him. 'Get off me,' I snivelled. There was snot on my face. 'Please, Mark. I—'

'What's going on? Sadie! Are you all right, Sadie?'

Anna. I was faint with relief. Thank God, thank God, oh thank God for Anna. My saviour. She was here at all the right times. And now she was wedged between me and Mark, pulling me inside the house, shutting the front door on him. I leaned against her and sobbed, raw, rasping sobs that hurt my throat. Safe.

For now.

Mark was battering on the door, inches away from us. 'I mean it, Sadie, you can't push me away like that,' he was saying. 'Wait till I tell Alex what you've been doing. Wait till I—'

'Go and fuck yourself,' Anna shouted through the letter-box. 'Before I call the police.'

Over the sound of my sobs and sniffs, we heard his foot-steps retreating, and then a car engine start up and drive down the road. He had gone.

Less than a minute later, Alex was back with the kids and bags of shopping. 'What are you doing out of bed?' he said crossly, when he saw me tear-stained and white-faced in the kitchen.

'My fault, sorry,' Anna said easily. 'Jamie's looking after the kids this morning so I popped over with some flowers. Just arrived, just leaving, don't worry.' She hugged me, and I looked up in surprise. Flowers. I hadn't even noticed she'd brought them, cellophane-wrapped tulips on the dresser. 'I won't stay. I can see you're wiped out, Sadie.' She kissed my cheek, and new tears rolled silently down my face. 'You look after yourself, my love. Give me a call when you're up to a chat.'

Wonderful Anna. She had saved me again. I nodded and tried to smile at her, and then she had gone.

'Back to bed at once,' Alex ordered. 'No, don't get up. Let me take you.'

He carried me up the stairs, not making a single joke about enrolling me for WeightWatchers classes, or breaking his back and needing to be in traction for a year. He laid me gently on the bed and pulled the duvet over my body. 'Now sleep,' he instructed. 'And then, when you wake up, I'll show you the treats I've got you.'

When he'd gone, more tears fell at the very thought that I could ever have betrayed him, good, kind Alex. *Wait till I tell Alex what you've been doing!*

Mark had been right: I was a bitch. A little bitch. I was the most ungrateful bitch alive, and I deserved everything I got. Although if anyone was going to tell Alex just what a bitch I'd been, he should at least hear it from me, straight from the bitch's mouth.

I was going to have to tell him. I was going to have to break his heart.

That night, when the kids had gone to bed, Alex came up with two dinner trays for us. He switched off the telly, lit a few candles around the room, and got under the duvet with me.

'There,' he said. 'A little sneak preview of what we'll be doing in thirty years' time.'

'What, eating off trays, in bed?'

'Yeah,' he said, shovelling in a forkful of pasta. 'You know, when the kids have packed us off to an old people's home because they can't stand us any more.' He shrugged. 'Something to look forward to, anyway.'

'Yeah,' I said. 'Cheers for that. You really know how to cheer a gal up, Alex.'

'You wait,' he said. 'Didn't I always tell you I'm right about everything?'

I rolled my eyes. 'Once or twice.'

'Actually,' he said, looking shifty all of a sudden, 'actually, there is something that might cheer you up.' He coughed. 'Or, at least, I hope it will. If I don't balls this up by picking a completely inappropriate time to be asking you, I mean.'

I stared at him. He was fiddling around with his garlic

bread and looking acutely embarrassed. Alex just didn't *do* embarrassed. Which meant that this had to be something really big. Oh, Christ. Was he going to . . .?

'What I'm trying to say is,' he started, and then stopped. 'No. Hang on. I want to do this properly. I've been doing a lot of thinking. About us. Good times and bad, and how much you mean to me. And what I'm trying to ask you is—'

'Don't,' I said in alarm. His face swung round to mine. Now he looked alarmed, too. 'Don't ask me. I mean, obviously I don't know what you're going to ask, but perhaps this *is* an inappropriate time.'

Alex's expression turned from alarm to dismay to something resembling relief. Off the hook for the time being, mate. 'Right,' he said.

'I mean . . .' Had he really been about to propose to me? I had never seen him look so uncomfortable in his life. Much as I'd longed for him to pop that bloody question for years and years, I could not sit there and listen to him do it, while I was planning to knife him with my betrayal, moments later. 'I mean, we've just been through a really horrible thing. We're still going through it. And I . . . I . . .'

He put his knife and fork down, and rubbed my back. 'I know. You're right.' He elbowed me in a jokey way. 'I suppose I'll have to ask the doctor instead.'

'What?'

'Oh, I was just going to ask how long you need to wait after a miscarriage before having sex again, that's all, but . . .'

I laughed. I really did. I laughed out loud. 'You tosser,' I said. Then I started to cry again.

'Oh, no,' he said in consternation. 'Oh God, sorry. That was so insensitive of me. I'm sorry, Sade. I'm such a prick, aren't I?'

'No,' I sobbed. 'I'm not crying about that. I thought that was f-f-funny. I'm crying because you're *not* a prick. Or a tosser.' I snatched up a wedge of tissues and blew my nose. 'I'm crying because I don't deserve you. You're too good for me, Alex.'

He looked utterly gobsmacked, as if I'd just told him I had been a secret Man United fan for years. 'What?'

'I don't deserve you.' I wiped my eyes, and looked at him. Time to come out with it – bludgeon him with the truth before Mark had a chance to do it for me. Oh God. The moment I'd been dreading.

I took a deep breath. 'I am so sorry for what I'm about to say. You're going to hate me and I don't blame you.' I flinched under the confused squint of his eyes. Christ, I could hardly bear to say the words to him. How on earth was he going to look when I'd told him? 'I . . . I had an affair. But it's over now.'

His body jerked at the words, and his fork went skidding off his plate. 'You what? You had an affair?'

I nodded. It was so hard to do this to him. If anybody else

had caused him to look quite as stricken and battered, I would have hated them for it. 'Yes,' I said. My voice was barely more than a whisper. 'I did. And I really regret it. And I'm so very, very—'

'An *affair*?'

'Yes.'

'You had an affair?' He had been looking at me, but he suddenly wrenched his head away as if he couldn't bear the sight of my face any more. He pushed himself away from me and sent his tray of food sliding off the edge of the bed and crashing down to the carpet. 'When? And who with? And *why*? Why, Sadie?'

It felt like we were acting out a scene from a TV drama. Right, OK, so this is the bit where I tell you about the affair, yeah, and you go mad and . . .

Only we weren't acting. It was really happening in our bedroom, the room where we slept and made love. The room where our son had been born only six months before. It was happening right now, a moment neither of us would ever be able to forget. I had spoiled both of our lives now.

I swallowed down the lump in my throat. I had to tell him whatever he wanted to know. 'For the last month or so,' I said. 'With Mark. Julia's husband, Mark.'

'With *Mark*? That posh twat we . . .?' His voice was shaking and he banged his fist down on the bed. 'Oh God. I can't believe this. I can't believe that you and Mark . . .' He looked at me then and his eyes were swimming with tears. 'Tell me it's a joke. Please, Sadie, tell me this is a joke.'

I couldn't bear that I had hurt him so much. I wished I could retract it, tell him yeah, it's only a joke, don't worry. As if I'd go off with 'that posh twat' anyway!

'It's not a joke,' I said miserably, hating myself. *You little bitch, Sadie. You little bitch.*

He was scrambling away from me, out of the bed, backing across the floor. 'I don't want to be near you,' he said. 'You . . . I don't want to know. I'm going.'

'Going?' I echoed. 'What do you mean, going? Can't we talk about this?'

'No,' he said. He was at the door. 'I don't want to talk to you. I need to go and think. I can't stand to look at you any more.'

I tried to go after him but my head was spinning as I got up. 'Please,' I said desperately, one hand at my temple, the other clutching on to the bed for support. 'Please don't go, Alex. I'm so sorry. I love you.'

He stared at me, as I swayed there pathetically in my pyjamas. 'Was it his?' he said hoarsely. 'The baby. Was it his?'

'No!' I went towards him. 'Please let's talk about this. Please. I . . .'

The door banged shut. I heard him thud down the stairs. The front door crashed behind him.

I heaved up one of the sash windows, leaned out over the road. 'Alex, come back. I'm sorry!' I wailed.

He ignored me. He was at the car, opening the door, sliding into the seat. Then the engine started, the lights clicked on. He drove away.

I had told him. I had finally told him the truth – and it had wrecked everything. From having a partner, a lover and a new baby inside me, I'd been left empty-handed. The eternal quadrilateral had become me, Sadie, on my own. The joke was on me. What sort of a fool was I to have lost everything?

I stood at the window staring out at the quiet street. Alex had left me. He'd been so devastated, he had left me. The shock and hurt in his eyes had been the worst kind of punishment. I couldn't see any way this was ever going to work itself out. And what the hell was I going to tell the children in the morning?

I didn't think I would sleep, but the painkillers the hospital had given me were so full-on, they knocked me into a stream of terrifying dreams. Then, the second I woke up the following day to Nathan's lusty yells from the next room, I felt the empty space next to me in the bed, and my heart sank. Alex had been out all night. He hadn't come back or phoned. He must really, really hate me.

Of course he bloody hates you, a voice in my head scolded, as I dragged on my dressing gown and hurried to get

Nathan. Of course he hates you, you utter fool. You've just told him you betrayed him with none other than his boss's husband. What is he supposed to do – congratulate you?

There was a tiny hope pulsing inside me that I'd go downstairs to find Alex crashed out on the sofa, but no. No sign that he'd come back, even to get some things. He'd literally gone out with nothing but his keys. Where could he have gone? Who could he be staying with? Would he have slept all night in the car?

I flicked on the central heating, whacked one of Nath's bottles in the microwave to warm, and filled the kettle. All the usual early morning things, yet there was no Alex upstairs in bed, brown hair sticking up against the pillow, murmuring in his sleep. I even used his sacred Leeds United mug for my tea in the hope that it would be comforting, but it wasn't. It was no comfort at all. It just reminded me that he wasn't there.

Dear Sadie,

Great to see you the other night. Sorry if I got a bit amorous on you at the end – well, I'm not at all sorry that I tried, actually, but I am sorry if it made you feel awkward. I couldn't help myself when you looked so gorgeous and we'd had such a laugh all night. Excuses, excuses. Hope we can do it again sometime. (The seeing each other thing, not me making drunken passes.) Perhaps next time we could lose the Bee Gees soundtrack, too.

Hope all is well with you and your kids. Still can't get over that. I feel a callow, pimply youth compared to your maturity. And of course, it's made my mum bang on even louder about how she's never going to be a grandmother, and why can't I stick with a nice girl for longer than two months, so cheers very much for that. You know you're now a legend in the Cooper household as The One That Got Away, I hope you realize?

The world of recruitment is as dynamic as ever. Applied for any jobs yourself lately?!

Keep in touch
Your partner in bullshit and Terry Jacks songs
Danny xxx

Molly, Nathan and I lay low for a few days. I still felt too weak and weepy to leave the house, and certainly had no desire to wash my hair or even brush my teeth, or, in fact, dress myself most of the time. Instead, we sat in and watched end-to-end videos and ate biscuits. Not something you'd find recommended in the good-parenting guide, but hey, it got us through. The buzz of the telly washed over me as I drowned in my thoughts.

People had been phoning – Mum and Lizzie and Anna and Becca and Rose – all tentatively asking after me and saying that if there was anything they could do, I just had to ask, blah blah.

I changed the subject instead, and asked about them. How's the job going, Rose? (Great, kicking media arse left, right and centre.)

What's the gossip, Bec? (Well, actually, there's this bloke at my gym, right, and . . .)

Is Theo crawling now, Anna? (Yes, but only backwards, commando-style at the moment – not hardcore just yet.)

My mum and Lizzie weren't quite so easy to fob off. I asked Mum something innocuous about her garden, and she sighed. 'I hope you're not trying to change the subject,' she said sternly. 'Listen to me, love. I know you're upset – of course you're upset – but please stop blaming yourself. You're a smashing mum, you really are, and—'

I nearly fell off the sofa. 'I'm a *what*?'

She chuckled. 'I said, you're a smashing mum. You're brilliant. A damn sight better than I was.'

I passed a hand over my forehead, reeling with shock. Or was I hallucinating? Had my own mother just said that to me? 'I don't think so,' I replied shakily in the end. Was this a wrong number, maybe?

'You know, I feel sorry for you mums today,' she went on chattily. 'All the expectations. All the choices. I mean, I'm as much of a women's libber as you, dear' – I stifled a snort at that – 'but at least when we didn't have choices, it made life simpler. None of this agonizing about work and what have you. We were mums and housewives and that was that.'

'Mmm,' I said, not sure where this was leading.

'And bloody boring it was, too,' she sighed. 'Now don't get me wrong, I loved you all to bits when you were babies. But . . .' She stopped herself suddenly. 'Why am I rambling on like this, when there's your lunch to make? I'll pop over in a bit with a casserole.'

'No, no, don't,' I said hastily. The only way out of this was a bare-faced fib. 'Er . . . Alex is making something.' I squeezed my eyes shut as I said it, hoping that would be my last lie for a while. There had been far too many of them lately.

'Is he? God love him,' she said warmly. 'I told you he was a good one, didn't I?'

A tear trickled down my cheek and splashed onto my lap. 'Yes, Mum. You did,' I said.

Lizzie was far less dissuadable. 'I'll come over and take the kids out to the park,' she said. 'Give you a breather. It's a lovely morning.'

'No, Liz, you don't have to do that,' I said weakly.

'I know I don't have to but I will,' she said. 'I'll be twenty minutes.'

'No,' I said again. 'Honestly. I think I just want them near me.'

She was silent for a moment. 'Fine, well, I'll come over and put some washing on for you, then. Clean your kitchen floor, that sort of thing.'

There was a lump in my throat at her kindness. 'Actually, Liz,' I said, clutching the phone so tightly, my fingers started to ache, 'could you just come round and talk to me? I really need to talk to you.'

'Of course,' she said. 'Absolutely. It's probably the best thing to do after what's happened.'

After what's happened? I thought. Then I realized she meant the miscarriage. I leaned my head back against the sofa. 'There's something else as well. Something worse. Please come, Lizzie.' I was crying all over again for the millionth time that morning. 'Will you come now?'

'I'm on my way,' she said. 'Hang in there, sweetheart. I'm on my way.'

She came on her own, having left Felix with a friend. She hugged me on the doorstep and I cried and cried on her shoulder. 'Oh, Sadie,' she said, stroking my back. 'What is it? What's happened?'

I knew that Molly was standing right behind me, so I tried to curtail my sobs. 'It's Alex. He's . . .' I sniffed. No. Mustn't do this in front of Molly. 'Sorry. Come in,' I said, trying to sound normal. 'Everything's gone wrong.'

I stood there in my own hall like a wooden doll while she hung up her coat and found a box of jigsaws for Molly to do on the living-room floor. Then she steered me into the kitchen and flicked on the kettle. Then, while the water boiled and she sorted out cups and tea bags, I told her. I told her the lot.

I had always thought that, if I was going to tell one of my sisters, it would be Cat. I hadn't wanted to talk about it with Lizzie, as I'd always felt that her life was so much calmer and better ordered than mine. Now I wanted her to understand the chaos of mine.

She listened to me all the way through without speaking, without judging, then she put her arms round me. We were both still standing at the kitchen worktop and I leaned gratefully into her.

'What a mess,' she said. 'Has he been in touch since?'

'No,' I told her. 'I haven't heard a thing since he stormed out on Tuesday night. His mobile's switched off, he's not at work and nobody seems to have heard a word from him.'

Pls phone, I had texted about five hundred times. **I am so sorry**. My ears had been straining for days, hoping to hear a replying beep from my mobile, but there had been nothing.

'He'll come round,' she said. 'He's angry. I know how he feels. He's hurt and angry. He needs to think about things before he can talk to you.'

I nodded. 'You know, I was so irritated by him when the Mark thing all kicked off,' I told her, drinking a mouthful of tea. 'I know that's not an excuse to go and have an affair, but it was like I just fell out of love with him for a while. I think he did the same with me. It was as if we were living together but we never *spoke,* you know? Or if we did, it was just about boring things like why the phone bill was so expensive or . . .'

'Boring things,' Lizzie repeated. 'Steve said the same to me.'

I clamped my mouth shut. I hadn't even *asked* her about Steve. What kind of a crap sister was I?

'And do you know what?' she went on, staring out of the window. 'I think he's wrong. I'm not a boring person. I think he was just looking for an excuse.'

'Yes,' I said hoarsely. Just like I had been, I thought with a jolt.

'It's got to the point where I feel angry with *him,*' she said. 'In fact, I've told him as much. I've told him he has to make his mind up – me or Jessica – and live with that. I don't want Felix – or me – to be messed around for another day, while he goes through his mid-life crisis, or whatever the hell it is. It's gone on long enough already.'

She spat the words out, a fire in her eyes. I hadn't seen her look so alive or determined for months. Years, even.

'Good for you,' I said timidly.

She looked at me then. 'I'm not having a go at you,' she said. 'I know these things happen. I just never wanted it to happen to me, that's all. So I've told him – make your mind up. I've taken back some control. Because there *are* boring parts of relationships, of every relationship. You just have to accept that. It's not sex and holidays for ever, is it?'

I goggled at her. I couldn't help myself. She didn't sound like passive, we-aim-to-please Lizzie any more. 'Right,' I managed to say. 'No.'

'I feel so angry with him for hurting me, you know,' she said. 'And now that I've got over the shock and the humiliation and all the rest of it, I've started thinking about what I want. And I don't want to compromise. He's either with me, or not. If he's with me, great. We'll try again. If he's not, then fine. I will manage.'

'I will survive,' I said, half-joking, half-serious.

'Exactly,' she said. 'Every woman's bloody theme song, I know. But it's true. Life goes on without men. It's true for you, too. I know you feel bad about Alex and I hope, for your sake and the kids' sake, he comes back. But if he doesn't, then you'll still be OK. We'll come through the other side, Sadie. We've got each other and our children and friends.'

Molly ran in just then. 'Help me, Mummy,' she said, holding up some jigsaw pieces. I followed her obediently. Bloody hell, I was thinking. First my mother shocks me with her mothering praise. Now Lizzie comes over all strong and angry. If I hadn't heard them with my own ears, I wouldn't have believed it. It just showed – you thought you knew someone but really, you never even came close.

*

The one thing that was really terrifying me about all this was the thought of Mark turning up and shouting at me again when I had sunk to such a vulnerable low. I scared myself by imagining him forcing his way into the house, frightening the children as well as me, pushing me about, hitting me, hurting me. I could take anything he wanted to do to me, yeah, bring it on, Mark, I would fight him all the way, gouge my thumbs into his eyes, rip his hair out, you name it. It was the thought of Molly's white, drawn face, eyes wide and fearful as she saw her mummy getting beaten up by 'that man'. That was what really did for me.

So far, though, he hadn't shown up. He hadn't even phoned. I toyed with the idea of writing him a letter and sending it to his office, but got stuck whenever I tried to put the words on the paper. What on earth would I say, other than 'Sorry. Goodbye'? There was nothing else that I *wanted* to say, more to the point, other than, 'Don't you dare come round to my house again, especially not if my kids are there, you psycho stalker.'

Somehow or other, I didn't think that would go down too well.

And then, suddenly, it was the weekend, and Alex still hadn't come home or phoned me. I felt faint with fear. I had to face facts: he might not be planning to come home at all. For the first time in days, I had a shower and washed my hair, dressed myself and the kids properly, and cooked a proper breakfast.

'Daddy home today?' Molly asked at the kitchen table. I had told her he had gone on another course, as the Wolverhampton trip was still fresh in her mind.

I shook my head, trying to find the right words. 'Not today, love, no,' I said, feeling the familiar catch in my throat at the thought. 'Actually, it's quite a long course so . . .' I took a mouthful of coffee. How should I say this? 'It might just be us three for a while, Molls. Me, you and Nath. But that'll be all right, won't it?'

'No,' she said. 'I want my daddy back.'

Clunk. I sighed, feeling a cold hand squeeze my heart in a painful tight grip. Christ. I couldn't believe I was seriously getting close to the conversation I thought I'd never have to have, the one about how Mummy and Daddy aren't living together any more, but how they both still love *you* and you're still the most important thing in the world to both of them . . .

I couldn't believe I had done this to my children, the very people I wanted to protect from all the hurt in the world.

I couldn't believe I was staring single parenthood full in the face.

'I know you want him back,' I said. 'I do, too.' I did, I really did. I wanted him back more than anything. He had his faults, sure, but so did I. And I'd hurt him far worse than he had ever hurt me.

I sighed again as I glanced over to the empty chair at the table. 'We'll have to do lots of fun things together, just us three until he comes back. OK? We'll just have to have a nice time without him.'

Chapter Nineteen

Dear Danny,

Glad you're still coping with the cut-and-thrust world of recruitment. It's a glamorous job but someone's gotta do it, that's what I say. And no worries about the amorous thing. I was more offended that you asked me to dance to 'Seasons in the Sun', to be honest. How could you even think such a thing? Have you no shame?!

Things have gone a bit strange here but it's not really something I can explain in an email. Let me know next time you're down south and we can have a proper heart to heart.

It really was great to catch up the other week. Big kiss to your mum. I always knew she was a woman with taste.

Love Sadie xxx

PS And you can leave out all that 'callow youth' bollocks. Don't give me that, Cooper!

☆

I only ever saw Mark once after our affair finished, and it was purely by chance. I had taken the kids out to the playground on Clapham Common for the morning, and after Molly had swung and slid and scaled the peaks of every climbing frame, we were strolling along the High Street looking for somewhere for lunch, when I saw him.

And her.

It was a sunshiny April day, T-shirt weather under the aquamarine sky, and all the cafes had put their dinky two-seater tables out on the pavement in an attempt to look Mediterranean, although, if you were a cynic, you could say that the effect was somewhat spoiled by the fume-belching West-End-bound traffic queuing back from the lights.

I saw him before he saw me. He was drinking coffee outside a French restaurant and wearing a crisp white shirt, sleeves rolled up. I could see the dark hairs on his arms. The way he held his cup with both hands. The light glancing off his rings. His suit jacket hanging on the back of his chair, sleeves dangling in a slight breeze. He was laughing at something his companion was saying.

I was waiting at the pedestrian crossing, a small island in the middle of the road. I watched the way his smile widened, how his eyes crinkled at the sides. His face seemed so familiar and yet so strange. I had kissed that face, held it in my hands. Now my eyes stung to look at it.

I punished myself by looking at the woman he was with

instead. The woman who once would have been my competition. Or had he been seeing her, too, all along? Were we both two of many conquests? Was it all a game?

She had dark hair, cut in a funky, gamine style, with coppery lowlights which shone in the sunshine. She was wearing a burnt orange shirt with a natty pointed collar and three-quarter-length sleeves. Silver bangles. French-manicured nails. Wedding ring. She waved her hands a lot when she spoke. She was teasing him about something, I guessed, from the mischievous grin on her face.

His lover.

People were crossing the road but I stood there, oblivious, watching them chatting and laughing and touching each other's hands across the table. My heart thumped painfully inside me, but I couldn't look away. I was transfixed, drinking in every detail. Her high-heeled boots. The sound of her laugh. The kitschy PVC handbag at her feet.

Go, go. Go, before they see you.

'We go, Mummy?' Molly inquired, drumming her feet on the buggy.

Then Mark looked up, just as the green man gave its last flash and vanished again. The red man appeared. Stop. Do not cross the road.

There was an air of triumph in Mark's eyes. *See?* they gloated. *I didn't waste any time getting over you. I've traded up to a better model, now – look!*

Just in case I hadn't got the message, he leaned over and whispered in the woman's ear, and then she was looking straight across at me, too, brown eyes curious. And she was laughing, and he was too, and then they were kissing, eyes closed, touching each other's faces.

Two cars zoomed between us and I shivered. I could no longer see them, but the kiss went on and on in my mind, playing endlessly like a loop of film.

Cheeks burning, I lumbered the buggy round and crossed back to the far side of the road, and then wheeled it to the row of bus stops. I glanced down at myself – cut-off jeans, old white T-shirt that had been over-washed and was now thin and greying, ancient, beaten-up trainers that smelled of ripe Camembert up close. I had no make-up on to cover my sleep-deprived skin and I knew that the dark circles under my eyes were like twin, crescent-shaped bruises. My hair needed cutting, my eyebrows needed tweezing, there was yellow poster paint wedged down the sides of my fingernails.

I sighed. I was out of the game as far as flirty coffees went. I was back where I belonged. 'Tell you what, Molls,' I said, leaning over to kiss her head. 'Let's go home and have a picnic lunch in our garden instead.'

It was the last time I ever saw him. Laughing at me with another woman. It was some kind of closure, at least. I certainly wasn't left in any doubt that we could ever be in love again. And that was a relief. He had moved on, and I had been left behind. It was over.

I didn't feel jealous. I felt as if I had escaped.

Alex stayed away until Sunday, when he appeared without warning, clutching a pile of Sunday papers, milk and bread. I stared at the milk and bread while Molly shrieked with delight to see her dad again. If he had brought groceries, surely that was a good sign? Surely that meant he was going to . . .?

'Hello,' I said. 'How are you?' We were standing a respectable distance from each other in the kitchen and all I wanted to do was fling myself across the vast chasm between us into his arms.

'I'm all right.' He looked me in the face and I examined him hungrily. He was unshaven and his clothes were crumpled, but other than that, it was Alex. In our kitchen. Home. 'You?'

'Yeah, OK.' I bit my lip. 'Apart from missing you and wishing I'd never been so stupid.'

He nodded. There was no light in his eyes, no spark of humour or anything that gave me any additional hope. I glanced back at the milk and bread just to reassure myself that they, at least, were there and I hadn't simply invented them as part of a crazed delusion.

'All right if I make a cup of tea?' he asked.

I started at the formality of his words. 'Of course you can! You don't have to *ask*!'

'Do you want one?'

'What, a cup of tea?' I was trying to joke, but it completely bombed. He stared at me as if I'd insulted him.

'Yes, a cup of tea.'

'No, thanks.'

Molly meanwhile was trying to tell Alex every single thing that had happened while he'd been away. 'I saw ladybird, Daddy. With spots. We had chips. I watch *Monsters* with Mummy. We played houses. And babies. And shops. Nathan had a bump.' She paused thoughtfully and then turned her face up to him, beaming. 'You had a nice course, Daddy?'

He said nothing for a few moments, just knelt down and cuddled her. 'I have missed you so-o-o much, Molls,' he said tightly. 'The best girl in the world.' He picked her up and swung her round so that she screamed with giggles. It was a noise I hadn't heard all week, and for some reason, it made me want to weep. It was a noise that had been part of the soundtrack to our life for so long, and I hadn't realized, until then, how much I had missed it. Only Alex could make her incoherent and hysterical like that. He was the only one. We both needed him here. We all needed him here.

Alex looked over at me. 'Do you mind if I take them out for a bit, Sade? Just to the park or something. It feels like ages since I've seen them.'

I bit my lip again. This seemed horribly like 'visiting rights', where Dad came along once a fortnight and took the kids to McDonald's and binge-fed them in the hope that it would make them love him for it. 'Yeah, 'course,' I said, in as bright a voice as I could muster, turning away so that he couldn't see my face.

'Hey, d'you hear that, Molls? Shall we go out to the park?'

'YEAH!' she cried. 'I get my shoes,' she said, racing out to the hall.

'Do you want to come, too?'

For a second, I thought he was asking Nathan, but then I remembered Nathan was actually asleep upstairs. So he had to be talking to me. 'Well, I . . .'

'Shall we all go? Get a bit of fresh air? Do the family thing?'

My heart sank. Do the family thing – that sounded so awful. Like we had to pretend to be a family, all of a sudden. 'Yeah, if you want,' I said tonelessly. Don't cry, I told myself fiercely. Don't start crying all over again. My eyes and cheeks still hadn't recovered from the tear-marathon of the week before.

'Yeah, I do want,' he was saying. 'I want to sort this out, you know.'

Something jumped inside me at his words. A tiny flicker of hope. I swung round to look at him. 'You do?'

His eyes were hard; he didn't look like my Alex any more.

This was the new, damaged version. 'Of course I do. We need to talk about it, try and find out where things went so wrong that you had to . . . That you wanted to . . .' He shrugged unhappily. His hands were flapping at his sides as if they weren't sure what to do. 'We need to talk. You need to tell me. I've been so angry with you for what you've done. I trusted you and you—'

'I know.' I didn't want him to say it. 'I know I hurt you. And I wrecked everything. And I wish that—'

'I wear my WELLY BOOTS,' Molly announced proudly, strutting in with her boots on the wrong feet. 'I put them on by MYSELF, Daddy.'

Alex came over and took my hand. Not a hug or a kiss, just his fingers around mine, but that was OK. That would do for now. 'We'll talk,' he said again. Then his voice rose as he smiled down at Molly. 'Aren't you clever? Wow! Look at those boots!'

'Thank you,' I said, trying to keep my voice steady. 'Thank you for giving me another chance.'

I would make it work, I vowed, pulling my own boots on seconds later, and wedging hats onto the children's heads.

I would so make it work, I told myself, unfolding the buggy and flicking the dried bits of mud off the wheels onto the pavement.

It *had* to work, I thought with a pang, watching Alex

nuzzling Nathan's belly with his chin until Nathan was helpless with chuckles.

'Right, kids,' Alex said, bouncing a football in his hands. 'Who's gonna kick this down the road with me? Are you coming, Nath?'

'No, ME coming, Daddy. I coming!'

'What, you? Molly? You think you can kick this ball, do you? Think you can get it off Hot-Shot Dad?'

And they were off, just like that, father and daughter, running and giggling and kicking the ball to each other down the road.

I pushed Nathan behind them with the sun on my face. 'GOAL!' Alex was yelling. 'And she's scored on the Ford Focus!'

We could do it, I thought, with a flare of optimism. Alex and I, Molly and Nathan. The very people I loved most in the world. We would talk later and we would start again. I watched him, the man I loved, as he showed our daughter how to dribble a football, and I was struck with the realization of how much I had missed him in my life. His smell. His laugh. His hands on me.

I smiled at the outrage on Molly's face as he tackled her and won the ball. He was so competitive, it was ridiculous. 'Come and get it, Molls,' he was shouting over his shoulder. 'Try and get it off me!'

I had nearly lost him, but now he was back. There was no

way I was going to make that mistake again. No way on earth. I picked up the pace in an attempt to catch up with the footballers, who were almost at the bottom of the road. Good times ahead. That was what Alex had said, wasn't it? Good times ahead. And hadn't I always said he was right about everything?

If you enjoyed

Any Way You Want Me,

you'll love these other books
by Lucy Diamond . . .

The Secrets of Happiness

The best things in life can be just around the corner

Rachel and Becca aren't real sisters, or so they say. They are step-sisters, living far apart, with little in common. Rachel is the successful one: happily married with three children and a big house, plus an impressive career. Artistic Becca, meanwhile, lurches from one dead-end job to another, shares a titchy flat and has given up on love.

The two of them have lost touch but when Rachel doesn't come home one night, Becca is called in to help. Once there, she quickly realizes that her step-sister's life is not so perfect after all: Rachel's handsome husband has moved out, her children are rebelling, and her glamorous career has taken a nosedive. Worst of all, nobody seems to have a clue where she might be.

As Becca begins to untangle Rachel's secrets, she is forced to confront some uncomfortable truths about her own life, and the future seems uncertain.

But sometimes happiness can be found in the most unexpected places . . .

Summer at Shell Cottage

A seaside holiday at Shell Cottage in Devon has always been the perfect escape for the Tarrant family. Beach fun, barbecues and warm summer evenings with a cocktail or two – who could ask for more?

But this year, everything has changed. Following her husband's recent death, Olivia is struggling to pick up the pieces. Then she makes a shocking discovery that turns her world upside down.

As a busy mum and GP, Freya's used to having her hands full, but a bad day at work has put her career in jeopardy and now she's really feeling the pressure.

Harriet's looking forward to a break with her lovely husband Robert and teenage daughter Molly. But unknown to Harriet, Robert is hiding a secret – and so, for that matter, is Molly . . .

'Stuffed with guilty secrets and characters you'll root for from the start, this warm and emotional novel about a family in crisis makes for delicious summer reading'

Sunday Express

'A great summer read from Lucy Diamond' *Hello*

'Enthralling drama about family secrets' *Heat*